"I want to save you," the Templar said. "But I can't." She howled in pain and shook visibly. "You need to get out of here. I can't control it much longer."

Heather took a step back.

"It's inside me," the Templar said. "Inside my mind." Tears slid down her face. "I didn't know. I swear I didn't know. I thought I could control it."

"Tell me," Heather said desperately. "Tell me where the safe places are."

"Get out of here." A paroxysm shook through the Templar.

"There are safe places," Heather said. "We've heard about them. The knights have them."

The Templar stopped quivering, looked up, and smiled. "There are no safe places anymore, fools. Now you'll pay the price for your stupid, pathetic hope."

Heather managed to turn and run, but she didn't take more than three steps before she felt the sword thrust between her shoulder blades. All sensation below her shoulders left her. Her legs crumpled and she fell to the ground in a kneeling position. Only the sword held her up.

Several inches of it stood out from her chest. She gazed at the weapon in disbelief. The knights—the Templar— were supposed to be good. Neil had told her they were helping everyone stranded in London, and that they were fighting the monsters.

Not true, Heather thought as she felt her body turn cold. *Not all of them.*

HELLGATE LONDON®

BOOK TWO OF THREE
GOETIA

MEL ODOM

POCKET STAR BOOKS
New York   London   Toronto   Sydney

Pocket Star Books
A Division of Simon & Schuster, Inc.
1230 Avenue of the Americas
New York, NY 10020

This book is a work of fiction. Names, characters, places, and incidents either are products of the author's imagination or are used fictitiously. Any resemblance to actual events or locales or persons living or dead is entirely coincidental.

First Pocket Star Books paperback edition March 2008

POCKET STAR and colophon are registered trademarks of Simon & Schuster, Inc.

For information about special discounts for bulk purchases, please contact Simon & Schuster Special Sales at 1-800-456-6798 or business@simonandschuster.com.

Cover art by Blur Studio

Manufactured in the United States of America

10 9 8 7 6 5 4 3 2

ISBN-13: 978-1-4165-2580-6
ISBN-10:   1-4165-2580-7

DEDICATION

For the University of Oklahoma gamers I've come to know this past year: Chris Borthick, Greg Hambric, Ben Wood, and Brian Burns.

And for my sons, Shiloh (who ventured into *Hellgate: London* in the game first) and Chandler (who's my companion in *City of Heroes*).

Game on, people!

ACKNOWLEDGMENTS

Thanks to Marco Palmieri of Pocket Books for keeping the demons at bay, and to Bill Roper and the fine game creators of Flagship Studios for bringing *Hellgate: London* to life and filling it with dead things!

HISTORIAN'S NOTE

This story begins fourteen years prior to the events depicted in the *Hellgate: London* video game.

PROLOGUE

LONDON, ENGLAND
SEPTEMBER 19
2024

Propelled by bloodlust, the Stalker demons scampered across the rooftops of the tall buildings along Fleet Street. There were six of them, all experienced slayers with a thirst for killing. They flung themselves across the rooftops. Legs bunched as they gathered themselves at the edge of one building to throw themselves to the next without hesitation.

Bright, hard moonlight burned down through the gray smoke that filmed the black sky. It left dangerous patches of light that would have revealed them to their prey, and other demons that would have killed them just for sport.

It didn't matter that a whole new world lay before them to conquer. The demons weren't equals. Their world didn't operate on principles of honor or diplomacy. Size and strength were the natural dividers among their kind. Creatures that were smaller or looked weaker became food or cruel diversion, and either was welcome at night when most of them were active.

Fear quivered through the demons as they regarded the light patches they had to navigate. It was just one of the tools in their survival arsenal that kept them alive night after night. Fear kept them alive and dangerous.

They paused on top of one of the buildings as the whirling gray smoke parted and left most of the rooftop exposed. Moonlight reflected in a silver sheen across the wet roof. The lead Stalker threw its ugly snout into the air and breathed deeply. The rain had turned to mist and made the air heavy.

The acrid scent of the smoke burned the demon's nasal membranes. It was an experienced predator and was familiar with the smoke. It was a byproduct of the process called the Burn, which changed the target world into one similar to the demons' homeworld.

This wasn't the first world the pack leader had helped invade and decimate. It was long-lived compared to most of the others in its pack. Usually, they served as cannon fodder, though the demon had no concept of that. It was a flesh-and-blood machine bred to hunt and kill.

Tonight they had fed well and now hunted for sport.

Long-limbed and thin as greyhounds, the Stalkers had a vaguely human appearance but usually ran on all fours. The chitinous blades that stood out along their forearms and lower legs immediately marked them as different from anything human.

The blades were sharp enough to cleave flesh, and the Stalkers had a stylized fighting system that made use of those projections. Hard chitin covered their bodies and shielded them from danger as much as Kevlar armor. Their heads were small, and their faces were tight.

They lay in the shadows of the rooftop and waited for the gray haze to obscure them once again. When it did, they scampered to the edge of the building and peered down.

A few humans roved the street. When the Hellgate had first opened and the demons had been allowed into this world, the hunting had been easy and plentiful. Now times were harder.

Few humans remained in the city. The ones that had survived had learned to be wary and clever. Many had escaped in the early weeks of the invasion, but millions had died and the streets had run red with blood for weeks.

The pack leader of the Stalkers drew in another breath as the breeze changed. Humans occupied the streets below. They hunted at night now too, for food and water to live out in the shadowed holes they'd dug themselves into.

With another sniff of air, the pack leader singled out one of them, a small female huddled in the dark. In the demon's vision, the female was a pulsing blur of orange and yellow contrasting with the purple-blue of the cool night. If the demon could have smiled, it would have. But it couldn't. Instead, it quivered, but this time it was from the killing urge that thrilled through its body.

It slipped over the roof's edge, dug its claws into the side of the building between the bricks, and moved slowly as it closed in for the kill.

Stay calm, Heather May told herself harshly as she remained within the safety of the shadowed alleyway just off Fleet Street. *Stay calm. You're going to find him.* But it was hard to remain calm out on the streets of London these days. Too many bad things happened there. She'd seen them. *You're going to find him, and you're going to get out of here.*

Cautiously, she peered out into the street. Overturned cars scarred by flames littered the block. Nearly every window in every building was broken. Some of the building walls were shattered, either by the demons or the military units when they had tried to fight back. War, though brief, had broken out inside the city and so many of the areas Heather had grown up in lay in ruins.

Here and there, other scavengers—humans, dogs, and cats—lingered in the shadows in the hopes of finding food that was still good and hadn't already been found. Meals had gotten harder to come by. Every few days they had to change where they were staying.

Weeks had passed since the last time Heather had seen sunlight. There were fewer demons in the streets and skies during the daylight hours, but there was almost no chance of hiding. Night was always filled with possibilities.

Twenty years old, Heather was slender and only a few inches over five feet tall. At a hundred pounds, she wasn't big enough to fight the demons. She'd survived the last four years in London by embracing her fear and letting it be her greatest strength. Her fear had never left her.

But it hadn't been like that for Neil. Her younger brother had gotten braver over the last four years. Or more desperate or numb. Survivor's guilt may have been driving him too. A woman Heather had talked to a month ago had suggested that when Heather went scavenging with her.

Neil was taller and bigger than her now, and he wasn't happy about taking direction from her. Lately, he'd fallen in with a group of older boys who had taken it upon themselves to range farther for food and water.

His bravery, his foolish confidence, was going to get him killed. Less than an hour ago, Heather had woken and found him gone. She'd known immediately that he'd gone out with the other boys and young men. Though she'd tried to stay awake to keep an eye on him, she'd failed.

When they had first started living in the underground train stations and supply rooms after the invasion occurred, Neil had been twelve. Nightmares had haunted him every night. He had been at home when the demons broke into the flat and killed their parents. He'd barely escaped with his life, and then only because the horrific monsters had chosen to stay and kill the others in the building.

Heather had been at a friend's parents' flat when the news about the demon invasion had hit the television news channels. She'd been sleeping over with Claire, talking about boys and watching dumb romance movies they had both giggled over.

The sound of the military jets screaming through the night sky and the rumble of the tank treads over the street had filled London that night. But mostly what Heather remembered were the screams of the wounded and dying. In the beginning, those things had been nightly and daily occurrences. Now they still happened but there weren't as many as before, primarily because there weren't as many victims left in the city for the monsters to find.

She wore jeans that had once fit her like a second skin but now had to be held up with a belt because she had lost weight. Skaters' elbow and knee pads provided extra protection. Protection was everything in her world now. She also learned to wear hiking boots and heavy leather gloves any time she was outside the Underground. Even down in the tube, debris created danger and obstacles. Without a chemist's shop, doctor, or hospital to go to, a simple infection could be life-threatening.

Four years ago, when she had been at school, she would never have left the flat in such a state. She kept her dark hair hacked off as short as she was able—to keep it from her eyes and to prevent it from being easily grabbed. She'd since learned both of those things could get her killed in a heartbeat.

She also carried weapons these days, something she had never done. A long-bladed hunting knife rode in a scabbard on her right hip. She carried a weighted length of pipe in her right hand.

After a final quick breath to steady her nerves, Heather slid around the alley corner and started down the cracked sidewalk. It would be morning soon. She didn't want to be caught out on the street in daylight.

She kept her eyes moving. That was a trick she had learned from a Special Air Services soldier who had stayed in one of the small group shelters where she'd kept Neil for a few weeks. That was back when large groups could exist for a while in relative safety. Those days were over.

During the soldier's stay, he had trained anyone who would listen in survival skills. One of the main things Heather remembered was that the human eye wasn't designed for nocturnal activity. In order to see things at night, humans had to keep their eyes moving and use peripheral vision to detect motion and shapes in the darkness.

She did that now. She also kept her ears pricked for the slightest change in sounds. Blood Angels, the female winged demons who controlled so much of the rooftops and airspace, sometimes mixed in with the gargoyles perched on buildings. Heather had trained herself to listen for the muffled subsonic flutter created by a Blood Angel's swooping descent. It was usually the last thing anyone ever heard.

Her left hand trailed the line of shops beside her. She didn't lose touch with the buildings. It wasn't enough to merely watch and listen to her environment these days; she had to remain in physical contact with changes in space as well.

She thought perhaps her parents had brought her shopping in the area before the Hellgate opened by St. Paul's. But she couldn't remember for sure. It seemed as though she remembered a lot more pleasant times these days than had actually happened.

A man stepped out of the darkness ahead of her. He turned to face her and grinned.

"You out here by yourself, love?" the man asked.

Heather froze, one hand on the wall and the other tight around the weighted pipe.

Even looking at him with her peripheral vision, Heather barely made the man out against the darkness. He was scrawny. It was as if fat people had disappeared off the face of the earth after the demons had arrived. Whiskers dirtied his lean wolf's jaws. A long duster covered him from neck to knees. Maybe the garment had always been black, or maybe it had gotten stained that way. He held his hands in his pockets.

There was a time, she told herself, *when running into a man like him was the most fearful thing you had to worry about.*

She didn't fear him now. But she was wary of him. If he hurt her in any way, or incapacitated her, she wouldn't be able to care of herself.

Or Neil.

"Did anyone ever tell you that it was rude not to speak to your elders when they spoke to you?" the man asked in a harsh tone.

"I'm not out here for conversation," Heather replied. She kept her voice neutral and offered no insult or hint of fear.

"Then why are you out here, love?"

"I'm foraging. Same as you."

"You should have someone watching your back. These are dangerous times."

Not just because of the monsters, Heather thought.

There was talk in the shadows of groups of humans that had gone feral. People said they were cannibalistic, that they'd started out eating the flesh of dead people but had acquired a taste for it. These days they took their kills fresh.

"I can watch my own back." Heather stepped toward the curb to go around the man.

"Then you've a fool for a partner, Doris," the man said in a child's sing-song voice.

Away from the wall now, Heather felt dizzy. She had noticed the effect several months ago and she thought she knew what it was. Agoraphobia was a fear of open places. Small animals—rodents, lizards, birds, and fish—all had the same inborn fear. All of them were used to being hunted. A long-ago science class she'd barely paid attention to had taught her that.

She shifted the weighted pipe to her left hand automatically. She had learned the hard way to never leave her weapon exposed to a potential enemy.

That habit saved her life.

The man reached for her and caught her arm. His long, thin fingers curved around her wrist. With a jerk, he pulled her to him.

"Well now, I guess you'll have to learn better manners, Doris. These are hard times, they are. If you're going to go along, you got to get along."

His foul breath collided with her face. It smelled like death, like the inside of the morgue Heather had found a few years ago. With the power cut off, the refrigeration units had stalled. The bodies inside the stainless steel vaults had spoiled.

While looking for anything salvageable, Heather had pulled one of vaults open. Her torch beam had revealed the horror within. She could still never say whether the body was male or female, only that it was covered with an infestation of maggots that writhed as they fed.

Even that could've been worse, she'd discovered. In some places, the dead lived again and sought only to feed on the flesh of a living.

The man touched her face with his free hand.

Heather's skin crawled at his touch. With a lithe twist of her hips, she brought the weighted pipe around in an overhand blow. The man saw it coming in time to raise his arm, but it didn't do any good. The weighted pipe snapped his arm like a twig.

The man screamed in pain and cradled his injured arm to his chest. He cursed at her between painful groans.

That was when Heather spotted the long forms of the monsters clinging to the wall of the alley. The lowest one was already at the second floor. Its lips pulled back and revealed double rows of serrated teeth.

Without hesitation, the monster leaped from the wall and landed on the man's back. The sudden weight dropped the man to his knees. He never had a chance to run. The monster's jaws open wider and latched onto the side of the man's neck. He screamed again, but this time it was in fear, not pain or anger.

Bones snapped and crunched, and it was frightening that she knew that sound from experience. Blood ran down the front of the man's duster.

Heather turned and fled. Even if the man had not tried to assault her, she wouldn't have tried to help him. Individuals only fell into two different camps these days. She only helped those in one of them. Neil was in that camp, and the rest of the world—whatever remained of it—was in the other.

Several blocks later, Heather reached a tube station. Her breath came in ragged gasps. She dug a minitorch from her pocket and flicked it on as she plunged into the stairwell. She jumped the last few feet and landed hard enough that for a moment she thought she'd broken her ankle. She ignored the shooting pain and made sure her foot worked.

"Turn that bloody torch off, you silly cow," someone said. "You're going to draw the demons down on us."

"They're already coming," Heather warned.

More cursing followed.

When she swept the torch's beam across the foyer, Heather saw three young men and two women standing in the tube station. They held pillowcases filled with canned goods.

Around them, skeletons picked clean of flesh lay in wild disarray amid piles of refuse. The foyer smelled like a urinal. Of course, the tube had reeked of piss on occasion even before the Hellgate opened, but the survivors now lived in its stations.

The men and women were young, no more than mid-twenties and worn-looking. Even then, though, Heather couldn't imagine living to be so old.

"Why did you bring them down here?" someone asked.

"It wasn't like I had a lot of choice," Heather retorted.

"We can't stay here, Byron," one of the young women said.

The man she talked to stood six feet tall. He carried an assault rifle. Heather felt certain he had gotten it from one of the military men who had fallen in battle. But he appeared to know how to use it.

Byron took the lead and walked back into the tube station as if he belonged there. "What are you doing here?" he asked Heather.

"I'm looking for my brother."

After he turned the corner, he followed the stairs down to the boarding platforms. His torch flicked on.

"Is your brother out there?" Byron demanded.

"I don't know."

"You lost your brother?" one of the women asked. Her

tone indicated she believed Heather was incredibly irre-
sponsible.

"I didn't lose him," Heather replied defiantly. "When I
got up, he was gone."

"Too afraid to go out and scavenge on your own?" the
other women taunted.

"No. Neil's my younger brother. I've been scavenging
for the both of us since this thing started."

Byron played his torch in both directions along the
tube line. "Feeling especially lucky?"

"No," Heather said.

"Make her go another way," one of the guys said. "If
she's brought bad luck, she needs to take it with her."

Heather held back a ripping curse. It wouldn't do to
alienate people who might offer a degree of safety.

"No," Byron said softly. "We stay together. If the demons have our scent, one more person can help. There's
safety in numbers."

No one argued.

Byron shined his torch both ways again, then moved
to the left. Within a few feet they were jogging. Heather
hated that because she knew the sounds would carry and
she wouldn't be able to hear the monsters coming.

"You called them demons," Heather told Byron when
they paused to catch their breath.

"Yes."

"Why?"

"Because they are demons," one of the women said.

"Demons aren't real." Heather hung on to that thought.
She didn't want to believe in demons. Despite everything
she'd been through during the last four years, it was easier—
more sane—to think of them as monsters.

"You're too stupid to live," the other woman said quietly.

"She's lived through this for four years," Byron said. "Leave her alone, Julie."

Heather was silently grateful for Byron's interference. But she resented it at the same time. She hadn't asked for help.

"The demons *are* real," Byron said. "Most people don't call them that. There are some who still think they're aliens."

"From another world," the other man said. "Not from across the channel."

Heather knew that. She'd talked to some of those people too. They tended to wear aluminum foil hats and tried to convince her that the aliens were sending out thought-control brain waves.

"We're down here foraging," Byron said. "But we're also looking for the knights."

Heather remembered the stories about the knights too. When her friend's parents had called them into the living room to watch the breaking news reports, there had been some coverage of the knights battling the monsters near St. Paul's Cathedral.

There hadn't been much. The reporting team covering the titanic battle between the knights and the monsters had been killed within minutes.

But the image of those knights, all of them standing tall—men and women—in their gleaming armor, had left an indelible impression on her. The impression had been left even more strongly on Neil.

He'd only been twelve. He'd still believed in super-heroes and good triumphing over evil. During the early days when they'd been hiding out, Neil had told her they needed to find the knights, that the knights would keep them safe.

The stories they'd heard about the knights guiding

people out of London hadn't helped. No one knew if the stories were true. All those who had managed to leave London had never returned.

Heather wouldn't have, either. But she didn't know where she would go. All of her family, her parents and her uncles and aunts, had died. There was no other place to go. And there were rumors that other Hellgates had opened up around the world too.

"The knights aren't real," Heather said. The pronouncement came out automatically. She'd told Neil that on several occasions. Neither of them could allow to get their hopes up. *She* couldn't get her hopes up.

"You don't even know the demons are real," Julie said. "The knights are real."

"Have you seen one?" Heather asked.

The young woman looked away.

"Thought so," Heather said. However, she regretted her words immediately.

They walked in silence for a time. Heather didn't want to stray too far from the neighborhood where she and Neil were staying. She had never known the city well, and too many things were wrecked that had once existed. Getting lost was easy.

She stopped at the next station. "I gotta get back. Neil's still out there somewhere. I need to find him before morning." He might even have already returned to the building where they were squatting and be worried about her. *It would serve him right.*

"Sure," Byron said. "We'll come up with you."

The two women protested his decision, but Byron ignored them.

Heather was grateful because she didn't want to be alone. She couldn't tell Byron that, though.

They went up slowly and without the torches. There was just enough moonlight to manage to get through the foyer and to the door.

Outside again, Heather glanced along the street. Something slithered above her. Panicked, she turned and looked up.

A monster clung to the wall only a few feet above the entranceway. Moonlight splintered against its ivory grin. It twisted its head from side to side, and she felt it was showing off, letting her know that she didn't have a chance against it.

It tracked me, Heather thought helplessly. Before she could step back into the foyer or take a fresh grip on the weighted pipe, it leapt.

White light suddenly flared through the night and a whirring sound of metal on metal echoed around Heather. Stunned, she watched as the monster's advance changed in midleap. A silvery ball slammed into it, then spread into a delicate spider's web that enveloped the creature. The bound monster dropped heavily to the cracked sidewalk beside Heather.

"Get back," a hoarse voice ordered.

When she glanced to her left, Heather saw an armored figure striding from the shadows. As the figure came closer, Heather made out the feminine form. She was over six feet tall. Some kind of metal covered her from head to foot. A blank faceplate disguised her features.

As Heather watched, the armor seemed to pulse. The night's darkness drained from the gleaming metal. By the time the knight reached Heather, the metal was silvery.

Above the tube entranceway, more monsters clung to the wall. One of them leaped from the wall toward the knight. Its jaws were wide open and its front forearms were poised to bring the jutting chitin blades into play.

The knight drew a long sword from her hip. Runes glowed along the double-edged blade. A gem or some kind of device mounted in the hilt glowed bilious green. The knight stepped forward and swung the sword in mailed fists.

After the blade met the monster with a great green flare that left spots dancing in Heather's eyes, the monster fell to the sidewalk in halves. The flesh smoked and showed burned spots.

Another demon had already been in motion and had leapt from the building as well. Unable to draw the sword back in time, the knight pulled one fist free and swung it backhanded at the monster. Just before the armored fist connected with the creature, it glowed incandescent green. Hooked spikes formed along the back of the glove. They sliced easily through the monster's flesh.

Driven aside by the blow, the monster flopped to the ground. Before the creature could recover, the knight raised one of her feet over its head. A spike suddenly jutted out the side of the armored boot. Mercilessly, the knight rammed the spike through the monster's head. The keen point not only punctured its intended victim, but also passed several inches into the pavement.

When the knight turned back to the creature bound in the gleaming silvery net, she flexed her hand and made a fist. Abruptly, the wire strands surrounding the trapped monster suddenly tightened and sliced through the scaly flesh.

The monster howled in terrified pain as the strands sank through its body. In seconds, though, the howls stopped and the creature had been reduced to chunks of meat and bone.

"Come on down," the knight taunted the monsters still clinging to the wall. "Come on down and die."

Heather didn't know if the monsters could understand words. Somehow the idea that they were clever enough to understand spoken language made it worse. If they were just animals hunting it was horrible enough. But if they were intelligent *and* malevolent, the situation seemed even more insurmountable.

The knight dragged her sword tip across the pavement in a half-circle. Green sparks shot into the air.

The surviving creatures all backed away. They howled in anger. In a few more seconds, they hauled themselves back over the lamppost.

Heather gazed in wide-eyed wonder at the knight.

"It's true," one of the women with Byron said. "The story about the knights is all true."

The knight raised her sword in both hands. She smiled fiercely as she turned to them. "Not knights," she said. "Templar. We are Templar."

As she looked into the knight's—Templar's—face, Heather saw the sickness in the woman's features. She looked wan and hollow.

As if something's eating her from the inside, Heather couldn't help thinking.

The device on the sword, mounted just below the cross guard, grew brighter green. The illumination lit up the immediate area and chased the shadows back from Heather and the others. A wave of nausea twisted through Heather's stomach.

Something's wrong.

"You can save us," Julie half-whispered. The words sounded too loud. "You can guide us out of London and get us to safety."

"I want to save you," the Templar said. "But I can't." She howled in pain and shook visibly. "You need to get out of here. I can't control it much longer."

Heather took a step back.

"It's inside me," the Templar said. "Inside my mind." Tears slid down her face. "I didn't know. I swear I didn't know. I thought I could control it."

"Tell me," Heather said desperately. "Tell me where the safe places are."

"Get out of here." A paroxysm shook through the Templar.

"There are safe places," Heather said. "We've heard about them. The knights have them."

"No."

Heather didn't know what the Templar was saying no to. "I don't understand."

The Templar stopped quivering, looked up, and smiled. "There are no safe places anymore, fools. Now you'll pay the price for your stupid, pathetic hope."

Heather managed to turn and run, but she didn't take more than three steps before she felt the sword thrust between her shoulder blades. All sensation below her shoulders left her. Her legs crumpled and she fell to the ground in a kneeling position. Only the sword held her up.

Several inches of it stood out from her chest. She gazed at the weapon in disbelief. The knights—the Templar— were supposed to be good. Neil had told her they were helping everyone stranded in London, and that they were fighting the monsters.

Not true, Heather thought as she felt her body turn cold. *Not all of them.*

The sword blade blazed incandescent green. Heather felt herself dwindle and grow small. Then she was sucked into darkness.

ONE

You *have found them, vassal. Now I want them dead.*

From the third-story fire escape, Warren Schimmer gazed down at his prey and tried not to think of them as human. Not that it would have mattered too terribly much. With his life in the balance against theirs, he would save his own life every time. That was how he'd done things for the last four years.

Do not hesitate or your own life will be forfeit.

The deep, rasping voice in Warren's head belonged to Merihim, a demon who had chosen Warren as one of his pawns in the demonic wars playing out over England. To disobey orders would be to die in a most horrible fashion.

Warren was afraid of dying. He'd nearly been killed by his stepfather when he was a boy. His stepfather had just succeeded in killing Warren's mother. The sound of the gunshots still haunted him at night.

But those dreams were less scary than the ones of the demon.

The five people below moved cautiously. Four of them, three men and one woman, were security guards. Warren knew that from the way they moved and the weapons they carried. They also wore hard-shell Kevlar vests and Kevlar helmets.

The fifth person was a man in his middle years. The

others had bundled him up in body armor, too, but he moved uncomfortably in it. He clutched a package tightly to his chest.

Merihim wanted the package.

Warren didn't know what it was. He rarely knew what Merihim sent him after. During the last four years, the demon's primary command had been to watch and grow stronger in his powers. Warren knew that Merihim often watched through his eyes. The demon's flesh bound them.

Occasionally, when Merihim's guards were down, or because Warren *was* growing stronger in his powers, Warren sometimes got glimpses of the things the demon saw. When Merihim caught him spying, as he did most of the time, Warren ended up getting migraines that left him sick and hurting for days.

Worst of all, those episodes left Warren defenseless. He'd had to rely on others to keep him safe. Dependence had never come easily to him. These days he hated it worse than ever.

Control had always been a big part of Warren's life. Now, what little control he did have was just an illusion. Merihim controlled him. But he also protected him.

It was a suitable trade-off. Most of the people Warren had met over the last four years had died hard deaths. Living, even as a demon's vassal, was better than dying.

Even when it meant killing others.

The five men entered the alley and walked beneath Warren's position. A small object, no larger than a racquetball, trailed them from a discreet distance.

Warren gestured. The object changed course immediately and came to him. He caught it in his right hand, the demon's hand that Merihim had given him after he'd lost his own in battle against a Templar named Simon Cross. It was the hand that bound Warren to Merihim so tightly.

Covered with silvery-green scales, the hand was proportioned to his own. In the first few months he'd had it, it had changed. Except for the coloration, the scales, and the black nails, most wouldn't give it a second glance. Unless they'd heard the stories about him.

The object squirmed inside Warren's hand.

"Stop," he said softly, too quietly for the men below to hear.

The thing stopped trying to escape.

Warren opened his hand and examined it. The object was an eyeball he'd plucked from a dying Blood Angel. As the demon had expired, Warren had worked the binding spell that Merihim had coached him in.

When he'd finished, the eye had been his and he could see through it as Merihim could see through his eyes. Over the years, he'd made more of them. He'd created other things as well. They sometimes moved and jerked in the demonhide bag he carried slung over one shoulder.

None of the other Cabalists he knew had been able to make such things. Of course, none of the others were bound to a demon.

He pushed the Blood Angel's eye into the bag and shook off the attempts of the other things in there to get free. None of them could escape the bag. His power bound them there.

Do not fail me.

Warren summoned the power within him. He felt strong. On those occasions when he directly obeyed the demon's orders, he had discovered that his reservoirs of power were a lot bigger. Tonight he felt especially strong.

He threw the demon's hand before him, fingers outspread. Force shimmered against his palm. He felt it, and he saw it as a rippling wave of smoke. With a flick, the force shot from his hand and struck one of the two rear guards.

The man went down without a sound. He sprawled in a loose tangle of limbs.

The other rear guard shouted a warning, then hunkered down into a half-crouch with his weapon raised in his hands. It was some kind of machine pistol. Warren knew that from countless online First-Person Shooters and RPGs he'd played.

One of the other two guards clapped a hand on the man's shoulder and jerked him into rapid motion. The man, overburdened by the body armor, almost tripped and fell. The guard managed to keep him upright and moving.

The other guard half-crouched as well and looked around the alley. His eyes drifted up and locked onto Warren. Too late, Warren saw that the man had flipped down lenses from the Kevlar helmet. Obviously they offered some kind of infrared or night-vision capabilities because the man had no problem spotting Warren.

Even as he felt the man's gaze on him, Warren leaped from the third-story fire escape landing. No human could have survived the drop without serious injury. Warren landed and barely flexed his legs to absorb the shock.

A line of bullets, interspersed with red tracer rounds, slammed into the fire escape where he'd been. Metal clanged and shrieked under the barrage.

That's going to draw demons, Warren thought sourly. *Maybe the police.*

Incredibly, ragged remnants of the London Metropolitan Police Department continued to live inside the city. In the beginning, they'd tried to keep order in the streets, thinking that the military would put things to rights in short order. When that hadn't happened, most of them turned as mercenary as everyone else trying to survive in the city.

But they still investigated disturbances. It was in their nature. Also, they'd claimed weapons taken from military stockpiles. Normally they weren't armed. Times changed. Equipped with the new weapons, the police officers had become more dangerous.

Warren held his fist out and popped it open suddenly. Flames jetted from his hand and enveloped the security guard with the quick trigger finger. The man surged up, dropped his weapon, and batted at the flames as he ran as though he could leave the fire behind.

"James!" the guard holding the civilian yelled. "Don't run, mate! It only feeds the fire!"

If the burning man heard his friend, he gave no sign. He careened into the wall and fell into a pile of debris that also caught on fire.

At that moment, Warren lost sight of the man as he concentrated on the other one who was even then turning on him with the machine pistol. Warren brought his hand up in front of him and pushed more energy into the spell he had ready.

The guard fired his weapon. Dozens of bullets spat from the machine pistol like a swarm of metallic bees. Muzzle flashes lit the alley like miniature lightning strikes.

Despite his confidence in his abilities, fear trickled through Warren. His senses sped up so much that he could see the bullets clearly as they streaked for him. Most of them wouldn't miss.

Afraid? Merihim taunted.

Warren ignored the mocking voice. He flicked his hand open over his heart. A shimmer passed over his body several inches from his skin.

The bullets struck the barrier he'd called up and froze in mid-air only inches from him. The lead projectiles were partially melted from the heat created in the barrel, and from the impact against the shield. They hung suspended as he gazed at them.

Then he realized his left shoulder felt as if it was on fire. When he looked, he saw that one of the bullets had evidently struck him and penetrated the flesh. The sensation of blood spreading down his back let him know the bullet had gone all the way through.

How?

It is a reminder, Merihim said. *I do not want you to get too complacent. You will not take for granted what I've given you.*

Silently, Warren wondered if Merihim had intentionally let him be wounded, or if the demon's powers weren't as strong as he'd claimed. The fact that he could question such a thing without Merihim knowing also proved the demon didn't have quite the hold he professed.

Of course, the possibility existed that the demon *did* know and only allowed Warren his misplaced confidence. Warren forced the thought away almost as soon as it dawned. He concentrated on survival.

He ignored the pain in his shoulder and focused on the guard that had shot at him. *Shot me,* Warren corrected.

The man brought his weapon up again. The bullets held in stasis before Warren created silvery-green waves of energy that bumped against each other like rocks in an incoming tide.

Warren swept his hand toward the man. The bullets immediately spun back toward the guard. Mushroomed and deformed from being fired, they wreaked havoc on the man's body. Impelled by greater forces than mere cordite, the projectiles ripped through the man's body armor and hurled him backward a dozen feet. He smashed against the wall behind him and slumped to the ground. Only blood, bone, ripped flesh, and shattered Kevlar remained of his face.

Warren strode to the two survivors. "Shoot me and you die," he told the guard.

The man hesitated, then dropped his weapon to his side.

Kill them all, Merihim ordered.

I don't have to, Warren thought back at him.

I have told you to. They die . . . or you die.

"All right," the man said. "What do you want?"

Warren stopped in front of the man and held his hand out. It hurt to move his arm, but he kept his right hand clenched and ready to unleash another spell.

"The book," Warren said.

"No," the man pleaded in a thin voice. "You work with the demons. You're one of the demon worshippers."

Warren didn't bother to correct the man. The Cabalists weren't demon worshippers. No one alive on the planet was fool enough to think that the demons bore any good-will toward humankind. Cabalists were fools who thought they could control demons.

The man wrapped both arms around the bag he carried. "Please. How can you do this? How can you turn against your own kind?"

"My own kind?" Warren's tone turned bitter and the old anger he had reared its head. "My own kind didn't care about me. My mother had me but cared more about learning witchcraft than rearing a child. I never knew my father. My stepfather tried to kill me when I was eight. After he'd killed my mother."

The gunshots sounded in Warren's head again. He should have died that night. But he hadn't. Instead, he'd commanded his stepfather to shoot himself in the head. It was the first time he'd ever used his power like that.

"The courts turned me over to foster care," Warren continued. "I won't bore you with the abuse that I suffered there . . . among my kind." He took in a deep breath and shook his head. "In this world, there's only me and you. And it's a bad day for you when I have power over you."

Tears coursed down the man's cheeks. "Please. You don't understand. This is important. This is something we need to know that the demons don't."

That interested Warren immediately. Knowledge was power. Especially when that knowledge was about secrets. He'd learned that at an early age.

"The demons know everything, mate," Warren said. "You're a fool if you think they don't." He grabbed the book with his left hand to leave his right free. Pain burned through his shoulder but he worked through it. With a wrench that nearly brought him to his knees, he yanked the book from the man.

The guard lifted his weapon and tried to bring it to bear.

Growling a curse, Warren thrust his right hand at the man and squeezed it viciously. Power erupted through his body and he knew Merihim was boosting his abilities.

The guard screamed in agony, dropped his weapon, and pressed his hands to his head. As he fell backward, his head and the Kevlar helmet blew up and spread over the wall behind him.

Warren took a ragged breath. Even after the horror of the past four years and everything he'd done in Merihim's name, he hadn't been prepared for the man's grisly death.

The other man collapsed into a fetal ball with his arms over his head. "Please," he whispered frantically. "Please. Don't kill me. I'm begging you."

Warren felt bad for the man. Despite his resolve to see to his own needs first, he knew with devastating clarity how it felt to be alone and vulnerable. The man in the alley was both those things.

He was also too weak to make it back through the city without ending up in some demon's gullet before daybreak. Killing him was merciful.

Warren knelt and placed his hand over the man's chest.

"Please," the man whispered.

"Sleep," Warren said, when what he meant was *die*. The man's ears heard one thing, but his heart heard another. It stilled within his chest and never beat again.

You should have let him beg more, Merihim said. *Begging is music to my ears.*

Quiet and contained, Warren pushed himself to his feet. "I have your book. Where do you want it?"

I'll let you know. For the time being, keep it safe.

The absence of the demon in Warren's head left a vacuum. It also left him feeling dangerously fatigued. He forced himself to move and to ignore the pain in his shoulder. He wanted to get back to his sanctuary where his sentries could watch over him.

And, since he had the chance, he wanted to know what was in the book he'd killed five men for.

TWO

Armored from head to toe in the magically reinforced palladium alloy armor his father and he
had crafted when he'd gained his full size, Simon
Cross paused at the entrance to the underground parking
garage beneath the Taylor & Loftus Building in the May-
fair District.

"Confirm comm link," Simon said.

"Reading you five by five," Danielle Ballentine called
back over the frequency immediately.

In swift order, the rest of the twelve-man unit counted
down.

Simon listened to them and tried to bank his fear for
later. The emotion was never truly useful except as extra
energy during an impromptu escape. But only if it could
be successfully mastered. Otherwise it simply drove a man
to foolish acts.

He wasn't there for a foolish act. They were there to
rescue teammates. Or avenge them.

Before stepping into the armor, Simon stood an impressive six feet five inches tall and weighed two hundred
fifty pounds. Clad in the armor, he gained three inches
and almost one hundred fifty pounds. The suit's Nanodyne microprocessors and "muscles" gave him the movement of an Olympic athlete and the speed of a racehorse.

Smithed primarily of palladium, the armor had also

been blessed and had spells of protection woven into it. It was the finest combination of magic, science, and faith that had ever been built.

It was primarily powered by solar energy streamed through a microfusion drive. Even under harsh circumstances, the armor could operate for eighteen to twenty-four hours nonstop. When those solar cells were depleted, there was a spell that provided a boost of arcane energy for a time. With any luck, the reserve system would hold out long enough to get a Templar to safety.

When all members of the team had been accounted for, Simon focused on the building. So far nothing had moved in or around the building. There weren't even any "gargoyles" present.

Checking for gargoyles had gotten to be second nature whenever Simon's Templar went into the city. So much of the architecture was Gothic, and gargoyles had been a prominent feature. But many more of them these days were Blood Angels and other demons from whatever Hell they'd crawled out of.

"Here we go," Simon said. He drew his sword, a double-edged great weapon forged of palladium alloy that presented four feet of gleaming, rune-etched razor sharpness. It was light enough, with the armor's boosted strength, to wield one-handed.

Simon scanned the street and immediate area one more time. The helmet's HUD provided a 360-degree panorama. He could literally see where he was going and what was behind him at the same time. A whispered command to the armor's online entity could change the view from normal to night vision to thermographic.

"Magnify," Simon said.

"Magnify," the suit's AI responded in the melodic feminine voice.

The HUD reflected the changes immediately. Simon was already using night vision. He scanned the building again. There was still nothing there to cause him to scrub the mission. He took a deep breath and took the first step.

Simon crossed the road and avoided the burned-out hulks of the vehicles scattered in the street like a child's toys. A red double-decker bus that itself had once been a sight to see in London lay on its side. Skeletons—adult and children, Simon saw—were scattered throughout.

The driver, still wearing his uniform, occupied the driver's seat. Most of his teeth had gotten knocked out during the wreck. A plastic Buddha figurine sat on the dash beside a Hawaiian hula girl. Stitching on the side of his shirt read: GEOFFREY.

Behind him, Danielle placed her hand on his shoulder and cued suit-to-suit communication only. That frequency was used for private chat and to circumvent anyone who might have the technology to break the encryption. The contact also provided an immediate medical readout on the other person.

"Simon," she said gently.

"Yeah," he replied.

"It's nothing we haven't seen before."

"I know." *But that's the bad part,* Simon thought. *Don't let me get used to this. Let every one of these sights strengthen my resolve to fight the demons.* He turned and moved on.

Danielle stayed close behind him. Her armor was colored green and black, but—like him—she had the camouflage function turned on and its surface rippled with the night's shadows.

The other two Templar flanked them and mirrored the placement of the second and third teams. All of them carried swords because of tradition and because the Templar had been training to fight the demons since the Crusades. That war—man versus demon—would always be fought in close quarters in the cities that men built. They knew no other way, but they had adapted. The Spike Bolter Simon wore at his hip proved that.

"Incoming signal," the suit AI announced.

"Who?"

"Unknown."

Simon signaled the teams to stand down. He squatted against the building and studied the 360-degree view of the street. He touched Danielle's forearm.

"I've got a communiqué," he said. "Relay that to the others. Tell them to stay alert."

"Yes sir." Even though Danielle's blank faceplate showed nothing but the reflection of Simon's own blank faceplate, tension tightened her voice.

Both of them knew they wouldn't have been there if they hadn't gotten tipped off. And they still didn't understand the role of the woman who had given them the information about the captured Templar.

"Acknowledge incoming signal?" the suit AI asked.

The fact that the signal wasn't simply jammed through spoke volumes to Simon. Either the sender couldn't take over the suit's comm array. *Or she's being polite,* Simon thought.

"Acknowledge," Simon said.

"Simon," the feminine voice said.

Simon recognized her voice immediately. It belonged to Leah Creasey, the young woman who had accompanied him back from South Africa when he'd heard about the London invasion. As it turned out, she'd been in Cape Town looking for him. He still wasn't sure why, or who had sent her, but during the last four years of hard-fought battles they'd learned to trust each other. They just didn't talk about who she was with.

Back in London after her arrival there with Simon, she'd temporarily spied on the Templar Underground, then disappeared when she chose to. He still didn't know what that was about either.

Later, when he'd split with the main group of Templar and set out on his own to rescue those he could that had been stranded in the country, she'd shown up in time to help him pull off that escape by train. He still hadn't figured out how she'd managed to know where he was or that he'd needed help against the Cabalist with the demon's hand. He'd only seen her a few times since then, hit and miss encounters that had left him asking even more questions about who she was and what she represented.

But he had learned that he could trust her when it came to survival issues. She—and whomever she ultimately worked for—wanted the demons gone as well.

"Leah," Simon said. "This is a bad time."

"It's about to get worse."

Simon paused at that. "How do you know?"

"Because you're walking into a trap."

Across the street from the front of the Taylor & Loftus building, Leah Creasey lay prone on the roof's edge. She had a cluster rifle snugged up against her shoulder and peered through a sniper scope down onto the street five stories below.

She wasn't supposed to be there. She knew she was going to be in a world of trouble if she was found out. But in a world that had suddenly been infested by demons, no trouble outside of that looked big enough to worry about.

So she'd shown up to see how Simon Cross and his group handled the problem she'd put into their laps. She'd felt bad about dropping it on him because it wasn't—at least in a way—his problem.

"How do you know we're walking into a trap?" Simon demanded.

Leah sighted on him through the sniper scope. He looked huge in the armor, like a human tank. But it was hard to see him with the camo effect engaged.

"Because I was just told that those Templar are being held as bait to pull you out of hiding," she replied.

"I haven't been hiding," Simon replied.

He sounds tired, Leah thought. "I know you haven't been hiding."

For the last four years he'd been building his own underground. All of that was without the resources the Templar had assembled over hundreds of years.

He'd also been saving lives where he could. That endeavor had dropped off steeply. It wasn't just that there were fewer people to save, but that it was harder to find them among the city's ruins. Simon had been weeks without saving anyone, and Leah knew he kept track of that. During the last four years, even with infrequent meetings, she'd come to know what kind of man he was.

And the kind of man he was . . .

Well that's what's brought you up on top of this bloody building in the middle of the night and breaking cover, which you'll catch bloody hob for if you're caught, isn't it?

From what Leah Creasey had seen, Simon Cross was the kind of man they didn't make any more. And she wasn't about to let him just up and die without lending a hand.

Or warning him off.

"Are there Templar inside that building?" Simon growled.

"There are," Leah told him. "But the demons holding them are expecting you."

"How do you know?"

"Because the bloody High Seat of Rorke, Terrence Booth, left them there as bait." When she'd been in the Templar Underground as a reluctantly admitted guest, Leah had met Booth. The man wasn't likable, and he held a huge grudge against Simon for bygone trespasses.

"Booth knew they were there?" Simon asked.

"Yes."

"And he did *nothing*?"

"They're still there, Simon. I'm sorry. But you can't go in there. They'll be ready for you."

"How do you know this?"

Leah couldn't explain everything. There was still too much that depended on secrecy. Even if they couldn't defeat the demons, the people she was with were determined not to let the death of the planet go unavenged.

She'd sworn an oath to uphold her station, and she couldn't breathe a word to anyone until she was released to do so.

"You'll have to trust me, Simon."

"You're spying on them, aren't you?"

Leah didn't bother to deny it. The information her superiors gleaned from the Templar Underground was important. The Templar were the only people to be truly ready to battle the demons.

And nearly all of them had died that first night of the invasion. The rest, everyone except Simon and his lot, had gone into hiding.

"Who are you with?" Simon growled.

"I can't talk about this," Leah said. "And this isn't the time or place even if I could." She paused and watched him through the sniper scope. Throughout her upbringing, she'd been raised on heroes, of men that would lay down their lives in a heartbeat for their country.

When she'd stepped into that world, she'd found most of the men—and women—there weren't that way. Most of them concentrated on getting out of their predicaments with whole skins first. Mission success came in a distant second.

There were some like Simon Cross and the Templar he'd drawn to his flag, but the majority of them were like the other Templar hiding in their Underground fortresses. Men like Simon Cross, she'd found out, didn't come along often and the world needed more of them. Especially now.

"What you need to understand," Leah said patiently, "is that you mustn't go into that building."

"It was your information that brought me here," Simon replied. His voice was a flat accusation. "I wouldn't have known about them if you hadn't contacted me."

"I know." Leah took a breath and tried to remain calm. Dealing with Simon and his simplistic do-gooder belief was often frustrating, she'd discovered over these past years. If someone else's life was on the line, he'd risk his every time. "Now I'm telling you that it's a trap."

"The bottom line," Simon stated quietly, "is that Templar—maybe friends of ours—are being held by demons inside that building. That's all we needed to know."

"Simon." Leah heard the click of dead air and knew he'd cut the communication link with her. She cursed him soundly, but she didn't abandon her post. Apparently Simon Cross's particular brand of stupidity was incredibly contagious.

She settled in behind the cluster rifle and waited for the action to start.

THREE

The decision to go, even with the new information that they were headed into a trap, was almost instantaneous. All of the Templar with Simon knew he had a mysterious source of information within London. None of them trusted her as much as he did. But they believed the information she'd given them: the bad news and the worse news.

As Simon had said, with Templar lives on the line—with friends, fellow warriors, and possibly relatives hanging in the balance—they could do nothing else.

However, it did change the tactics.

"The first team will go in for a brief recon," Simon said. "If we can get in and out without anyone the wiser, we're even better off. But if not, we get them out into the street where we'll have a chance to save ourselves."

Then he led the first team down into the underground parking garage while the other two teams set up in flanker support positions for a hasty withdrawal.

Simon unlimbered his Spike Bolter as he strode through the darkness of the garage. The pistol was specially encrypted to his armor and wouldn't operate for anyone other than another Templar.

The weapon looked ugly, with a pig's snout for a business end. Six rapidly rotating barrels could fire up to sixteen hundred rounds per minute. The rounds were palladium needle bullets that could shred even the densest demon hide. With so many rounds spewing from it, the Spike Bolter wasn't the most accurate handheld pistol and had to be used primarily for close-up engagements, but it more than made up for it with the barrage capability.

The carnage from the street had spilled down into the garage. More cars sat abandoned. Many of them were locked in eternal collisions that had jammed up whatever escape their owners might have wished for.

The elevators leading to the upper floors and to the basement were on the right. With the power grids out across the city, they wouldn't be working.

Using the night-vision capability of the HUD, Simon gazed around the garage. "Bring up the garage schematic," he said.

"Accessing," the suit AI said. At almost the same moment, the blueprint overlaid the garage visual. The elevators and stairwells were clearly marked.

The stairwells were on the left side of the garage. Simon led the way. Fear lurked inside him. It always did these days. It was another thing to take into account when he had to face the demons. When he'd been a child and later a teenager growing up in the Templar environment, he hadn't really known fear.

When he'd been small, the first stories all Templar children were told of the demons had scared him and given him nightmares. That was normal. Templar children were raised with the idea of bloodthirsty demons waiting to take over the world. That definitely wasn't the same kind of upbringing other English children enjoyed.

In his teens, however, he'd ceased believing in demons. After all, no one had truly seen one. Even the stories of demons were hundreds of years old, told by men who'd traveled from England and France down to Constantinople, before it was renamed Istanbul. They'd been warriors that had prided themselves on their prowess.

And wouldn't stories of defeating demons be a grand tale?

That was how Simon had come to think of the Templar beliefs when he was a teenager. He'd alternately frustrated his father and broken Thomas Cross's heart. In the later years, they'd grown apart. Simon had developed a love for *parkour*, BASE jumping, and skateboarding as well as other extreme sports, and he'd never known real fear during that time. Even when he'd broken limbs in attempts, he'd been just as ready to try it again.

Now, though, he knew the demons were out there. And they were waiting.

At the door to the stairwell, Simon sheathed his sword down his back. He kept the Spike Bolter in his left hand. With his right, he gripped the door's handle and pulled it gently.

It swung out almost soundlessly. That wasn't a good sign. The door had been getting used.

He held up and listened. Only silence echoed in the narrow walls. He scanned the floor and checked the metal staircase leading down into the basement.

"Clear," Danielle said.

Simon knew she was accessing the video from his HUD. Groups were able to do that over close distances. The Templar had been thorough in their armor upgrades. They'd been planning from the start to fight a vastly superior opponent. Some of the upgrades they'd managed over the years had been given to military forces. And Templar armorers had borrowed just as heavily.

After a last quick glance up, Simon started down. He

knew Danielle would cover him as she came down. Walter, the fourth man down, would also cover the top while Kevin covered the bottom with Simon.

The stairs corkscrewed down. Graffiti covered the walls. Some of it was funny. Some of it was offensive. The sad part was that none of it mattered any more. The people who had written the missives and the reasons they'd written them were all dead or didn't matter any more.

With the audio enhancers turned up, Simon heard the soft impacts of the Templar behind him. Nothing human probably would have. They'd learned how to go quietly despite the armor.

Two landings farther down, they reached a doorway marked PRIVATE.

"What did they keep down here?" Simon asked. Danielle had been responsible for the research.

"Files," she replied. "Extra office furniture. Cleaning equipment."

Simon examined the schematics. The room was thirty feet by forty feet.

He tried the door.

It was unlocked.

"Ready?" Simon asked. He packed away the last of his fear and concentrated on the adrenaline that was hammering his system. He needed it to keep himself stoked, but too much of it would—

"Warning," the suit AI said. "Adrenal output beyond optimum. Preparing partial sedation. Stand by for—"

"No," Simon said. "Abort slap patch."

The suit came with built-in medical and psychological aids. If a limb was lost, it was designed to truncate the injured area and preserve the blood flow. If a Templar started to hyperventilate or panic, slap patch prescriptions could level the Templar's emotional state.

If that failed, some of the suits—for those that relied more heavily on magic—spells provided the same results.

I've got it, Simon told himself. He needed the adrenaline flow. He always had. That was why he'd taken up extreme sports. His father, God rest his soul, never understood that entirely.

The others stood waiting.

Simon swung the door wide, shoved the Spike Bolter inside, and cautiously followed it.

Boxes and office furniture filled the room and created a virtual maze. Most of it was stacked taller than Simon. Automatically, before he entered the room very far, he checked the ceiling. Far too many of the demons they fought seemed able to cling to any surface.

The ceiling was clear.

He went forward slowly. The Spike Bolter led the way.

"Send distress response," Simon told the suit AI. "Identify me."

"Acknowledged. Sending."

The distress response was a low-level communications tag that infiltrated all the frequencies open to the Templar. It was designed for search and rescue missions for Templar whose suits had powered down due to battle damage or malfunction.

"There are two responses," the suit AI said.

"Onscreen," Simon said.

Immediately two starburst blips appeared on the HUD. They were close together, straight ahead of Simon.

"Confirm one other human body temperature," the suit AI said.

"Onscreen."

Another starburst, this one red in warning, formed beside the two.

"Can you identify the new signal?" Simon asked.

"Negative. Parameters are human."

Human? Simon pondered over that but he kept moving forward. A last wall of crates and office equipment blocked the way. He shouldered his way through and heard something shift ahead of him.

Despite his preparation and the four years he'd spent prowling through the obscene landscape London had become, Simon wasn't prepared for the sight that greeted him. He pointed the Spike Bolter automatically and reached for his sword, then stayed his hand when he realized the quarters were too close.

"Hello, Templar," the thing before him said. Once it had been human, but it was warped and twisted beyond anything human now. Instead of four limbs, the creature had eight. All of them were arms. It stood on four of them with the other four raised before it. Reddish-violet scales covered it in the place of skin. Foot-long black mandibles thrust from its misshapen mouth. Jagged yellow teeth backed those, and there were far too many to be human. Two eyes remained on either side of its head, but they were farther apart than they should have been. They were also segmented and bulbous like a fly's. Other eyes covered its head like satellites to the main two.

"What is that?" Danielle whispered over the suit comm.

"I don't know," Simon replied. In the Templar Underground, they'd studied the demons' strengths and weaknesses. But they'd worked almost totally from stories handed down over generations and the information had become bastardized.

They had learned more about the demons while battling them after the invasion. As it had turned out, their list of demons and what the demons could do was short compared to what they actually were and were capable of.

"The body has been possessed and corrupted," Walter said. He was one of the older Templar. He'd found his way to Simon's group only lately. His primary field of study had been magic.

"That thing has taken over someone's body?" Kevin asked. He was nineteen and still training. When Simon had split off from the main Templar, Kevin had joined them weeks later. Like Simon's, Kevin's father had been killed in the massacre on All Hallows' Eve at St. Paul's Cathedral. In the beginning, he'd burned for vengeance, but he'd learned to pace himself.

"Yes," Walter said. Wonderment filled his voice. "There are stories about this, but none of them had ever been confirmed."

Until now, Simon thought.

"What about the host?" Danielle asked.

"His mind was burned out when the demon took possession," Walter said.

The demon cocked its head and made a series of anticipatory clicks that couldn't have come from a human throat.

"You're sure there's no chance of saving the host?" Simon asked.

"None," Walter replied. "His mind is gone. Whoever that was before the demon seized possession of him, nothing's left of him."

Simon hoped not.

"Where are the Templar?" Danielle asked.

Guilt flooded Simon when he realized he'd forgotten about the Templar they'd come to save. But the sight of the demon had been overwhelming.

The two Templar lay on the ground to Simon's right. Both of them had been cocooned in silken strands that looked as black as oil. Neither of them stirred. The only thing that told him they were alive was the constant body temperature. Nothing dead would register on the suit AI's sensors. Simon took heart in that.

He thought he recognized the blue and green coloring of the armor on one of the Templar. The other, gray over green, was new to him.

"Welcome, Templar." The demon tilted its head. Yellow ichors dripped from its mandibles. "We knew that some pathetic few of you still existed and chose to fight. A few of us were sent to run you to ground." The mandibles spread. "I shall not be merciful. You will have a harsh death. Just as these two will."

"Not today," Simon said as he squeezed the Spike Bolter's trigger.

FOUR

The Spike Bolter jumped like a rabid hound in Simon's armored fist. Without his enhanced strength and training, he wouldn't have been able to hang on to the weapon. Twenty-six rounds a second thudded into the arachnid-demon's body. He started them at the demon's center of mass and allowed the Spike Bolter to track upward. Even with the suit's strength he couldn't prevent that.

The bull-fiddle moan of the weapon reverberated inside the enclosed room. A moment later the demon's screams joined the noise.

It vaulted toward Simon almost effortlessly. Green blood dripped from hundreds of wounds. One of the arms dropped away as the needle bullets chewed through it.

The arachnid-demon grabbed Simon and pressed its face against his faceplate. The mandibles clicked against the polycarbonate-based liquid metal that made up the faceplate. The composite material in its natural state was liquid, but when it had electricity running through it—or magic—it firmed up harder than steel. The suit's AI kept templates stored in memory for the faceplate's shape.

Small cracks appeared in Simon's faceplate as the mandibles increased pressure.

"Warning," the suit's AI stated calmly. "Possible breach."

Simon's vision blurred a little as the faceplate grew thicker. The fissures disappeared as if they'd never been. Simon brought his right hand up and wrapped his fingers around the demon's neck.

"You're going to die, Templar," the demon snarled. "You'll never get out of here alive."

Simon made no reply. He holstered his pistol, drew his sword, and whipped it forward. The blade cleaved deeply into the demon's flesh. A moment later, the demon went limp in Simon's grasp. All seven of its remaining arms hung lifelessly. He cast it from him and it fell into a tangled heap in the corner among copy machines that were decades old.

He strode forward and put his hand on the nearest Templar. "Life signs," he said.

"Accessing," the suit's AI replied. "ID confirmed. Elizabeth Stevenson."

Simon recognized the name. She was one of the young Templar. If he remembered rightly, she would have been twenty-one, eight years younger than he was. She was of the House of Rorke, the same House Simon's family served. And it was the same one where Terrence Booth now sat as High Seat.

Numbers and values spun across the left corner of Simon's vision superimposed over the basement scene. The heart rate, blood pressure, and respiration all fell within normal ranges for a sleeping person.

Simon guessed that was normal. The demon wouldn't want a prisoner capable of defending herself. That was especially true of one with a Templar's capability.

"Was the armor breached?" Simon asked. The only way Elizabeth could have been sedated was through a breach.

"Negative," the suit's AI said.

Accessing Elizabeth's suit's AI was impossible suit-to-suit. That had to be done back in the safety and security of a lab, with full authorization from the suit's wearer. Or it could be done once the wearer was dead.

Simon figured he'd know soon enough what had happened to the two Templar. He looked at Danielle, who knelt beside the second Templar.

"Who's that?" he asked.

"Justin Fitzgerald."

"Do you know him?"

"No."

"What House?" The Templar were divided up into eight different Houses that administered the needs and the edicts of the Templar Order.

"Sumerisle." Danielle's voice held a note of reverence.

The House of Sumerisle always found favor and respect among the Templar. The last Grand Master, Patrick Sumerisle, died fighting the demons on All Hallows' Eve. Simon had known and respected the man.

"So he's one of the royal nephews," Simon said.

"Grandnephew or great-grandnephew is more like it," Danielle replied. "He's only seventeen."

Simon shook his head. "What were the two of them, as young as they were, doing out here on their own?"

"We were that young," Danielle said softly. "Not so long ago."

"They might not have been out here on their own," Walter added. "This could be all that's left of a group."

That sobering thought struck Simon sharply. He didn't like wondering if there were a line of dead Templar that led to this place.

"Simon." The voice came from one of the Templar outside the Taylor & Loftus building.

"Yes."

"There's movement inside the building."

"What?" Simon stood.

"Zombies, mate," the Templar said tensely. "The parking garage is full of them."

They decided to leave the Templar trussed up in the spider webbing. Walter and Kevin carried the unconscious warriors slung over their shoulders while Simon and Danielle led the way back up the stairwell.

By the time they reached the second landing, the zombies had crowded in after them. Hideous and disfigured, the zombies lurched after their prey, bearing down on them inexhaustibly.

Blood covered the zombies in the stairwell and promised all manner of infectious diseases with any contact on an open wound, eyes, nose, or mouth. Remnants of clothing clung to them and hinted at what they might have been before their lives had been snuffed out and their bodies claimed by the demonic spell that brought them back.

Simon pointed the Spike Bolter and fired. The palladium rounds chewed through undead flesh and tore limbs, heads, and pieces from the bodies. He swung his arm like club and battered them out of the way. His pace slowed from steps to inches.

"Simon," Danielle said, "my Shockwave is prepped."

With a lunge, Simon grabbed one of the zombies in the midsection. He felt its flesh tear and its ribs snap as he held it. The undead creature flailed at him with decomposing fists that shattered against his faceplate.

"Do it," Simon ordered.

The Shockwave was another handheld weapon the Templar carried in their arsenal. It operated on HARP (Harmonic Resonance Projection) technology, which had been developed under Templar guidance. HARP technology used electronic and sonic generators to emit a static field that conducted sonic waves.

Designers intended HARP technology to help in mining operations and search and rescue efforts. The sonic waves generated by the HARP blasters shattered nonorganic items by altering frequencies too fast for those things to survive. Wood, stone, and steel items in the path of the sonic blast ruptured under the assault. Caves survived the punishment because they were too large to lose their integrity. But loose debris went to pieces.

Living matter—plants and animals—had their neural systems disrupted. Plants sometimes went into shock, but animals and humans blacked out under the assault.

Danielle triggered the Shockwave. It was a cut-down version of the HARP rifle. In order to get the reduced size, the designers had sacrificed room for the electromagnetic pulse gatherers and capacitors which had lengthened recharge time considerably. The area of effect was also cut back to fifteen to twenty feet and there was no way to aim the weapon. It discharged in a radius burst that went in all directions.

The Shockwave clicked loudly, then hummed. A moment later it fired. The sound even affected the ambient light. Particle waves became brighter and blistered in a blinding blue-white flash.

Simon's HUD adjusted to the light assault immediately. He experienced only a momentary discomfort and blank screen because the suit's AI was programmed to compensate for the Shockwave's effect. His vision returned in time to see what happened to the zombies.

In life, the zombies had been composed of *living* organic matter. In death, that composition changed. Blood no longer flowed and the body's internal rhythms were silenced. Inert corpses suffered the same fate as inorganic materials struck by the HARP waves.

The zombies froze like statues for a moment. The ones behind those affected by the Shockwave kept struggling to get to their intended victims. A moment later, the zombies shook and quivered, then flew to pieces and disappeared as they were reduced to energy waves. Some of those dead a short time were only blown back into the others.

Simon's right hand suddenly grasped nothing but empty space. He surged forward at once and barreled into the next line of zombies. The Spike Bolter leaped and howled in his hand. Palladium rounds chopped the zombies to pieces. He lowered his shoulder and slammed into the knot of undead trying to fill the vacuum at the doorway.

He tripped over a tangle of dead limbs and rolled forward to take advantage of his weight and momentum. Adroit as an Olympic athlete or not, the armor still had a lot of inertia to account for.

The undead buried him before he could get to his feet. Their combined weight threatened to crush him to the ground.

These are the quick ones, Simon thought. Even though he was outnumbered and outmassed, potentially looking at death, a savage joy hummed to life inside him. No matter what happened, no matter how the fight ended up, he knew he was where he was supposed to be. He'd trained all his life for the battles ahead of him.

He pushed himself up to his knees with his right hand. The suit strained to comply. The undead horde pressing him down shifted. He brought the Spike Bolter up in front of his face and squeezed the trigger.

A hole opened up in the undead flesh. He shoved himself toward it as the panoramic view through the HUD showed nothing but zombies around him. On his feet now, he whirled to the right with the Spike Bolter roaring in his fist. He reached for the sword sheathed between his shoulders and raked it free.

Four feet of gleaming steel sprang free in his hand. Since he'd learned to walk, his father had taught him the way of the sword. Bladework came as naturally as breathing.

He spun back to the left and hacked through the zombies with a horizontal slash that sliced through undead flesh and bone almost effortlessly. As he drew the sword up over his left shoulder to ready a backhand slash, he stepped into the crush of his enemies and brought up the Spike Bolter.

The HUD marked the three Templar in the building with him, and it marked the four Templar that had started in from the underground parking garage's street entrance. The Spike Bolter yammered as he blasted down the enemies to his left. With a hard pull, he yanked the sword from his shoulder in another level swing that emptied the ranks of the zombies to his right.

"Team Two, Team Three," Simon ordered. "Hold your positions. We're coming out."

The four advancing Templar pulled up and retreated. "Then come on," Drake said irritably. "You look like you're infested down there."

FIVE

When Simon looked to check their progress, Danielle, Walter, and Kevin came from the basement door. Walter and Kevin added their own small-arms fire.

Walter's Scorcher set zombies on fire as if they were dry tinder. The magical elements of the Greek Fire that fueled the hand flamethrower disrupted the control of the zombies' master. They lumbered and lurched in all directions, no longer intent on anything except the orange and red tongues of flame that consumed them. Kevin carried a Spike Bolter like Simon's, and he used it with deadly skill.

In the darkness, Danielle's Molten Edge sword burned through the zombies. It was a solid shaft of yellow and orange coal. The metal hilt and spine of the sword gave the eldritch energy its shape. The fiery blade left ash and cauterized flesh in its wake. Several of the zombies caught on fire and spread the flames to their mates.

But as many as the Templar destroyed, more arrived. The trap had been well set and well stocked.

Simon saw a Jaguar XKE-2 overturned ahead of him. He fought his way toward it. He holstered the Spike Bolter and chopped through the zombies between him and the sports car. When he reached the car, he caught hold of the bumper and yanked once to test it. Satisfied that it would hold for his purposes, he set himself.

"Anchor right foot," he ordered.

Immediately the suit's AI changed configurations and fired a spike into the concrete from the ball of his right foot. Only the ground anchor allowed him to use the suit's full strength to accomplish his goal. Otherwise the XKE-2's mass would have been too great for him to manage.

He spun and pulled with all the armor's strength. Metal shrieked in protest as he yanked. When a suit of armor was made, no two suits ended up the same. They were designed to enhance a Templar's natural abilities. Bigger, stronger Templar ended up even bigger and stronger.

At six feet five inches tall and built broad and thick, Simon was a human tank to begin with. In the armor, he became a wrecking machine. It would have been impressive if some of the demons weren't bigger and stronger.

The XKE-2 shrilled across the pavement as it came around. Simon pivoted on the anchored foot and threw the car. The vehicle didn't go far, no more than thirty or forty yards, but it cleared the way of zombies almost to the entranceway of the parking garage.

"Go," Simon shouted as he pulled the Spike Bolter free again. "Danielle, you've got the point."

"Understood." Danielle sheathed her Molten Edge and pulled the twin Spike Bolters she carried on her hips. The pistols roared as she picked up the pace to an open field run in the wake of the thrown XKE-2. "Stay on me. Stay on me."

Walter and Kevin, their burdens slung over their shoulders, followed Danielle. Their pistols fired continuously.

"Retract anchor," Simon said.

"Retracting anchor."

His foot came free of the pavement. He pushed himself forward and drew his Spike Bolter as he covered the retreat. The remaining zombies hurled themselves in pursuit. The palladium rounds mowed them down like a scythe. When they got close enough, he cut them down with the sword.

Simon fought and spun to meet the challengers. With the HUD guiding the way, he never lost his sense of direction or his teammates' positions.

With a lithe leap, Danielle reached the top of the overturned XKE-2. Spinning in a circle, she fired into the advancing ranks of the zombies. They went to pieces all around her.

"Regroup," she yelled. "My Shockwave's recharged." She holstered one of the Spike Bolters.

Walter and Kevin took cover on the lee side of the XKE-2 as Simon reached them. Almost immediately, the blue-white burst of the Shockwave blast took shape around them. The zombies within fifteen feet—and the XKE-2—vanished into displaced particles. The floor and ceiling remained because they were part of large structures.

Danielle landed effortlessly and swept her pistols toward the wave of zombies that separated them from the street entrance. Walter and Kevin were at her heels.

For a moment, Simon thought they were going to make it easily, then he saw the winged demons approaching the teams waiting in the streets. He didn't know if Leah Creasey was on-scene, but from what he knew of her, he felt certain she'd be nearby.

"Leah!"

Atop the building across the street, Leah saw the demons swoop down from the dark sky. They hadn't been there a moment ago.

And that means someone called them in, she thought

grimly. Then she heard Simon's voice echoing through her comm-link.

"I see them," she told him calmly. She sighted down the Cluster Rifle and took aim at the demon closest to the Templar teams holding positions on the street.

At first glance, Leah had thought the flying demons were Blood Angels. Those things were among the deadliest in the demon hierarchy.

These looked like pterodactyls from the natural history books Leah had studied as a girl. Back then, she'd loved the idea of dinosaurs and blamed it on Steven Spielberg's movies. Velociraptors had been great movie monsters, but they paled in comparison to the demons in London these days.

Instead of triangular heads, these flying demons had massive wedge-shaped heads that looked like they were all mouths and teeth. Horns clustered on the demons' heads over their eyes and along the backs of their necks. No lips framed the curved mouths. They were harsh, razor-edged beaks. The eyes were long and the pupils filled them, a certain indicator that they were nocturnal predators. Bat wings sandwiched massive bodies that had four limbs and tails that doubled the demons' length. Mottled dark scales covered them.

Four of the demons descended in a diamond shape on the unsuspecting Templar.

Leah heard Simon's warning cry over the Templar frequency she monitored. She put aside her fear and anxiety for the Templar and concentrated on the shot.

The onboard computer built into the small backpack unit she wore fed information to her helmet. Her sighting ocular flipped into place over her right eye as she lined up the shot.

In less than a heartbeat, the computer adjusted for the

demon's descent rate, the prevailing winds, the light, and
the distance. The ocular pulsed and turned Leah's vision
blood-red to let her know she had target lock.

Her finger caressed the Cluster Rifle's trigger long
enough to send a full salvo of missiles streaking toward the
demon. The Templar were only then reacting to Simon's
frantic instruction.

Coolly, Leah shifted targets before the first salvo struck
the demon. The Cluster Rifle's tri-barrel chugged as it rotated and fresh missiles were loaded. After acquiring her
new target, she squeezed the trigger again as the first target
was hit.

All the missiles sailed true and hammered the mark.
Leah had come prepared for quick takedowns. The missile
sequence loads were comprised of a sabot round designed
to penetrate a demon's hide and explode the secondary
charge within, Greek Fire, and a shotgun blast of palladium flechettes to slice and dice.

The flying demon buckled in the air under the impact.
The fletchettes opened gaping holes in the batwings and
sliced through several of the smaller support bones. The
wings turned to shredded meat. As the demon fell, the
Greek Fire caught and it became a comet on the way to the
ground. Only a few feet before the demon hit the ground,
the sabot round exploded and blew a great hole in the center of its back.

Even then, when the demon hit the ground, it was still
alive. It wobbled uncertainly on its back legs and focused
on the Templar. The demon stood two feet taller than
the Templar. Its serpentine neck lashed out as the wedge-
shaped head split into a huge mouth.

The second demon was in freefall as well. Leah kept
her attention focused on the two flying demons still in
the air. Hopefully the Templar could handle them on the

ground. The demons were more dangerous when they could streak in.

Unfortunately, she'd drawn the attention of the two surviving demons. They skirled high in the air, then flipped over like fast attack fighter jets and came screaming at her. Literally screaming. The noise was like fingernails on a chalkboard, and Leah's audio receptors struggled to knock down the decibel level and provide her with auditory contact.

One of them opened its mouth just as her ocular flared red to let her know she had the target. Roiling flame twisted from the demon's mouth and rained down on her. She hadn't seen that coming.

Free of the zombies, Simon ran for the nearest demon. It had its back to him and struck savagely at the Templar in the street.

Without giving quarter, Simon ran toward the demon. He sheathed the Spike Bolter and took a two-handed grip on the sword. Some preternatural sense warned the demon of his approach. It swiveled its massive head and tried to turn. A belch of flame hissed out over Simon as he swung the sword.

"Warning," the suit's AI said. "Critical damage taken."

Simon set himself, almost blind in the fire as the HUD sensors struggled to keep up with the assault, and swung the sword. He didn't aim for the demon's head or neck, even though those were tempting targets, because they moved too much.

Instead, he cleaved through the demon's spine. As long as a demon or demonspawn wasn't undead, basic anatomy applied. Provided an attacker could sever the spinal column through the scaled hide, the damage would render the demon paralyzed.

The demon toppled, but it didn't give up. It propelled itself forward with its front legs and managed to grab Simon's left leg in its mouth.

"Warning," the suit AI said in the calm female voice. "Structural integrity at risk."

Although the armor was so form-fitting as to be unique, there were still hollow places. A Templar couldn't gain weight without compromising his ability to fit into his armor, but weight loss was sometimes a problem during a campaign. The hollow spaces also created weak areas.

To neutralize those voids, the Templar smiths had created a special hygienic chemical "liquid" protein that filled in those areas and flowed all around the Templar's body. That way if a Templar was in his armor for days or weeks at a time, the "liquid" massaged the body and skin, keeping both healthy. The fluid could also be appropriated by the suit's AI and used to patch cracks and even holes from the inside in case of emergency.

It was also used to reinforce targeted areas to prevent damage from impact and crushing. Electrical impulses "hardened" the fluid in Simon's leg and provided extra strength.

Ignoring the pain in his leg, Simon reversed his sword and thrust it into the demon's eye all the way up to the hilt. The other end of the blade protruded through the demon's head. Then Simon twisted the blade.

The demon quivered convulsively. Its jaws went slack and it dropped.

The demon still blazing, Simon put his foot on its head and freed his blade. The other demon toppled as he glanced up. But the HUD showed there were two more. Both of them closed in on one of the nearby rooftops. As he watched, one of them breathed fire onto the rooftop. In the same moment, a salvo of missiles struck the demon and knocked it from the sky.

A black-suited figure rose to one knee on the rooftop and took aim at the last surviving flying demon.

Leah! Simon knew the young woman at once from their long association.

But he'd never seen her on fire before.

SIX

On fire, burning up, Leah stayed with the target. She fired twice and the Cluster Rifle bucked hard against her shoulder both times. Both salvos struck the flying demon in the back and knocked it from the sky.

As it fell, no longer a danger to her continued survival, she turned her attention to the flames that engulfed her. The armor she wore didn't compare to that of the Templar. Even during the years of investigating the secret order of knights as well as the Cabalists, her people had never learned the technology behind the armor.

What she wore was the best military grade there was, strictly eyes-only hardware, but it couldn't bear up like Templar armor. The flames peeled away her defenses. The first to go was oxygen. Her suit didn't carry an oxygen filtration and backup reservoir as she'd learned the Templar armor did.

And whatever the demon had spat on her, magic-based pitch resin or some kind of natural oil, it wasn't going out. She dropped the Cluster Rifle and beat at the flames with her gloved hands. All she succeeded in doing was spreading the flames.

Her lungs burned for air, but every time she tried to breathe in, there was nothing there. Heat battered her face as the flames sucked in close to her mouth and nose.

Don't panic, she told herself. But it was one thing to tell herself that while driving on icy roads or deep in enemy territory with security guards nipping at her heels. It was quite another to be calm while asphyxiating.

"Leah!"

She focused on Simon's voice. Surely he knew she was in trouble. Then again in the heat of combat, he might not have even known. Her senses swam and she knew from experience that she was about to black out.

She tried to choke out his name and couldn't. She stumbled toward the rooftop's edge and hoped there were no more demons.

Movement on her right side brought her around. She tried to draw the pistol at her side, but her hands failed her. In the next moment Simon was on her. He wrapped his arms around her and started back down the fire escape he'd climbed.

She was barely aware of him breaking through the window of the apartment there and grabbing the curtains. Leah was surprised they were still there. Curtains, especially heavy brocaded ones like this one, could help people stay warm during the bitter winters spent with no electricity or coal.

Simon called her name but she couldn't answer. He wrapped her in the curtain and she knew that he was trying to snuff out the flames. She didn't know if he was successful because she passed out.

"Leah." Simon pulled the curtains from the young woman cautiously. He thought he had all the flames out, but it was possible that fresh air could cause combustion.

She didn't respond, but the oily substance clinging to her armor didn't catch fire either. His cursory examination of the lightweight personal armor she wore, which fit her like a catsuit with reinforced contact areas at elbows, knees, sternum, and groin, didn't appear burned through. That was good. However, the flesh on the other side of the flame-retardant barrier could be parboiled.

"Simon," Danielle called.

"Yes."

"We have to get out of here."

"I know."

"Now."

Simon didn't blame Danielle for wanting to leave, but Leah had put her head on the block for them. He wasn't going to leave her behind. However, he didn't want to try to move her if it was only going to cause further injury.

"Go. I'll catch up."

"That's not how we—"

"No, it isn't." Simon swiveled his head and glared down at her. He knew she could spot him easily up on the fire escape landing through her HUD. Her suit's AI would have him tagged to make that even easier. "Nothing out here goes as planned every time. You've seen that. Get the team home. Get them safe. I'll be right behind you."

Danielle hesitated for only a moment, then she showed the good judgment that he'd promoted her to his field second for.

"If you're not," she warned, "and I have to track you down, I'm going to kick your butt."

Simon grinned a little at that. Danielle was a frequent sparring partner. It frustrated her that he was better than she was.

"Good luck," she called.

"And you." Simon watched her for any sign of life. He breathed a sigh of relief as he saw her chest rise and fall—slightly—but in steady rhythm.

* * *

Simon searched the black mask and thin helmet that covered her face for a seam or some locking mechanism that would allow him to remove it. None were apparent. When he saw the headset and ocular built into the helmet, he suspected the suit had built-in circuitry much like his armor's.

With his hand on the side of her head, Simon said, "Access."

"Accessing," his suit's AI responded.

Feedback suddenly juiced across Simon's HUD. The imaging feature rolled.

"Warning," the suit's AI said. "Shock deterrent employed. Access failed."

Frustration chafed at Simon. He didn't know if Leah was critically injured or only passed out from shock. There was no way to know if smoke had gotten trapped in her lungs and was damaging them as she struggled for breath.

And he certainly didn't know how anyone could know he and his team could be set up through her. Or who would want to.

Tenderly, he gathered her into his arms. He didn't know what she meant to him in this time and place. She was a beautiful woman, and independent. If they'd met at another time or another place, it might have been interesting to see how things would have turned out.

He climbed back to the top of the building long enough to pick up her rifle, then carried her against his chest as he went quickly down the fire escape stairs. With the armor boosting his strength, she was practically weightless.

At the bottom of the steps, the 360-degree vision allowed him to see the zombie lurch out of hiding. Its right arm was missing below the elbow. Its face was a wreck. It drew back the long knife it fisted in its remaining hand.

Effortlessly, Simon spun and delivered a reverse kick that crunched through the zombie's chest and knocked it to the ground. He stepped close to it and raised his foot, intending to smash its head and put an end to the twisted arcane power that gave it a semblance of life.

The thing's head suddenly shivered and melted. It re-formed almost immediately as new features rose from the bloody mess of diseased, dead flesh.

The new face looked angular and raw. The jawbone was long and ridged with a row of bony scales. The mouth was a knife-blade slash. Black eyes glinted with cold indifference beneath a forehead of twisted horns.

"This isn't over, Templar," the zombie said.

The voice reminded Simon of the demon down in the basement. He was certain whoever had possessed the man in the building and raised the zombie was also possessing this body now.

"I will find you again," the demon threatened.

"Tell me where you'll be," Simon replied. "I'd be happy to meet you halfway. Until you have the courage to face me, don't make hollow threats." He rammed his foot down and smashed through the zombie's head. When he turned to go, he didn't look back.

One more demon looking to kill him in a city full of them wasn't going to make a difference.

Leah continued to breathe all the way to the Bond Street tube station. Simon listened to her, but knew it wasn't what it should have been.

Bond Street had once been an affluent part of the May-fair District. It had risen to prominence during the May Fair market days, when the annual trade fair was moved there for a time; then it had evolved into one of the most prosperous places in all of London.

Simon had gotten to visit the area a few times with his father. The Templar had invested their money and speculated in the markets. Thomas Cross had dabbled in some of those investments.

As a boy, Simon had enjoyed the arcades on Old Bond Street and, later, watching the pretty young women that shopped along Savile Row. Now he wished he'd spent more time listening to his father. After four years, the pain of losing his father on All Hallows' Eve while he was squandering his rebellious youth in South Africa remained sharp.

He pushed those thoughts out of his mind as he descended the tube's stairs. He kept Leah from banging against him.

The tube no longer operated. He was pretty certain that since he'd gotten the train loaded with escapees out of the city four years ago no other trains had moved.

Several of the tube lines led to Underground complexes. Many of the Templar areas remained hidden, but the demons remained on the alert for them. If the Templar hadn't maintained an interest in the city's architecture, aboveground and below, those hiding places and underground fortresses wouldn't have existed.

Those places remained hidden for the most part, though the demons had ferreted out some of them. The sacrifices the Templar had made at St. Paul's on All Hallows' Eve had been to protect those resources. By dying in such great numbers, they'd hoped to lull the demons into believing the Templar threat was gone.

For the most part, the Templar threat was. Except that it hadn't been eradicated as the demons would have wanted. They'd merely moved more deeply underground to reconvene the war at a later date.

When Simon had seen the proposed plan in action, he

hadn't been able to follow through on it. Too many helpless people had remained in London and merely waited to die. In the end, he had taken his leave of the Templar Underground to follow a more proactive stance in helping the survivors reach the ships that ran the coastline in those days.

Those times were long gone now. Other Hellgates had opened up in other parts of the world. The struggle was no longer just for the survival of London, but of the planet.

Danielle and the others waited in the tunnel. They stood ready and waiting around two ATV trucks that had been specially modified from gasoline-powered engines to electromagnetic springwheel power plants. They were based on the Panther MLV but sported several upgrade packages. As a result of the conversion, the ATVs had more power, ran silently, and supported anti-aircraft guns and cannon. They were only one small step removed from tanks.

"Is she still alive?" Danielle asked as she reached down for Leah.

"Yes." Simon handed her up. "Be careful with her." He vaulted up into the cargo area after her. "I need some O_2 from the medkit."

One of the other Templar opened the medkit and took out the O_2 tank and a mask.

"Open helmet," Simon ordered. His faceplate dissolved in front of him as it receded to the reservoirs inside his helmet. He suddenly couldn't see as well in the dark, and the noises in the tunnel sounded different. The air stank and felt hot and doughy against his face.

Leah's breathing sounded more raspy and desperate to him, but he heard it with his own hearing, not the amplified sound pumped through his sensors. Her efforts sounded strained, but he could better judge how she was doing.

He lifted her head gently and fitted the face mask over

her mouth and nose. He knew from past battlefield experience that the suit wasn't self-contained like his armor. Her mask filtered out a lot of toxins. He just hoped enough O_2 could get through the material covering her lower face offset the smoke she'd inhaled. If he could clear her lungs out enough, they'd resume normal breathing. After a nod to the Templar manning the O_2 tank, he listened to the hiss of the gas filling the mask. She started breathing with less stress as the O_2 saturated her blood.

The ATV got under way with only a slight acceleration. The heavy-duty suspension, also an improvement over the old design, made progress almost smooth and rapid despite the debris left in the tunnels.

Templar manned the machine guns on either side of the vehicle and over the cab.

As he held the mask over Leah's covered face, Simon leaned his head back against the side of the truck and tried to relax. Their complex, the one he'd help build with his own two hands three and a half years ago, was miles outside of London. Although the trains no longer ran, the tracks still remained.

While he sat there, he tried to think of the names of any enemies he might have made that would have troubled themselves to put a demon onto his trail. Or who would have been able to.

So far none of the demons had made the war between them personal. But a man, although he didn't have a complete name, did come to mind.

The first time Simon had met him, he'd cut the man's hand off. When he'd found him again, the man had been wearing a demon's hand in place of his own.

Simon wasn't sure where to go looking for a man like that, and wasn't certain if that effort would be all that helpful. Whoever the man was, he was powerful and deadly.

SEVEN

For the last eight months, Warren Schimmer had made his home in an older building that had been a brothel on Old Compton Street in the Soho District in the center of the West End of London. Back before the Hellgate opened and he'd been a part-time college student and full-time employee of minimum wage jobs, he'd walked by the place several times while shopping in Chinatown. The prostitutes and their pimps had cleared out as soon as the demons had arrived. Locals had always claimed the area was going to Hell before, but they had no idea of how bad it would actually get.

The zombies he'd raised as his personal guard sat around him on the fine furniture. The building he'd chosen stood five stories tall, narrow and boxy.

In the early days, human squatters had tried to move in on Warren. But the zombies had stopped all those attempts. And there were occasional demon patrols, but most of them were Stalkers and others with minimal intelligence. The zombie presence indicated to them no human was there. A typical zombie could wander randomly through much of London these days. Warren's skills kept his in place, preventing another demon calling them away. They weren't good company, but at least Warren felt safe among them.

The rooms were elegantly furnished in red lacquer and

black onyx. Improbable portraits and carvings of Chinese heroes and demons decorated the walls. All of it seemed laughable now. There were far worse monsters moving through London these days than had ever been pictured in Chinese mythology.

Warren had chosen a suite of rooms on the fourth floor for himself. He assumed the room had been for special guests. It had a wet bar, which no longer worked but the alcohol supply was intact, a living area, and a balcony. He'd enjoyed the balcony for a few days until he'd nearly been killed by a demon once and almost shot by a London policeman a few days later.

It didn't do to flaunt his territory to either side locked in the struggle.

So he'd pulled the steel security bars down and settled in to make the brothel his home. With the zombies he left on guard there night and day, the building was clearly off-limits to anyone human that might want to steal what they could of from the desperate people who lived in such places.

Only Warren lived there now.

For a time, he had lived there with Kelli. She had been one of the three flatmates he'd had before the demon invasion. After Merihim had burned him and nearly destroyed him when the Cabalist contact had pulled him into this world, Warren had used his power to make Kelli his guardian. She'd become his zombie thrall, and lived only to care for him.

Almost a year ago, Kelli had given her life protecting Warren while scavenging for food. An Imp had shot her through the heart with some kind of weapon Warren still hadn't managed to identify. After Kelli had fallen, all without a sound, Warren had used his power to raise her up again.

During the three years he'd held her in thrall, she'd lost most of her personality. Warren had never believed she'd had a personality anyway. She'd always just been loud and argumentative in the flat. He hadn't cared for any of his flatmates, and they'd suffered with his presence because he paid more than his share of the bills

After he'd raised her from the dead, he'd brought her back to the brothel house. She hadn't fared as well as the other zombies he'd raised. He'd noticed differences in the zombies he'd raised. The ones from the older graveyards, the ones interred before embalming became a staple of most funerals, tended to fall apart quickly. If they were together to begin with.

Since Kelli hadn't been embalmed, natural decomposition had set in. Magic slowed the process, but she was slowly and quietly going to pieces.

Warren could no longer truly bear the sight of her, but he couldn't get rid of her either. With his childhood a shambles after the murder of his mother and his stepfather blowing his brains out in front of him, followed by a succession of foster homes where he'd only been a monthly stipend and not anything remotely human, Warren clung to familiar things.

Books and movies were his favorites because both were passports to other places that he'd found far more pleasant than his real life. He had vast libraries of them now, and had found generators that allowed him to play them. The soundproof basement—where "special" services involving whips and chains had been rendered—provided a safe place to watch them. But it was also a trap for him if anyone discovered him.

At this point, Kelli's zombie was a familiar thing, too. He couldn't get rid of her, but he knew at some point she'd be gone. She sat quietly every day in one of the lower rooms and slowly withered away. He only checked on her every now and again.

Seated at the ornate desk in the suite, Warren opened the nylon bag the man had carried the book in. Warren reached inside and took the tome out.

The book was large and thick, eighteen inches by fourteen inches by six inches. The leather binding had been dyed virulent purple, but the result—by accident or by design, Warren wasn't sure—had left the book marked by lines that looked like blood veins.

Then he felt it pulsing in his hand, like the echo of a heart beating slowly and strongly somewhere deep inside.

Fear touched Warren then. Some books had lives of their own. Some were traps. He'd read about them and heard about them from other Cabalists.

All of the books of power were designed to protect themselves.

He ran his hand, his demon's hand, over the book. A purr vibrated through the still air at the contact. The book *felt* pleasing to Warren's touch.

"Are you alive?" he whispered to the book. Even though he'd read about such things, he'd never actually seen a living book.

An eye opened in the center of the book.

Warren slowly drew his hand back.

The eye bulged from the book's surface and glanced around. Warren almost expected it to sprout legs to run away or wings to fly off. He wouldn't have truly been surprised.

A mouth opened below the eye. Jagged fangs and a forked black tongue filled it.

"Who are you?" The voice was deep, somber, and slow.

Warren thought about his answer for the briefest moment. True names often carried power, and Merihim had enough power over him.

"A friend," Warren said.

The eye looked around the room again. "I don't know this place."

"You're safe here."

Suspicion narrowed the eye's focus as it studied him. "What do you want?"

That was a dangerous question too. The book doubtless had protective spells, but how did the other man hold it?

"Only to know," Warren said.

"What do you wish to know?" the book asked.

"Everything."

The mouth below the staring eye smiled. "Then know."

The book cover flipped open and struck the table a resounding blow that echoed in the cavernous room. The first page was a full-color illustration that had to have come from Hell itself. As Warren stared into the picture, he sank into it.

In the blink of an eye, Warren stood on that battlefield. Demonic roars, the shrill, frightened cries of the wounded and dying, and the clanking of iron-bound wheels spinning across the rocky ground screamed into his ears.

All around him, fearful demons engaged frightened human warriors mounted on horseback and in chariots. Most of the demons towered above the humans. Some breathed flames and incinerated humans, horses, and chariots alike. Flying demons struck from above with spells, weapons, claws, and teeth.

Warren turned his head in an effort to look away from the book. All he saw was more of the battlefield. He didn't know how he'd entered the scene in the book, and he definitely didn't know how he was going to get out.

"Demon!" The harsh cry ripped through the air behind Warren. "Foul thing from the pits of Hell! I'll send you back!"

Warren turned and saw a charioteer riding straight for him. In the chariot, a man with a square-cut beard, an olive complexion, and violet eyes drove his team furiously. He plucked a javelin from the quiver mounted beside him. The two horses that pulled the chariot were wide-eyed with panic and frothing at the mouth from being run too hard for too long.

Stand still, Warren told himself. *Just stand still and let him run you through. That will break whatever spell you're under.*

The chariot raced toward him. The horses' hooves thundered on the hard-packed, bloodstained earth. The iron-bound wheels rolled over the bodies of the dead. With a lithe flick of his arm, the charioteer sent the javelin shooting toward Warren.

Self-preservation won out over Warren's decision to stand his ground. Years of looking out for himself and fearing nearly everything and everybody wouldn't be denied. He stepped back and sideways to let the javelin pass within inches of him. No one human could have moved so fast. Merihim's hand blending with Warren's own flesh and the spells he'd laid on himself had increased his physical abilities.

Undeterred, the charioteer whipped his horses mercilessly and drove them straight at Warren. Either the horses' flashing hooves or the churning wheels would wound or kill him.

Warren gestured at the horses' feet. Their legs tangled and they fell. The harness jingled and rattled as the chariot overturned and slid along the ground. The wheel trapped under the vehicle shattered as the driver sailed forward and landed on the ground. Before he could get up, the chariot rolled over him and the broken wheel spokes tore into his chest and stomach.

Another human rider rode at Warren and swung the short-hafted ax he carried in one scarred hand. With his right hand, Warren caught the man's wrist as he swung the heavy blade at his head. With a brief twist, Warren pulled the rider from his saddle and flung him away.

A riderless horse ran beside Warren. Effortlessly, Warren caught the saddle horn in his left hand and hauled himself into the saddle.

He was surprised at his actions. He'd never ridden a horse before in his life, and he'd only seen the maneuver he'd just performed in movies and television shows.

He leaned down and caught the reins, then pulled them back hard enough to make the horse rear. The blood that built up in the steed's lungs from the exertions of battle caused pink foam to fleck his nostrils.

The horse wheeled at his command, and he looked down the long hill where the battle raged. Fetid Hulks towered twelve feet tall as they marched slowly through the horsemen and chariots to smash the ballistae the human forces had gathered to combat the advancing horde. Ill-shaped and ghastly green, the brutes hammered men, horses, and chariots to pieces. They stopped on occasion and spewed the virulent toxin they carried in the sack below their gaping mouths.

Carnagors, thickly muscled and armored with almost impenetrable gray-black hides, erupted from the ground as they tunneled under the battlefield to surprise the defenders. When they came aboveground, their massive heads snapped out at those luckless enough to be around them, gulped them down, and retreated once more into the earth.

Blade Minions swung their spiked forearms against their foes as they took on the front-line defenders. The armor that the humans wore shredded like paper under their blows. Ripped and torn bodies lay scattered behind them as they drove forward.

Occasionally the defenders got loads of rock airborne. When they did, the rocks crushed and injured the imps and demons that made up the bulk of the invading force. Huge crossbow bolts flew across the battlefield and speared through the Fetid Hulks and other large demons.

But those victories were too few to even begin to turn the tide of battle.

From horseback, Warren watched the battle. Part of him wanted to see how things turned out even though he was certain he knew. But part of him wanted to return to his room in the brothel.

The thing that scared him most was that he didn't even know if that was possible. He could be trapped in the book forever. He was certain that was where he was.

Do you know now? the voice asked. *Do you wish to know more?*

Before Warren could answer, he looked farther up the hill the demons were taking and saw a castle high among the jagged peaks. A narrow dirt trail wound back and forth across the foothills to reach up into the mountains. Warren assumed the trail led to the castle, and he wondered who lived there.

Do you wish to know more?

Warren almost answered yes before he had time to think. *Is that part of the glamour? Does curiosity bind you to the book? And what happens to you when you stay here?*

"Not yet," Warren answered. "Let me know more later."

As you wish.

The landscape swirled then went black. Dizziness wrenched Warren's stomach and he would have purged if only his stomach and throat were still connected. He was certain they weren't.

Then everything faded away.

Warren roused as if from a heavy sleep. He gazed blearily at the book before him on the desk. At the moment it only looked like a book again. Curious, wondering if he'd only imagined the whole thing, he lifted his hand and laid it on the book.

The eye and mouth didn't reappear. He wondered if he could call it forth if he wanted to.

"Warren?"

Startled, Warren snapped his head around.

EIGHT

Ill at ease, Warren rose from the chair at the desk. He thought about putting the book away, but knew that doing so would only draw more attention to it. Instead, he focused on the woman who had intruded into his sanctuary and wondered how she'd been able to do that.

Naomi sat on the unmade bed in the center of the room. Covered in tattoos and piercings, the woman was a couple years older than Warren. Two short, curved horns stood out on her smooth forehead and gave her an evil look. Petite and womanly, she wore dark red leather pants, hiking boots, and a sleeveless, high-necked blouse.

At one time she'd been more skilled in the ways of demons than he was. That was no longer true. These days he was the teacher. From the beginning, he had more power.

"Is anyone else here?" Warren demanded. He rose from his seat and gazed around the room for anyone that might have accompanied her.

No one else was there.

"I came alone," Naomi said in her soft contralto.

Warren glared at her. She was the kind of woman that wouldn't have given him a second glance before the Hellgate opened. If he hadn't been as powerful as he was, and definitely more powerful than her, she probably still wouldn't have given him the time of day.

"How did you get in?" he demanded.

"Through the front door. It isn't locked."

It wasn't locked because it had been broken down. Fixing it would only have drawn attention to the fact that someone lived there. And zombies didn't repair doors.

"The zombies should have stopped you."

"They didn't," Naomi replied casually.

When he'd first met her four years ago, Naomi had been among the hierarchy of the Cabalist sect that had taken Warren in and explored the power he'd possessed that had drawn Merihim forth. Most of those people were dead now, some of them at Warren's hand.

"Why?"

"You've had me here with you."

Warren had. She'd since become a sometime lover. At first he'd been excited. Then he'd learned she was only truly with him to learn what he knew. The passion had quickly cooled, and he hadn't wanted to let her know she'd hurt him by being so mercenary.

"They didn't know they were supposed to keep me out," she said.

"I need to tell them to guard against you," he said.

Naomi frowned. "Do you see me as a threat?"

"No. Of course not." Warren said that quickly, a gentle rebuke to remind her of how much power he wielded rather than any form of endearment. "But this is my sanctum." He'd always liked that word when he'd read it in the comics.

She smiled a little at that. "I would have called if I could. Niceties like announcing yourself are a thing of the past, I'm afraid."

Warren walked to the window and looked out over the city. Darkness had given way to light, but it was far past dawn. He couldn't help wondering how long he'd spent ensorcelled by the book.

"What are you doing here, Naomi?" he asked.

"I came to see you."

He leaned a hip against the window and gazed at her. "You don't do that often, and only then to get something from me."

"You make me sound selfish."

"You are."

"But you still like me."

"Sometimes." Warren felt irritated at the game she played. Before, when he'd first met her, she'd been intimidated and fascinated by him. Now she'd grown familiar with him. And maybe more than a little jealous of his power.

The Cabalists observed and—sometimes—captured demons. They catalogued and grouped them to explore their natures and weaknesses. But mostly they coveted the demons' power.

Before the Hellgate had opened, humans—*some* humans—had possessed powers that some believed came from an earlier contamination of demons touching this world. The histories were more like fables and stories regarding those times, but the powers had existed. The closer the time came for the Hellgate to manifest, the more prevalent the powers became.

Warren's mother had been drawn to the dark powers, and she'd neglected every other aspect of her life for them. Warren had never wanted them, and he'd tried to ignore the fact that he'd had them.

"Do you like me now?" Naomi asked coyly.

"I liked you better four years ago," Warren said. "You had more tact in those days."

Stung, Naomi stood. Her cheeks darkened. "You thought I was innocent?"

Warren had. He also wondered if she had been more

innocent in those days and if the power she strove to attain was corrupting her.

"It doesn't matter what I think," Warren replied. Though he resented her intrusion, he didn't want to see her go away angry. Or maybe go away at all. "I like you fine now. But you shouldn't come here."

"I usually like coming here."

"What would you do if the zombies weren't the only things I had guarding this place?"

"I don't know."

"You could end up getting killed."

Naomi crossed the room to him and took his demon's hand in both of hers. She kissed the scaled flesh tenderly. Warren couldn't help wondering if Merihim felt that kiss as well, and if Naomi suspected the demon might.

"I don't think you'd ever kill me," she said.

"I would," Warren said, "if I ever had reason to."

"I will never give you reason to."

Warren hoped not. He hadn't had any friends before the Hellgate opened. He didn't have any now, but Naomi was as close as it came.

"Why did you come?" he asked.

"To see you." Naomi released his hand and stepped away.

Warren waited. He didn't like playing games with her.

"First Seer Cornish would like to speak to you."

"About what?"

"He didn't say." Naomi frowned at that. "It appears he likes keeping his secrets too."

First Seer Cornish was new to the post. Not many who wanted to become the leader of the Cabalists remained in that position. He'd been an aristocrat before the arrival of the demons and had conducted his studies into mysticism on his own. He still remained something of an elitist, and Warren didn't care for him.

"I'm surprised he's still alive," Warren said.

"The current First Seer has a way of giving ideas to others and convincing them they thought of them," Naomi said disdainfully. "Several people have died as a result."

"Do you think he wants to *convince* me of something?"

"He might." Naomi smiled. "But I don't think he will."

"Did he convince you to come here?"

"I didn't need convincing." Naomi came to him and wrapped her arms around him. "I only needed an excuse. It's been days since I've seen you." She kissed him deeply.

"I've been meaning to ask you, where do you get the water to bathe?"

Warren stood in the bath and toweled himself dry. "I had the zombies dig a well in the basement. They pump it up to the hot tubs on the fifth floor."

"You had a well built?"

"Dug. Yes."

"I didn't know you knew how to dig wells."

"There are books that tell you how to dig wells." Warren pulled on black jeans and a red, white, and blue Rochdale Hornets rugby jersey. The garment, an official jersey, was something he'd never have been able to afford before the invasion. "You can find pumps at the stores."

The city's survivors made use of everything they could find, but there were far more supplies than there were survivors.

"The water tables are dropping. Soon it's going to be hard to get drinking water."

Warren knew that. All a person had to do was look at

the River Thames to see that. The effects of the Burn had lowered the river to the point that it now flowed backward in from the North Sea. Once that had happened, the water had turned brackish, fresh water mixing with salt water, and became undrinkable. Wells near the riverbanks had also become tainted because they weren't able to filter out enough of the salt.

Despite that knowledge, Warren didn't feel guilty about bathing. When he'd grown up in the foster homes, hygiene had been ignored. Baths were a creature comfort he demanded.

Dressed, Warren surveyed his reflection in the mirror. The scars from the burns left him with patches of demon skin. His mates would have ridiculed him as ugly, but among the Cabalists he was looked upon with envy.

Though Cabalists could—sometimes—transplant demon horns as Naomi did, few of them could transplant limbs or organs successfully. Those who tried and failed died horrible, agonizing deaths. The number of those who wanted to try were even fewer.

He turned from the mirror and returned to the suite.

Naomi sat at the desk and pored over the book.

"What are you doing?" he demanded.

She still hadn't dressed and sat there naked in the chair. She'd suggested that the First Seer didn't have a definite timetable in mind and they could be a little later. Warren hadn't wanted the physical encounter because he always felt weak afterwards for giving in to her. It was like admitting she had power over him. But he hadn't been able to ignore it.

"Looking at this book," she replied. "Where did you get it?"

Warren ignored the question. He walked over to join her, surprised that she was still sitting there.

"What do you see?" he asked quietly.

"Shapes. Shadows. The pages look like they were wet and the ink smeared. I don't know why you haven't thrown it away." Naomi regarded him. "You see something else, don't you?"

On the page, the battle between the humans and the demons continued. The skirmish line had receded farther up the hill. The image began to waver.

With an effort of will, Warren looked away and closed the book with his human hand. "No."

Naomi looked at him for a moment, then said, "You don't lie very well."

"I'll get better at it," he replied.

NINE

Leah came to with a start. Almost immediately a headache throbbed between her temples. The bright light shining down into her eyes didn't help. Something bound her above her breasts, at her midsection, and across her knees.

When she tilted her head up and opened her eyes, she discovered she was lying on a hospital bed in a sterile white room. Thick leather bands held her against the bed. She was still clad in her black armored one-piece.

She attempted to gain leverage against her bonds and either break them or slither out through them. Either was possible. Her one-piece, besides being bullet- and impact-resistant, also accentuated her strength and speed. It was nowhere near what the Templar armor did, but she was a lot lighter on her feet and could hide easier.

The door opened and a young woman in scrubs walked through. She was pretty and demure, with short dark hair and freckles across her nose.

"Easy there, miss." The young woman's tone was officious but nonthreatening. "I'll have you loose in a minute. If you'll give it to me."

Leah powered up a taser charge in her right glove. One slight flick would send an electrified dart winging across the distance and deliver a fifty-thousand-volt charge that would drop the woman in her tracks.

"Where am I?" Leah demanded. Her voice sounded muffled through her mask.

"Simon Cross brought you in, miss." The woman unfastened the belt across Leah's chest. "We only belted you in so you wouldn't fall off the bed and injure yourself further."

Leah made herself lie still and take calm breaths. Her throat was sore and her lungs ached. "You didn't say where I was."

"You're in the retreat. Outside of London." The woman unfastened the last belt. "Do you need help sitting up?"

"No. I can manage." Leah felt incredibly weak. If her strength hadn't boosted by her suit, she knew she wouldn't have been able to bring herself to a sitting position on the bed. "Thank you."

"You're welcome." The woman stood nearby.

Leah tried to get off the bed and fell. Enhanced strength didn't help her sense of balance, and accelerated reflexes only meant she could grab for the bed twice and miss both times.

The woman caught her. "Easy does it, now." Gently, she eased her back onto the bed. "Maybe you'll want to go slowly for a minute."

As she sat on the edge of the bed and waited for her head to stop spinning, Leah chafed to be up and moving. She'd been gone too long. Her supervisor was going to have a proper fit. She couldn't blame him.

"Maybe you could remove the mask, miss," the nurse suggested. "We weren't able to do that. It made getting you enough oxygen troublesome."

"Not yet. I want to see Simon."

The young woman nodded. "All right. He'd asked to be notified as soon as you'd regained your senses." She started to turn away, then turned back. "I'd like to suggest that you allow us to check you over before you get too active. We weren't able to x-ray you through your uniform."

Leah nodded. She wanted to make sure she was physically fit as well. "As soon as I talk to Simon."

The nurse left.

As she sat up straighter, Leah tried to draw breath deeply into her lungs and breathe it out. She remembered being on fire, and trying to breathe the acrid smoke. Nightmares had haunted her while she'd been out.

"Time," she said.

Her ocular flipped into place and brought up the current time. It was 3:43 p.m. She was long past check-in time. Anxiety thrummed through her. The increased blood pressure intensified the pain in her head and the pounding in various bruises scattered around her body.

The armor held an inner layer of HardShel nanobots that worked together like fluid. They were a step up—a *big* step up—from the liquid body armor that had been brought out twenty years ago for military forces. Those garments had weighed in the neighborhood of four pounds apiece. The one-piece she wore weighed ounces more than the normal clothing would have.

The nanobots were designed to keep a constant flow around the body of the wearer. Any sudden shock, such as a bullet impacting against the one-piece or someone stabbing the one-piece, would be absorbed.

Leah kept breathing slowly. Smoke had to have gotten down into her lungs and she had to work to breathe it out.

"GPS location," Leah said.

The ocular flashed almost immediately. Tiny letters printed out on the screen but she could read them.

UNABLE TO ACCESS

Great, Leah thought, irritated. *GPS is blocked.* She had no idea where she was, other than at Simon Cross's hideaway. In the last few years, he'd gotten better at being hidden. She had no idea where she was.

"Simon."

Waking instantly at the touch, Simon briefly touched the sword sharing his bed. He gazed up at the belled underside of the hammock above him.

Space was at a premium in the redoubt. This particular bunker hadn't been built with long-term occupancy in mind.

When he'd set up general quarters, he'd devoted most of the room to women and children who were noncombatants and support staff. In the Templar Underground, everyone had lived with cramped space because room was at a premium.

In addition, the Templar Underground had had hundreds of years to make bigger places and train all their people to use space efficiently. Simon had to balance everything carefully in a camp that held both refugees and soldiers, where disciplined Spartans ate and slept side-by-side with frightened civilians.

"Simon."

"I'm awake," he said, and pushed himself out of sleep to a sitting position on the side of the hammock. The concrete floor was cold against his feet.

The Burn heated London up, but the rest of the world seemed cold these days. The magic reshaping the city had disastrously affected weather patterns. A light frosting of snow covered the ground outside the bomb shelter they were currently holed up in. Normally, there wouldn't have been snow on the ground for months.

"The woman you brought in," Nathan Singh said. "She's awake. She wants to talk to you."

"All right."

Nathan extended a flask. "Hot tea, mate. It'll help get the blood going."

"Any cream and sugar?" Simon asked.

"No," Nathan quipped, "but I've some lovely cabbage rose print china back at my bunk."

Simon grinned, took the flask, and drank deeply. The tea was strong and dark, and hot enough to clear his sinuses. "Thanks."

"No problem." Nathan put the flask back on the hammock above Simon's.

Simon abandoned hope of any more sleep for a time. Leah would have a lot of questions. And then he'd have to decide what to do with her. Having her at the camp compromised the camp's location. He thought he could trust her, but he had over four thousand lives hanging in the balance if he was wrong.

You can't be wrong, he told himself. *However you handle this, you can't be wrong.*

He stood and pushed the blankets to the foot of the hammock. He was nude. All Templar slept nude because they couldn't wear clothing under the armor. It was made to fit exactly without any hindrance.

The question was whether to see Leah as a Templar, or as himself. As a general rule, he'd ordered every Templar to keep his or her armor at hand no matter where he or she was.

"Get dressed," Nathan said. "Street clothes. I'll bring your armor along in a bit."

Simon nodded. During the last three years, Nathan had proven himself to be a good friend and dedicated warrior. He was from the Templar House of Darius, and normally they were at odds with the House of Rorke.

Ruefully, Simon admitted that the rebelliousness was probably still in order. High Seat Booth was all in favor of the Grand Marshal's current edict that the Templar remain in hiding for the most part. Like many of the others that had abandoned the Underground, Nathan hadn't been able to stomach the idea of staying safe while so many people were hunted by demons every day.

Nathan was almost six feet in height and bulked up from lifting weights. A black gunslinger mustache he took a lot of kidding about framed a generous mouth. He wore his hair short and had a tattoo of a dragon that covered his left arm from shoulder to elbow. He claimed it was the dragon St. George slew.

Simon kept a small selection of clothing in a chest under his hammock. He pulled on cargo pants, tennis shoes, and a dark blue T-shirt that fit him like a second skin. He belted a Spike Bolter around his hips.

Rule #1 was that no one went unarmed in the redoubt.

When Simon reached the medical bay, he found Leah sitting on the edge of the bed. He entered the room and looked at her.

"How are you?" he asked.

"Alive. That's pretty surprising." Although the mask covered Leah's face, Simon thought he could hear a smile in her voice.

"It surprised me, too," he admitted. "I didn't know if you were going to make it." He leaned against the wall with his arms folded over his chest. "For a while there I didn't know if any of us were going to make it."

"Did you get the Templar out of there?"

Simon nodded. "We did."

"How are they?"

"Still unconscious. The medics have worked on them. They don't know what's wrong. Their physical health seems all right, but there may be some brain damage."

"Did you lose anyone rescuing them?"

"No. We were lucky."

Silence hung in the room for a moment.

Simon had a hard time guessing what thoughts were going through Leah's head. He had a hard time figuring that out anyway even without the mask hiding her features.

There were too many things he didn't know about her. Why she was down in South Africa looking for him. How she even knew to look for him. How she got as competent at fighting as she was. How she was so familiar with weapons.

And where she'd gotten the black one-piece uniform she wore.

"You need to get out of that armor," Simon said. "The medics haven't been able to properly examine you. There could be some internal damage or a broken bone. They couldn't get the uniform off you or x-ray through it."

"No, they wouldn't be able to do that. And it's a good thing for them they didn't try too hard."

"Who are you with?" Simon asked.

The blank features of the mask regarded him for a moment. Then Leah lifted her hands to her head and ran her palms over the tight-fitting headpiece. The mask separated and rolled down to her neck.

Leah hadn't changed much during the four years that Simon had . . . *been aware* of her. He couldn't say he knew her. She had captivating violet eyes and short-cropped dark hair that hung just past the line of her jaw. Her skin was pale, no longer possessing the tan he'd seen her with on that plane out of Cape Town.

"I can't answer that," Leah said.

"I may be endangering the lives of everyone here if I let you go," Simon said. He tried to keep his voice easy and light, but he knew the threat was there all the same.

"If I decide to leave," Leah stated quietly, "you won't stop me without someone getting hurt."

"I know. That's what makes the situation difficult. I shouldn't have brought you here. But if I'd left you, you might have died."

"You couldn't do that."

Simon hesitated. "No."

Leah showed him a faint smile. "Do you guys have a code against that?"

"Yes," he answered honestly. "It's part of the Templar charter. We defend the helpless and the weak. Originally it was intended for travelers met on the road."

"I'm not exactly helpless and weak."

"You're not," Simon agreed. "You still needed help."

"Not all of the Templar believe the way you do, Simon," she said. "I know they don't, and you know they don't."

Simon was quiet for a moment. When he'd first taken her into the Templar Underground, he'd thought she was just a young woman in need of protection. But the biggest reason that he'd taken her there was because it didn't matter. The Templar Underground, at least in the House of Rorke's area, was easily defensible. More than that, there'd been no reason to believe the demons would talk to any human. Or that humans would betray the Templar.

"I was told you wanted to talk to me," he said.

"I wanted to thank you for bringing me here," Leah said earnestly. "You probably did save my life. But I needed to talk to you about more than just those two Templar."

TEN

"Have you heard of a man named Archibald Xavier Macomber?" Leah asked.

Simon stared into those violet eyes and thought about the name. Something worried at the back of his mind but he couldn't pin it down.

"No," he answered.

"Macomber's a linguistics professor," Leah said. "He was a child prodigy when it came to languages. He traveled the world and worked on old scrolls, illuminated manuscripts, and other things that needed translation. He got quite a bit of fame out of the work he did."

"He was on the American History Channel," Simon said, remembering where he'd heard the name. "There were a series of specials that he did showing the flow of language along trade routes."

Leah nodded. "The Silk Road. The Salt Road. The Slave Trade. He covered all those areas."

Simon remembered then. Thomas Cross had loved knowledge simply for the sake of knowledge. When he'd been younger, he'd enjoyed watching several of those episodes—especially the ones involving medieval weapons—with his father.

"As I recall, Macomber seemed to disappear overnight," Simon said.

"In most people's opinions, Macomber started to lose his grasp on reality."

"I don't recall that."

"He started insisting that there were demons loose in the world," Leah said. "He claimed to have uncovered proof."

Simon remained quiet. Although the Templar had known of the demons' existence, even they had been hard pressed to prove their case. In the end their belief had cost them their fortunes. The king of France, Philip the Fair, accused the Templar Order of heresy and had prodded Pope Clement V to declare them to be heretics. As a result, they'd been stripped of their titles and privileges in 1307. Philip drove the Templar into exile and burned Grand Master Jacques de Molay at the stake.

From that time on, the Templar had operated out of the public eye and away from the royal courts. But they had remained tapped into the aristocratic families and learned all the news they could of far-off lands. When an artifact or proof of the demons came to the surface, Templar were dispatched to recover them.

"Nobody wanted to hear about demons before the Hellgate opened," Simon said. "The news broadcasts we've watched are still full of stories about aliens from outer space and a global terrorism effort."

"I know." Leah frowned. "The group—" She stopped herself. "The people I'm with are still struggling with the idea of demons. Terrorists, or even aliens from another world, are far easier for most of them to understand. But some of the things Macomber was talking about, some of the writing he showed—which a lot of people thought he'd made up—is like the writing of the demons that are here now."

We should have known this, Simon thought. Then he realized that the Templar may have known it and chosen not to act on it.

"My . . . *friends* wanted to talk to Macomber," Leah said. "They've been searching for him."

"Did they find Macomber?" Simon asked.

"We found him. He was in an insane asylum outside of Paris, France."

"Why France?"

"His wife at that time was French. She wanted him sent there for 'help' so the French courts would make certain she would get his estate."

"She divorced him?"

"Not until the money was all gone." Leah took a breath. "Macomber spent eight years in the asylum. Four years ago, after the Hellgate opened, the asylums were opened and those people were released. Nineteen months ago, he came to the attention of the group—"

Simon resisted the impulse to ask what group that was.

"—and efforts were undertaken to track him down," Leah continued. "Last week, Macomber was found."

"Where?"

"Inside Paris. He was living in one of the universities and had some of his papers. He was working on the translations when we located him."

"Translations of what?"

Leah shook her head. "No one knows."

"What kind of shape is Macomber in?"

"He's lucid. Intelligent. And convinced that he's onto something."

"He knows about the Hellgate?"

"They have one in Paris now, too."

Simon was briefly taken aback. There had been rumors of other Hellgates, but this was the first confirmation he had heard of the one in Paris. He imagined the Champs Elysées in ruins, and the Eiffel Tower toppled and smashed like Lord Nelson's Column in Trafalgar Square.

"What is Macomber saying about the demons?" Simon asked.

"That's just it," Leah said. "He's not. He's insisting he's not going to talk to anyone until he talks to the 'knights' first."

The knights. Simon let that sink in.

"Where's your lady friend, mate?"

Simon paused the video feed on the old tri-dee that one of the salvage crews had brought in from one of their excursions. The crew had rescued it for the children who stayed with them till they were able to arrange passage out of Great Britain.

These days no ships or boats ran and such passage was scarce. Simon had heard that most of the vessels had been destroyed, but he'd also heard that there were no safe places to take anyone. The demons were everywhere.

"Back in the infirmary," Simon said. He sat in one of the small public gathering places scattered throughout the redoubt.

The building had originally begun life as one of the fallout shelters built during World War II. In that war, all the children had been sent off to the countryside to get them out of harm's way. Back then, the greatest thing a person had to fear was a bomb landing in their house. Nobody had ever thought about demons pouring in through a Hellgate until it happened.

"Thought you might like a bite to eat." Nathan placed a big bowl of oatmeal on the desk beside Simon. "I know how you forget things like that."

"Thanks." The oatmeal smelled good and made Simon's stomach growl. He scooped it up and looked at the butter melting on it. "Butter? Hand-churned?"

"Hand-churned. Next time you'll be getting your tea with cream and sugar in a china cup. And biscuits. Shall I fetch you a cushion?"

"Ponce," Simon replied as the unfamiliar feeling of a smile crept into his face.

Nathan laughed. "There are still a few cows running round in the wild, and we've been fortunate enough to have a few people among us who know how to make do from scratch."

Simon knew that was true. The survivors they'd dug from the wreckage of the city had contributed as much to the sanctuary as the Templar. A few of them were even learning how to make Templar armor and use it.

"So how is she?" Nathan asked.

"She appears to be well enough."

"Did she say where she got that uni she's wearing?"

Simon briefly considered the uniform Leah wore. None of their technology had yet penetrated the suit's defenses. "No."

"Do you want to take a guess?"

Simon swallowed oatmeal. "My guess would be military."

"Not exactly what the soldier boys were wearing while they were fighting the demons in the streets."

"I know."

"But it's definitely mil-spec." Nathan smiled. His background, before the invasion, had been military. Although he didn't want to choose between his military duty and Templar duty, Nathan had decided to follow the Templar. When he had been one of those assigned to stay in hiding, he had taken the command hard. "Makes her all the more interesting, eh? Popping into and out of your life as she sees fit. Telling you what she wants you to know."

"I don't take her on blind trust."

"I didn't say that you did." Nathan looked at the computer chips on the desk. "But she's responsible for this, isn't she?"

"She is."

"Want to tell me about it?"

"Have you ever heard of a man named Archibald Xavier Macomber?"

Nathan thought for a moment, then shook his head.

"He was a linguistics professor who believed he'd found—and partially translated—a demonic language."

"Now someone like this, I should have heard of."

"That's what I thought." Simon took another bite of oatmeal. "Leah's people—"

"Who shall remain mysterious."

Simon ignored the comment in continued. "—found Professor Macomber down in France. He'd been in a sanitarium for the last eight years."

"Lovely."

"His wife had him committed once he started talking about demons."

"A lot of people talked about demons, mate," Nathan said. "Normally most people would just walk on the other side of the street and talk behind the backs of those who admitted such things. Now it's downright fashionable. What made Macomber so much the target?"

"There was money involved."

"Ah, so it was financially rewarding to lock up the professor."

"Right." Simon put the empty bowl on the desk. "I've been through the Templar files regarding Macomber. We—meaning the Templar—knew about Macomber."

"Then why didn't we—meaning the Templar—talk to him at some point?"

"It was decided that Macomber was too controversial and too public at the time."

"When was that?"

"Twelve or thirteen years ago."

Nathan smiled. "I was still stealing kisses from the girls in the Underground. And you, as I recall, were planning BASE jumps off prominent London buildings."

"Not quite then." It has been those BASE jumps that had brought Simon to the attention of the Metropolitan Police Department and almost caused a huge investigation. Simon hadn't had any papers. There wasn't a record of his birth on file in the country. He'd almost been deported as an undesirable immigrant. Only his father's hand in the matter had smoothed things over.

"You probably weren't paying any more attention to the goings-on of the Templar intelligence department than I was," Nathan said.

"No, I wasn't."

"So we must have missed mention of Macomber."

Simon nodded.

"Even if we'd heard of him, we'd probably have ignored him as much as everyone else did."

"Probably."

"So why did your lady friend—"

"Leah. Not my lady friend."

"My apologies. Why did Leah bring Macomber up to you?"

"Macomber," Simon said as he looked at his friend, "is in the hands of Leah's people. Or will be soon. They're sailing him in from the French coastline in a couple days."

"Sounds intriguing, but if they're trying to be mysterious and everything, should she be telling you?"

"Macomber is refusing to answer any questions about the demons. He wants to talk to a 'knight.'"

Nathan grinned. "Ah. She supposes that would be us."

"Yes."

"So are we going to talk to him?"

"Macomber claims to know of a weapon that we can use against the demons."

"Advantageous. I don't see how we can pass that up."

Simon silently agreed.

"When do we leave?" Nathan asked.

"Soon."

ELEVEN

Rather than retreating underground as many of London's survivors had done, the Cabalist Septs had taken up residence throughout the city in abandoned buildings. They put up wards that hid them from demonic eyes and from human ones. Occasionally the spells were penetrated by the demons anyway and some of the Cabalists were killed, but it was hard to observe the demons while the Cabalists were locked away and hidden.

The observation groups tended to be small so they could move quickly. And so that losses were manageable when they invariably occurred.

Warren and Naomi followed the Piccadilly Line from the West End to Islington. Once there, they abandoned the aboveground railway line and picked their way through ominously silent suburban streets until they made it to Enfield. At that point, they followed the Ponders End Railway line to Enfield. With frequent rest stops and pausing to avoid demon patrols, it was almost nightfall by the time they reached their destination. The only way to safely get around inside the city these days was on foot.

They talked a little along the way, but both of them concentrated primarily on paying attention to their surroundings. They also shared the food Warren had brought from his sanctum.

By the time they reached the suburb, Cabalist lookouts had spotted them and sent word to the others. A small group of horned and tattooed men and women met Warren and Naomi in short order.

Naomi took charge of the brief conversation. Warren hung back to watch those who watched him. He knew that during the last four years he had become much talked about among the Cabalist Septs. None of them had ever talked to demons and lived to tell the tale.

After brief discussion, they were once more on their way.

First Seer Cornish held court in Ponders End in the Enfield district in one of the civic buildings surrounding Enfield Green. The building was austere and stark. Most of the windows were broken. The Cabalists living there had made no effort to replace them. Doing so would have drawn attention to their presence.

Armed guards met Warren and Naomi at the main doors. The men and women carried handguns in a few submachine pistols. The Cabalists preferred spells over weaponry, but not everyone was capable yet of using the magic that had returned with the demons. Those just in training were usually selected for guard duty and had to carry weapons.

Despite Naomi's protests, the senior guardsman insisted on searching Warren.

"It's all right," Warren said. He stood still as the man searched him. "I don't have anything to hide."

Naomi was still livid. "He's here as our guest. The First Seer sent for him."

"I'm just doing my job." The senior guardsman took the long dagger from Warren's right boot. He slipped the dagger into his belt.

Warren hated to lose the knife. It was his only weapon outside of the pistol he could use. He had never been much of a fighter, but over the last four years he had learned a lot. Still, he had no chance against the group around him. He had never liked feeling helpless.

Even though his weapon had been confiscated, the senior guardsmen and the other security people seemed content to give Warren plenty of space. At least they didn't try to restrain him. However, his reception strengthened his immediate impulse that he had made a mistake in coming to see the First Seer.

What is your name?" Naomi demanded.

"Cedric," the grizzled old warrior stated. If he was uncomfortable about giving his name, it didn't show.

"Your job isn't to offend our guests," Naomi said sharply.

"No, ma'am, my job is to keep the First Seer alive." The senior guardsman removed a coal-oil lamp from a nearby peg and nodded toward the doorway. "If you'll follow me I'll take you to the First Seer."

From the look on her face, Warren knew Naomi wasn't through with the argument. He touched her arm with his human hand and caught her eye. He quickly shook his head.

Naomi shared her anger with him. She took her arm out of his touch and folded both over her chest. With a sigh, Warren turned and followed the senior guardsman into the building.

The interior of the building had been gutted. A few remnants of papers and plaques—things that had once been part of the activities there—remained, but they were scattered. Smashed cases that had held civic awards and trophies hung on walls. Documents hung askew behind broken desks. Evidence of squatter nesting showed in piles of material gathered in corners and against the walls. Ashes remained of small campfires. The bones of small animals and empty tins mixed in with the debris.

Cedric skirted the piles of refuse of and headed to a stairway that led down into the basement. More guards held positions at the entranceway to the stairs.

The basement area was far larger than Warren would have guessed. Lit only by coal-oil lanterns, the hallways didn't reveal much but Warren noticed evidence of expansion. Someone had worked long and hard to excavate extra space under the building.

Part of him wondered how the work had been carried out. It couldn't have been easy. Making the space required moving a lot of earth, and that dirt had to have been put somewhere. Signs of building would have drawn the demons immediately.

A lot of effort had gone into the construction. Warren saw that immediately when he took note of the many hallways that shot off the main one they traveled. Cedric went without hesitation, twisting and turning along the path. Warren gave up trying to memorize the route when he realized that Cedric brought them back through the same tunnels more than once.

The hallways also connected the basements of other buildings. Along the way, Warren saw various earthworks that he suspected could be collapsed to block of tunnels. Some of them could block off a tunnel at either end to create a deadly trap.

The underground wasn't just a sanctuary, it was also a carefully sculpted battlefield.

Eventually, they arrived at one of the larger rooms. Coal-oil lanterns hung on the walls and filled the area with

dulled yellow illumination. Someone had made an effort
to turn the area into a reception room. Tables and chairs
stood neatly arranged in the center of the room.

A man, watched over by a half-dozen fierce looking
men and women, sat at the center table and stared into a
circular mirror on the tabletop. Although he'd hadn't seen
him before, Warren knew this was First Seer Cornish.

The man was younger than Warren would have
guessed. He was probably no more than thirty. It made
sense, though. The younger Cabalists tended to have the
most power. They harnessed it far more easily and more
naturally than older Cabalists.

As a result, many of the Septs and the Voices among
them tended to be young. Warren had heard of many
splits among the Cabalists over power issues. The youthful
often commanded the raw power, but their seniors knew
more about the demons and the nature of the magic they
used.

First Seer Cornish looked up. He had a thin, sallow
face, but the tattoos were the first features most onlookers
noticed. They were so black and so thick that at first Warren wasn't sure what race the man was. His eyes looked
hollow and glassy. Black and shiny rams' horns curled on
either side of his head. His scalp had been overlaid with
demon's skin that was mottled and covered in protrud-
ing spikes like those of a porcupine. He wore dark robes
covered in symbols.

Cornish turned away from the circular mirror on the
tabletop and smiled a little. His gums looked black, and
it wasn't until then Warren noticed Cornish had replaced
some of his teeth with demons' fangs. Warren had never
heard of the procedure, but he knew the Cabalists were
using extreme measures to tap into the same power the
demons used.

"Naomi." Cornish smoothed his robes with a hand. "I see you were successful in arranging a visit."

Naomi only nodded.

Cornish turned his full attention to Warren. "I've wanted to meet you for some time."

Warren didn't respond. Since he had entered the room, he'd felt uncomfortable. At first he had thought it was the circumstances he was there under. Now he realized there was an overpowering sense of wrongness inside the room. He wanted out.

Cornish tilted his head a little and studied Warren curiously. "Do you feel well?"

"I feel fine," Warren lied. He opened his mind the way he had learned from Merihim and felt for the troubling sensation that lay within the room.

Almost immediately, a powerful blow struck Warren hard enough to almost buckle his knees. Dizziness swam through his head. For a moment he couldn't focus. Double images filled his vision. He felt hot all over and perspiration coated his skin. The scratches Naomi had left across his back during their earlier lovemaking burned like fire.

"Perhaps you'd like to sit." Cornish gestured to one of the chairs.

"No," Warren responded. He wanted out of the room. He knew that with certainty.

A small smile pulled at Cornish's thin lips over the demons' fangs. Warren couldn't help wondering if the fangs all came from the same demon, and if they actually helped the First Seer harness the magical energy that coursed through the city these days.

"May I see your hand?" Cornish asked. He extended his own hands.

Warren understood immediately which hand Cornish wanted to see. He didn't move.

"Please," Cornish said.

Instead of reaching out to the man, Warren merely lifted the gift he had received from Merihim. He held the hand open. Lamplight glittered along the scales.

Curious and hesitant, Cornish reached for Warren's hand. Tattoos covered the First Seer's hands and even his fingers. Some of them glowed a deep purple that burned brighter the closer the tattoos got to Warren.

The sense of wrongness vibrated even more sharply within Warren. The scratches along his back burned more fiercely. Before the First Seer could touch him, Warren rolled his hand into a fist. Cruelly curved claws sprang out along his knuckles. Warren gazed at the new manifestation in wonder.

Cornish hesitated and withdrew his hands. "Has it ever done that before?"

Anger and frustration swirled within Warren. Now was not the time for the hand to be independent of him. "Yes." He lied guilelessly. But, in truth, he didn't know if it was he who lied or the essence of the demon he carried within him.

"You've been an inspiration to us," the First Seer stated. "Although we've been successful transplanting some features of the demons, we've not yet demonstrated the success involved in your own transplant."

This wasn't a transplant, Warren thought. *Merihim claimed me with this hand.* Still, he suspected that it wouldn't be long before the Cabalists successfully transplanted other limbs. They were becoming too attuned to the wild magic loose again in the world.

"Many have volunteered to undergo the process," Cornish said. "Instead of success, all we've created is a series of cripples." He paused. "Despite our best efforts to recreate the treatment you received, we've not been able to duplicate the result."

Warren concentrated and tried to bring the two images of Cornish together as one. He only had partial success. The two images resolved now and again into one, but for the most part they remained separate and distinct. Strangely, one of the images looked more human than the other.

"We've managed several transplants that have all augmented powers and abilities," Cornish went on. "But nothing like what I've been told you're capable of."

"I don't know what you've been told," Warren said quietly.

Cornish grinned and revealed the demon's teeth again. His black gums gleamed. "I've been told you can speak to the demon. I'm also been told that, upon occasion, you can manifest the demon and channel its power through your body."

"No," Warren replied. "I don't speak to the demon. He speaks to me. And I don't manifest him." He didn't want to discuss the power he was sometimes able to tap into. That was no one's business. And it gave the Cabalists one more reason to be envious of him.

"I think you're being too modest about your abilities, though I'm not sure why you would choose to be so." A note of irritation crept into Cornish's voice.

"I'm not being modest," Warren said. The sense of unease reached new heights within him. The two images of Cornish contrasted sharply.

"We'll have to disagree about that," Cornish said. "Unfortunately, I'm in a position that I need to know what you can do."

"I didn't come here to be a test subject." Warren glared at Naomi.

"Oh, you're not here as a test subject," Cornish said. "You're here as a donor." He pointed at the demon's hand. "I've come to believe that it wasn't the treatment you were given during the attachment of the hand that's the source of the success you've enjoyed. I think it was because that hand was given willingly by the demon that nearly destroyed you."

The nausea that filled Warren's stomach suddenly turned sour. He realized then that he had been betrayed. He looked around the room wildly and sought an avenue of escape.

Both doors that lead out of the room, one on each opposite wall, were blocked by guards. As he whirled to face them, they closed ranks.

"This will be easier if you don't struggle," Cornish said.

The words reverberated inside Warren's skull. He swayed on his feet and barely kept standing.

"You've already been drugged. Naomi can be quite persuasive when she's properly motivated." Cornish grinned knowingly. "You'll be unconscious in minutes. I'm actually surprised you're still standing now."

Warren shook his head in an effort to clear some of the narcotic from his system but only succeeded in throwing his balance off. He dropped to one knee and slammed his hand—the hand that Cornish wanted—against the floor barely in time to keep himself upright.

At Cornish's order, the guards closed on Warren.

TWELVE

L eah luxuriated in the shower. It was the first time in months that she'd had more than a chem-bath. The water was hot and no one had mentioned any short supply.

She guessed that Simon and his Templar had tapped into an underground stream or lake, or had drilled several wells. It was possible, though, that the water supply was pre-existing and the Templar had merely taken advantage of it.

The underground structure they were in showed signs of previous, earlier, habitation. A few storerooms held furniture and books from decades before. She'd assumed the Templar hadn't thrown it away because they hadn't yet needed the space. The physical debris would also be hard to get rid of. And, if left lying around, it could draw the demons to them.

Leah felt certain Simon had chosen a base outside of the city to protect the civilians he'd gotten out of London. That was how he'd operated for the last four years. He'd risked his life on a daily basis to save the innocents that had been trapped in the city.

Even from the short times she'd been with him over those last few years, Leah knew Simon Cross wasn't a man who would easily change his nature. His whole goal was to protect the defenseless.

The way he'd thought he's been protecting you.

Leah sometimes felt guilty about the way she'd deceived him in order to get inside the Templar organization. But it was what she did and she was good at it. Normally, though, the organizations she penetrated offered some threat to Great Britain. The Templar had become a target solely because no one knew anything about them.

And if it hadn't been for Thomas Cross dying on All Hallows' Eve and being recognized by a police inspector who'd had previous dealings with him, no one would have known about Simon Cross and his ties to the Templar. Leah wouldn't have picked up Simon's trail in South Africa. And if she hadn't already been assigned there, she'd never have crossed paths with him.

It was all a matter of luck. Some good and some bad. As it was, the Templar posed no threat to England and, in fact, might well be her greatest weapon against the demons.

Except that the Templar who were left were reluctant to engage the demons.

All but Simon Cross and his fellow warriors.

And if he accepts the mission you've put before him, he'll be in harm's way again.

Leah told herself she wasn't going to feel any guilt. She knew that was a lie, but if she couldn't feel it till after she was gone, till after Simon was gone, that would be best.

Finally, feeling guilty about the water, she turned the faucets off and stepped from the shower cubicle. Simon had assigned her room within the underground complex. He had also assigned guards to watch over her.

She toweled off, then walked to the mirror and wiped a patch of it free so she could see her reflection. She wasn't happy.

You look gaunt and tired, and not attractive at all. Then

she chided herself for being foolish. She wasn't there to be attractive. She was there because she had a message to deliver. Now that it was delivered, she needed to go.

If she was allowed. And if she wasn't allowed, she'd leave shortly after that. No matter how good the Templar were, they couldn't hold her if she didn't want to be held.

In the sleeping quarters, Leah dressed. She pulled on the spandex "onesie" that insulated her from the rough interior of her stealth suit. She knew that the Templar armor had fluid that rejuvenated the wearer's skin and provided antibacterial topical medications. The fluid also helped cushion impacts and drastic changes in the outside temperatures.

The door opened just as she reached for the armored pants. Simon stopped immediately.

"Sorry," he said. "I should have knocked."

Unselfconsciously, Leah stepped into the armored pants and pulled them on. She wasn't embarrassed about her near-nudity. From her short time in the Templar Underground, she knew that nudity was accepted as necessary with so many people living so close together in a constant state of readiness to go to war. She had seen Simon naked and it hadn't fazed him.

Of course, with the way he was built he had nothing to be ashamed of.

Thinking like that is going to get you into trouble, Leah told herself. She reached for the armored blouse.

"It's all right," Leah said. "I'm almost dressed."

"You look better," Simon told her.

"Inferring that I looked terrible earlier?" Leah was conscious of her effort to secure a compliment as soon as she spoke. She felt embarrassed and a little put out with herself. It wasn't like her to be like that. She had known men before. But none of them were ever like Simon Cross. The Templar was as deadly and dangerous as any of the men Leah knew, but something vulnerable and innocent clung to him.

Those were qualities that Leah wasn't used to. He was exactly what he acted like. Not one of the social chameleons that Leah worked with.

"I didn't mean it that way," Simon said. He even had the decency to look embarrassed. "I just meant you looked rested and healthier."

"I owe that to you. So thank you for caring for me. And for the compliment." Leah prodded the inside of her left forearm with the fingertips of her right hand to activate the suit's circuitry.

Immediately, the onboard electromagnetic generators locked the armor pieces together. The suit almost became another layer of skin and fused at the seams so the pieces couldn't be easily separated. Once she pulled on her helmet, that would lock in as well.

"That armor's very interesting," Simon observed

"I've always thought so," Leah agreed. "Beyond that, however, I can't tell you anything."

"Can't?"

"Won't."

"Same difference?"

Leah shrugged. She knew she presented a puzzle and a worry to him. Part of her enjoyed that. In addition to being brave and loyal, Simon was curious.

"What are you going to do about Macomber?" she asked.

"If we don't go get him, what would your people do with him?"

Leah recognized the question as a feint. Simon couldn't pass up the chance for more information about the demons. As informed as the Templar were, they didn't know the demons' complete history.

"I'm not privy to that information," she answered. Calmly, she sat on the bed and waited. The Cluster Rifle she'd used was nowhere to be found, but she had several defensive and offensive measures built into the suit.

"Will your superior be with Macomber?"

"I don't know who'll be with Macomber." Leah understood immediately that Simon was fishing for information about the architecture of the organization she belonged to.

"What guarantees do I have that Macomber will be at the rendezvous point?"

Irritations chafed at Leah. The longer she stayed at the Templar Underground, the more questions she'd have to face and the more trouble she would be in. Her supervisors already had doubts about her when it came to Simon Cross, but she was the only one who could approach him.

"Paranoid much?" she asked. Before he could answer, she sighed. "Ignore that. I'm not in a good mood. Paranoia is pretty much the state of the world these days."

"If you want to stay alive," Simon agreed.

"You'll have to trust me that Macomber will be there."

He was silent for a moment. "You know where this base is. If you send me off on a wild-goose chase, you'll split the defensive forces here."

"Why would I want to do that?"

"I don't know. Why did you follow me back from Cape Town? Why did you go with me to the Templar Underground?" Simon shook his head. "I have a lot of questions about you."

"Mostly, I've helped you," Leah reminded.

Simon took a deep breath and let it out. Then he nodded. "I know."

"Can I just walk out of here? Or am I being held?"

Simon hesitated for a moment. If he hadn't, Leah would've been suspicious. His nobility and honor had placed those he was trying to defend in a precarious position when he'd refused to leave her behind. He had to trust her more now than he had at any in the time in the past.

And that was without the information about Macomber hanging in the balance.

Most of the men, and many of the women, whom Leah worked with would have preferred simply putting a bullet through her head either when she'd gone down or when she'd proven difficult here. Death came with unconditional trust.

Unless a demon found the body and reanimated it, she thought sourly. Of course the body can always be destroyed as well. People within her organization had already thought about that and often destroyed their dead when they couldn't take them with them. There was no need to supply the enemy with additional weapons. Ultimately, with the powers the demons wielded, that was what corpses were. And no one wanted to see their friends or family desecrated in such a manner by the demons.

"You're free to go anytime you want," Simon said.

Leah stood. "Then I really should be going."

Simon's eyes locked on hers. "If you don't go with us, we're not going after Macomber."

The ultimatum stung. Leah hadn't been expecting that. "That's mad. I've told you that what he knows can help you."

Simon said nothing for a moment, but his gaze held steady. "That's the way it's going to work, if it's going to work at all."

"You need the information Macomber has. He's not going to give it to anyone else but you."

"You don't know that he's going to tell me anything. You're just guessing."

That was true. She was guessing. So were the people who'd passed that information on.

"You don't even know if Macomber has anything of value to tell."

Leah couldn't refute that either.

Simon put his hands together in his lap. "Your people need and want that information as well."

"So what? I'm to be a hostage?" That possibility angered Leah even further. She hated feeling helpless. What right did Simon Cross had to usurp her freedom of will?

"Not a hostage. Our negotiator."

"Simon, look. I was never supposed to be here. The people I'm responsible to wouldn't have wanted me here. Both of us are going to face problems as a result of this."

"But I'm having to trust you more," Simon said softly. "I'm not just trusting you with my life, Leah. I'm trusting you with the lives of every man, woman, and child that are noncombatants in this war against the demons. If your people decide that revealing the location of this place will do them any good—either as a bargaining tool or a delaying tactic, or even as bait in a trap like those two Templar were yesterday—it'll be my fault for trusting you."

Leah wanted to assure him that none of those scenarios would happen. She couldn't. The lie wouldn't slide past her lips despite all her training. She could have lied to anyone else in the world.

She took a deep breath and considered her options. Her primary objective had been to get Simon Cross to pick up Macomber. After all the medications, shock therapy, and other horrible things that had been done to the man in the Parisian sanitarium, no one in Leah's organization was fool enough to believe that Macomber could stand up to more of the same.

Therefore, the primary objective on this mission hasn't been completed. Leah felt guilty because she knew she was skating the rules.

"All right," she said. "When do we leave?"

"Now. Everything has been made ready." Simon stood and carried his helm in one hand.

None of Simon's warriors trusted Leah. She understood that perfectly and quickly. The way they lined up around her, boxing her inside a loose two-by-two formation that somehow wasn't quite aggressive enough to trigger a response, told her that.

She deliberately paused to adjust one of her boots even though it didn't need it to see how they would react. All four men stopped dead in their tracks and maintained the two-by-two formation. When she looked up at them, they didn't even try faking reasons for why they too had stopped. They'd been caught and they knew it.

Okay, Leah thought. *Now everybody knows we're all wise to the game.*

That knowledge brought her a little peace of mind and more than a little self-satisfaction. She wasn't stupid, and now they knew that. It wouldn't change the rules of the game, but it felt good knowing that the players were now meeting on equal footing.

Simon led the way through a twisting tunnel at least two miles long. Leah's suit generated an infrared beam that she picked up through the lenses of her helmet. NanoDyne capacitors built into the suit allowed her to charge the infrared beam simply by walking. Kinetic energy was an important source for the suit, but there were backup systems that allowed continued use for dozens of hours without movement.

The initial tunnel had been a short one directly from the underground area. It had looked new. The section they were in now looked positively ancient.

"Is this part of a coal mine?" Leah asked over the suit's radio frequency.

"It is," Simon replied. "One of the reasons we chose this location was because of these mines. Only a few tunnels were required to give us access to miles of underground hiding areas. We've since instituted hydroponics farms to raise vegetables, and we're mining leftover coal from some of the areas to process fuel."

"I thought the mines in the area had all been abandoned because the coal had been exhausted back during the Industrial Revolution."

"It was," Simon agreed. "For conventional tools of the nineteenth century. Also, the mining companies needed a lot of coal. We only need a little."

Leah was impressed. She'd guessed the Templar and the people they protected would be living a hardscrabble existence. Instead, the Templar seemed to thrive when the situation got hardest. It was easy to understand why the people Leah worked with feared and mistrusted the Templar.

Only a little farther on, the tunnel widened into a cave. Electric floodlights lit the cave. Three sleek ATVs with matte black finishes occupied center stage. All of them had six wheels that stood at least as tall as Leah's shoulder. Clearance beneath the vehicles was nearly three feet and they were built low and sloping at both ends so they were very few surfaces for brush or anything else to cling to.

"Where did you get these?" Leah asked.

"One of the primary developers on this design was a

Templar," Simon answered. "Three of the manufacturers were Templar."

"But these are military vehicles."

"The military wouldn't have had them if it hadn't been for the Templar." Simon swung a duffel up onto the forward deck of one of the vehicles.

"I thought the Templar were strictly hands-off regarding the rest of society."

"The Templar organization tried to keep a low profile," Simon agreed. "But they also knew that the only way to keep abreast of emerging technology was to be part of the research and development companies. Ever since the organization's inception, Templar engineers have been part of every major undertaking regarding weapons of war and medicine. Those two fields generally overlap in a huge way."

"The Templar *stole* the technology?"

"Sometimes. When they had to." A pained expression filled Simon's face. "You don't obey the letter of the law when you're at war. If you do, you'll just die slower. The Templar succeeded from the beginning because they were politically, economically, and technologically savvy. They help create the idea that became incorporation. They've also apprenticed to engineers and designers." He gazed at the ATV. "This was designed by a Templar engineer. The design was given to the military so that Templar vehicles wouldn't be so noticeable."

"Do you really expect me to believe that?"

Simon shook his head and gave her a thin grin. "I don't see that it matters. Believe what you want. But these ATVs are armored in palladium, not steel or reactive armor." He gestured to the step hanging down from the deck. "Do you need a hand?"

Instead of replying, Leah grabbed the handhold and

pulled herself up in a lithe vault. She turned and offered him her hand. "No, I'm fine. Do you need a hand?"

Simon leaped to the deck easily. The faceplate on his helmet irised shut.

The cramped quarters of the ATV promised misery. Simon took the chair in the center at the top while four other Templar took stations. One of them sat in the driver's seat, and others in the weapons control center, the communications center, and the gunner's mate position.

Leah was familiar with the setup. Although she had never occupied a fast-attack vehicle, she had been trained on FAV simulators.

She was impressed, even though she knew she shouldn't have been. Simon and the Templar were incredibly well equipped.

Simon quickly went through a pre-ops checklist that included weapon readiness and communications with the other vehicles. When he was satisfied, the convoy started.

Leah sat back in the sling-seat with the other six Templar who made up the crew. All the Templar sat relaxed and slept, talked, or played games built into the suits' AIs. Leah had similar software built into her own armor. Boredom was a healthy warrior's greatest enemy.

Only a short distance farther on, Leah peered at the vidscreen above Simon's head. The vidscreen was a redundant system that backed up the Templar HUDs. Normally the crew operated the ATV from inside their armor and used those systems rather than the ones provided for regular military operators. The FAV simulators she had trained on worked in the same fashion.

The vidscreen showed night all around the ATV, but the onboard infrared systems lit up the landscape. Sensors constantly swept the rolling countryside for any signs of life.

In the distance, the dark clouds above London hung heavily over the tall buildings. Seated in the sling seat, Leah kept watch and silently hoped all of them made it back from the coast alive.

THIRTEEN

As the guards closed in on him, Warren tried to stand his ground, but the drug in his system kept his senses spinning. He couldn't focus enough to direct an attack. They were on him in seconds and beat him to the ground. Their hard fists slammed into his face and body. Even though it shook him physically, he didn't feel most of the assaults. Likely, the same drug that weakened him also removed most of the pain. It was an unexpected benefit, but not one that was going to save his hand from being cut off.

They forced him prone, facedown on the floor. Men sat on his legs and his back to keep him helpless. Someone screwed a pistol into the back of his neck. The barrel was cold and hard.

"No one said you have to be alive when they remove your hand," a man yelled into Warren's ear. "They'll take it off your dead body even easier."

The Cabalists had never truly taken Warren in as one of them. He had barely known them when the initial group he had met summoned Merihim. Few forgave him the deaths of all those people. Naomi had been the only one to show him any kindness or respect.

Now it looked as if Kelli was more true to him while she was rotting away in one of the rooms of his sanctuary.

Fear ran wild within Warren, like a rabid animal jacked up on amphetamines.

"Get his arm up here," Cornish ordered.

At least three men struggled to pull Warren's arm up from his side. He yanked and pulled against them with all the strength that he had. Since the demon hand had been grafted onto his arm, he knew he had become faster and stronger than anything human. At least, faster and stronger than any human he had so far met.

In the end though, he was one man against several. They pulled his arm forward.

"Hold it still," someone ordered.

Even with his senses ricocheting inside his head, Warren realized they had made a mistake. He almost laughed. Except that he knew they would correct the mistake as soon as they caught it. To make matters worse, they might not catch that mistake until it was too late. He might end up with no hands at all.

"It's not this hand," a man said. "This hand is human. Get the other hand."

The guards struggled to bring Warren's other arm forward as they took his other arm back. Warren stopped fighting when he realized that struggling against them also served to break his concentration.

It was hard mastering the panic within him enough to shove it away and allow him to focus on building his energy. He tried to ignore the trapped feeling he had as he lay on the floor with his arm stretched out. He gathered his power and envisioned what he wanted to do.

"Do you only want the hand?" a man asked. "Or do you want part of his arm too?"

"Just the hand," Cornish answered as coldly as though he were ordering a cut of meat from the local butcher.

"Someone pass me that bone saw."

When there was no time left, as he felt the cold bite of a sharp, serrated blade against his wrist, Warren unleashed the power within. A violent shockwave exploded from Warren's body and hurled his attackers from him.

They sailed in all directions, many of them yelping at the sudden contact against the floor or walls.

Surprised by how well the attack succeeded, Warren pushed up from the floor and stood swaying. He faced Cornish and pointed the demon's hand.

Flames poured from Warren's fingers and streaked for Cornish. The First Seer crossed his hands in front of him. Flames encircled Cornish and filled the room with heat. Still struggling to stay on as feet, Warren tried to peer through the flames but couldn't see anything. He fully expected nothing to be left of the man but charred bone, and he didn't know how the other Cabalists were going to deal with that.

But in the next moment, Cornish stepped through the flames. His robes smoldered in several places. Smoke eddied up from his hair and clothing. He patted several embers out and smiled.

"Well, after that, I don't know if I'll be needing your demon's hand if that's all you can manage," Cornish declared.

It might be different if I weren't drugged, Warren thought. He summoned his power again, but it was hard to manage because it kept slipping through his fingers.

Cornish gestured. In the next second, Warren felt as though he had been kicked in the chest by a mule. He left his feet and flew backwards into a group of guards. All of them went down flailing.

Several of the guards tried to hold on to Warren. He broke their attempts to hold him while he rained blows on exposed faces. Eventually, they let him up.

No longer able to bear the drug in his system, Warren changed tactics. He concentrated on the drug, visualizing it as a liquid in his bloodstream, as a poison that wasn't part of him. He'd never tried to affect anything in his body. Once he had the image smoothed out, he used power to burn out the poison inside him.

Almost immediately, he began to feel better. His head cleared and he was better to able to focus.

Cornish gestured again, and once more Warren was driven backwards. This time, though, he kept his feet through sheer willpower.

It wasn't going to do any good, he knew. Ultimately they were going to have what they wanted. Cornish gestured again, and Warren rebounded from the wall behind him. His breath left him in an explosive rush. Black spots whirled, flared, and died in his vision.

Panic escalated within him. What he felt now set off the old fear that he'd had as a child when his stepfather had beaten him and his mother. The medicines and counseling he'd received as a child after he'd caused his stepfather's death—the police investigators had ruled the shooting a suicide, but Warren knew he'd caused the man to shoot himself—had taught him to wall that fear away. He'd never been able to rid himself of it.

Now it was back. He didn't want to be afraid. He didn't want to be hurt. And he didn't want to die.

Then don't die, Merihim whispered into his mind. *You're not as valuable to me dead.*

For one hideous moment Warren realized that he wouldn't be free of the demon's control even in death. Merihim could animate his corpse and order him to serve him still further.

As he stared at the Cabalists regrouping to come at him again, Warren's vision cleared. His breath returned as his heart rate slowed to more manageable levels. He felt Merihim's strength within him.

Your enemies are my enemies, Merihim stated. *There's more to this encounter than meets the eye.*

Warren didn't worry about that. He wanted out of the meeting alive. He pulled himself together and stood a little straighter.

The Cabalists noticed the change in his demeanor. A few of them hesitated.

"Give up, you fool," Cornish ordered. "Accept your fate and I'll make it as painless as possible."

Painless? Anger grew stronger in Warren. *There isn't anything painless about being too weak to take care of yourself.*

The demon's hand rose before him, and he couldn't honestly say whether it was through his effort or Merihim's. For the moment they were one.

A shimmering wave passed from Warren's hand. The Cabalists braced themselves for a violent attack. Instead, the shimmering wave touched the first four Cabalists. They stood in surprise as it wound around them.

Then one of them laughed. "I guess he doesn't have anything left."

In the next instant, though, the blood veins in the men's flesh turned black. The patterns, looking like streets and roads that crisscrossed each other, stood out against pale and dark flesh alike. Then, the men's flesh turned putrescent green and they started screaming in agony.

The other men stepped back from them, as if whatever their comrades had might be contagious.

The four men dropped onto the ground. Their faces writhed in anguish as they tried to hold themselves up. Their efforts only delayed the inevitable. In the end, they fell to the floor and slumped bonelessly.

Warren knew they were dead. He'd felt the life leave them.

The Cabalists stepped farther back from Warren. They looked to Cornish for guidance.

"Don't hesitate, you fools!" Cornish exploded. He gestured and a wave of flame spewed from his palm.

Warren knew he couldn't get out of the way in time. He also knew he hadn't ever seen anyone else wield that much power. Something was wrong. He remembered Merihim saying there was something else going on.

Instinctively, Warren held his hand before him. The whirling mass of flames halted only inches from him, then it blew out as effortlessly as a birthday candle.

Fear showed on Cornish's face then.

Warren turned his attention to the four dead men on the floor. He tapped into the dark energy that Merihim passed through his body. At his silent command, the four dead men reanimated. Their limbs jerked and shivered.

The Cabalists drew back to the entrances to the room. The dead men lurched to their feet and stood before Warren. Their flesh showed virulent green with corruption.

Even though Warren had raised a great number of zombies from the graveyards and from the dead he'd found lying in the street, he'd never seen any like this. Like a pack of hungry wolves, they sprang at Cornish.

The First Seer tried to turn and run, but it was already too late. He was slower than the zombies. They grabbed him and bore him to the floor on his back.

"Stop!" Cornish yelled. "Get them off me!"

A couple of the more stalwart among the security guards rushed forward. They wielded truncheons, but they had no effect on the zombies other than to draw their attention. The zombies rose and lashed out with arms that struck like battering rams.

One of the zombies punched through the chest of a Cabalist. The man died in an instant, and his skin turned the same mottled green with black veins by the time he sank to his knees. When the zombie that had killed him yanked his arm back, the newly dead man rose as a zombie as well.

The other man tried to break free of the second zombie's grip. Despite the kicks and punches, the zombie took him to the ground and threw itself on top of him. His teeth found the screaming Cabalist's throat and savaged it like a wild animal.

"Warren!"

As he cut his eyes to Naomi, Warren caught sight of the man dying then returning almost immediately as a zombie. It was all he could do to watch.

"Warren." Naomi approached him slowly. She held her arms out to her sides. Frightened tears shimmered in her eyes. "I had nothing to do with this." Her gaze implored him to believe her.

One of the new zombies stepped quickly to intercept her and keep her from reaching Warren. Naomi drew back. She had no defensive powers. Her talents primarily lie in divination.

"Please," she said in a tight voice. Tears streamed down her face. "Please don't hurt me."

Let her die, Merihim whispered.

No, Warren said. *She's my friend.*

She led you into this trap.

She said she didn't know. Warren felt the hunger within him to see Naomi dead. He knew it wasn't his own; it was feeding into him from Merihim. It was everything he could do to restrain it.

You're a fool to believe her.

Warren didn't believe her. At least, he didn't believe her entirely. But he didn't want to kill her.

"Don't hurt her," he told the zombie.

The creature froze in place.

Hesitantly, Naomi lowered her hands from in front of her. "Thank you," she whispered hoarsely.

One of the Cabalists pulled a pistol from his robes. Apparently not all of them believed their spells and powers were answers to all problems.

FOURTEEN

The Cabalist guard leveled the weapon in front of him. Warren saw that it was a traditional handgun that fired bullets, not flames or sonic waves or anything else used by the Templar or the special commando units that occasionally still fought within London.

Warren flicked the demon's hand in the man's direction. A wave of fire leaped forward just as the man squeezed the trigger.

The harsh detonation of the pistol sounded overly large in the enclosed space. The wave of fire flared briefly as it caught the bullet and burned it up. The man was caught flat-footed as the whirling flames engulfed him. He managed one scream before the flames stabbed greedy fingers down his throat and seared his lungs. Dead already, he collapsed.

Warren walled away his fear and leaned on the demon's strength. "If any more of you raise your hands against me, I won't rest until I kill you all."

The surviving Cabalists looked at the smoldering and poisoned bodies before them and quickly fled the room.

Merihim's mocking laughter roared in Warren's head.

Bruised and aching from the pummeling he'd received, Warren stepped toward the First Seer. Cornish stared up at him with frightened eyes.

"Do you want me to beg for my life?" Cornish asked.

Yes, Merihim told Warren. *Let him beg. You never feel as empowered as you do when you have someone begging for his life before you.*

The thought sickened Warren. He didn't want to hear the man beg.

You're too weak, Merihim told him. *You have all that anger stored up inside you, all that fear, and you don't utilize it to its full advantage.*

"I'll . . . beg if you . . . want me . . . to," Cornish said. His voice was soft and hoarse.

He'll lie to you, Merihim said. *He'll beg for his life today, then he'll plot to take yours tomorrow.*

Warren didn't doubt that. He'd seen Cornish's kind all his life. Bullies who made the most of their power, whether they were a manager at a quick mart he'd worked at or the building super where he'd shared the rent of a flat.

So many people with just a little power let it go to their heads. Having power only made them worse.

"I . . . beg you," Cornish said.

Even lying there in the grip of the zombies, the First Seer had trouble saying the words. Warren knew the man would never recover from the ignominy of his rough treatment at Warren's hands. He would live only to send more people after him, and he would never risk being this close again.

Warren knew that because it was what he would do if the roles were reversed.

And still he stayed his hand.

You're a fool! Merihim exploded. *This man offers you nothing in return for any kindness you might show him, and he'll harbor only a thirst for revenge. If you let him live you're only signing a death sentence for yourself.*

Warren turned away before the fear overcame him

and he did what the demon wished. Naomi stood nearby watching him.

Look at her, Merihim ordered. *Look into her eyes. Does she think she sees a man willing to be forgiving? Or do you think she sees a man afraid to seize his destiny?*

Warren didn't know. He didn't want to think like that. He wished he could be gone from that place immediately. He wished he'd never come.

You came because you wanted to impress her. How impressed do you think she is?

Warren ignored the voice and tried to walk through the door. He didn't know if he would even live to walk outside. But he couldn't move.

No, Merihim said. *There's more here than you think.*

Abruptly, the mirror on the table that Cornish had been gazing into turned molten red. At first Warren thought the smoke rising from it was caused by the table burning. Then he saw that the smoke came from the mirror's gleaming surface.

Merihim took shape in the climbing smoke pooling against the ceiling. He formed with his back to Warren as if he were ashamed of his chosen vassal.

The demon had a blunt face and a square jaw covered with red scales. Two horns jutted from his forehead and towered above him, adding another foot of height. Scars ridged his brow and cheeks from past battles had turned black with age. Massively muscled and broad, the demon stood almost eight feet tall. Blue-green armor made of lizard scales from a vanquished monster covered his body. A long, heavy broadsword hung at his hip.

Naomi shrank back. She'd only seen the demon in visions, never in the flesh.

Merihim ignored Warren and strode to the First Seer

spread-eagled on the ground by the poisoned zombies. The zombies all hummed like children at the demon's approach.

Warren knew from his own use of the zombies that the response was more a generation of the power they sensed than out of any emotional well. Zombies held nothing over from their former lives. They were automatons that awaited orders from whoever had raised them.

Effortlessly, Merihim dropped into a crouch beside Cornish.

"What secrets do you hold, little man?" the demon asked.

"Don't kill me," Cornish begged. "Please don't kill me. I can serve you better than he does. I can be more than he is."

Warren didn't know what to say. He hadn't expected Cornish to try something like that. And if the demon took the First Seer up on his offer, what would happen to Warren?

He glanced over his shoulder and saw Naomi staring at him. If his life was forfeit, she knew hers was too.

"No." Merihim's voice was flat and mocking. "You already serve another. That's the problem. You already staked your life with the one you chose to serve." The demon traced the ridge of Cornish's left eye with a thick talon. "I doubt your master would let you live after your offer."

"Please. You can protect me. I know you can protect me. You're stronger than she is." Cornish struggled fiercely but hopelessly against his zombie captors.

Merihim grinned, and the expression was totally without compassion. "How could I ever trust you? You change sides as soon as the way becomes difficult."

"I won't. Take me. I will always be yours. I will always serve you."

Warren felt sorry for Cornish because he knew the demon wouldn't show mercy. But Warren also felt afraid because he knew Cornish's fate could one day be his.

"No," Merihim said. "And that's enough begging." With a simple flick of his hand, the demon drove his talon and then his finger into the First Seer's eye.

Blood spurted from the eye socket and Cornish's wails filled the room. Naomi sat with her back against the wall and her knees curled to her chest, arms wrapped around her legs.

A moment later, Cornish shivered all over then relaxed and lay still in death.

Nausea whirled through Warren's stomach. For a moment he thought he was going to throw up. Sour bubbles of bile burst against the back of his throat.

Merihim's work wasn't finished. He hooked his finger behind Cornish's cheekbone and pulled. The muscles along his arm rippled with the effort but he made it look like child's play.

The front of the First Seer's face shattered. Ivory bone suddenly jutted up through bloody flesh. Naomi got sick at that point and turned her head away as she threw up.

Merihim glanced back at Warren. "Come here."

Unable to disobey, Warren walked over to the demon. The scent of burning rocks and decay clung to Merihim. Heat resonated from his body. Some of the Cabalists believed that the demons came from a much warmer environment and that was why they had started the Burn to terraform the areas they had dominion over.

"You never sensed the *other* within this one, did you?" Merihim asked.

"No," Warren replied. He still didn't know what the demon referred to.

"There's still so much I need to teach you."

Warren relaxed a little of that. If Merihim was going to teach him, that meant the demon didn't have plans to immediately kill him out of hand.

Unless he was lying.

"You should have known he wasn't alone," Merihim continued. "No one, especially not a foolish human, would dare attack someone I had named as my own." The demon waved a hand over the dead man's ruined face.

In response, that one flesh and broken bone shifted. The soft gliding of tissue and slight rasping of bones sounded loud in the room.

A moment later, a new face took shape in the blood and wreckage of Cornish's features. The face wasn't human. It was demonic. Ridges of bony scales moved along the long jaw. The mouth was a mere slash carved beneath the hooked nose. Malice turned in the black eyes that moved from Merihim to Warren and back. The torn flesh of the dead man's head shifted slightly until they resembled horns.

"Fulaghar." This time the smile on Merihim's face did hold humor. But it held the promise of pain and death as well.

"You know me, then," the demon rasped.

"I do," Merihim replied. "This was your idea?"

Fulaghar smirked. "It almost worked."

"But it didn't. And now I know you as my enemy. It didn't have to be that way."

"Ah, but it did, o Bringer of Pestilence," Fulaghar taunted. "You're in this place without sanction. You have no business here."

"The business I have is my own."

"Wrong." Fulaghar's face turned angry. "Everything you do affects what we're doing here. Unfettered and unsanctioned, you are a danger to us in this place."

Warren's thoughts spun. He knew that the Cabalists

had summoned Merihim to London and that the demon hadn't come through the Hellgate like all the others had. From everything he had seen, Warren knew that the invasion was a carefully orchestrated maneuver. It was surprising to learn that the demons didn't want if an interloper even if he was one of their own kind.

And what did unsanctioned and mean? Obviously the other demons would destroy Merihim if they have the opportunity. The question was, why?

Merihim laughed at Fulaghar's assessment. "I'm no danger to any except those who trespass me or have what I want."

"What you seek isn't in this world," Fulaghar stated.

Again, the horrific smile spread across Merihim's coarse features. "You're a demon. How can I trust you?"

"You would be a fool if you did." Fulaghar smiled. "Then again, I might lie to you by telling you the truth and lets you search endlessly for that which you seek."

"I have one of the Books of Qhazimog," Merihim said.

The smile drained from Fulaghar's borrowed face. "You can't have one of those books."

"Then . . . I'm lying and I don't have one."

Fulaghar hesitated. Warren saw indecision and fear in the bloody face.

"How did you find it?"

"Because I know what I'm looking for here. I know what was lost all those years ago, and I know where it can be found."

Warren listened to the demon's words carefully, but he couldn't separate lie and truth. His thoughts turn immediately to the book back in his sanctuary. If the book was so important—especially if all of demonkind was searching for it, or at least demons as powerful as Fulaghar—why had Merihim left it with him?

Fulaghar's voice took on a more serious note. "Those books are dangerous. Even to you, Merihim. Or have you forgotten?"

Dangerous? Warren's heart beat a little faster. In all of his studies of Merihim during the last four years, he had read no mention of the Books of Qhazimog, or of anything that might threaten the demon's life or existence in this world.

"I've forgotten nothing," Merihim snarled. "I haven't forgotten the Books or the fact that I was betrayed."

"You were betrayed for just cause."

"I had every right to seize the territory I wanted."

"If you had the right to those territories, no one would have challenged you. Now you're in this place—again where you don't belong—and you'll be dealt with. There will be no simple banishment this time. This time they will end you."

"I choose not to be ended," Merihim growled. "And you can tell all those who try that I will deliver unto them permanent death."

"You give voice only to empty threats," Fulaghar scoffed. "You'll never be strong enough—"

Without another word, Merihim wrapped his large hand around the dead man's head to cover the demonic features of Fulaghar. The other demon's voice became muffled. When Merihim squeezed, the tattered flesh and broken bones turned to bloody pulp. They head ripped from the neck and he threw it against the nearest wall.

Naomi shuddered as the head bounced away only a few feet from her. Blood splattered over her. Tears tracked her face. She shivered in fright.

Merihim stood, then breathed flames over his bloody hand. It was the same hand that he had sacrificed for Warren, then grew back in minutes. The blood turned to ash and fell away from the scales.

"Go away from this place," the demon ordered. "I want you to find Fulaghar, or his minions, and I want you to destroy them when you do."

New fear filled Warren. He couldn't imagine how he was supposed to destroy a demon as powerful as Fulaghar was. If it had been that easy, why hadn't Merihim done it while he was talking to him?

Instead, Warren chose to say nothing. He didn't even ask how he was supposed to find the demons he had been charged with destroying.

Without another word, Merihim walked back to the table and lay his hand up on the mirror. Almost at his touch, his body turned to smoke and he was drawn back into the reflective surface. In less than a moment, except for the headless dead man on the floor, it was as if he had never been there.

Warren's legs quivered and threatened to give way. He remained standing with effort. His mouth was dry with fear.

Naomi looked up at him. "What are you going to do?"

"I don't know." Warren looked over his shoulder at the dead man's body stretched out across the floor. "Anything to keep from ending up like that."

"But to kill a demon . . . " Naomi left the rest unsaid.

"It's too late to run." Warren knew he was telling himself that more than her. He turned to the zombies and brought them to heel. They moved around him and remained waiting his orders. "Demons have been killed before. They all fear it. I'll just have to find a way to kill this one." He looked at her. "What about you?"

"What do you mean?" Naomi stared at him. "This has nothing to do with me."

"Will you be safe here?" Warren nodded toward the shadows clustered around both the doors where Cabalists hid and stared at them.

Naomi glanced at the shadows, then turned back to him. Her face turned hard. "Do you care?"

Warren chose to ignore the immediate scathing response he had in mind. "I asked," he reminded.

"Will I be any safer with you than here?"

"They're going to blame you for the First Seer's death."

"He asked me to bring you here. This isn't my fault."

"All right." Warren turned to go.

"Wait."

When Warren turned back to her, she was struggling to inch up the wall to a standing position. He offered his hand, the human one. For a moment she hesitated, then she took his hand and allowed him to help her to her feet.

Together, surrounded by the zombies, they walked back out of the building and into the night. Warren didn't even think of asking the Cabalists for a night's shelter. They would have better luck sleeping among the monsters that prowl the darkness along the way.

Even if he survived the return trip, he didn't know how he was supposed to survive assassinating a demon as powerful as Fulaghar.

FIFTEEN

S imon spotted the demons on his HUD only a second
before the suit's AI called his attention to them.

"Warning," the feminine voice announced.
"There are hostiles in the area that are converging on your
position."

As he leaned forward to take a fresh position in the seat,
Simon opened the frequency they were using between the
ATVs. Suit-to-suit communication was strong, but all data
exchanged between the two vehicles needed to be instantly
absorbed and calibrated by the onboard ATV AIs.

"Do you see them, Nathan?" Simon asked.

"I do," Nathan responded.

"Autopilot disengaged," the suit AI relayed. "Human
driver has control of this vehicle."

The slight shift of control as Nathan took over was
small but Simon felt it. The ride became less smooth and
more directed. The AI's reaction time was faster, but its in-
terpretive skill regarding dangers and opportunity lagged
a little in comparison. Plus, hands-on steering provided a
degree of unpredictability.

"Weapons?" Simon called.

"All systems green," Danielle replied. Her voice held an
edge.

Tension filled Simon. During the last four years, he'd
gotten some experience with engagements from inside the

ATV. Although the vehicle was well armed and armored, he preferred to be in the open and standing on his own two feet with a sword and pistol in hand. That was how Templar were most taught to fight.

Armored vehicle engagements on the simulators were a low protocol. But they had practiced them for times when rapid deployment was needed, or for quick supply runs. He had practiced with the ATVs—every Templar had that had access to them—and had thought they were totally cool at the time.

It's different when you're laying your life on the line in one of them.

Simon glanced at the corner of the HUD to see behind him and make sure the rest of the Templar were aware of the situation. All of the warriors shifted in their sling-seats as they checked weapons and readied themselves. Leah was in motion also.

"Billy," Simon said, "give Leah her rifle."

One of the Templar reached back and brought out the Cluster Rifle. He handed it over to Leah, who gave him a nod of thanks.

Simon turned his attention back to the HUD. The demons were less than a mile away now. They had been picked up by the long-range sensor drones that were tied into the comm array.

The sensor drones were something the British military hadn't gotten access to. The Templar had wanted to keep that surprise to themselves. Generally, each ATV carried six units that operated in threes to provide adequate triangulation. They referenced GPS satellites in deep space in low earth orbit for spatial recognition.

Covered in palladium armor, the drones were designed to be hard to destroy. They were wedge shaped with wide wings and a low profile that presented an almost nonexistent radar signature. Powered by nanospring technology, the sensor drones offered an operation life of four-hour shifts. They only had to return to the ATV for thirty minutes on a charger to return to full readiness. As one came in, another went out to take its place in rotation.

The sensors operated on a wide video and audio spectrum. With access to databases on board the ATVs, they could quickly sort out potential enemy targets.

There was no mistaking the demon forces lying in wait.

The question was whether the demon patrol was random or there by design? Simon knew every Templar warrior was asking himself or herself the same question.

And he didn't have an answer.

"Can we take evasive action?" Simon asked. He looked at the maps of the area available to him through the HUD.

The area was overgrown with trees and brush. They had stayed off the main roads intentionally, in hopes of lessening the chances of encountering demons. From the reports that had reached them, Simon knew demons still patrolled many of the main thoroughfares and the coastal areas.

Demon numbers had steadily increased over the last four years while human population in the area had decreased. Simon didn't know for sure how was in the rest of the world, but he was pretty certain that everyone else was suffering the same problems.

"We can try," Nathan said. "But you're looking at a lot of broken countryside out there. Rocks, fallen trees, and dense brush. If we veer from the track we've laid out, we're going to be out in no man's land."

The caravan was operating on recent information from Templar groups who had made recent pilgrimages to the coast of in hopes of finding rescue ships for survivors they had pulled from the city. During the last four years, the countryside had grown up and become more volatile.

In addition to the demons, several strange beasts had come through the Hellgate as well. They had flourished in the wild and rendered most of the local wildlife extinct through constant hunting. All of those creatures, like the demons, were carnivorous and lived to hunt.

"Can we backtrack and take another route?" Simon asked.

The HUD indicator showed less than a half a mile to the encounter point. The red numerals flickering onscreen quickly dwindled.

"We could try," Nathan said, "but they could overtake us. If we've sensed them, you can bet they sensed us. We'll only be putting off the inevitable."

"Leah," Simon said, "can you talk to your people from here?"

She answered instantly. "No."

"Are they out of range or can you not hail them?" If the people holding Macomber were already dead, chances were good that Macomber was already dead too. Pursuing the matter would have been foolish.

"Even if they were there," Leah said, demonstrating that she knew exactly what Simon was thinking, "they wouldn't answer. I'm not supposed to be along on this little jaunt."

It's not exactly a little jaunt when we're racing headlong into a demon ambush, Simon thought unkindly. He took a deep breath and released it.

The distance remaining was less than a quarter-mile. They were fast approaching the point of no return.

"Well," Nathan asked calmly, as if they were out for a

lark and not about to get bloody, "what's your druthers, mate?"

"We meet them on their chosen territory and kick their bloody arses," Danielle said softly.

Despite their predicament, Simon couldn't help smiling. The attitude was pure Danielle.

"We meet them there," Simon said.

"Do we stick around to introduce ourselves properly?" Nathan asked. "Or do we just barrel on through without so much as a by-your-leave?"

"We came for Macomber," Simon said. "We take as many of them out as we can now, and maybe hope they're still hanging around when we come back this way."

Only the muted rumbling of the tires across the broken terrain cracked the strained silence inside the ATV's command center. The nanofluid suspension kept the interior practically floating motionless. For all intents and purposes, the personnel carrier was a separate unit from the drive and the base vehicle. Electrical connections carried through the nanofluid.

Simon sat forward in his seat. His elbows rested on his knees as he watched the activity on his HUD. The land outside the ATV was thick with brush and covered in loose soil and rock. The large ATV tires churned through it.

The blips on the screen that identified the demons separated into dozens of targets as they neared. As Simon watched, the suit's AI sorted the information gathered by the sensor drones and translated it into real data he could use.

The demons appeared to be a group of Gremlins accompanied by Blade Minions and Ravagers. The Gremlins tended to be blunt, squat creatures with flat faces, multiple eyes, and horns crowning their heads and trailing down from their jaws. Blue-white scales provided a thick defense against traditional weapons. They were incredibly dangerous and knew how to work in groups.

Blade Minions stood between seven and nine feet tall. Built like flesh-and-blood tanks, with massive heads on short necks and auxiliary flesh around their features that made a protective hood, they were terrifying opponents. Blades along their forearms allowed them to slash through most armor. Black and gray scaly hide covered them.

Ravagers ran on all fours and possessed the native intelligence of pack animals. However, they could be controlled by handlers and guided psychically. They were built like armored lions, six to ten feet in length, and possessed huge, gaping maws filled with serrated teeth.

As Simon watched, seven flying demons flew in behind the ATV caravan.

"Warning," the suit AI broke in. "Seven bogeys have been detected by sensor drones."

"I see them. Center screen and magnify to identify." Simon watched as the suit AI used the sensor drones to lock on the unidentified flying objects. A glowing orange rectangle bracketed the seven figures. Then the rectangle broke into seven individual rectangles, each marked with its own GPS coordinates.

One of the orange rectangles suddenly exploded and filled the HUD screen. The figure was vaguely and horribly female humanoid, but the addition of two huge bat wings identified it immediately as a demon. Runes marked the demon's flesh and glowed bright crimson in the darkness.

"There are seven Blood Angels within the potential combat zone," the suit AI announced.

"Nathan," Simon called.

"Seven bogeys that are Blood Angels," Nathan said. "I got them, mate."

"Weapons," Simon said softly.

"Weapons ready and standing by."

"I want a full array of Greek Fire missiles deployed from the forward launch tubes when I call for them."

The gunner's mate spun in his seat and loaded the selected missiles into twenty-cylinder firing tubes. When he was finished, he gave a thumbs-up.

The motion was redundant, of course. Simon's HUD displayed the information that the missiles were confirmed and the loading had been completed.

The distance separating the ATVs from the demon army closed to within a few yards. Simon couldn't believe they hadn't been attacked yet. Then he remembered the demon's face that had materialized back in London.

For a moment, Simon's mind was filled up with the possibilities surrounding the nature of the demons. Not enough knowledge and too much curiosity often caused problems.

Nathan's voice brought Simon back to the present.

"The Blood Angels are attacking," Nathan said.

Simon changed the HUD view into the full 360. The seven Blood Angels dropped from the night sky on a direct attack flight path on the Templar ATVs. Simon shifted from the overhead panorama of the scene to the vid relay from the top of the ATV.

At his vocal commands, the view sharpened and locked on the lead Blood Angel. The demon was a monstrosity. The large, angular head seemed aerodynamically designed for swift flying. As the demon swept closer, wings beating savagely at the air, the red numerals in the lower right corner of the screen spun downward toward zero.

"Impact imminent," the suit AI announced.

"Brace for impact," Simon warned. He gripped the

seat's restraints and held on tightly. "Weapons, you have point blank range. *Fire.*"

The lead Blood Angel dropped onto the second ATV. It crouched there like a great hunting beast, arrogant and powerful. Then the Greek Fire missiles ripped from the launch tubes and slammed into the Blood Angel.

SIXTEEN

Greek Fire enveloped the Blood Angel. Gold and green, with flashes of livid red, the flames charred the demon's flesh from its bones. It leaped from the ATV and screamed loud enough to be heard over the vehicle's audio dampers.

The other two Templar ATVs loosed a barrage of Greek Fire missiles. Most of the weapons found their targets. Five of the seven Blood Angels turned into burning comets and shot across the sky in an effort to escape immolation before losing that battle and dropping like stones. One of those two still living landed in a tree in the path of the ATVs.

"Reload," Danielle ordered calmly as she swung and searched for targets.

"Reload complete," the gunner's mate called.

Nathan steered immediately for the tree with the flaming demon sitting in it. "Hold on," he warned.

"Impact imminent," the suit AI warned.

For a moment, Simon wondered if Nathan had been too ambitious in his attack. Even with the ATV's momentum and mass, it was possible that the vehicle would be blocked or receive damage.

Or get jammed up. That particular thought was chilling. The demons would cover them like ants on prey.

Then the ATV hammered the tree and knocked it over.

The vehicle clambered over the collapsed tree, then ran over the Blood Angel while the flaming demon tried to scamper away. Nathan roared in triumph.

Simon took control of the large Spike Bolter mounted on top of the ATV. He tracked the Blood Angel's panicked run through the forest, brought the gun to bear, and opened fire. The palladium spikes ripped through the Blood Angel and dropped her in shreds to the ground.

At his command, the HUD displayed the locations of the other two ATVs in relation to his. Both vehicles ran closely behind his.

Without warning, the remaining Blood Angel landed on the nose of the ATV. It hunkered down and tried to peer through the reinforced observation window.

"Simon," Nathan called. "There's a—"

"I've got it," Simon responded. He adjusted the Spike Bolter and opened fire just as the Blood Angel punched the observation window with a knotted fist. The impact-resistant glass shattered but held. However, Simon was pretty sure that it wouldn't withstand another such blow.

Palladium spikes filled the air and the Blood Angel. Pieces of the demon ripped off and blew away as the ATV raced through the forest. The dead body toppled over to the side.

"Close call, mate," Nathan said.

Simon didn't respond. They weren't out of it yet.

Less than a minute later, they engaged the main body of demons. The creatures stood thickly packed in the middle of the route Nathan had laid out. More than that, they had piled fallen trees across the narrow gap. The walls on either side were ten or fifteen feet high.

"Hold on," Nathan warned. He accelerated and steered to the left.

The realization of what Nathan was about to attempt turned Simon cold. It was a risky maneuver at best, but under the circumstances possibly the only thing they had open to them. Stopping would have left them open to immediate demon attack, and the probability of getting through the barricades was slim.

The ATV's NanoDyne electromagnetic engines, which weren't standard on the British military versions, whined at a higher pitch. A glance at the speed indicator readout on Simon's HUD revealed that the ATV was traveling at 148 KPH, and still accelerating.

The Gremlins opened fire and bathed the ATV in corrosive acid, explosive toxins, energy discharges, and fiery blasts. The impact-resistant windscreen shuddered under the attack but thankfully held.

"Warning," the suit AI stated simply. "ATV armor has sustained damage. Integrity levels down to eighty-two percent."

The armor was holding up better then Simon had hoped. Given time, they had the tools to repair the armor and the supplies to get it done. But time was a rare commodity on the battlefield.

Then the ATV roared up the left hillside and went almost perpendicular as a shot over the barricade. Only the centrifugal force caused by the high speed held the vehicle into the hillside. Even then, the wheels on the ATV drifted dangerously close to losing traction. Simon felt the positrack transmission shift to drive only the wheels on the right.

Someone cursed, but Simon didn't know who it was. He thought it might have been himself.

Just as it seemed that the ATV would inevitably flop over onto its top like a turtle, Nathan cut the wheels sharply and guided them behind the barricades. The luckless Gremlins in front of them were mown down like wheat before a thresher. Their bodies bounced from the front of the ATV.

One of them exploded through the weakened windscreen and sent shards of Plas-glas spinning. If the crew hadn't been armored up, some of them might have been mortally wounded in the barrage.

Simon checked his HUD and pulled up a quick medical report on the team. No one had been injured.

Incredibly, the demon caught in the window remained alive. Only its head and one arm were inside the control compartment. It reached for Nathan at the controls.

Calmly, but quickly, Nathan fisted the Spike Bolter holstered at his hip and shoved it into the demon's face. When he pulled the trigger, the Gremlin's face and head crunched and fell to pieces. Still driving by instruments, Nathan holstered his weapon and shoved the Gremlin back through the window.

A quick check of the HUD showed Simon they were through the worst of it. He linked with the Spike Bolter and targeted the nearest demons.

At the same time, Danielle unleashed the Blaze Cannon mounted on the front and rear decks. Greek Fire spewed over the demon army and turned them into burning pyres.

Simon watched as the second ATV on the right hillside to negotiate the barricade. The tires dug in and threw rooster tails several yards behind the vehicle. Liquid fire in energy bursts caught up to the ATV. Several of the trees along the ridge line caught fire.

The ATV returned fire with blistering accuracy. Then it suddenly sailed free of the hillside and shot through the air. Simon watched in dread as the ATV rotated in mid-air, obviously out of control. He pulled up the comm-link to the other vehicle.

"Jennifer," he called.

Jennifer Mapleland was a friend from Simon's childhood days. Only a year apart, they'd grown up together and trained together. She'd only recently left the Templar Underground to join his group as they actively sought out survivors in the city. Both of her parents had died at St. Paul's Cathedral.

"Carnagor," she called back. "Came up from the ground. Sensor drones didn't detect it."

Simon saw the Carnagor then. The huge demon reared on two legs from the hillside as if in triumph. Its efforts only served to dislodge it, though, and it tumbled down onto hapless Gremlins below.

Jennifer's ATV hit the ground on its side then rolled over onto its top. It spun in a loose circle as it tilted back and forth. The demons started for it at once.

"Simon," Jennifer called, "we've got to abandon the ATV."

"No," Simon replied. "Stay with it." They'd never make it out of the engagement alive if they left the vehicle. "We're coming back for you."

"Thank God," Nathan said. He cut the wheels sharply and brought the ATV around in a tight turn. "I'd have had real trouble with you if we'd bailed on them, mate."

Simon hailed the third ATV. "Borden."

"Yes." Borden was an older Templar who was seasoned as an ATV commander with the British armored units.

"We'll need covering fire."

The third ATV roared up the same hillside Nathan had chosen.

"You've got it, mate," Borden replied grimly. "Whatever you're going to do, you're going to have to be bloody quick about it."

Simon silently agreed.

* * *

"Danielle, lock on the Carnagor." Simon watched the demon gather itself and start for the overturned ATV at a distance-eating lope. With its speed and proximity, it was going to reach the trapped Templar before Simon's vehicle could reach them.

"I have target lock," Danielle said.

"Fire at will."

Immediately, missiles bearing Greek Fire launched from the forward tubes. Simon tracked them for only a second and knew they were on target. He turned his attention to the overturned ATV.

"Borden, see if you can slow up the ground forces," Simon suggested.

"I'm on it," Borden replied. His ATV's guns erupted and spilled death across the demons' frontline.

"Nathan—"

"Ram Jennifer's ATV and hope we can right her, right?" Nathan asked.

Inside the suit, Simon nodded then caught himself. "Yes. We're only going to get one attempt at this."

"I know, mate. No prob, right?"

"No prob," Simon repeated, but his words were more hope than declaration. He bracketed the Carnagor—already on fire from Danielle's marksmanship—in his sights and fired.

The demon stumbled and Simon thought he might have mortally wounded the Carnagor, but Danielle's next salvo of missiles removed all doubt. For a second, the demon vanished in the huge sheet of twisting flames. Then it stumbled through the fire and stretched out on its side, skidded several feet, and lay prone within inches of the overturned ATV.

"I thought it had us," Jennifer said.

The demons may still have you, Simon thought before he could stop himself. He pushed the thought of his mind and concentrated on the effort they were about to make.

"Brace yourself," Simon suggested.

"Impact imminent," the AI reported in her cool voice. "Altering course."

The safety systems. Simon cursed himself for forgetting those. Even when the ATVs were on manual control, there were defensive safety overrides in case the driver couldn't see a disaster looming under battlefield conditions.

The ATV started to slide away from Jennifer's vehicle.

"Abort safety overrides," Simon ordered.

Immediately, Nathan recovered control of the ATV and drove into the other vehicle. Even though he was braced for the collision and was in his armor, the impact jarred Simon soundly. If not for the seat restraints, he would have been hurled forward and possibly through the broken window.

Nathan had hit the other vehicle a glancing blow on the side. Simon's ATV rocked up as if it was going to overturn, then settled back to the ground. A brief glance at his HUD revealed that Jennifer's vehicle was slowly swinging up. For a moment, it seemed to hang and Simon was afraid that it wouldn't flip back onto its wheels. Then the apex passed and the ATV dropped right side up.

A brief cheer carried over the radio frequency, and it was coming from all of the ATVs. The celebration was short-lived because the pressing matter of survival was once more quickly at hand.

Nathan's course took him into the demons. Simon had his hands full for the next minute or so burning through ammo in the Spike Bolter. Most of the demons went down before the palladium spikes and the Greek Fire missiles.

The exterior vid showed that the ATV was on fire as

well. The tires were pretty much fire-resistant but Simon knew they weren't completely so. Having a blowout—or multiple blowouts—would leave them stranded and as vulnerable as Jennifer and her team had been.

The ATV bumped and shivered as it rode over demons. Blade Minions leaped to the attack as Nathan downshifted and cut sharply back toward the open area. The demons' sharp forearm blades grated against the ATV's palladium armor. Simon knew the vehicle was taking damage that would have to be repaired at some point. Left to their own devices, the Blade Minions would have peeled the ATV open like a tin can in spite of the armor.

"HARP shield ready and standing by," Danielle said.

When Simon switched to an exterior view of the ATV, he saw that it was swarming with demons. Inside London, he wouldn't often get caught like this. The countryside was far too open to provide adequate cover for a small group of warriors outnumbered by a larger force as they were now.

The HARP shielding would blanket the entire ATV but seriously drain the batteries. Another charge couldn't be ready for another eight to ten minutes. By then they could all be dead.

Using the shield was his call.

"Energize shield."

"Energizing," Danielle replied.

A distinct keening whine echoed throughout the control compartment. For a moment, when the HARP discharged, Simon's HUD went blank. The charge was powerful enough to temporarily take the HUD and comm offline. Only a second afterward, though, the AI brought the HUD and comm systems back up.

Nathan had kept the wheels churning through dead demons and broken landscape. A moment later, he burst through the line and raced to the other two ATVs.

The demons followed and fired volley after volley that lit the surrounding forest on fire and scored intermittent hits on the ATVs. They weren't going to be able to keep up.

Simon ran a quick aerial reconnaissance with the sensor drones but no airborne demons were detected. For the moment, they were free and running safe.

"We could dog them for a bit," Jennifer suggested. "Take down a few more of them."

Knowing they had the upper hand, even if only for a short time, made the idea attractive. Simon give it consideration. They hadn't had a truly decisive victory against the demons in months.

"It would be foolish to pursue that course," Borden said. "We've got a job to do it we need to see it done."

Almost regretfully, Simon agreed. But he knew that it wouldn't take long for the demons to call in reinforcements. Then the battle advantages would change again. They were lucky they had been able to handle the seven Blood Angels.

"Withdraw," Simon said. "Let's stick with the game plan."

SEVENTEEN

An hour and seventeen minutes later, they reached the rendezvous point at Dover. Simon positioned the ATVs in a triangle with his own vehicle heading up point. Sensor drones swept through the surrounding mountains and even out over the English Channel.

They weren't far from the cliffs at the point which plunged down fifty feet and more to the sea below. It was the perfect place for an ambush, and Simon and his Templar would be their targets.

The uncomfortable itch at the back of Simon's neck told him he was being watched even though none of the sensors showed the presence of anyone.

"Leah," he said.

"Yes." Her voice was small and quiet.

"Are they out there?"

She hesitated. "I don't know."

They sat in silence a moment longer.

"Well, mate," Nathan said, "there's really only one way we're going to know for sure."

"Cover me." Simon reached up for the roof access hatch and released the lock with his retina print and voice. When the vacuum-seal hissed open, he shoved the hatch up. It fell open with a clank.

He reached up and hauled himself through the tight

opening. Had he been much broader chested, the ATV wouldn't have been an option for him.

When he was outside the ATV, he stood on the rear deck to take advantage of the low profile if it came to that. He fisted his sword hilt as he scanned the surroundings.

"I'm Simon Cross," he said. The suit boosted his voice.

A preliminary search of the area had revealed no demons, but he still felt the people he'd brought there were exposed and vulnerable. More than that, he didn't know what was happening back at the camp he'd established. The demons had systematically destroyed most of the ground-based satellite relays to the network out in space. Access to those satellites was difficult and uncertain at best.

Losing those satellites had been one of the hardest things Simon had been forced to adjust to. All his life he'd grown up with technology that allowed him access to the world. Despite his Templar training, he'd taken that access for granted. Everything now felt too separate, too far apart, to make any sense.

A shadow moved to Simon's right. Even with the advanced vid capability available to the suit, Simon barely made out the figure.

"Mr. Cross," a man's clipped voice greeted. "Welcome. We were told you might be joining us."

Simon remained on the deck. It would be easier to get back inside, and he could use the tank's bulk for defense if he needed to.

"Maybe you could join me down here," the man said. His voice held a tinny quality that let Simon know it was being amplified.

"I can hear just as well from here," Simon countered.

"I thought perhaps we could at least be civil about this."

"Hiding in the shadows isn't my idea of civil."

The figure hesitated, then reached up to his head. The tight-fitting helm split at the back and he pulled it forward off his face.

The man looked as if he was in his thirties. His black hair was cut short, a military high-and-tight style that had been around for decades. His face was thin and gaunt, and old scars that looked like wear marks webbed his left cheek and temple.

"Forgive me," he said. "I don't like being unprotected these days."

"Neither do I." Simon stepped off the ATV and dropped to the ground with the same ease a man would have stepped from the lowest rung of a stepladder. He commanded the faceplate to iris open and immediately relished the cool sea air blowing in from the Straits of Dover. After the effects of the Burn, it had been a long time since he'd felt an honest chill. "I especially didn't like the demon army we ran into not far from here."

The man grimaced. "Sorry about that, but we're under orders not to break cover."

"Whose orders?"

"I'm afraid I can't tell you that."

Secrecy seemed to be second nature to Leah and her cohorts. Simon understood that, though. The Templar existed in the same environment. He continued walking toward the man, but he was sure the man wasn't alone. But that was all right; he wasn't alone either.

"I have Leah Creasey with me," Simon stated.

The man regarded Simon without expression. "I don't know anyone by that name."

Simon couldn't tell if the man was lying. Neither could his armor's AI, and it held programming to detect false-hoods in most people. Even before the technology had been invented, Templar had been trained in body language to detect lies.

There was a rumor, among those who had believed in the Templar before the bloody battle on All Hallows' Eve, that no one could successfully lie to a Templar. In times past, the Templar had encouraged such beliefs while they'd stalked demon artifacts through black markets in various countries involved in the Crusades.

If the man before him had ever heard that, he didn't show any sign of being impressed.

"Fine," Simon said in partial disgust. "Let's get on with this, then, shall we? I've got things to tend to."

The man flashed a brief smile. "As you will." He gestured in the darkness.

Immediately two men dressed in the same kind of armor stepped forward. They ushered a third man forward between them. The two on either side of the third never said anything.

But the third figure lurched forward.

"A *knight*!" The voice was hoarse with disbelief. He came forward with his hands lifted.

Without thinking, Simon drew his Spike Bolter and aimed it at the man. "Stay back," he commanded.

"Don't shoot," the first man admonished. "That's Macomber. The man you've come all this way to see." He reached forward and caught the man by the shoulder to halt his progress.

Simon lowered the pistol but didn't put it away. Even after four years, he didn't completely trust Leah or her mystery group. The almost silent hum that had taken place behind him told him that Nathan or one of the other Templar had taken aim with the ATV's arsenal.

"Not exactly a friendly overture," the man commented dryly.

"It's not exactly a friendly world any more," Simon said. He focused on the man in the middle. "You're Macomber?"

"Dr. Archibald Xavier Macomber, yes." The man might have nodded, but with the helmet it was hard to tell. "Who are you?"

"Simon Cross."

"Ah. You're Thomas Cross's son. I see the resemblance now. Your eyes are the same. But you're bigger."

The announcement surprised Simon. For the most part, he'd always known his father as a quiet, solitary man. At least, as quiet and solitary as a man could be living among the Templar. And Simon stood four inches taller than his father.

"You knew my father?" Simon asked.

"I did. Sadly, only for a short time. But he left a huge impression. Thomas is a very impressive man."

"*Was*," Simon corrected automatically. Four years later, and that correction was still hard to make.

Macomber hesitated. "I'm sorry to hear that. I didn't know."

"Thank you."

"I suppose we need to talk."

The crash of the waves below the cliff echoed through the forest around Simon as he hunkered down on the lee side of the ATV. The nameless man who had come forward sat with him. Both of them watched Dr. Archibald Xavier Macomber.

The professor had taken his helmet off and it lay forward on his armored chest in a loose pool. Macomber was in his sixties and looked frail. Obviously the sanitarium he'd been locked away in had robbed him of a lot of his health.

His face was a pale oval in the darkness. A silvery beard

hung in ragged tatters from his jaw, mirrored by the long mop of hair that brushed his shoulders.

"Why did you want to see us?" Simon asked.

Macomber looked as though the question surprised him. "I wanted to see your father."

"What business did you have with his father?" the quiet man asked.

Simon hadn't made up his mind yet how he was going to deal with the man's presence. Although he wanted to get Macomber off to himself, he wasn't yet ready to challenge the quiet man for custody of the professor.

Besides that, since the ATVs' and his armor's sensors couldn't detect the men surrounding the meeting place, Simon wasn't sure how costly such a maneuver might prove to be.

"His father knew about the demons, of course," Macomber said. "Before the rest of the world learned about them."

"How did he know they were coming?" the quiet man asked.

Suspicion only cast a light stain on the man's question, but Simon was certain distrust ran bone-deep in the man.

"Because of the manuscripts, of course." Macomber sounded old and tired, but also a little like an innocent child.

Simon wondered if the man's mind was still healthy. He'd seen what shock treatments, ice-water baths, and radical medications could do to people's minds.

"What manuscripts?" the quiet man persisted.

"The ones I'd located in France." Macomber blinked. "I need to rest. Really I do. These past few days have been hard on me."

"In a little while, Professor," the quiet man said. "Tell us about the manuscripts."

"They were part of an estate sale outside Paris," Macomber explained. "I sometimes help out with such things. By that time I was living with my wife, Jeanne. Does anyone know what happened to her?"

"We'll try to find out," the quiet man said. "Why were the manuscripts important?"

"The manuscripts aren't gone," Macomber said. "They still exist. And they're still important. They may be the only way any of us are ever safe again."

"How can they make us safe?"

Macomber looked at Simon. "Why aren't you asking any questions?"

"Because he's asking the same questions I would," Simon said. "How can the manuscripts help us?"

"Because they're books of magic, of course." Macomber looked put out, as if everyone should know that. "There are a lot of books out there that claim to be magic, but as you know there aren't that many."

Simon remembered the book he'd helped locate four years ago that had opened up and eaten a Templar standing next to him. *Maybe you don't know all the books that are out in the world, Professor.*

EIGHTEEN

"What made this book so special?" Simon asked the old man. The professor still hadn't acknowledged him with a look. He only stared out into the night sky. "Professor?"

Macomber didn't answer. His eyes stared off into the darkness.

"Professor," Simon said gently.

Unmoved, Macomber sat like a statue.

Simon looked at the quiet man.

"He has episodes," the quiet man said. "After we found out about him—about the work he did in the field of demonology and linguistics—we tracked him down."

"Where was he?"

"Living in one of the universities."

"How did he get out of the sanitarium?"

"Evidently when the generators went, there was a fire. The built-in safety measures opened all the cell doors. Most of the patients remained within the building or within the surrounding neighborhood." The quiet man was even quieter for a short time. Sadness touched his eyes. "Even before the Hellgates opened and the demons arrived, that sanitarium was a bad place to be. The thing that kept most of the residents there was the food. That appeared to be plentiful."

"How did you find him?" Simon asked.

"There was an investigation into your father's past. Someone found out that your father had visited Macomber in the sanitarium. They sent us to find Macomber."

"What did they know about my father?" Simon felt awkward asking the question, as if a stranger would know more about his father that he did.

"Your father's body was found and identified at St. Paul's Cathedral only a few days after of the attack during All Hallows' Eve."

The news hurt Simon. He hadn't known his father's body had been recovered. By rights, if he was able, he was supposed to lay his father's bones to rest in the family crypt in the Templar Underground.

"Where's my father?" he asked.

The quiet man paused before answering. "He's in a medical examiner's vault. If it's still there."

"I need to know where."

"I'll see if I can find out where it is."

Simon nodded, unable to speak. He only hoped his father hadn't been raised as zombie by one of the demons. He turned his attention to Macomber. Gently, Simon laid his armored hand on the old man's shoulder.

"Professor," Simon said.

The old man started at Simon's touch. Macomber put his hands up to defend himself. "Don't hit me! Please don't hit me again!"

He's not here, Simon realized. *He's there, still stuck in the past.* He kept his hand firmly on the old man shoulder and called his name again.

"Professor Macomber. I need to speak with you about Thomas Cross and the book."

The old man's eyes focused on Simon. "Ah, there you are, Thomas. I've been wondering where you'd gotten off to."

Simon didn't bother to correct the man and hoped that the mistaken identity worked out. "Tell me about the book, Professor."

Macomber smiled. "It's a wonderful book, Thomas. I think you're going to be pleased."

"Why am I going to be pleased?" Simon asked.

"Because the book has their *names!* It's like we've always agreed. If we know their names—the names of the demons—we'll have power over them. We won't have to fear them, Thomas. Even if they come to this world, we can save ourselves from them."

"What's the name of the book?"

"Don't play me for the fool, Thomas. You know exactly what book I'm talking about. It's *Goetia*." Macomber set heavily on the ground. "I'm tired now, Thomas. I want to go home. Do you know why Jeanne has not been here yet to pick me up? When they put me in this awful place, she told me she would be back for me as soon as she could." The old man snuggled against the ATV tire and pulled his arms around himself. "Would you watch over me, Thomas? Would you wake me when Jeanne arrives? I don't want to miss her."

Without another word, Macomber closed his eyes and slept.

Simon reached for the professor, but the quiet man stayed his hand.

"It won't be any good to try to wake him at this point," the quiet man said. "When he gets like this, he goes to sleep for a few hours. Even if you succeed in waking him up, all you would probably get is gibberish."

"What's wrong with him?"

"I think they Swiss-cheesed his mind in the sanitarium with all the drugs and treatments. My personal opinion is that he wasn't very strong when he went in. A lot of what he's said while he's been in my custody has been insane stuff." The hint of a smile pulled up the quiet man's lips. "At least, if demons weren't even now running rampant throughout London, I would've thought him insane."

"I want to take him with me." Simon watched for any signs of resistance or baiting. He had to figure that whoever Leah was with would just as likely prefer Simon took the old man. After all, the old man could provide a trail as well. He might even be faking his senility.

"He's yours," a quiet man said. "And I'm glad of it. He's a hard man to be around. Especially with all the talk of demons." He studied Simon. "Do you know what book it is he's talking about? *Goetia*?"

"I do," Simon said. "Have you ever heard of King Solomon?"

"Of course. H. Rider Haggard's pulp novel about Allan Quatermain. *King Solomon's Mines*."

"The historical figure," Simon said.

"No."

"Solomon was the son of David."

"The *David* of David and Goliath?" the quiet man asked.

"That's the one," Simon said. "He was reputed to be the wisest man ever born. During his reign, he wrote the book of *Goetia*. In it, he penned the names of all the demons."

"But that had to be a couple thousand years ago," the quiet man protested incredulously.

"Longer ago than that," Simon said. "He was supposed to have a magical seal—a ring—that gave him power over the demons." He decided not to get into the tale of Asmodeus, the demon that had temporarily tricked Solomon out of the ring.

"A ring?" the quiet man asked doubtfully.

"It's a story," Simon said. "But many stories have some basis in facts."

"Do you really believe there's a ring that can bind the demons?" the quiet man asked.

"I don't know," Simon said. "There was a time when I didn't believe in demons so much."

"I thought you people always believed in them."

"No," Simon answered, but he didn't bother to explain his personal journey to the truth. "Solomon also wrote a book called *Goetia*, also known as *The Lesser Key of Solomon*. The book is supposed to be a compendium of demons' names. Scholars think he called forth seventy-two demons and imprisoned them in a bronze urn of some kind."

"Do you think that's true?"

"I don't know."

The quiet man frowned. "I thought you people knew everything there was to know about the demons."

"No," Simon replied. "We just know more than you do at this point." Before it was over with, he was certain they would know everything together. *Or we'll all be dead.* "The question remains, do I get custody of Macomber? Or was this just an interview you arranged?"

The quiet man looked at the professor sleeping against the oversized tire. The old man looked completely innocuous.

"For the time being, yes, you get him."

Simon squelched his immediate impulse to tell the quiet man that he had asked only out of politeness, not out of necessity. After all, no matter how many men were hidden in the forest, the Templar still had three armored ATVs present.

"I'd suggest keeping him sedated," the quiet man went on. "He travels better that way."

"Giving him more drugs isn't going to help his frame of mind," Simon objected.

"Agreed, but it might just keep you alive. He's been fairly lucid tonight. That isn't always the case. While we were traveling with him, he became extremely agitated and attacked two of my men. We were on a ship and there wasn't anyone to hear. You're traveling overland through dangerous country, and demons' hearing is acute." The quiet man shrugged. "It's just something for you to consider. I'm not telling you how to do your job."

Simon nodded.

"I hear you people have some pretty well-equipped medical facilities," the quiet man said. He touched a section of his armor over his heart. A hidden pocket opened up and he took out a small data chip. "A gift. To show goodwill on our part."

Simon took the chip but didn't point out that he wasn't overly interested in slotting the chip into any hardware the Templar possessed.

"I know you'll have your suspicions about this," the quiet man said. "And I don't blame you. What you got there are Macomber's complete medical records. Maybe it will help you get him straightened away." He smiled sadly. "Before all this mess happened, I had an uncle who had Alzheimer's. I knew him before and after the onset. I hate to see somebody in Macomber's shape."

"Thanks." Simon closed his hand over the chip. "We left a lot of demons back there. Are you and your men going to be okay getting back to London?"

The quiet man grinned. "Didn't say I was going back to London, now did I?"

They were, Simon reflected, as secretive and directed as the Templar. In a way, it made him respect them more. However, it also made him more wary of dealing with them.

"What about Leah Creasey?" he asked.

The man shook his head. "Like I said, I don't know anyone by that name." He looked back the way Simon had come. "You've got a long way to go. Good luck and god-speed."

Simon watched as the man folded his helmet back over his face. The armor sealed immediately and Simon's own armor registered the slight flicker of the energy signature.

The man offered a brief salute, then turned and walked into the treeline. Within three or four steps, with Simon watching him, the man faded from view and disappeared from his armor's sensors.

Just like a ghost, Simon thought.

Simon carried Macomber back to his ATV. Nathan and Danielle helped take the man aboard. They stowed the professor, still sleeping, in one of the sling-seats.

Leah looked curious, but she didn't ask any questions. As Nathan wheeled the ATV around, she pulled her helmet up over her face. It sealed and she was once more expressionless.

With a final look at Macomber, Simon temporarily pushed past the problem the professor presented and focused on getting back to London alive. That would be problem enough for all of them tonight.

Nathan contacted him on a private frequency. "So what's the skinny, mate? Have we got something here, or have we just picked up extra baggage?"

"I don't know," Simon answered honestly.

"If this man is for real, what does he have to offer that makes them worth the risk?"

"He claims to know where *Goetia* is."

"The book of demons?"

"One of them," Simon agreed.

"Do you believe it?"

"I don't know."

"And if it is true, is that book's existence going to make matters better or worse?"

That was the question, Simon thought.

NINETEEN

"**W**hat do you know about the demon Fulaghar?"

Warren hunkered under the eave of a three-story building near his destination and waited out the rainstorm that had blown in shortly after they had returned to the city. He had never much cared for the rain even before the demons had invaded. Melancholy by nature, he felt that the rain seemed to make his moods even darker and more desperate.

Now, though, the rain could often be deadly. Tainted by the Burn, rain usually carried harsh and caustic acids that scorched skin and caused rashes that could chafe to the bone. Warren had seen instances of both cases. People and animals had died from the rain.

Fat raindrops splashed pools out in the uneven streets and tapped incessantly against the metal eave. Nothing else seemed to move throughout the city. Warren suspected that even most of the demons, the lesser ones at least, avoided contact with the acid rain as well.

"I've heard the name," Warren replied in answer to Naomi's question. "He's supposed to be one of the more powerful demons in the lower hierarchy."

Naomi pulled her raincoat more tightly about her. During the long walk back from Ponders End, she hadn't spoken much. That had suited Warren perfectly because he hadn't wanted to talk. He had spent those hours trying to wrap his head around everything Merihim had commanded him to do.

"He's evil," Naomi whispered just barely loud enough to be heard over the rattle of the rain.

"All the demons are evil." That ability of the Cabalists to distinguish one evil from another had always confounded Warren.

"Some of them are more evil than others."

Warren didn't bother to argue the point. When it came to matters like this among the Cabalists, he'd found it to be a losing proposition and a waste of time.

"Fulaghar is dangerous," Naomi said.

Warren refrained from pointing out that all the demons were dangerous. The fact that the majority of the Cabalists chose not to acknowledge that was sheer stupidity and had gotten more than a few of them killed.

"He's called the Shadow Twister because of his ability to alter perception, and because he's rumored to have caused people's shadows to attack and kill them," Naomi said.

"Sounds like that would be a good reason to live in the dark," Warren pointed out.

"How are you going to destroy something like that?"

Warren let out a breath and was relieved to see the rain finally coming to an end. Only a few drops struck the street in front of him now.

"I don't know yet. I'll figure it out."

"But—"

Warren turned and shot her a harsh glance. "I need you to help me, not tell me how impossible this is. If you're going to do that, you might as well go away."

For a moment, he thought she might do exactly that. It was what he would have done.

She reached for him and placed her palm against the side of his face. "I'll help you. It's just that I feel so . . . overwhelmed by this. By *all* of this."

"But this is what you trained to do."

Naomi shook her head. "We believed. We had tapped into them over the years. But we never believed that anything like the demon invasion would happen. At least, I didn't."

Warren looked closely at her and stared into her eyes. "If this thing becomes impossible—" He couldn't finish, and he couldn't believe that it wouldn't turn out to be impossible.

"Then I'll leave you and save myself." Naomi at least had the decency to look ashamed and sorrowful. "It's the way it has to be, and you need to know that."

Warren took in a deep breath and let it out.

Naomi smiled a little and took her hand back from his face. "If I had answered any other way, you wouldn't have believed me."

That was true.

"I'm staying for now because I care about you, and that's the truth whether you believe it or not. But I also want a chance to get more power, Warren. You need to know that too."

Actually, Warren could understand that perfectly. He nodded toward the street. "The rain's stopped. We can go." He turned from her and stepped into the street.

Warren followed a twisting maze of alleys and deadend streets. He had memorized the path a long time ago. When he'd been a child, his mother had dragged him all over the London looking for books on magic and spell casting. There had been dozens of small businesses that had catered to the quiet, but ever-growing, section of the city's population that had gotten interested in arcane matters.

His destination was one of those.

When he reached the place, he found it was far smaller than he remembered. It was a third-story walk-up above a consignment shop and photography studio.

The name of the bookstore, Horowitz Archives, was neatly lettered on the small brass plate beside the stairwell. Memories churned within Warren as he stepped through the broken doors and headed up the stairs.

The stairwell was dark and smelled of urine. That wasn't new, because those details were in his memories of the place.

He couldn't remember how many times his mother had hurried him through the hallway. She had always been afraid that her husband, Warren's stepfather, would find out she was their spending what little money she made on books about magic. The memory of her hand shaking in his was so strong that for a moment Warren felt certain he could close his hand and slow her down the way he had back in those days.

That's over now. Let it go. Otherwise you're going to be as dead as she is.

At the top of the stairs, Warren turned to the left and spotted the simple, frosted pane glass door. The glass had been broken out for the most part. A few jagged shards remained in the frame. Beyond that, the room was filled with books.

Nearby, what Warren had believed only to be a bundle of rags stood up and became a man. The man was scruffy and gaunt, and his complexion gone to a grotesque yellow, like he had been jaundiced.

He held a gun, which he pointed at Warren. "You people need to get out of here. This is my place. All *mine.*"

Warren came to a stop and glared at the man. "I'm not here to take your place. I came to visit the bookstore."

"Bookstore's closed for business." The man cackled madly at his own sense of humor. He waved the pistol meaningfully. "Now I'll see the backside of you leaving this place, or I'm going to put a bullet in the front side."

With a slight twist of the power that filled him, Warren changed his vision to night sight to better see the man. What he saw surprised him.

"You're yellow," Warren said.

The man shifted defensively. "I've been sick."

"You haven't been sick." Warren stared at the man, then shifted to the pile of ragged blankets and quilts lying on the floor.

Long bones, too long to belong to a dog or cat, like partially concealed within the material. Horror twisted Warren's stomach when he realized what the bones belonged to.

"You're a cannibal," Warren accused.

"No I'm not." The man's voice turned shrill and desperate. "Don't say that. You've got no reason to say that."

Cannibalism, though not rampant, did happen within the city. Warren had seen cases of it. The yellow coloration of the skin generally came from the hepatitis infection that was carried through the blood. If the victim did not have hepatitis before getting killed by demons, they often did at the time of death. Most demons carried all sorts of infectious diseases.

The man raised his pistol and in his shaking fist. "No more warnings! Get out bloody well now or I'm going to kill you!"

Warren concentrated for a moment to consolidate his strength, then pushed at the man with his open palm.

The man flew backward as if he'd been hit by a double-decker bus. Bones crunched under the magical impact, and it was all punctuated by the loud bark of the pistol. After he hit the wall, the man hurked and gasped for a moment, then shivered and lay still.

"Are you—" Naomi began.

Warren halted her question with a raised hand. He listened to the silence, straining his ears for the sounds of human feet or demon claws or hooves.

There was nothing.

He let out a tense breath and turned toward the bookstore. A gouge in the wall showed where the bullet had hit. From the angle, Warren knew the bullet hadn't missed him by more than a few inches.

If he hadn't been afraid of Merihim and the task that lay before him, Warren would have gone home. He only hoped the trip to Horowitz's Archives hadn't been in vain.

"What are we looking for here?"

The question irritated Warren. "This is a bookstore, right? We're here looking for a book."

The glow from the minitorch Naomi used to search with brightened her features and showed her own disconsolate feelings. "I knew that. I meant, was there a particular book you were looking for?"

Warren reined in his anger. He didn't want to be alone right now. He didn't like being alone and had never done well during those times when he had to be by himself. That was why Kelli still rotted in his sanctuary.

"Any book on Fulaghar," Warren said. "I need more information about him."

"How did you know about this place?" Naomi kept the minitorch moving and searched the shelves.

Even before the invasion, the bookshop had always been only partially organized. An old man had owned and operated the place. He had seemed to have a genuine affection for kids and sometimes performed magic tricks, actual feats of legerdemain and not arcane efforts, for Warren.

As he went to the shelves now, Warren thought about the old man and wondered what had happened to him. He hoped the old man had died quietly in bed before the demons had come.

"My mother brought me here," Warren said.

"She was interested in the arcane arts?"

"More like she was obsessed by it. All I remember of her from the time I was small was her reading these books. I didn't like them. I saw some of the pictures inside and they . . . scared me."

"A lot of these books can be quite intense for the younger mind." Naomi held up a book on sacrifices and shined her minitorch on the cover.

The artwork showed several demons gather around an altar made of black marble. A winged demon with an angelic body and scanty clothing held a stone dripping blood in one hand and the head of a man in the other. Intense fear showed on the man's face even though he had to be dead.

"Of course," Naomi went on, "several books written on the subject are pure malarkey."

Warren remained silent and kept looking. He sorted through boxes of books, and though he found some he wanted to investigate further, he didn't find what he was looking for. He tried not to feel hopeless, but that was an old unfamiliar feeling that he had never been able to shake. The feeling settled onto him now, ran its tendrils into his bones, at leached away his confidence.

TWENTY

Ultimately, only shortly before dawn, Warren gave up the search. When he left the bookstore he saw the dead man's body still slumped against the hallway wall.

The acid rain had departed, but the coming heat of the day caused by the Burn had already started making itself felt. The streets were muggy and steamy fog filled the city.

Alerted by the grinding sound of ironbound wheels against the pavement, Warren caught Naomi's arm and pulled her back into the safety of a nearby doorway. He held her flat against the door as the grinding sound came closer.

Farther down the street, a horse-drawn carriage rolled through the steamy fog and emerged in full view. Despite all the macabre scenes Warren had seen played out over the last four years, this one was a total surprise.

Six zombies lurched in the place of the horses that would normally pull the carriage. They held on to the double-tree rigging and stepped mostly in unison. The top was pulled back on the cab and the occupants sat for all to see.

Three Darkspawn demons—broad-shouldered and narrow-hipped, with impossibly long legs that had two oppositional knees, and a multitude of blue-green eyes set into heads that joined their shoulders without benefit of a neck—sat in the carriage. Their scales looked like striations of yellow, orange, charcoal, and red. That coloration marked them as Diabolists among their kind. As such they tended to use both the arcane and technology.

During the invasion, the Darkspawn had become the part of the occupation forces. They kept regular patrols over areas while other demons hunted.

While watching them, Warren had noted that the Darkspawn were insatiably curious and inventive. Where the other demons tended only to destroy things, the Darkspawn explored areas, examined things, and tried to make sense of them. They were also inventive, and made their own weapons.

That curiosity made them even more dangerous. While other demons bored easily without stimulus or fixated on whatever it was they were attempting to do, the Darkspawn thrived on the new and different, and had roving attention spans.

Evidently now the three Darkspawn Diabolists were conducting experiments or amusing themselves.

After they were gone, Warren led the way out of the building and stayed within the deepest shadows as he made his way back to his sanctuary.

Once he was inside his building again, Warren started to feel safe. That didn't last long when he checked the magical binding that tied him to Merihim. The demon was there, just within reach.

"I have a room for you," Warren told Naomi.

She and looked at him with a hint of surprise. "I thought I would stay with you."

Warren didn't bother to explain that sharing the bed with someone while he was awake was a totally different matter than of even thinking of sharing one while he was asleep. He didn't trust anyone that much.

"It's a good room," he said. "We both need a good night's sleep."

Naomi just stared at him for a moment, then nodded. "Maybe you're right."

"I am. We both need to be thinking clearly later." Warren walked her to the room, one of the more upscale rooms in the building. Only briefly did he think about what he was walking away from.

At the stairway, he reached into his shoulder bag and took out one of the Blood Angel eyes he'd cast a binding spell on. He pictured Naomi in his mind as he held the eye in his demon hand.

"Watch," he commanded. Then he tossed the eye up into the air.

The eye bounced for just a moment, blinked twice, then floated up into one of the dark corners of the hall where it could watch over Naomi's door.

Warren activated the spell that bound the eye to him. Immediately what the eye saw overlaid his vision. With a little concentration, he shifted his vision to that afforded by the spell. He saw himself standing in front of the door to the room he had let Naomi borrow.

Satisfied, he went up the stairs to his own room.

In the large suite, Warren undressed and took a quick shower. Attending to his personal hygiene always made him feel more in command of himself.

Instead of remaining unclothed, he dressed in black khakis and another rugby shirt. He also tossed a thigh-length leather jacket on the bed so he could find it quickly if he had to.

He added two 9mm pistols and a sheathed knife. The pistols wouldn't do any good against the demons, but not everything out there that hunted and killed was demonic.

Fatigue ate at him and he wanted to lie down but his mind just wouldn't rest. Thoughts kept banging away inside his skull. The old fear that had always been with him stirred anxiously.

He lifted the heavy drapes and peered outside. Nothing moved out on the streets. A quick check of the Blood Angel eye watching over Naomi showed him that the door was still shut. If it had opened the eye would have alerted him.

"Warren."

Startled, Warren gazed around the room. No one else was in the suite besides him.

"Warren."

This time, Warren tracked the voice to the other side of the room. As he walked in that direction, he picked up one of the 9mm pistols from the bed, fisted it, and flicked the safety off with his thumb.

"Who called for me?" Warren asked quietly.

"Do you wish to know?"

When he reached the wall, Warren opened the hidden safe area he'd found only a few days after his arrival. The pressure release that popped the cover of the safe had to be pressed in the correct order in order to reveal the hidden area. Otherwise it looked just like the wall.

The book lay inside.

As Warren watched, the eyes opened on the book cover and looked down at him.

"Do you wish to know?" the book asked again.

"Who are you?" Warren asked.

The book regarded him, almost looking as though it were looking down its nose at him due to the angle.

"I can be your friend. If you allow me."

"Friendships cost too much." *More than that,* Warren told himself, *demons lie.*

"You've never had a friend like me before."

Warren remained unconvinced.

"I know about Fulaghar," the book said.

Instead of immediately asking about the demon, Warren chose to pursue the line of questioning in his head. It was more important to find out who was helping him for one, and who all the other players were.

"How did you find out about that?"

"Because I am one of the Keepers." There was a note of pride in his voice.

"One of the keepers of what?" Warren asked.

"One of the Keepers of the Secret Histories."

Warren waited, certain there was a trick involved. "What are the Secret Histories?"

"Things that the demons do not want known." The book continued to stare at Warren. "How can you not be a friend with one such as I? I can help you attain everything you desire. I can give you a world."

"Merihim called you a Book of Qhazimog."

"The demons call us that because Qhazimog was the one who first wrote the Secret Histories."

"I've never heard of him."

"Before the demons came, there was a lot you hadn't heard of. There's still a lot you have heard of. Besides that, Qhazimog wasn't from this world. He was from another. Those who studied the arcane arts millennia ago brought me and other Books into this world. They were given by other worlds that were consumed by the demons and by the Burn."

Suddenly Warren was even more afraid that he had been. "This is a trick," he rasped.

"If you believe it is so, then it must be." The book closed its eyes.

"Wait." Desperation filled Warren. For the last four

years his life had gotten harder to live and the risks greater.

"What?" The book opened its eyes again.

"If you are what you say you are, then why would Merihim allow you to fall into my possession?"

"Your demon lord doesn't know everything. None of the demons know everything."

"How did he know to send me after you?"

"He knew only that I was a book important to the Cabalists."

"I don't believe you."

"Then how am I here, talking to you? Demons don't care for books. They never have. For them, books have always presented power to destroy them. I am one of those books. There are others. That's why demons have sometimes disguised monsters as books to destroy scholars who can read the lost languages."

"What lost languages?" Warren asked.

"Like the language we're using now."

"But you're speaking like me."

"No," the book said. "You're speaking like me. This is my language, and I'm sharing it with you. I would never do that with a demon."

Warren thought about that, but the distrust and fear wouldn't leave him. Still, his entire life had been lived within those shadows. The trick was to embrace the lives and sort out the truths he needed, the truths that would keep him alive.

Gingerly, he reached into the safe and took the book out. "You can tell me about Fulaghar?"

"What do you wish to know?"

"I need to kill him."

The book laughed, and the effort caused it to shake and vibrate in Warren's grasp. The noise was dry and hollow.

"Your demon lord does not care much for you, does he?"

"Can you tell me about Fulaghar?"

The book's expression turned serious. "Yes, I can."

Warren sat at the desk and opened the book. For the first time he saw that the face was not bound to the cover, but instead was free to roam throughout the book. The eyes now opened on every page to look at him and to talk to him.

"Here is Fulaghar," the book said. "Wrapped in his terrible glory, the Shadow Twister—as he is known by many—has always been vicious in battle. He is even feared within the demon ranks."

The page showed a towering figure of truly demonic proportions. He stood head and shoulders above the humans who fought in vain against him. They stood on a bare hillock beneath a blazing red sun. Fulaghar wielded a mighty double-bitted battle-ax. The blades ran crimson with blood, and ropes of it stained the white sand beneath the demon's feet.

Fulaghar had wings and a crown of horns that stood straight as spears a foot above his head. His visage was grim, not truly human as it had been when it had borrowed the First Seer's face back in the Cabalist lair. Mottled green and yellow scales covered him from head to cloven hoof. The scales were deeper green toward the center of his body and grew gradually more yellow as they flared out to his limbs. Scars stood out on his body and created a map of past battles. A belt of human skulls ringed his waist.

As Warren watched, the battle came to life. Fulaghar couldn't be stopped and was totally merciless in his attack. The screams of dying and wounded men filled Warren's ears, punctuated by the ring and rasp of steel on steel.

The demon looked impossible to kill.

"Fulaghar can be destroyed," the book said. As it spoke, the moving figures on the page came to a stop.

"How?"

"All you have to know is his name."

"That can't kill him." Warren didn't believe that for a moment. The demons were too ferocious and too hard to kill. He had seen lesser demons destroy the armored knights that he sometimes saw in the city trying to save survivors.

"Knowing his name makes him vulnerable. The demons have other weaknesses, but this is one that I can give you."

"You know Fulaghar's true name?" Warren didn't dare hope, but some part of that emotion took root within him anyway.

"I don't," the book said. "But there is another book that will have Fulaghar's true name listed."

"Will it also have Merihim's true name?" The question was out of Warren's mouth before he knew the question had even taken shape in his mind. Sickness twisted within him as he waited to be struck down by Merihim.

The book gazed at him from the page with Fulaghar on it. "When you talk to me, your demon lord cannot hear your thoughts."

But what about when I'm not talking to you? Will Merihim know what we've been talking about? Warren wanted to ask that question but wondered how best to pose it.

"I can shield those thoughts from Merihim," the book said. "Just as easily as I can read your thoughts now. As I said, I can be the best friend you've ever had."

"What price am I going to have to pay for that friendship?" Warren asked. "The one thing I've learned in this world is that nothing comes for free."

The book stared at him with serious, ancient eyes.

"When the time comes, Warren Schimmer, you will be my friend. You'll help me escape this bondage I have been in for thousands of years." He gave him a small, sad smile. "The Books of the Secret Histories were not made without tremendous sacrifice. I would be free before I die a true death."

"But how—"

"No. We'll not talk of this matter now. That's too far off and we have much to do before such time arrives." The book gazed at him. "I'm trusting you as much as you're trusting me."

Warren still didn't believe that was true, but for the moment he didn't contest the veracity of that statement. The time would come, he knew, when he would learn the truth that was being hidden between them.

All that mattered, given his present circumstances and the impossible task before him, was that he needed a friend who could tell him the things the book promised to reveal.

"All right." Warren studied the obscene figure of Fulaghar on the page. "Tell me about this book that lists the names of the demons."

"It's called *Goetia*, also called *The Lesser Key of Solomon*. And it's somewhere within the city. I can guide you there."

TWENTY-ONE

"Simon, the old man is awake."

The communication came over the armor's frequency so Simon knew their guest wouldn't take offense. "His name is Archibald Xavier Macomber," he corrected. "When you address him, address him as Professor Macomber."

Although he could see Macomber plainly in the HUD, Simon turned to face the old man and opened his faceshield.

Macomber looked disoriented and frightened. He rubbed at one ear like a child.

"Professor Macomber?" Simon said.

The old man looked up at him. "Thomas?" then he caught himself and shook his head. "No, you're not Thomas. Forgive me. Sometimes it's hard to wake up."

"Some days it's hard for me to wake up too. Would you like anything to eat or drink?"

Macomber hesitated. "Something to drink, perhaps. My stomach doesn't do very well these days. Perhaps after we get settled and things are not so uncertain."

One of the Templar pulled a plastic container of water from the ATV stores and handed it to Macomber. The old man fumbled with the seal and couldn't quite manage it.

Leah opened her helmet. "Allow me to help you with that, Professor."

Macomber stared for just a moment, then passed the water flask over to Leah. "Thank you, my dear."

Leah opened the flask and passed it back to the professor. He nodded his thanks and took a sip. Some of the tension left his face.

"Where are we?" Macomber asked.

"Twenty-five miles east of London," Simon answered. "We'll be safe and secure in just a little while."

"I don't think anywhere is truly safe," Macomber commented. He smoothed a hand through his wispy white hair. "We did talk about *Goetia*, right? I didn't dream that?"

"No," Simon replied. "We talked about the book. But not enough." He felt sorry for the old man, and for everything that he had been through, but if he had information about the demons that they needed he had to get to it. "Do you know where the book is?"

Macomber fidgeted. "I've never seen the book, but I know it exists. I've read sections of it. But none of those sections ever had the names of the demons." He paused. "That book is important. It can help in the war against the demons."

"I know," Simon said. "If it's everything that it's said to be."

Macomber sipped his water again, but Simon sensed that it was a delaying tactic rather than a want or need. The old man was clearly hesitant to trust him.

"You knew my father. He gave his life fighting these demons," Simon said. "I've spent four years of my life fighting them and trying to save those people still trapped within London. I've seen the bodies of those people I couldn't save—men, women, and children—and I've held friends who died in my arms." Surprised at how thick his voice had gotten, he took a deep breath and pushed those sharp emotions away. "I will never betray any trust you invest in me. I swear that to you on my father's name."

"I know." Macomber nodded. "I know that you do. Your father swore an oath to me as well."

"Templar oaths are not lightly given," Simon said. He was surprised at the touch of anger in his words, but he didn't like having to defend his honor or that of the Order. Honor was a sacred thing, a privilege and a duty. It was also to be respected.

"I know that. But I also want you to know that the oath I gave was not lightly given either. The man who gave me the knowledge about *Goetia* impressed upon me the manuscript's importance." Macomber looked at Simon. "You're familiar with the history of the book?"

"It was written by King Solomon and was also known as *The Lesser Key of Solomon*. Some say he used the power in the manuscript to bind seventy-two demons into a jar."

"It wasn't a jar," Macomber said. "What Solomon did was bind seventy-two demons from this world. The Templar have searched for this book for a long time. They first found out about the book when they took up residence under Solomon's temple after the first crusade."

"I knew about the Templar being there then," Simon said. "But I didn't know they were searching for a book."

"Not everyone believed *Goetia* existed. Not even the Templar. During that time, the manuscript's existence caused a great deal of consternation among the Order."

"But it dealt with the demons."

Macomber nodded. "The Harbingers—the demons who always first come forth from a Hellgate—had arrived in this world. Solomon had the names of most of those demons that tried to force their way here. He used the knowledge of those names to keep them from arriving and shut down the Hellgate."

"Can the demons only come through the Hellgates?" Leah asked.

"No." Macomber shook his head. "The Harbingers and some of the lesser demons come through first to anchor the Hellgate in whatever world the demons are invading. They're heralds of a sort. Dark and deadly things."

"Then why use the Hellgate at all?" Leah asked.

"Because only a few demons can come through without it. The majority of them, especially if they're arriving in number, must use the Hellgate. That's how we know about the demons. A few of them have always lurked in this world. Now and again, some of them are found, but very few. Part of their glamour, at least of the ones that lurk here, is that no one will believe in them."

Simon understood that. Phillip the Fair had used that disbelief against the Templar to steal their fortunes and their honor.

"Only the Templar and a few other people over the course of history have believed in the demons," Macomber said. "Most of them were tried and convicted of heresy. Which at many times in history meant those convicted would be burnt at the stake, drowned, or imprisoned in a madhouse. In the case of the Templar, they were stripped of their riches and their dignity. So you see, even those who believed in demons were reluctant to admit that."

"There are still some who believe the demons here now are aliens from another world," Leah said.

Macomber shook his head. "This is the power the demons wield. I fear for all of us."

"How did Solomon learn about the demons?" Simon asked.

"He didn't learn about the demons. Others who knew about them told him. King Solomon came to believe through their belief. He didn't write *Goetia*, but he caused the manuscript to be written. He claimed credit for authoring the manuscript so no one would challenge its authenticity." Macomber sipped his water. "Of course, you see how that turned out. No one even believes the manuscript exists."

"There are some who claim that manuscript was never written during Solomon's time," Simon said. "It's reputed to be a thinly veiled political attack on nobility, which didn't exist in Solomon's day."

"Those were other versions written later," Macomber said. "They were nothing more than a smokescreen, possibly created by those in league with the demons or those who used Solomon's name for their own purposes. The true manuscript has become a thing of legend, myth, and make-believe. That's what the demons do best: cause you to doubt yourself."

"You said you'd seen sections of the manuscript," Leah said.

Macomber nodded. "I have. Even those copies that I saw carried the twisted power that is inherent in the demons. I don't know how anyone can read those manuscripts, let alone *write* those manuscripts or copy them. I was reading them—more of them after I had talked with your father, Simon—when I had my first . . . *episode*."

Although he was anxious to find out the rest of the story, Simon waited as patiently as he could. It wasn't easy, but he saw embarrassment and frustration tighten the old man's features.

"I'd read other sections of the book," Macomber continued. "There had been adverse reactions before—sickness, nightmares, and periods and I couldn't remember at all—but nothing like what happened that time. I lost days of my life to the madness. I don't even really remember much of it. But I do remember that there was a demon in the pages. How it got there, I don't know. It's hard to remember. But I do recall that it promised me things. Wealth. Long life. Power. All the things that demons offer so casually. And when I resisted, it threatened to kill my wife and my children."

Only the hum of the NanoDyne electromagnetic engines filled the ATV's interior. Simon couldn't help remembering his own experience with demonic books.

"That was when I snapped," Macomber said. "I burned the manuscript. Unfortunately, I also apparently burned the apartment where I was living and set the building on fire. I'm told that the fire department almost didn't get the blaze out in time." He paused and took a sip of his water. "My wife, bless her, didn't know what I had been through. She had me committed. I didn't blame her then, and I don't blame her now." Tears showed in the old man's eyes. "The television news stories made her out to be some kind of monster. But she wasn't the monster. I have seen monsters."

"It must have been very hard," Leah said gently.

Macomber turned his head to focus on her. He smiled. "You're very pretty."

Leah smiled back. "Thank you."

"Do you know where to find the book?" Simon asked. "I don't mean to sound insensitive, but—"

"You're not insensitive," Macomber said. "I saw the pain in your eyes when you told me about your father's death. It's just that these are hard times. We have to acknowledge that and go on." He drew a breath. "As I said, I've never seen the true manuscript, but I do know where it can be found."

Simon stared at the map of the city of London on the wide-screen monitor in front of him. If Macomber had known how to use the armor's AI system and if Leah had been privy to all the Templar systems instead of just the comm frequency, they could have worked over the HUDs.

But the ATVs carried redundant systems. The monitor was one of those and intended for use in times that non-Templar personnel were aboard.

"When you're in a madhouse," Macomber said with all seriousness, "you meet all kinds of people. There are some in there who have serious problems. I can tell you truthfully many times the medication, the treatment programs, and the lack of empathy on part of the personnel contribute to those problems." He leaned closer to the screen. "There's a sanitarium somewhere around the East India docks. I believe the name is Akehurst Home for the Criminally Insane."

Simon initiated a search onscreen. The results came back in seconds. There was no Akehurst Home for the Criminally Insane, but there was an Akehurst Brighter Days Rehabilitation Clinic.

"I guess the new name might seem more hopeful to patients," Leah said. "Or at least to their families. Probably more likely, though, the insurance companies felt more at ease writing out the monthly checks for care and rehab."

Voice commands brought up the history of the place as well as images. Property records indicated that Akehurst Brighter Days Rehabilitation Clinic had until 1953 been doing business as Akehurst Home for the Criminally Insane. According to the tax records, the same family owned the property and the business.

The images showed a gray box of a building that squatted like an ancient dog in the middle of landscaped grounds surrounded by a high wrought-iron fence. Three smaller outbuildings surrounded the main building.

The map showed that the rehab clinic was only a few blocks from the Thames. With it in such close proximity to the river, Simon knew demon patrols would be a serious problem.

"Why is the manuscript there?" Simon asked.

"You have to understand that it's not the original manuscript," Macomber said. "It's only a copy."

"Will a copy work?" Leah asked.

"What I read, what drove me insane there for a time, was just a copy." Macomber looked at both of them. "You need to understand the kind of power you're dealing with. Replication doesn't dull that power or dilute it in any way." He paused. "Understand also that if you choose to go after this manuscript—"

"We don't have a choice," Simon said.

"—your lives will be in the greatest jeopardy you can imagine."

"They already are," Leah said.

The suit's AI broke in as Simon tried to assemble his thoughts and put a plan together.

"Warning. Nine unidentified vehicles are on an approach path with this convoy," the female voice said. "Efforts to communicate with them have failed. All precautions should be taken at this time."

Simon closed his faceshield and pulled up the HUD's radar screen. The sensor drones had already reached the unidentified vehicles.

A schematic of one of them popped on screen. The design was immediately familiar.

"It's an ATV," Nathan said.

"Military or Templar?" Danielle asked.

Simon studied the ATVs. The indicator display showed that they were two miles out and closing rapidly.

"Hail them," Simon said. "Let's see if they answer."

As soon as hail went out, there was an immediate response. Terrence Booth's image formed to the right on the HUD.

Booth was the High Seat of House Rorke, the hereditary leader position within that house. The last four years had evidently been more demanding on him than Simon might have guessed. Although he was only four years older than Simon and currently in his early thirties, Booth's dark hair and goatee now showed silver streaks. His face and gotten more round and his dark eyes looked more close-set, and lent him a sour look.

The broken nose hadn't changed a bit. Simon took pride in that. He had been the one to break Booth's nose. Both times. Once when they were younger and then again four years ago when Simon had last seen the High Seat.

There had been no love lost between them when they were teenagers, and there was less so now. Four years ago, Simon had disobeyed Booth's direct orders and left the Templar Underground. Several of the Templar had accompanied him.

Simon couldn't imagine what had brought Booth out of the Underground. But even more puzzling was how Booth had found him here now.

Booth's presence could only mean that Simon had a traitor in his midst.

TWENTY-TWO

S imon opened a public comm channel rather than going private as Booth's communiqué had requested. During his leadership role, Simon had chosen to keep all his people informed and up to date. There weren't going to be any secrets, no divisions of loyalty.

And yet, he told himself, *you've still managed to bring along an informer.* He pushed the thought off. It was something to be dealt with at a later date. And he wasn't going to go on a bloody witch hunt to find out the informer was.

"You've come far afield of your normal stomping grounds, haven't you, Booth?" Simon asked. He offered no sarcasm, but it was there in his words all the same.

Booth frowned. "I don't want to make this complicated. And you don't have to be egregious."

"No, I don't have to be. I throw that in for free." Simon muted the comm for a moment. "Nathan, see if you can break this interception path."

Immediately, Nathan took a new heading. The ATV crashed through underbrush of an over small trees. The ride became decidedly more bumpy.

On the HUD, Simon watched as the other two ATVs changed course to follow Nathan's lead. They plunged through the night in single file.

Just as quickly, though, Booth's vehicles altered course and again pressed for an interception.

"You're not going to get away that easily," Booth threatened.

"I wasn't aware that I was trying to get away," Simon said. He motioned for Leah and Macomber to resume their seats. "The last time I saw you all, I was under the distinct impression you never wanted to see me again."

"If I had my way, I wouldn't see you again."

"What can I do for you, Booth?"

"Since you haven't seen fit to die fighting the demons, and you haven't left well enough alone, I'm forced to have this little meeting with you."

"And if I should decline?"

"That's not one of the choices," Booth said.

The indicator figures showed that 0.473 miles remained between the two groups of vehicles. That distance diminished quickly.

"It's come to my attention that you've been dealing with that young woman you brought to the Underground," Booth said. "I've been told that you've got a man named Archibald Xavier Macomber with you. A professor of linguistics who was, until late, a guest of a Parisian sanitarium."

Simon was surprised that Booth knew who Macomber was. As a young man growing up, the current High Seat of Rorke hadn't been one to study. He hadn't had to. The position was hereditary and his father had been young. At the time, Booth hadn't figured on becoming High Seat until he was an old man himself.

"That's none of your business," Simon said.

Booth shifted in his command chair easily, then leaned forward so that his face filled the vidscreen. "Tonight it is my business. I'm making it my business."

A chill threaded down Simon's spine despite the even heating and cooling supplied by the armor. Anger wrenched at his stomach and made his head hot.

"What do you want?" Simon demanded.

Booth shrugged. "I want the professor."

"Why?"

"For the same reasons you do, of course."

Simon doubted that. During the last four years the Templar Underground had chosen to remain invisible. They remained hidden within the vast subterranean complexes and kept separate from the living and dying that happened within the ruins of London.

"You'll understand why I choose not to believe that," Simon said. "I haven't seen you take part in striking out against a demon in the last four years."

Anger mottled Booth's features. He didn't like being castigated, much less in public. It hurt even more, Simon supposed, when what was said was true.

"You don't have a choice about turning the professor over to us." Booth's words were cold and threatening. "If you don't turn Macomber over to me, I'll take him by force."

Simon broke off the communication with Booth's vehicles. He looked around and his team. He couldn't help wondering if one of them was Booth's informer.

"Someone sold us out, mate," Nathan said.

"That isn't the problem we have to deal with right now," Simon replied. He watched the progress of the two waves of vehicles approaching each other. They were less than thirty-seven seconds apart.

"You can't give me to them," Macomber said hoarsely. Panic echoed in his words. Terror widened his eyes. "I don't know them."

"Can we outrun them, Nathan?" Simon asked. Then he activated the defensive shields.

"We're evenly matched," Nathan replied. "And if Booth really wants to push this to a physical encounter, we're outnumbered three to one. Not only that, but after that encounter with the demons, we're limping back home."

"Warning. Impact imminent." The AI's voice sounded strangely calm in spite of all the tension that filled the command center.

Before Simon had time to say anything, the proximity numbers relaying the distance between his vehicle and the lead ATV of Booth's forces zeroed out. The thunderous crash echoed within the command center.

Simon knew from the sensor drones that the collision pushed the ATV up on its side. The onboard computer revealed that the armored vehicle rose up to a twenty-nine degree angle. Despite the impact, the command center revolved within the nanofluid environment, keeping everyone inside in their upright positions.

The ATV's defensive shields took a seventeen percent loss. Even as he registered everything going on with his own vehicle, Simon saw the other two ATVs get struck as well.

The vehicle that had hit him stayed locked on and pushed the ATV sideways into a copse of trees. Some of the trees shattered on impact and bared white flesh under the bark. Others stood firm.

The seat restraints bit into Simon's shoulders as they called him up short. The ATV came to a sudden stop.

"Weps ready," Danielle reported angrily. "I have a target and can fire on your mark."

"Warning," the AI said. "Other vehicles have target lock on this vehicle."

Before Nathan could reverse the electromagnetic engines, another ATV slid in behind them and blocked them. Nathan tried to break free of the trap but couldn't. The tires chewed the turf but couldn't find enough purchase to dig out with the extra weight of the other ATV.

Simon opened the hail he received from Booth.

The High Seat grinned. "Give him to me. You don't have a choice. Give him to me and I'll let you and your people go free. Fight me and I'll take you all down. That's a promise."

A glance at the HUD's radar image relayed from the sensor drones showed Booth's ATV well back of the firing line. Disgust weighed heavily on Simon. He'd had no way to expect what had happened, no way to prepare. He had been blindsided.

"We can stay inside," Nathan pointed out. "They'll still have a hard time peeling us open."

"They don't have to peel us open," Danielle growled. "All they have to do is wait until we get hungry or thirsty. Then we'll come out on our own."

"With the provisions we have, we can stay inside for three or four days," Nathan said. "More if we want to stretch them. If I know Booth, and I do, he's not going to want to wait around out here that long because he'll be worried about demons finding us." He turned from the steering section and looked at the Simon even though he didn't have to with the HUD operational. "In a game of nerves, we'll win."

Simon looked at the High Seat's image. "This isn't about nerves. For whatever reason, Booth thinks he has to win. That's always when he's at his most dangerous." He paused, but in the end knew that they had no real choice. "If he has to, he'll kill us."

"There are a lot of Templar who wouldn't put up with something like that," Nathan said. "Despite the fact that we've defied orders, we've got friends there. They know what we've been doing in the city and how many lives we've saved."

Simon felt certain that was true. But if they forced the issue, Booth would be able to get his troops to open fire.

"That's probably the only reason Booth didn't try to have us killed outright," Simon said.

"Then we brinkmanship him," Danielle stated.

Simon glanced at her.

"We, and the other two ATV crews, train our weapons on Booth's vehicle and tell him where going to shoot him if he tries anything. He doesn't particularly care to have his neck on the chopping block."

"That would also mean firing on other Templar," one of the warriors in the sling-seats said. "I'm not comfortable with that."

Neither am I, Simon told himself. He racked his brain for another way out of the situation, but just couldn't find one.

"Simon." Macomber's voice was soft and unsteady. He looked sick and gray. "These are other Templar, correct?"

"Yes."

"Why, then, are you at odds?"

"Because Booth and most of the other Templar want to remain in hiding and pretend they have been defeated," Simon said. He felt compelled to tell the old man the truth. Macomber deserved to know what was going on.

Macomber nodded. "To grow their strength back from all they have lost."

"Yes."

"It's a good plan."

"Except the demons are going to be growing stronger too. And the Burn is going to be changing our world more and more, providing them even better and more user-friendly terrain to find us on." Simon shook his head.

"Waiting isn't a good idea. Waiting isn't going to save people still trapped in the city."

"I understand that, and I empathize with what you're trying to do." Macomber took a deep breath and shuddered just a little. "These men—this man Booth—none of them wish me any harm, correct?"

"I don't think so," Simon answered.

"If they did, they would have already attacked us with their weapons."

Simon nodded, and hoped that he was right.

"What do they want from me?" Macomber asked.

"I don't know. Maybe they want to know what you know. Or maybe they just don't want me to know what you know."

"They want to stop you?"

"Booth and the others are afraid I'm going to make things worse."

"How can you make anything worse?"

"I don't know."

Macomber cursed in English and French. "That man is a fool. Everything you can find out about the demons early on is better. That was one thing your father and I agreed on. That was why he came to me when I started translating the demon texts. Knowledge *is* the best kind of power."

"My father used to say that knowledge was the sharpest weapon you would ever have in your arsenal," Simon said.

"Intelligent man, your father."

"Smarter than I thought he was. But I never got the chance to tell them that."

Macomber unbuckled his seat and walked over to Simon. The professor put his hand on Simon's shoulder. "I'm sure your father knows."

Simon hoped so.

Macomber drew a deep breath into his lungs then let it out. Of he offered Simon a smile. "Then let me be as brave a man as Thomas Cross was in this instance. Let me out of here and I'll turn myself over to this man Booth."

"I can't let you do that," Simon said.

"You don't have a choice. Not from your enemy, nor for me. This is my undertaking. Let me do it while I'm still brave enough."

"Simon," Leah said, "what he says makes sense."

Simon knew that, but it still made him angry that he was forced into the situation.

"Please," Macomber said.

In the end, there really was no choice.

TWENTY-THREE

When Simon gave the command to open the control center and allow Macomber outside the ATV, he went with the professor. As Simon stood on the rear deck and stared at Booth's ATV, the guns of the other vehicles tracked on to him. If he was wrong and Booth decided to eliminate any further problems from him, Simon knew there was a chance that the first round to hit him might not penetrate his armor and only knock him from the ATV.

If. That was suddenly a big word standing there out in the open. It was almost easier standing up to demons. At least those were guaranteed to attack and he didn't have to wonder.

He left his faceshield open, which was another risk, but he didn't like the idea of simply presenting the armor's blank face to Macomber as the professor left. It was a small personal touch but Simon needed to do it.

Macomber looked up to him and spoke in a whisper. "I've told you where you can find the *Goetia* manuscript. I will hope that you do." He looked over his shoulder as the nearest ATV's control center hatch opened. Two Templar stepped out onto the ATV's deck. "I will forestall them as long as I'm able. But, if I were you, I wouldn't take too long."

"Understood, Professor. Take care of yourself."

"Until we meet again." Macomber offered his hand.

Simon took the old man's hand gently for just a moment, then released him.

Macomber negotiated stepping from one ATV to the next with ease. It helped that the vehicles were butted up against each other.

Neither of the Templar spoke to Simon as they watched him. The faceshields were blank and offered only dim reflections of Simon in them.

"What do you think you're doing out there?" Nathan asked. "Get back inside the vehicle before Booth orders someone to light you up."

It was good advice, and Simon knew he should have taken it. But he couldn't. Maybe it was pride on his part, or maybe it was defiance. Either way, he stood his ground till Booth's vehicles backed up and rolled away.

"You have an incoming communiqué," the suit AI announced.

Simon knew who it would be from. He closed his faceshield and pulled up the HUD. The communiqué came over a private frequency. Simon allowed it to connect.

Booth's gloating face formed on the HUD. "You've been saving people for the last four years. You'd probably be better off sticking with that and staying out of my way."

"It's hard to be in your way," Simon said. "You're not going anywhere."

An unpleasant scowl darkened Booth's features. "I hope the demons don't get you. Honestly I do. One of these days there'll be an accounting between you and me."

"It can be today if you like," Simon offered. "I'm here."

Booth cursed ferociously for a moment, then blanked the screen and broke communications.

Behind the faceshield, Simon grinned. *Okay, maybe that was childish, but it felt good.*

But helplessly watching Booth's ATVs roll away took some of the joy out of it.

Once more seated in the command center, Simon watched as Booth's ATV units headed back toward London.

"We know where the *Goetia* manuscript is supposed to be," Nathan said. "Do we go there?"

"Not tonight," Simon answered.

"Do you think it's wise to wait?" Danielle asked.

"It's almost four a.m. If we went there now, we'd arrive at daybreak. And we're not set up for an insertion into the city."

"You're gambling that Booth won't send a team into the sanitarium before we can get there," Leah said.

Simon felt tired. Tonight had been a series of mixed blessings. Hope had been offered and taken away, and he wasn't exactly sure what the final balance between the two was. He suspected that he'd come out on the short end.

Unless the Goetia *manuscript is at Akehurst and it really does offer a weapon against the demons.*

"No, I'm gambling that Macomber will keep quiet as he promised he would. Going into London right now the way we are—tired and not properly prepared—that's just asking for a death sentence." Simon took a breath. "We'll do it tomorrow night."

If it's to be done at all.

When he woke, Warren found a dead woman standing beside his bed. The sight startled him so much that he drew back across the bed and almost unleashed his power on her. Then he recognized her.

Kelli.

She looked worse than ever. He hadn't seen her in days. Putrefaction has settled into her flesh and her skin tones were beginning to change colors, showing greens and yellows now. The stench was horrible and her body moved with the things that lived within her.

"What are you doing here?" Warren asked.

Kelli only turned her head and silently regarded him. He couldn't remember when she had ceased speaking. Then again, she hadn't had much to say in a long time.

Warren wanted to tell her to go away, but he didn't have the heart. She was with him because he'd wanted her to be with him. And she was dead through no fault of her own.

Without a word, Kelli sat on the edge of the bed. She had one leg folded up under her, and the flesh was torn so that he could see bones beneath. She creaked when she moved and there was the rippling sound of leather.

Unable to bear sitting on the bed with her, Warren got up and pulled a house coat on over his pajamas. With the fullness of day outside it was too hot to be clothed, but he'd always been modest. He was even more so now with his body scarred and alien to him.

Besides, he had a plan to put into effect.

An uncomfortable itch at the back of his mind alerted him to the silent warning of the Blood Angel's eye. He chose to see through it for a moment, and watched as Naomi left her room and came up the stairs toward his.

Warren glanced back at Kelli and knew things weren't going to begin well.

Naomi at least had the good manners to knock before she barged into his room, but she barged all the same. Then she stopped stock still in the doorway and stared at zombie on Warren's bed.

"What's she doing here?" Naomi asked.

"I woke up and she was here." Embarrassment stung Warren. He could only imagine what thoughts first ran through Naomi's mind. "I can't get her to stay away."

Kelli's dead gaze focused on Naomi. Kelli had never liked Naomi when she'd been alive because Kelli had felt threatened that Naomi would take Warren away from her. Evidently that dislike had run deeply enough to carry over into death.

"She's dead?" Naomi's voice carried curiosity. She walked closer to get a better look at the zombie.

"In the shape she's in, I certainly hope so." Warren took a bottle of water from the box against the wall. There was no way to keep it refrigerated. He admitted that the thing he most missed about the early days of the invasion was when the beer was still good. Unfortunately, like Kelli, there'd been an expiration date.

"Did you kill her?"

"No." Warren felt angry and ashamed that he had been asked that question.

As Naomi neared her, Kelli stood to face her.

"When did she die?" Naomi asked.

That was an even worse question.

Warren shook his head. "I don't remember."

Naomi shifted her gaze to him and looked incredulous. "How can you not remember?"

"You've seen her. Even when she was alive she wasn't very talkative."

"What about *before* you messed with her mind?"

"She wasn't very bright to begin with."

"I can't believe you."

"She's *dead*. There's nothing I can do about that."

"You could have at least cared enough to notice that she was dead! Or better yet, that she was *dying*!"

Warren cursed. "This wasn't a relationship, Naomi. I didn't love her and she didn't love me."

"No, you just used her are so you wouldn't have to be alone."

"Would you listen to yourself? This isn't some chick lit drama. I'm trying to stay alive. And so are you. That's why you're here."

Naomi folded her arms. "If I had any sense, I'd be *any-where* but here." She glared at him.

Without provocation, Kelli attacked and flailed her arms at Naomi. Caught flat-footed, Naomi didn't have a chance to defend herself or move away.

Warren threw a hand out and *pushed* with all his might. The shimmering wave of force jetted from his fingertips and hammered Kelli.

The zombie suddenly looked as if she had been thrown through a jet engine. Pieces of decaying flesh and shattered bone flew toward the other side of the room.

For a moment, Naomi stood frozen. Then she doubled over and was sick.

Warren figured that everything had officially just gotten worse. He went to get a trash bag and a broom. And a dust pan. Looking at all the little pieces, he figured he would need one of those too.

TWENTY-FOUR

Simon stared at the blueprints of the Akehurst Clinic. He had downloaded everything he could from the computer database regarding the building. His eyes burned from the sustained effort over the last few hours.

"You should get some sleep."

Changing his perception of the large wide-screen monitor in front of him, Simon spotted Leah's reflection in the surface. She wore hospital scrubs, which was one of the more accepted modes of dress up in the underground fortress.

Simon wore gray sweatpants, joggers, and a navy muscle shirt out of deference to the civilian population. There were a lot of children within the walls of late. It still amazed Simon how they had managed to survive the last four years.

Bruises from the previous night's encounter with the demons had turned a nice shade of blue and purple. In a few more days they would change colors and fade away.

"I could say the same thing about you," he said.

Leah leaned her hip against the desk and folded her arms. She stared down at him. "I've got six hours of sleep. Nathan tells me you haven't slept yet."

"Nathan talks too much."

"If you don't rest, you're going to lose your edge. If you lose your edge, you're going to die."

"Thanks for the pep talk." Simon felt angry at her and knew that she didn't deserve his ire. What she said was the truth. He let out a breath. "I'm going to go to sleep in just a little bit." He shook his head. "If I tried to go to sleep right now, with everything in flux, I'd just be wasting my time anyway."

Leah directed her attention to the monitor. "So what's in flux?"

Simon looked at her. "I thought you had somewhere to be."

She lifted a speculative eyebrow at him. "Would you let me leave here? Do you think I would leave not knowing if that manuscript that's supposed to be in that sanitarium is really there?"

Simon held her gaze for just a moment. "No."

"I guess that means both of us are in a flux." Leah studied the blueprints. "Where did you get access to all these blueprints?"

"The Templar have been involved in the architecture of London since the city began. All the files of every building, every house, and every railway tunnel are in our files."

"Where did you get the files? This isn't the Templar Underground."

"One of the volunteers from the Templar Underground brought a copy with her when she joined us. Having that kind of information has been helpful."

Leah went back to its studying the blueprints. "The architects and builders remodeled the building."

"Several times." Simon used the touchscreen to blow up various sections of the blueprints. "There appears to be an underground labyrinth under the building that later contractors neglected to mention."

"Why would they do that?"

"Probably so they wouldn't have to bring all the underground sections up to code as well. It would've been expensive."

"What did they do with the underground sections?"

"Walled them over for the most part." Simon pointed at three different areas. "These used to be entrances to the underground. In later blueprints—" He touched the screen and the blueprints changed. "—they're not shown."

"Could they have filled them in? When some of the older buildings developed flooding problems, it was easier to simply fill the basements with concrete and forget those areas ever existed."

Simon shifted back over to the initial blueprints he had been studying. "There were four floors beneath the main building. An undertaking like that would have been huge. People would have noticed."

"Why so many floors?"

"London has never been fond of her lunatics. The Victorian era was filled with people who resented and rejected the sexual repression that was going on. According to the files I've looked at, if you had a relative who was a homosexual, a nymphomaniac, or simply had another way of looking at the world that was considered dangerous or embarrassing, you could put them in Akehurst and plan on never seeing them again."

"Lovely bit of history you found there. Gives me the chills."

"The truly depressing part is the number of individuals that were locked away. Disappeared. And after they had finally died, they were buried unmarked in some graveyard for indigents."

"I trust knowing this isn't one of your hobbies."

"No. I hadn't known how prevalent the problem was until I accessed these files."

"Australia wouldn't have existed if not for the London poor, thieves, prostitutes, alcoholics, and the great unwashed. But for those who couldn't get to Australia, I guess there was Akehurst."

"And other places just as bad." Simon brought up another section of the blueprint. "The four subterranean levels are all primitive. They're not rooms; they're caves carved into the limestone underbelly of the city. Iron bars covered the front of the caves." Sour bile burned at the back of his throat as he thought about the conditions Akehurst's *patients* had suffered through.

"That's where Macomber said the manuscript was?"

"Yes."

"And we've got to go there?"

"*I* have to go there," Simon corrected.

Leah rolled her eyes at him. "What? And leave me here?"

"Actually, I was thinking that once I had the manuscript, you can be freed."

"Awfully generous of you."

"It is. Especially since I don't know who tipped Booth off about Macomber."

She frowned at him. "You'd be a fool if you thought it was me."

"Just for the record, I don't think it was you. It could just as easily have been one of those men that met us last night."

"Whatever would they do that for?"

"To keep the Templar divided."

"As if you couldn't manage that on your own."

Simon held off on an angry retort.

"Look, I'm sorry. I didn't mean to speak out of turn like that." Leah looked genuinely regretful. "I'm just tired, and I wouldn't like to see you throw your life away on a fool's errand."

"I wasn't trained to throw my life away. I was trained to fight and sell it dearly if it came to that."

"Do you know what your problem really is, Simon?" she asked in a soft voice.

Sensing that he was on dangerous ground, Simon chose not to answer.

"You still believe you can win this war."

"What other way is there to think about it?"

Leah looked away from him. After a moment, she replied. "You make the other guy lose just as much as you do. That way it's a draw. Nobody wins."

Simon didn't know what to say about that. Even after everything that had happened at St. Paul's Cathedral, he couldn't let go of the idea of defeating the demons.

"Do you know what's truly foolish?" he asked. "Fighting without thinking you're going to win. The demons are the hardest thing I've ever faced, but there's nothing and no one that exists in this world that can't be beaten. All we need is the proper advantage."

She stared at him for a long time and didn't say a word. Then, finally, she said, "Get some sleep. Soon." Then she turned and walked away.

Simon watched her go. She was beautiful. He had recognized that the first time he had seen her on the plane from South Africa.

She was also an enigma.

That was dangerous.

After he had swept up the last of Kelli's remains, Warren tied off the lumpy trash bag and worked hard to breathe as little of the stench of as he could. He carried the bag to the window and he heaved it outside. It joined several other bags at the bottom of the long fall.

The bag, like its brethren, burst on impact and spread

Kelli all over the alley. For a brief time he watched to make sure the pieces of her didn't try to get up and come back.

He followed up with a mop bucket and a pine-scented cleanser. When he finished, the gore was gone but the stench lingered as a pine-scented version of itself.

"I can't believe you just did that," Naomi said.

Warren picked up the broom and dustpan, looked at them and realized that he would *never* use them again, and tossed them out the window as well.

"I can't believe you didn't help. After all, it wasn't me she attacked."

Naomi regarded him silently for a long time. Warren grew uncomfortable with her intense attention.

"You've changed," she said.

"I've lost my hand and been horribly disfigured. And you're just now noticing?" Warren shook his head. "Four years ago when this happened, I was still naive. When I was going through the worst of it, as I recall, you chose to stay away. It wasn't till the First Seer, who is now dead after trying to kill me, sent you to contact me that you seemed to remember who I was. I moved on and became someone else because I had to."

"That's not fair," she protested. "It wasn't like that. *All* of us had to learn. *All* of us had to change."

"You had company. The only friend I had, I just swept up in the dust pan and tossed out the window. Now that I think about it, maybe I should have let her toss you out the window." The emotion of what he had just done hovered in the back of Warren's mind. He didn't let it get close to him or touch him in any way that would make him weak. That was for when he was alone.

"All of the Cabalists were—and still are—afraid of you. None of them talk with demons."

"If they did, they wouldn't want to nearly as badly as they think they do."

"None of them know what you know," Naomi said. "What you know is incredible."

"What I know is that if I don't obey Merihim, he's going to kill me."

"But to kill a demon? Do you truly think you can do that?"

"I don't have a choice." Warren looked at her. "But you do."

She looked at him without comprehension.

"I can't do this without help," he explained. "I need someone to anchor me when I use the arcane energy I'll need to use to get to them."

"If I help you . . . "

"Then I'll teach you more than you know now."

"Will you teach me everything you know?"

Warren looked at her. She was easy to lie to. She wanted him to lie to her. So he did.

"Yes. Everything."

"Fulaghar has three bodyguards," Warren explained. "All of them are old demons with names. They're not Dark Wills as Fulaghar is, but they are Greater Demons who have earned their names."

He sat across one of the tables in the abandoned restaurant on the second floor. All the tables and chairs were made of metal and glass. The paneling and other wooden furniture, including the bar, had been ripped out years ago by scavengers looking for enough wood to fuel a fire to get them through a long winter. The winters weren't as long these days, and nowhere near as cold as they had been with the effects of the Burn taking place.

Besides that, fires drew the demons.

"In order to get to Fulaghar, I have to kill the body-guards." Warren couldn't believe how calm he sounded as he talked about killing demons.

"You can do that?"

"I will. With your help."

Naomi hesitated, obviously realizing that such action on her part didn't come without risk. "All right."

A small knot inside Warren's stomach released. If she didn't agree to help him, he couldn't force her. It would be impossible to take control of her will and still allow her enough autonomy to help him if he needed it.

"Then let's begin." Warren got up from the table and walked to an open area of the floor. He reached into his shoulder bag and took out a small pouch of blue powder. The book had provided directions on how to make the powder. The ingredients were simple, but the arcane force that united them was incredibly strong.

"What is this?" Naomi asked.

"A protective spell. Sit down." Warren pointed at the floor.

Naomi sat but didn't look happy about it. Warren said nothing as he poured powder from the pouch around the two of them. When he had finished, they sat close in the circle of powder.

"If this works properly," Warren said, "we should be able to see the demons, but they won't be able to see us." When he was satisfied with the thickness of the circle, he put the pouch back in his bag and laid the bag to one side. He sat down cross-legged opposite her and held out his hands.

After a moment she took his hands. He felt her trembling. The vulnerability touched a softness inside of him that even four years of hardship and horror hadn't been able to eradicate.

Even though he didn't want to, Warren said, "It's going to be all right."

Naomi nodded, but he didn't think she believed him.

Warren took a deep breath and felt for the power within him. When he touched it and had a solid hold, he pushed in at the ring of powder. Instantly the powder glowed and pulsed, then created a shimmering half-dome of incandescent sapphire light. He felt the power of the protective energy surrounding him and the concrete floor beneath.

"What's going to happen?" Naomi whispered.

"I'm going to find the first of Fulaghar's bodyguards." Warren closed his eyes.

"How are you going to find him?"

"Merihim has marked him for me. Finding him will be easy. Killing him is another matter entirely." In his mind's eye, Warren watched as a translucent copy of himself stepped out of his body. He had a curious sensation of being in two places at one time. He looked down and his hands—the hands of the self standing beside the self sitting—and felt them empty as well as Naomi's flesh against his.

He concentrated on the translucent self and felt for the doorway that he knew should be there. A shimmering crimson ellipse not quite two inches across appeared in midair in front of him. Lips formed in the ellipse, pushed out, and opened.

"Will you go?" the same voice the book used asked.

A momentary fear quivered through Warren. He calmed himself, then answered. "Yes. Take me there."

"Don't be afraid," the voice said. "I will be with you."

Warren ignored the statement. His fear was his greatest weapon. It kept his senses sharp and made his power strong.

And until now, it had kept him from taking too many chances.

The lips parted and widened till he could step through. He entered and felt the arcane energy sweep him away.

TWENTY-FIVE

At the time it was opened in 1897, the Blackwall Tunnel was the longest underwater thoroughfare in the world. It was eight hundred feet short of a mile. Two passages, both of them originally built for horse and buggy, ran side by side under the River Thames.

Simon stood in the shadow of the Millennium Dome and studied the southern portal to the Blackwall Tunnel. Akehurst Sanitarium lay at the other end of the tunnel. Demons lurking in the area made the passage under the river dangerous.

There was no way Simon wanted to cross the river, though. The effects of the Burn showed prominently on the Thames. The last four years, the river had shrunk lower and lower. It was now almost possible to wade across the Thames in many places. Huge, rust-covered cargo ships sat mired in the mud and leaned at dangerous angles. Some of them had even fallen over.

With the depletion of the river, the North Sea had started rolling in. Mixed with salt water, the water was no longer fresh or fit for human consumption. Even the animals stayed away. For a time demons had gathered there to take their pick of prey when thirst drove them out of hiding. Lack of water had driven many survivors out of the city and into the surrounding forests.

The Isle of Dogs now seemed to thrust up from the

brackish river like a promontory rather than a peninsula as it had been. One it had been home to the Canary Wharf and the tallest habitable building in all of London. Rich and poor people had lived there, not together but separate, and eked out lives for themselves.

No one lived there now. Fire had destroyed most of the homes and buildings. The Canary Wharf office building was a burned-out shell that remained home to several demons.

Simon shifted views to the line of Templar standing behind him. Although he had had some reservations, he had allowed Leah to join them. A few of the Templar had voiced similar reservations about the woman's presence. Simon had made sure none of them had been picked for his recon team.

"Ready?" he asked.

After the confirmations came quickly, Simon freed his sword and Spike Bolter, then swung into a steady jog for the Blackwall Tunnel.

The tunnel didn't run straight. Twists and turns created blind spots that slowed the approach. Simon remained aware that demons could lie in wait around each of those.

All along the way cars sat abandoned. When the demons had arrived, many motorists had been trapped underground. Skeletons on the ground testified that not all of those had gotten free. Many of them have been stripped of clothing by later survivors who had gotten desperate for extra garments.

No dignity had been left to the dead. Rats scurried through the shadows and wreckage. Compared to the demons, the creatures almost seemed like kindred spirits.

Slowed to a walk now, Simon went forward carefully. The HUD washed the darkness from the scene with the night-vision capability. His auditory receptors were turned up to the point that he heard the rats shifting through the ruins and the breeze blowing through the tunnel.

Only eighteen minutes later, the Templar group reached the northern portal of the tunnel. Simon paused and peered out at East India Dock Road to the north.

The darkness only blunted the destruction that had been done to the area. Besides the ruin of Canary Wharf, the row houses lay in disarray.

Simon hated to see all of the destruction. There had been so much of London's history that had been preserved either out of sentimentality or necessity. There was no other city ever like her, and now she was torn and sundered. But London was also a city marked by disasters. For a time the largest city in the world, London had undergone many hardships and changes.

When the demons are gone, Simon told himself, *she'll stand straight and tall again.* He just didn't know if he would live to see that day.

In the distance, a few flying demons sailed silently through the sky. None were close enough to worry about. After checking the map on the HUD, Simon pressed on and led his troops toward their destination.

The wrought-iron fence around Akehurst Sanitarium remained standing and provided a gloomy introduction to the building behind it. The sanitarium stood five stories tall. The gray brick exterior exuded cold indifference. It was in a place Simon would ever have wanted to bring a family member.

Most of the windows had been broken out, and they gaped like empty eye sockets. Something had torn the ornate front gate from its hinges and cast it to one side of the entrance. A security kiosk stood on one side of the gate. No one was there now.

A simple brass plaque on an arch over the entranceway announced the name of the place in gothic script.

"I take it we're not going in through the main gate," Nathan said.

"No." Simon glanced up at the fence. It stood ten feet tall and had sharp tines at the top of each bar. He crouched and leaped over, easily clearing the top of the fence by inches.

On the other side, he landed with his feet spread and dropped into a low squat with the Spike Bolter braced over his right wrist while he held it with his left. The move wasn't for accuracy, but to help provide extra coverage for his face and shoulders in case of attack.

Nathan, Leah, Danielle, and the other Templar followed in quick succession. Simon jogged easily to the rear of the building.

Macomber hadn't known it, but the clinic had shut down two years after he'd gone into the Parisian sanitarium. All the patients had been transferred elsewhere when the corporation finally went financially bust after several civil cases put them out of business. With the state of disrepair the building had been in, and all the problems inherent in the age, no one had purchased the property and it had sat in escrow.

Hopefully, that meant whatever had been in the building still remained there.

Someone had already broken the locks on the rear door. It stood ajar a few inches.

After he sheathed his sword, Simon pushed the door open with his free hand and followed it inside. The night-vision capability stripped away the darkness.

The doorway opened onto a storeroom that was partially sunk into the ground. Simon had to navigate a short flight of stairs to get to the bottom. Metal wire shelves lined the stone walls. Nothing cosmetic had been done to make the walls more appealing. They were bare stone. Halfway underground as the room was, there hadn't been a real need for insulation beyond the stone.

Bottles and jugs of industrial strength cleaner littered the floor. Clothing, bedsheets, and other things that survivors could use had been stripped and taken years ago.

Simon crossed the room and peered through the open security door there. It too had been burgled, but the scratches on the inside of the door told him whoever had broken in had done so from outside.

"So where is this concealed stairway to the lower levels?" Nathan asked.

"Other end of the building," Simon replied. He stepped to the doorway and crept along the hall. A transparent map of the underground section he was in tracked through his HUD. Differently colored blips on the screen marked his position as well as the other Templar and Leah.

"Why didn't we just break into the other end of the building?"

"Because we'd have had to break in through a wall," Leah said. "It would have probably been more conspicuous that way."

"A little antsy, are we?"

"Not at all. I love poking through madhouses in the middle of the night. Especially when there might be demons here and the people I'm with insist on conducting a travelogue."

Nathan laughed, and the chuffing sound it made coming over the comm took away some of the tension Simon was feeling. It reminded him that he was there with experienced warriors. If anything went wrong, these were the people for it to go wrong with.

* * *

The stairwell in the center of the hallway went upstairs. Simon took an independently powered button cam from one of the cargo compartments built into his armor. He pressed the button cam to the wall and hit it with a charge of static electricity from the suit. The button cam adhered to the wall.

A quick check through the HUD showed that the miniature vid camera was online and available to him and the rest of the team. He went on.

Hospital rooms—though Simon thought of them or as prison cells—lined the hallway on both sides. A few of them held mummified bodies and enough dust to prove that no one had been there in years. Simon took a little hope in that.

The door at the end of the hallway was locked from the outside. It was a rectangular section of ugly, dented metal that showed years of hard use. A sign in the middle of it announced:

AUTHORIZED
PERSONNEL ONLY
STRICTLY ENFORCED

"Sounds properly mysterious, doesn't it?" Nathan asked. "What's supposed to be on the other side of that door?"

"Another storeroom." Simon tried the nod and found it was locked.

"Takes a key to lock that, mate," Nathan observed. "Makes you wonder why they bothered, doesn't it?"

It did, and Simon thought about that for only a moment before he pressed the forefinger of his free hand to the door lock. "Key," he said.

Immediately, the nanofluid inside his suit squirted a stream into the lock mechanism. A visual popped up on the HUD and showed the locking mechanism's interior as well as the nanofluid's progress into it.

"Key is ready," the AI announced.

Simon twisted and felt the tumblers rolling over as the key worked the lock. He let the Spike Bolter nose into the room ahead of him, of that never far enough that anyone could easily take it away from him.

An oozing tendril suddenly wrapped around Simon's wrist and yanked. As the AI loosed a warning, Simon tried to set himself. But it was too late. Whatever had hold of him of was incredibly strong. He left his feet as he sailed into the room and the waiting darkness.

And in the darkness, something *huge* moved.

TWENTY-SIX

H eat slammed into Warren as he was pulled through the dark current that gripped him. He didn't know how much time had passed. Fear throbbed electrically inside him. Usually he could change his vision so that he could see wherever he was. That had been one of the earliest uses of his powers he discovered. But when he tried to use that power now, nothing happened.

He reached for Naomi's hands. Although he could feel them almost within his grasp, he couldn't quite take hold of them.

"Don't struggle," the voice said. "You're only making things more difficult."

"Where are you taking me?"

"To meet Fulaghar's first lieutenant. As I said I would."

Warren tried to catch hold of Naomi's hands again, but failed. He called her name. There was no answer.

So much for being able to pull me out in case I get into trouble, he thought.

"The spell will work when it needs to," the voice said. "At this point you don't need to fear anything from me."

"Are we going where the book is?"

"Yes. Fulaghar has recently found out where it was."

"How?"

"Fulaghar has many resources. He's struck many deals

with demons and humans alike. Merihim isn't the only one to use humans to suit his purposes."

Neither of them are, Warren thought.

"All of us have uses for other people. You have Naomi waiting for you within the protected circle. Before that you had Kelli."

Guilt stung Warren again at the thought of destroying the Kelli zombie. She had been gone before he knew it.

"Prepare yourself," the voice warned. "I can't protect you here in this place. You'll have to care for yourself."

Nervous anxiety thrummed through Warren as the darkness around him seemed to grow less dense. "Where will you be?"

"I can't go with you here. You'll be on your own. Fulaghar's lieutenant, Hargastor, searches the underground labyrinth for the manuscript at his master's request. If you find him there, he'll know you."

"How? We've never met."

"Fulaghar has your scent. Once he knows you, all of his people know you."

"How will I kill Hargastor?"

"Don't confront him. Kill him from behind."

"I can't just ask him to turn around."

"There are others down here. Be careful."

The sensation of moving ceased. Warren hung in the empty blackness for just a moment. He still distrusted the voice.

"We're inextricably linked, you and I. I've waited over a thousand years to be able to speak to someone again. I cherish you. I don't want anything to happen to you."

Warren wanted to believe that. He held on to that thought as the darkness around and dissipated. He felt the voice leave his mind, but he still felt Naomi with him.

In the next instant, solid ground was once more beneath his feet. He felt like gravity had increased tenfold because his legs would not hold him. Despite his best efforts, he dropped to one knee. And when he blinked his eyes open, he saw horror all around him.

The creature that held Simon suspended in the air was so malformed that he had first didn't recognize it. The Templar had never learned a proper name for the monstrosity before him. It was a thing of nightmare, and for a long time Templar historians believed that was what it was: a fever dream on part of a warrior next to death.

Except that the description had kept occurring. Again and again, warriors that had sought out the demons had heard stories about creatures like the one that held Simon. In the end they had simply called it a Grotesque. The name suited, even if it didn't aptly describe the monster.

Grotesques came in different sizes, depending on the materials they had at hand when they were assembled. None of the Templar knew how the horrible things were brought to undead life in the fashion that they were, but they had seen them on occasion in the streets of London these days.

This one was as big as a cargo van. Simon guessed that at least thirty or forty corpses had gone into the Grotesque's manufacture. Although he had never seen a Grotesque put together, Simon had seen them come apart. Even through the palladium armor, he felt the buzzing pulse of the arcane energies that bound the corpses into one large entity.

The demon was a mass of roiling flesh. Arms and legs, heads and trunks, all writhed across the monster. Hands grasped Simon and feet lashed out at him. Some of those hands held weapons and the Grotesque somehow accumulated intelligence as a gestalt that was not present in the individual parts. The whole was greater than the pieces.

A pair of arms swung a fire ax into Simon's faceshield. The impact drove Simon's head back, but the faceshield received no damage. A misshapen head with stumps of broken teeth grinned at him. The head was so battered and ragged that Simon could no longer tell what the original gender had been.

Simon tried to swing the Spike Bolter toward the head, but a leg kicked out and pinned his arm against the ceiling. Three rough hands with no more than eight fingers between them caught hold of Simon's head and yanked at his helmet.

"Simon!" Nathan roared over the suit comm.

A glance at the HUD showed Simon that the other Templar were still outside the room. He was facing the monster on his own for the moment.

"I'm here." Simon swung his arm across the leg of the corpse. Bone broke and dead flesh shredded. He pulled the Spike Bolter into line with the head. A target reticule ghosted onto the HUD screen. As soon as he had target lock, he squeezed the trigger.

Palladium spikes erupted from the pistol barrel and chewed into the Grotesque.

"On our way." Nathan slammed his shoulder into the door and ripped it off its hinges. For a moment the Templar sprawled off-balance, then finally went forward into a roll and came up on one knee with a Blaze pistol in his fist. "Duck and cover, mate."

Simon wrapped his free arm around his head to add further shielding.

The *whumph* of Nathan's pistol flared into the room for just a moment. The arrowlike projectile thudded into the Grotesque. As it was designed to do, the shaft fragmented and sank into the demon's undead flesh in a wider area than the impact shaft would have done. An instant later, the shaft head and the fragments ignited. Greek Fire chewed into the demon and chased the darkness from the room.

Affected by the fire as well as the detonation and the damage Simon had done with the palladium spikes, the Grotesque started to go to pieces. Body parts fell away from the center mass and the floor became covered in arms and legs as well as a few heads. They all continued to act independently but they were without any real control. The sight was horrid but the pieces couldn't act in concert. They were largely ineffectual.

However, the Grotesque's attacks weren't merely physical damage dealt out by various limbs. It gaped open its maw, that center of itself it maintained no matter how large it got, and spat out fistfuls of flesh-eating parasites.

Normally these parasites, known as death maggots, were no longer than a finger's length and feasted on the Grotesque's victims. In extreme cases, like when the creature thought it might be beaten and was fighting for its unlife, the Grotesque used them as weapons.

The death maggots plopped wetly against Simon's armor and stuck. In the next moment, the creatures swelled nearly ten times their original size and exploded. If not for Simon's armor, the acidic goop hurled by the maggots would have seared his flesh and poisoned him. Civilians in the streets died almost instantly from exposures to the small demons. Those who didn't were horribly scarred for life.

Simon opened fire again and tracked the bulbous head as it sought to evade him. The palladium spikes opened great bloodless wounds in the undead flesh but didn't even slow the Grotesque. The demon swung Simon up against the ceiling. He struck in a bone-jarring crash that the armor wasn't quite able to mute. His senses spun for a moment and the air left his lungs.

Then more of the Templar were in the room. Upside down now, Simon braced his boots against the ceiling and said, "Fire boot anchors."

In response, the suit's AI fired palladium anchors into the ceiling. They bit deeply into the rock and held Simon's boots to the ceiling.

All a Templar needs is solid footing. Thomas Cross had told his son that nearly every day of practice. Simon had become a believer early on. His father had also taught him how to fight from many different angles. Upside down was just one of them.

Simon put the Spike Bolter away and drew his sword in both hands. The Grotesque was fighting against the damage that had been dealt it. Although that effort was a losing one, the demon still remained dangerous.

From his new vantage point, Simon swung the sword with all the strength. The sharp blade cleaved into the undead flesh. Arms and legs were lopped off in the single swipe. He managed five more attempts before he split the head that he deemed to be the one controlling the rest of the huge body.

The head fell away from the Grotesque. In response, the creature fell apart.

"Fire in the hole," Nathan warned. He pulled the the sleek Scorcher pistol from its holster and fired into the squirming mass of flesh on the floor.

The flame erupted from the end of the weapon with a flash that Simon's HUD barely blocked. Bright lights stabbed painfully into his eyes. When he looked back, the pieces of the Grotesque were all on fire.

"God, I hate those things," Danielle said fervently. Even in her armor she brushed at herself as if something foul had clung to her. "I'm definitely going to need a bath after this."

"Retract spikes," Simon ordered.

When the spikes retracted, he dropped to the ground. He spun in mid-air and landed on his feet. He kept the sword in hand as he walked to the fiery bits of undead flesh.

"Just be glad the suit filters out all the noxious fumes," Nathan said. "There's nothing worse than throwing up inside the armor. I mean, you can only get so much of it out."

"Be grateful you've got biohazard scrubbers built into the suit," another Templar said.

"Yeah, but that takes bloody hours to get done properly." Nathan kicked a flaming leg out of his way. "And the stench you have to put up with till that takes place is stomach-churning, I tell you. I'll pass on that little treat."

"At least now we know why the door was locked," Leah said.

"You got that right," Nathan grumbled. "Somebody wanted to keep that bloody thing in here. If we could have given it another few weeks, it probably would have digested itself trying to keep those maggots perky."

"Oh, and now it isn't that a fine image." Danielle snorted in disgust. "Maybe you can just keep those all thoughts to yourself."

"One thing's for certain: if that thing was in here chances are good that no one found the stairway down to the lower levels." Simon peered around at the floor.

"The floor seems to be intact," Leah said. She walked over to the northeast corner of the room. The directions were clearly indicated on Simon's HUD. "If the blueprints are correct, this is where the stairway should be."

"All right then," Simon said, "let's see if we can peel the floor back and find it."

TWENTY-SEVEN

Cages—little more than caves hewn out of solid limestone with a panel of iron bars slapped across them—surrounded Warren on all sides. He stared in disbelief and stumbled forward to the nearest cage.

Since he didn't have a hand torch, Warren used his own enhanced vision.

Inside the cage, a dead man lay sprawled on the floor. One of the skeletal arms was stretched forward as if his last act had been to reach for something. A metal bowl sat in the forward corner of the cage.

He knew the history of the place he was in. And he even knew a little bit about the history of sanitariums in England. He just never expected to see one.

There was no way to tell how long before this the unfortunates in the cages had been there. Long enough to die, that was evident.

"Warren," Naomi called across the connection that stretched so thin between them. Her voice was just the tiniest whisper in the back of his mind. Then again, "Warren."

She tugged on him then, and he barely had to resist in order to keep himself at rest. He knew that if something happened to him she wasn't strong enough to pull him back by herself. That knowledge rekindled the sick fear in his stomach.

"I'm here," he told her.

"Are you all right?"

As he gazed around the cages, Warren wasn't sure he knew how to answer that. "So far," he replied.

"Have you found Hargastor?"

"No." Warren expanded his senses, trying to find the demon. He felt nothing. He also felt for the voice from the book that gotten him here. He felt nothing there either.

"Where are you?"

Warren took a firmer grip on the tenuous thread that connected them. He pictured the cave in his mind and pushed the image at Naomi.

Her startled gasp told him she had received the image.

You're wasting time. Get on with it. The voice was Merihim's, and the demon sounded like he was standing at Warren's shoulder.

"How do I find Hargastor?" Warren asked.

Hargastor is there. He searches for a legendary manuscript that Fulaghar believes is located there.

"Is it?"

That doesn't matter. You were sent there for other reasons.

"And if I should find such a manuscript?"

You won't.

The certainty in the demon's voice bothered Warren. How could Merihim not know about the book? Or did the book not truly exist?

"Warren?" Naomi called.

"I'm busy right now. Stay in touch and stay ready."

"All right, but hurry. I'm getting tired."

According to the information the book gave, there were four underground levels in the sanitarium. Like this one, the other three had been carved from the limestone. The book had brought up drawings of the underground sections and the sanitarium itself, but Warren didn't know if he could trust those records.

He needed a guide.

As he circled the cages, he gazed inside and felt for the aura of those who had died there. That was another skill that he had manifested over the last few years: he had an affinity for the dead and could tell from their bones something about what they had been in life.

The men in the cages had been murderers and sexual predators. Some of them had only had carnal appetites that hadn't been accepted in Victorian London. Those appetites wouldn't have been given a second glance in the present world.

Warren felt saddened by his tour.

Finally he stopped at one cage. He got confusing emanations from the dead man inside. There was a sense of loss and a sense of authority. The man had belonged to the sanitarium in more than one way.

Warren put his hand on the locking mechanism of the gate. "Shatter," he ordered. Arcane energy blasted through his hand.

The large padlock burst into pieces and fell to the ground. Metal tinkled against the stone. When he pulled on the gate, it opened on rusty hasps that screamed into the silence.

The dead man sat hunched in a corner. He had died sitting up. There had been no room to do anything else. An additional arm bone lay on the floor beside him. When Warren checked the neighboring cells, he found that one of the skeletons inside was missing an arm.

There was no doubt from where the dead man had gotten the extra arm.

An iron manacle encircled the skeleton's right ankle. Wear on the bone showed that the manacle had worn through the flesh. Whoever had put the man in the cage hadn't fully trusted the cage to hold him.

Warren laid his demon's hand upon the man's skull. "Wake," he commanded.

At first nothing happened. Warren started to repeat the command, something he had never had to do before, when the skeleton shivered all over. Bones clacked and clinked as if someone had pulled a hammer down a xylophone.

The dead man's skull, wisps of hair still clinging to the ivory bone, swiveled and looked up at Warren. Red malice gleamed in the eye sockets.

The skeleton moved with more speed than Warren had ever seen in the newly revived. It lunged at him with hands opened wide to stretch around his throat.

Simon knelt on the floor above the area where he believed the staircase had been hidden.

"You're only guessing that the concrete was poured a few inches thick in this area," Nathan said. "You could be wrong."

"I know," Simon said. "We'll find out in a moment." He drew back his fist and slammed it against the concrete floor. He immediately pressed his palm against the floor section and waited.

The HUD measured the sonic waves that went through concrete. The application was similar to ground sonar. The suit's AI ciphered the various permutations of the information that came through Simon's glove after the blow.

"Based on information available, the density of this material is less than eight inches thick. It is backed by a wooden surface no more than an inch thick and probably made of oak."

Simon smiled and sent the information around to the rest of the group. "Looks like all we need is a little muscle." He drew his arm back.

"Wait," Leah said. "There's an easier way. You don't want to risk injuring the armor."

Simon glanced up at her. "This isn't going to hurt the armor. The armor can take a whole lot more than this. If it didn't, I'd have been dead years ago."

Leah dropped to her knees. She's moved her armored hands over the floor surface a few times. "If you hit the concrete and splinter it—even if you don't hurt the armor—you're going to make a bloody lot of racket."

Simon couldn't argue that.

"With the stairway open below this, sounds will travel a long way." Leah stopped moving. She placed her hands flat on the concrete. "How wide would you say the stairway opening is?"

A quick glance at the schematic gave Simon the measurements. "Forty-seven, one-half inches."

Leah spread her hands again. She leaned forward to put her weight on her shoulders. "Watch yourself."

"Why?"

"Because if you're wrong about those measurements, or the placement, you may just get a freight express ride to the bottom of the next room." Despite the situation, Simon heard the grin in her voice.

Before he could move, the floor seemed to shake violently beneath him. Jagged cracks suddenly showed in the concrete section between her hands. Some of the cracks ran between Simon's knees. Others ran for the Templar standing watch.

Nathan and Danielle stepped backward quickly.

The measurements had evidently been off. One of Simon's knees sank through the floor. As he started to fall, he slapped his right hand against the wall next to him and ordered the suit AI to anchor him. A spike drove into the wall and kept him from falling into the abyss below.

Leah wasn't so lucky. She dropped like a rock. Before she could fall into the room below, though, Simon grabbed her and held her suspended.

"Guess those measurements were off a little," Simon said sheepishly.

"Do you think?" Leah asked sarcastically.

Simon took the fact that nothing launched out of the darkness to try to kill them was a good sign. Effortlessly, he pulled Leah up and sat her on solid ground again.

"I suppose you've got sonic pulsers in those gloves?" Nathan asked.

"You'd be surprised how many times they come in handy getting into and out of places," Leah applied.

"Bloody brill." Nathan surveyed the hole in the floor. "Can you go through walls with those things?"

"I found them to be good for up to a foot of concrete."

"I've definitely got to start thinking about some upgrades on my armor," Nathan said. "Maybe I could work in sonic pulsers of my own."

"Yeah, it works great on regular concrete," Danielle said sarcastically. "Throw some rebar into the mix, and you'll have a much different turnout. And now, if maybe we're through with mutual admiration society? It would be just nifty if we could follow Simon."

As soon as he was certain that Leah was safe, Simon had retracted the anchor from the wall and started down the steps. His thermographic vision revealed nothing waiting below. Anything that had of an internal temperature above or below the ambient temperature in the rooms would have registered.

Concrete debris littered the steps as they corkscrewed

down into the lower levels. In the HUD, Simon saw the others fall into step behind him. Their order had been prearranged and they followed it now. Two Templar always waited behind to hold the rear guard in case they had to retreat in a hurry.

The HUD map has overlaid what Simon was seeing with what he had downloaded from the blueprints. There were inconsistencies and irregularities, but for the most part everything was the same.

The cages the mental patients had been kept in were horrifying. Many of them were still there. Skeletons occupied most of the cages.

"Do you think they just left them here?" Danielle asked. The somber tone in her voice was unusual. "Just let them starve to death?"

"They would have thirsted to death first," one of the other Templar said.

Gradually, the conversation fell to a close. Simon led the way through the first level into the stairway to the second. The underground sections were laid out in ovals that were basically circular tunnels with holes cut in the outer walls and rooms hollowed out of the center sections.

The room they had come to find, the one that Macomber had insisted was there given the clue as to where the *Goetia* manuscript was, was on the second floor below. Simon took the steps and headed down.

TWENTY-EIGHT

The skeleton wrapped his bony fingers around Warren's throat and squeezed. Black spots danced in Warren's vision. He almost passed out at the shock and a sudden pain. His demon hand rose almost of its own volition and clapped onto the skeleton's skull.

"Back!" Warren rasped through his bruised throat.

Shimmering force hammered the skeleton backward and broke its grip on Warren's neck. Warren sucked in a deep breath and heard it whistle into his lungs. He stepped back as the skeleton lunged at him again.

This time the chain around the creature's ankle drew him up short.

"Warren, are you all right?" Naomi asked.

Warren took another breath before he answered. "I'm fine. Stay out of my head and let me work. I'll call you if I need you."

With single-minded purpose, the skeleton lunged again and again at Warren. The undead creature's naked palms and bony fingers snapped together like bare winter branches in a high wind.

"Don't stand back there, boy," the skeleton snarled. Since it had no lungs or voice box, the effort was quite impressive. "Come closer."

"I brought you renewed life," Warren said. It hurt to speak. "You will obey me."

The skeleton lunged again.

Warren gestured and another wave of shimmering force slammed into the creature and knocked him back into the cave where he had died. Before the skeleton could get up, Warren gestured again. This time the slack length of the chain wrapped around the skeleton and pinned his arms to his sides.

The skeleton cursed cruelly.

"How are you able to think and speak?" Warren asked. Over the last four years of he and raised dozens of zombies to do his bidding. Most of them had served as guards and ended up getting destroyed by demons or the knights.

"The same way I always have," the skeleton answered.

"How long have you been down here?"

"Since Dr. Featherstone ordered me placed here under custody in 1923." The skeleton's efforts to free himself subsided. His strength was no proof against the steel chain.

"Do you have a name?"

"'Course I have a name. I carry me father's name." The skeleton's Cockney accent showed a little now.

"What's your name?" Warren asked.

The skeleton hesitated for a moment as if struggling to recall. "I'm Jonas."

"What were you here, Jonas?"

"I was a guard for a time."

That fit with the authority impression Warren had gotten. "How did you come to be a patient?"

"A prisoner, you mean."

Warren made no reply.

"Dr. Featherstone decided he didn't like the job I was doing. He accused me of . . . abusing some of the patients."

"Were you?"

Jonas the skeleton lifted and dropped his shoulders. The chain loops rattled as he did so. "Maybe a few. Some of the women that were brought here was pretty. They wasn't as friendly as they should have been."

Warren felt disgust rise within him. "While I'm here, you will acknowledge me as your master."

Jonas doffed an imaginary hat and his bones rattled with motion. "Of course, yer lordship. What will yer pleasure be?" His accent was thick and sarcastic.

"You know your way around in this place."

"Of course I do. I lived much of me life here and seems like even longer in death."

"Cross me and I won't just kill you all over again."

"And just what is it you'll do, your lordship?"

"I'll leave you here just as you are. Alive. And chained in this cell."

Jonas kicked his leg and tested the chain links. "I don't think this manacle will hold me forever."

"Your choice. But make it quickly."

"Then aye, I'll come with you and be your guide, yer lordship. Just you mind your back."

Warren gestured at the manacle. The metal ring vibrated and shook to pieces.

"Well now, that's a fancy trick, it is. And where did you learn that?"

"I thought you'd think being brought back to life would be more amazing."

Jonas regarded Warren with his empty crimson gaze. "And who's to say I wasn't just resting and waiting here for your arrival, yer lordship?"

The thought chilled Warren. If the skeleton had merely come to life, that would have been expected. Kelli, after she'd died, had lost what little personality she'd had in life. Warren had heard stories about undead that were more than simply animated. Many of them maintained their personalities. But he had never before seen such a case.

"Where is it that you wish to go, yer lordship?" Jonas asked.

"Up," Warren answered.

"And what is it you're looking for then?" Jonas turned on one bony heel and started forward. Evidently he had no trouble seeing in the dark.

Warren followed. "A book."

"That's good. Because we've always been a little short on treasure." Jonas cackled at his own joke.

The room Simon searched for was located on the left side of the circle on the second floor. They walked there without interruption or incident. He left button cams on the walls and ceiling as they passed. The vid relays provided constant overlapping fields of view.

So far as he could tell, they were the only ones in the abandoned sanitarium. It looked as if Macomber had held true to his promise not to tell Booth or any of the other Templar about the manuscript.

A brass plaque mounted on the stone wall above the gate and the cave entrance identified it as 213.

"Thirteen, eh?" Nathan asked. "I'm not exactly superstitious, mate. You know that. But I have to admit I don't like that number. Twice thirteen, that's bad luck for anybody."

"Just be glad it's not on the third or fourth floor," Danielle commented softly.

"I will then," Nathan returned.

A few of the Templar laughed.

Simon tried the gate and found it locked. He crushed the padlock in his armored glove and let the pieces drop. They tinkled to the floor. The gate opened with a screech.

"You're sure this is the place, mate?" Nathan asked.

"I am," Simon responded. He held up his hand, activated the torch projector in his palm, and switched over to the light multiplier application.

The inside of the cave became as bright as day. A skeleton, dressed in rags, lay on a thin, rat-gnawed pallet at the back of the cave. In its day, Simon had no doubt that the bedding had also been infested with insects.

"Who was he?" Leah asked.

"His name was Marcel Duvalier," Simon replied. He knelt and surveyed the man.

The body was nothing more than patches of skin wrapped around a bundle of bones. The face was a hideous, ill-fitting mask that gone gray and looked so thin that it could be read through.

"Who was he?" Danielle asked.

"A scholar. A linguist like Macomber." Simon reached down and picked up one of the dead man's hands. "Only something a little more." He spread the dead man's hand out for all to see.

Marcel Duvalier had possessed six fingers on his right hand.

"Birth defect, mate?" Nathan asked in the silence that followed. "Six fingers, six toes. Happened a lot among the royals due to all the intermarrying. The gene pool got thin."

"This wasn't a birth defect." Simon pulled on the second forefinger and it separated easily. "The finger was grafted on." He held a finger up. "It also had three articulated joints, not two."

Leah knelt beside Simon. She took the forefinger and studied it. "This isn't human."

"Macomber entered into a dialogue with a psychology

student who was studying the journals of the doctor who treated Duvalier," Simon said, repeating the story that the old linguistics professor had given him aboard the ATV. "When he discovered that Macomber was working on much the same project, the student contacted Macomber. Since he was a student, access to Macomber was fairly easy to get. Macomber said the student was fascinated."

"I'm fascinated, mate," Nathan said. "Do you know what the chances are of them ever even meeting each other? Or even knowing they were working on the same materials?"

"Astronomical comes to mind." Simon looked at the forefinger in Leah's hand. "Both of them, Duvalier and Macomber, had been studying the same manuscripts. And they had both continued their studies inside the sanitariums."

"Inside separate institutions?" Nathan asked.

"The student kept papers and letters going back and forth between him and Macomber," Simon said. "But Macomber felt certain that it was only this dialogue that existed between Duvalier and the student that kept him sane. They were both trying to solve the same problem."

"To interpret the demon language," Leah said quietly.

"That's right," Simon replied. He lifted his palm and shined the torchlight over the walls. Writing covered the irregular surfaces.

Every square inch of space was overlaid by symbols and letters. The hand wasn't always steady, but it had obviously been determined. Simon saved images of the writing through his HUD interface.

"If I didn't know better," Nathan said, "I'd think a madman had been at the walls."

That drew only a few dry chuckles from the Templar. The atmosphere inside the cage was to somber and sad for much more than that.

"Macomber didn't know how Duvalier been able to translate as much of the demon language as he had," Simon said. "The student at first had believed that Duvalier was creating an artificial language."

"The student thought Duvalier was only having on his doctors and contemporaries?" Nathan asked.

"Yes. It was only when the student studied the papers Macomber had written before the professor had been locked away in the sanitarium that the student realized the language wasn't just localized to Duvalier."

"Duvalier grafted the demon's finger onto his hand." Simon followed the haphazard columns of letters written on the walls.

"Where did he get the idea for that?" Leah asked.

"Macomber didn't know. I don't think he knew that Duvalier had grafted on this extra finger. At least not then. After he escaped the Parisian sanitarium, he saw some of the Cabalists in Paris that had demon parts grafted onto their bodies. He suspected then because it had been mentioned in the doctor's notes that Duvalier had a sixth finger on his right hand."

"When did that sort of thing start?" Leah asked.

"I don't know," Simon answered.

"Transplants have always been a source of mystery and the medical field," Danielle put in. "Some of the first things that were tried were teeth and larger body parts like hands and arms."

"Yum," Nathan said sarcastically. "Nothing I like more than having this kind of conversation after battling a Grotesque while we're stuck in a grotto of dead serial killers and mass murderers."

"They weren't all serial killers and mass murderers," Daniel replied.

"Enough of them were, if you ask me."

Leah stood beside Simon. "These are Duvalier's translations?"

"Yes." Simon studied the wall.

"Duvalier isn't exactly an English name," Nathan observed.

"It's French," Simon said.

"Glad we got that cleared up, mate."

"Duvalier came to England to study some of the texts that were here. When he tried to steal them from the Royal Libraries, he ended up killing a guard. At his trial he talked about the demons and the need to protect humanity from them."

"It's a wonder he didn't get a trip to the gallows."

"The university he taught for preferred the idea of him being a madman rather than a murderer. A deal was worked out."

"What are we looking for?" Leah asked.

"According to Macomber, Duvalier blackmailed a colleague into bringing a copy of the *Goetia* manuscript into the sanitarium. Duvalier also paid off guards to let him work on the manuscript. At the time, bribery was a major source of income for the police and guards."

"Besides Duvalier was just a mad Frenchman and it didn't matter," Leah said.

"Either way," Simon said. "There is supposed to be a copy of the manuscript down here."

"In this room?" Nathan turned to survey the walls.

"The clues as to the location are supposed to be here," Simon replied.

"Mate, if you can make sense of this gibberish, then you're a better man than I. If it's written in code—*and* in French—we're not going to—hello. What's this?"

Simon abandoned the wall he was looking at and went to join Nathan. "What?"

"What did you say the name of that manuscript was?" Nathan asked.

"*Goetia,*" Leah said as she joined in.

"Okay, but it had another name, right?"

"*The Lesser Key of Solomon,*" Simon answered.

"Maybe it's just wishful thinking on my part, but this looks like a map of the underground section of the sanitarium." Nathan rested his finger on three concentric circles drawn and in isometric scale so they were shown at a thirty-degree angle and 3-D presentation to the viewer. An arrow pointing upward was drawn to the center them.

At first glance, the drawing could have easily been mistaken for some of the other writing Duvalier had done. The second concentric circle had a stick figure drawing of a man with a book in hand.

But on the third concentric circle there was a small, unmistakable drawing of a key.

"A *lesser* key, right?" Nathan asked.

It was as good a guess as Simon could make. If it was wrong, they could come back.

"All right," he said. "Let's go."

TWENTY-NINE

Go carefully in this place.

Warren froze as soon as he heard Merihim's warning in his head. Flattened up against the wall at the curve of the stairway leading to the third floor of the subterranean section of the sanitarium, he ordered the skeleton to halt as well.

"What?" Jonas asked.

A *scritching* noise could be heard in the darkness ahead.

"Rats," Jonas said. "That's all it is. Nothing to get riled over."

"This place has been closed down for a long time," Warren whispered. "There's nothing left down here for rats to eat."

"Maybe you're not as brave as you think you are."

Warren ignored the skeleton and quietly made his way up the staircase. He peered around the corner and saw movement in the shadows halfway down the hall. He enhanced his vision further and saw the monstrous shape prowling the hallway.

Judging by the height of the hallway, assuming that it was as tall as the previous one, Warren guessed that the demon stood twelve feet tall. Since the hallway only went to seven feet, Hargastor had to lean forward and walk on his knuckles like an ape. The gait suited the demon, though. He was broad and blocky.

Four horns stuck out from the sides of Hargastor's bullet head and flared slightly upward like a bull's horns. His skin was muscled purple and black with threads of scarlet running through it. He carried a massive war hammer over one shoulder. Several Darkspawn trailed at his heels.

Warren's immediate impulse was to turn and run. He didn't stand a chance against a group like that. He felt for Naomi and found her there. She called his name but he quieted her. But he readied himself to spring back across the distance that separated them.

If you run, I'll strike you down, Merihim warned.

Regretfully, Warren stood his ground. *You can back out of this anytime you get ready to,* he told himself. He held on to that thought.

You won't live to regret it, Merihim warned.

Plaintive cries sounded from one of the cells near the demon. Two of the Darkspawn lashed out with truncheons and battered pale faces that stood just behind the iron bars.

"Please," the hoarse voices croaked. "Please. We need water."

"No water," Hargastor replied in a thunderous voice. "You're here to die at my leisure. I want your pain writ upon these walls."

Warren stared into the cells till he could penetrate the darkness. Human vision was blind in the darkness and he knew the people inside the cell couldn't see anything.

"Hargastor lives to torment," the quiet voice said at the back of Warren's mind. "He's no different than his master. Fulaghar has allowed him his *pets.*"

Judging from the clothing worn by the fourteen prisoners and the nine dead ones lying at their feet, they were all London survivors. Five of the fourteen sat at the back of the cave cell and conserved their strength. Warren "felt" that they were military. A few of Great Britain's police and military yet remained in the city as well. They listened attentively to the demons out in the passageway.

"You're wasting your breath," one of the soldiers stated quietly. "There's no mercy in any of those devils."

Hargastor laughed, and the sound of it filled the passageway. "You have meat to eat and blood to drink," he rumbled. "The weaker ones among you have died and left you their pitiful offerings."

"We're not cannibals," a woman cried out.

"Then you're dead sooner rather than later," Hargastor said. "And those of you determined to live will feast on you."

One of the military men cursed the demon, but most of the others broke down and cried.

"Let me hear the joyful noise of your lamentations," Hargastor snarled. He lumbered toward the bars on his knuckles and rapped one big fist against them hard enough to make the door ring.

"You're an ugly brute," the military man said. "Foul and filthy. And one day you'll get what's coming to you. The knights will make sure of that."

"The knights? You mean the Templar?" Hargastor cursed. "They're dead and gone. Only a few remain, and they'll die like rats when we find them."

"They've killed better than you," the man taunted.

Warren couldn't believe the man was still talking. Surely he knew the demon could kill him.

"That's what he wants," the voice said. "He's a warrior. He would rather spend his blood in battle than to die caged like an animal kept for slaughter."

That mindset seemed alien to Warren. All his life he'd struggled to survive, and that meant never drawing attention to himself.

Except he was here now, and he was supposed to somehow destroy the behemoth before him.

Hargastor laughed, and the evil sound echoed along the passageway. Then the demons stopped and snuffled like a dog taking scent.

Warren eased back into the shadows.

"He has your scent, yer lordship," Jonas whispered. Amusement colored his words. "You've still got flesh on your bones. And you stink of fear. Even I can smell it, and I don't have a nose."

"Shut up," Warren commanded.

Jonas's jaws snapped shut with a click.

Darkspawn turned in Warren's direction. They raised their weapons in readiness.

"Stay," Hargastor ordered.

Warren's bowels turned to water as he tried to press himself into the stone wall.

Hargastor shuffled on his knuckles. "I smell you, human. You might as well step out of hiding. There's no place to run."

Warren tried to leave but couldn't. His legs wouldn't go in that direction.

Do not retreat before him, Merihim ordered. *You represent me. I will not have my enemies think I am a coward.*

Then why aren't you here? Warren wanted to ask. But he only hoped he hadn't thought that too loud.

"I am with you," the voice said. "You aren't alone."

But Warren didn't trust any of the voices inside his head.

"Come out, human," Hargastor said more forcefully. "If I have to come after you, things will go much harder for you."

Before he could stop himself, Warren stepped into the passageway. He knew he hadn't moved his legs. Merihim had moved him. The demon hand knotted into a fist.

"Come to me," Hargastor ordered.

Even though he didn't want to, Warren stepped forward. Fear rattled so badly inside him he thought he was going to be sick. He swallowed bile and tried to remain focused.

Kill this abomination, Merihim ordered. *Let his death be a message to Fulaghar.*

"Bring him to me," Hargastor ordered. "I'll kill him to provide a banquet for those among the prisoners who would live."

The Darkspawn started forward.

Warren thought desperately. He saw the faces of the imprisoned humans lining the metal bars of their cage. If he could free them, even if he didn't have an army he at least had a means of splitting the demons' attention.

He concentrated on the lock that held the iron bars shut till he could picture the mechanism in his mind. He formed a blacksmith's hammer in his mind and *pushed*.

Instantly, the lock on the cell door shattered. Pieces of metal jangled against the stone floor.

Whipping his demon hand forward, Warren threw a ball of fire over the first two Darkspawn. They ignited at once and twirled around madly in an attempt to douse the flames. Their screams ripped through the passageway.

"You're free!" Warren yelled, impressing that suggestion to the prisoners in the cave/cell. "Run for your lives!"

He wasn't sure where they were going to run. From what he'd learned of the sanitarium, no one knew the lower levels existed.

The military men forced the other survivors up and through the door. Darkspawn turned toward them at once. Three of the military men closed on one of the Darkspawn. The demon fired a strange-looking red and gray weapon that belched red-gold bursts that ricocheted from the passageway floor and walls.

The creature managed only a few shots before the military men overwhelmed it and knocked it to the floor. One of the men took a direct hit and stumbled forward only a couple steps before dropping to his knees. He covered his chest and tried to scream.

Then his chest melted and took away his lungs. His face and head followed, sloughing into the chest cavity as the corpse fell forward.

With guttural curses, the warriors battered the demon to the floor and turned the weapon onto the Darkspawn. Several more bursts sailed through the passageway. One struck a fleeing prisoner and dropped the woman to the ground when her legs folded under her. She screamed hoarsely until the destruction caused by the weapon rendered her unconscious or dead.

Panicked, Warren dropped to the ground. A burst missed him by inches before disappearing down the hallway.

"Get them!" Hargastor ordered. "Don't let them escape!"

Three Darkspawn surged forward.

The two men left struggling with the Darkspawn fired several bursts into their opponent. The Darkspawn screeched defiantly and lashed out with a handful of claws that tore through one man's face and left it a bloody mess. The man staggered back, but the demon didn't live to see its victory. The energy burst turned it into a mass of seething protoplasm that leaked through its bones.

The man who had seized the weapon fired at the nearest Darkspawn and hit the demon in the head. Instantly the Darkspawn's head blew up like a balloon, then fell inside its neck. Already dead, the demon stumbled to the ground and sprawled.

Before the man could use his weapon again, two other Darkspawn fired at him from point-blank range. The bursts chewed holes in his body before he hit the ground. The other man wiped blood from his eyes and dove for the weapon. He managed to get it up, but couldn't fire before more bursts hit him.

Hargastor whirled toward Warren. "You're going to pay for the inconvenience you've caused, human. I'll give you a slow and painful death."

"Get up," the voice said in the back of Warren's mind. "Get up or you'll die on your knees."

Three Darkspawn closed on Warren as he pushed himself to his feet.

Simon led the way down the spiral staircase that had been hewn through the limestone. The HUD chased the shadows from the area. At the bottom, the hallway ran in both directions.

"Any guesses which way?" he asked.

"No," Nathan said. "The man—or woman—that made that drawing might not have known. Or could have gotten confused."

"We could split up," Danielle suggested.

"No," Leah and Simon said at the same time.

"Not exactly my favorite idea either," Danielle admitted. "But I thought we might be able to cover more ground that way."

"We go together," Simon said. "Whatever is down here has waited for a long time. It can wait a little while longer." He chose the passage to the right, thinking that the wall offered protection for his weak side.

More skeletons littered the floor. Most of the cages had been occupied. Mummified corpses lay sprawled on the other side of the iron bars.

"They didn't even try to get these people out of here," Danielle said in a soft voice.

"Their families paid for them to be locked away," Nathan said. "You didn't think they wanted them back just because the sanitarium was closing, did you?"

"Did anyone ever find out what the sanitarium staff did to these people?"

"I don't know," Simon answered. "None of the research I looked at talked about any of this."

"Seems to me we've had plenty of evil here before the demons arrived," Danielle said.

No one argued with her.

The unmistakable voice of a demon rang out in the passageway ahead. Then a human voice ordered others to flee for their lives. Feet slapped against stone as fearful cries echoed through the hollow throat of the hallway.

Simon waved the others into defensive positions. They occupied the hallway in stacked two by two formation. He and Nathan took kneeling positions with their swords across their knees and their Spike Bolters in hand. Danielle and another Templar stood behind them so they could fire over their heads.

It was a close-in tactic designed to break a frontal assault.

"Protect the rear," Simon said. "Pull back to the staircase and keep the way open. Remember that this hallway is a ring."

Two Templar broke off and jogged back the way they'd come. Simon kept track of all their positions on the HUD.

"I have identified one of the voices," the suit's AI informed him.

That surprised Simon. He hadn't recognized any of the voices, but he knew the AI kept track of everyone he'd come in contact with.

"Display," Simon ordered.

"His name is Warren. I don't know if that's a first name or last." The AI ghosted an image on the HUD.

Simon didn't recognize the young black man onscreen. "I don't know him."

"You met him before," the AI said. "When you were attempting to retrieve Balekor's Hammer."

Simon remembered the man then. He'd chopped his hand off when he'd called forth a demon to kill them. The nightmare of taking the man's hand had been only one of those that chased through Simon's dreams. He was surprised to learn that the man was still alive.

They'd gotten Balekor's Hammer that night, and they'd gotten away. Most of them. The weapon was in the Templar Underground now. At least, the last time Simon had seen it the hammer had been.

But what was the man doing here now? The last Simon had seen of him was the night the man—Warren—had tried to kill him aboard the train four years ago. Simon had felt certain the Cabalist had died in the river that night.

Shapes appeared around the bend in the hallway. Even with the HUD's amplification Simon couldn't tell if they were demon or human.

"Hold," he ordered calmly.

In the next instant he saw that they were human. Four of them fled for their lives. But Darkspawn followed at their heels.

Nathan cursed.

"Up," Simon ordered. "We let the people through and we hold the demons." He leaned into a run and brought the Spike Bolter up as he closed on the fleeing humans.

THIRTY

Warren summoned the dark energy that swirled within him. He threw his demon hand forward and imagined thousands of predatory insects. No actual insects manifested, but it was how he'd learned to shape the power. A shimmering wall collided with the advancing Darkspawn.

Sparkles glistened across their scaly hide. They jerked to halts as if stung by bees and started slapping at their flesh. Then Warren pushed again.

The energy had embedded dozens of explosive nodes in the Darkspawn's bodies. His secondary casting set them off. The resulting detonations shook and shattered the Darkspawn. Gobbets of flesh flew free and slapped against the walls, ceiling, and ground.

Only one of the Darkspawn survived with little injury. The demon aimed its pistol and fired.

The drain from the previous effort left Warren lightheaded. He'd used that attack only a few times before and it always had that effect on him. But it was always effective as well. He focused and held his palm out flat before him.

The energy bursts struck an invisible barrier in front of Warren and ricocheted back. Some of them struck Hargastor, who howled in rage as massive sores opened on his broad chest and one of his arms.

Startled, the Darkspawn turned toward its master as

if fearing retribution from that front. While the demon was distracted, Warren thrust his hand out and twisted violently. An invisible force caught the Darkspawn's head and twisted to mimic Warren's effort.

Bones snapped and the demon dropped to the ground and remained still.

Hargastor cursed and roared in pain.

"You can't kill him head-on," the voice whispered in the back of Warren's head. "His back is his weakest point. If he sees you, he can defend against you."

Hargastor waved his hands over the sores on his body. They healed almost immediately.

"He's almost invincible."

Warren believed that. He thought about diving for one of the weapons dropped by the demons he'd destroyed, but the idea of using a mechanical weapon bothered him. More than that, he'd seen Hargastor recover from those wounds in seconds.

"Those weapons aren't an answer," the voice said. "You have the power within you."

As he gazed at the huge demon before him, Warren knew that wasn't true. "No. I can't. Hargastor is too strong."

"You have to choose the moment to strike. Until then, you just have to stay alive."

Easier said than done, Warren thought helplessly.

Hargastor pinned him with its baleful gaze. Nearly a dozen Darkspawn yet remained around their master. They took aim and fired.

Warren ducked around the bend of the passage. He found himself standing beside Jonas.

"A bit nasty out there, ain't it?" the skeleton asked.

"Is there a way out of here?" Warren demanded.

Don't run, Merihim ordered.

Then help me, Warren entreated. *I'm not strong enough to stand against Hargastor.*

Down the passageway, Darkspawn ran toward Warren's position.

"There's a way out," Jonas said. "At least, there used to be. Stairway at the other end of the passage like the one we came up."

"If you try to leave, Merihim will strike you down," the voice said.

Warren hesitated, torn about what he should do.

"You can wait around if you like, mate, but I'm not." Jonas took off before Warren could stop him. The skeleton's bony feet smacked against the stone floor. He didn't manage twenty paces before the power animating him left him. The spell worked only in close proximity to Warren.

As Warren watched Jonas drop to the ground in a tangle of bones bound by desiccated ligaments, he knew he didn't have the power to animate the skeleton again. Warren clung to the thought that there was a way out. He reached for Naomi and felt her there.

"I'm here," she told him.

"I don't know if I'm strong enough to come back on my own. I may need you to do it for me."

She hesitated. "I'm tired. I don't know if I can."

You'll never come out of the darkness, Merihim promised. *It will swallow you whole, and I will allow it. Finish what you were sent there to do.*

Warren wanted to hide. It was what he'd always done while dealing with his stepfather. Just hide until it all went away. No matter how much power he had, or all the arcane knowledge he learned, he knew he'd never get far from that small boy he'd been.

"You will learn strength," the voice said. "I will teach you."

"Then teach me now," Warren said.

From the nearness of the running footsteps, he knew the Darkspawn were nearly upon him. He marshaled his reserve strength and set himself.

He couldn't run. There was nowhere to go that something wouldn't get him.

Then a barrage of weapons fire opened up in the hallway back in the direction of Hargastor. Warren recognized the sound from previous encounters during the last four years. Those were Templar weapons.

"Yes," the voice whispered. "Now prepare yourself. There's still a lot you must do if you would live."

When the last of the humans were by him and only Darkspawn remained before him, Simon opened fire with the Spike Bolter. Nathan joined him less than a heartbeat later.

The palladium spikes tore into demon flesh and broke the Darkspawn's charge. They howled in pain as they stumbled and fell. Simon holstered the Spike Bolter and took up his sword in both hands. He cut through the remaining Darkspawn and limbs dropped like tree branches in a storm.

One of the Darkspawn raised its weapon and blasted Simon full in the face before he could move. He'd tracked the creature on the HUD, knew the attack was coming, but couldn't do anything about it.

The energy blast rocked Simon's head back and blanked his HUD.

"Visual systems off-line," the suit AI stated. "Working to reroute program." The armor was designed to cannibalize parts of itself to support primary systems.

"Nathan," Simon said, "I'm blind."

"It's okay, mate," Nathan said calmly. "I've got you."

As he dropped to one knee to clear the field of fire, Simon heard Nathan's blade cleaving flesh, then there was a burst from the Spike Bolter. The sound of a body hitting the stone floor echoed in the hallway.

"Simon, let me see your hand," Danielle said.

Simon lifted his hand and felt it taken. She guided it to her shoulder.

"Open your sensor array," Danielle said. "Feed off mine."

"Doing that will limit your sensors," Simon said. All the suits were hardwired with symbiotic natures. The subset had originally been intended for medical analysis on the battlefield, but the use had broadened.

"I know. But we're underground. I don't think either of us will notice much loss."

Simon opened his sensor array to take in Danielle's open channel. He wouldn't have been able to access her sensors unless she'd left them available. His HUD "sight" returned to him.

The symbiosis wasn't perfect, though. His perception was slightly off, centered more on Danielle's point of view rather than his own position. Also, there was a good chance that both systems would experience slower processing that would take them out of real-time. In a battle, even a split-second could mean the difference between life and death.

"Your armor can share data?" Leah asked.

"Yes." Simon lifted his hand from Danielle's shoulder. Now that the connection had been made, the wireless interface kept the exchange running smoothly. As long as he remained within thirty or forty feet of Danielle, with no metal obstruction between them, the signal would continue uninterrupted.

"Doesn't that leave the interface open to outside attack?"

"Maybe right now, with demonspawn all around us, isn't the appropriate time to get into a technical discussion," Danielle stated. "And no, the suit systems aren't as easy to hack as you might think."

The question made Simon uneasy. It reminded him again that Leah was an outsider and that he might have made a mistake in bringing her.

The four people that had run past them cowered in the hallway twenty feet farther down.

"Who are you?" one of the men asked.

"Friends," Simon replied. He realized from the way the people stood that they were blind in the darkness. He took a lightstick from the supply pack he'd carried in. Since they'd been going underground, he'd packed accordingly.

Lightsticks made sense in case the HUD systems failed out or had problems functioning. Leaving the faceplate open hadn't been a choice he'd have voluntarily made, but if it meant life and death, he knew they'd need an alternate light source.

Simon slapped the lightstick against his thigh. A pale yellow glow stretched across the passageway.

"Knights," one of the women whispered.

"I thought they were just legends," one of the men said.

"I saw one once before," the other man said. "But only one. Not a group like this."

The second woman, a young one barely out of her teens from the look of her, shook her head and stepped back. "The light isn't good. It'll draw the demons."

"What demons?" Nathan asked. "We killed the demons." He indicated the bodies of the monsters lying around them.

"There are more," the other woman said. "A lot more. They've been holding us down here for days."

"Why?" Simon asked.

"Because they could," one of the men answered.

Then there was no more time for questions. More demons ran toward them and set up an offensive line.

"Simon?" Nathan asked.

"Repairs query," Simon said.

"Repairs at seventeen percent," the suit AI replied. "Estimated time of repair: six-point-three-two seconds."

"Take them," Simon ordered. "We'll try to buy the fugitives time to get clear."

Nathan's head swiveled toward the four people. "Run!" he ordered. "The stairway's ahead of you! Don't stop till you're clear of the building!"

Simon drew his Spike Bolter and charged the demon line as the Darkspawn opened fire. His reflexes felt awkward as he struggled to adjust to Danielle's point of view. The farther he got from her, the worse the perspective became. His feet thudded heavily against the stone floor.

A few energy bursts struck his armor and left scorch marks. Most of the others scored the walls and ceiling as the Darkspawn tried to hold the line.

Simon threw himself at them the last few feet. He flailed his arms out and took down three of the Darkspawn. Up close, he didn't depend on visual acuity. Close-in martial arts honed to perfection over years of training in the Templar Underground took over.

He forced himself to one knee and shoved the Spike Bolter into the face of one of the Darkspawn. When he pulled the trigger, the demon's face fell to bloody pieces. The skull fractured and fell inside itself.

He lunged to the left and swung his sword in a backhand arc that chopped into another Darkspawn's head. When he shifted to bring his other foot under him and stand, he brought his left knee to his chest and kicked straight out at the Darkspawn whose skull he'd cleaved.

The corpse shot backward and rebounded from another demon. Both bodies slammed against the wall. Nathan, Danielle, and the other Templar waded into the attack. The Demonspawn fell back but there were others behind them. In minutes the hallway was slick with blood.

"Trouble," Nathan growled. "Look ahead."

Simon did. He was almost twenty feet from Danielle, and the sensory deviation made it hard to focus easily. The subsystem had been designed primarily to allow a stricken Templar to fight in tandem with another Templar, or to allow them to help rescue themselves if they were able. They weren't supposed to fight apart.

Danielle approached Simon and the vision cleared to a degree.

A huge demon nearly filled the hallway. "I am Hargastor!" the demon roared. "Know me and fear me!" It drew back a hand and threw it forward. A flaming ball streaked like a comet toward the Templar.

Warren focused his power and released it in a shimmering wall. The force struck the three Darkspawn and knocked them backward. The effort nearly wiped Warren out. He felt a warm trickle down his upper lip. He knew from experience that if he wiped the liquid from his face, his hand would carry crimson stains.

"You're falling apart," Naomi said. Her voice sounded like a whisper inside his skull. "Come to me."

Warren wanted to. He wanted to leave this place more than anything.

"If you do, Merihim will destroy you," the voice said.

Warren blinked and focused his vision. Behind Hargastor the Templar weapons erupted into a new barrage of fire. The demon glanced back.

For a moment Warren thought Hargastor was going

to abandon the fight and investigate the sounds. Warren readied himself to take advantage of the demon's exposed back. He was reaching for the dregs of his energy when Hargastor whirled back around and flung a hand out.

"Die, human!"

An incredible force like nothing Warren had ever felt before knocked him from his feet. He felt the bones in his chest shatter and crumple inward. When he struck the wall behind him, the breath left his lungs in a rush and his senses fled.

THIRTY-ONE

"**B** oot anchors," Simon said. He felt the impacts of the boot anchors shooting into the stone floor. They bit deeply as he twisted his right side toward the whirling gout of flame.

"Warning," the suit's AI stated. "Combustible fluid approaching exceeds acceptable temperatures. Take—"

Whatever the AI might have said was lost in the thunderous roar that enveloped Simon's mind. The audio receptors shut down to preserve his hearing, but he lost the auditory connection with the AI at the same time. The intense heat nearly broiled him, and he wondered if he'd been parboiled inside his armor anyway.

Pain returned first, then the instinct to live. The HUD showed that the demon was advancing at a run. Simon lifted his Spike Bolter and aimed at the demon's horrible face. He squeezed the trigger and refused to give ground. Danielle, Leah, and the other Templar hadn't yet recovered.

The demon—Hargastor, Simon remembered—lifted its empty hand to ward off the palladium spikes. It never broke stride. Hoping to take the creature off-balance, Simon flung himself forward and met the demon, going chest-to-chest. At the last moment, Simon activated the boot spikes again and butted into the demon.

Hargastor hit Simon so hard that he broke the stone

floor that was anchored to the Templar's boots. Simon felt the extra weight at the ends of his legs. He withdrew the spikes and the stone chunks dropped away.

Senses reeling, vision through the HUD not reading true, Simon discovered he'd lost the Spike Bolter. He still held his sword, but using it was problematic. Instead, he looped one leg inside the demon's leg and tripped the massive creature. They collapsed to the floor and rolled over Danielle, who had been blown from her feet.

The demon rolled and tried to come up on top of Simon. Gripping his sword tightly, Simon slammed the haft into the inside of the demon's support elbow. The joint gave way to the blow and folded. As Hargastor fell, Simon butted him in the chin with the top of his helm, then caught the buckling arm with his free hand and pulled.

Hargastor fell to the side and Simon pummeled the demon in the face with the sword hilt. He was too close to employ the blade.

The demon roared in rage, but Simon heard pain in there as well. His attack had hurt the demon, but he knew it would have killed most lesser demons.

"Offensive flea," Hargastor snarled. He closed his own fist and hammered Simon.

Stunned by the blow, Simon shot backward and collided with Danielle. Both of them went down. Simon immediately tried to get up, but the demon was faster.

Hargastor backhanded Simon while he was still on his knees. Simon flipped over backwards and felt the breath leave his lungs. His borrowed vision reeled sickeningly. The demon came for him immediately.

"You're going to die, Templar. You should have stayed away from here. You should have stayed away from the book."

Desperation filled Simon when he realized there was only one book the demon could be referring to. It was one thing to fight for his life, but if he lived and the demon got the manuscript, he'd lost everything. Before he could move, Hargastor picked him up in both hands and slammed him into the wall. Stone smashed and cracks ran for several feet in all directions.

The demon's head suddenly rocked sideways as an explosive round from a Cluster Rifle struck home. One of the horns snapped off and went flying. Bloody ichors ran from the horn stump and stained the side of the demon's neck.

Howling with rage, Hargastor turned to face his newest opponent.

While standing less than thirty feet away, Leah calmly took aim again and fired. This time the round sped harmlessly by until it hit the passageway wall. Hargastor launched himself in pursuit of Leah.

Nathan tried to push through a mass of Darkspawn but couldn't reach Hargastor in time. Danielle was still trying to recover, and the remaining Templar was down, dead or unconscious.

Simon pulled himself out of the deep impression made by his impact against the wall. Small rocks and dust spilled out around him as he got to his feet. He took four quick strides and threw himself headlong at Hargastor as the demon drew back a hand that suddenly filled with swirling fire and black smoke.

When he reached the demon, Simon curled his arm around Hargastor's ankles and pulled tightly. The demon tried to complete his attack against Leah even as he fell. Rifle to her shoulder, she tracked her opponent as the demon rebounded from the floor, then fired.

The missile struck Hargastor in the chest. Acid burned

deeply into his skin. Some of it splashed over Simon's armor and set off alarms inside the HUD.

"Warning. Armor shielding is at sixty-one percent capacity."

Simon ignored the announcement. He was in the thick of it now and knew that he had no choice about giving up. If he released the demon, Hargastor would undoubtedly try to get to Leah because she was the least protected among them. Demons could sense things like that.

Hargastor's eyes blazed as he turned on Simon. "You're annoying me, pest. Can't you just die?"

"You first," Simon replied. He slammed his fist against the demon's burned and acid-eaten face. Even as he watched, though, Hargastor's wounds were healing. Simon struck again and again, willing the bone to break and the flesh to split.

Abruptly, the demon surged to its feet, though it remained hunkered over because of the low ceiling. The thing's strength was incredible. Simon knew that if they were out in the open, the fight might already be over.

Nathan attacked with his Spike Bolter and sword from the other side. Palladium spikes struck home from point-blank range and the sword slashed the demon's hide.

The demon picked Simon up by one foot and swung him into Nathan like a club. Both of them went down. Simon clung to consciousness by his fingernails. He felt the warmth of chemicals—stimulants as well as pain relievers—flood his system before he could call the suit's AI off. The medical subprograms were struggling to keep up with everything being done to his body as well.

Even as the demon released Simon, Leah fired once more. Another bone-shaking explosion filled the passageway. Dust fell from the ceiling, followed quickly by a shower of rocks blown free by the impact.

Hargastor rocked back on his heels for a moment. Then he stood. And he smiled while his head and features burned. Blackened flesh pulled back from his fangs and streamers of blood mixed with them.

"Weaklings!" the demon roared. "I am invincible!"

Shaking, nerves jangling from the pain and from the chemicals stampeding through his bloodstream, Simon forced himself to his feet again. He fought to suck in a breath and couldn't.

"Airway partially blocked and closing down," the suit AI said. "Administering epinephrine."

The adrenaline-enhancing injection flooded Simon's body. Some of the pain went away. His heart pounded rapidly and caused his temples to throb. But his throat opened up.

"Cardio-pulmonary operation within acceptable tolerances," the AI informed him. "Video sensor arrays are still being repaired."

Simon took a deep breath and stepped between Hargastor and Leah. He was certain his armor still provided a better chance of survival than hers. He fisted his sword and readied himself.

Warren woke with Naomi's voice in his head. She called to him over and over.

"I'm here," he said automatically. He struggled to remember where *here* was. His body felt like it was coming apart as he stood.

Get moving, Merihim ordered. *Hargastor can't be allowed to get away.*

Farther down the passageway, Warren heard the sounds of the Templar weapons. He didn't know which he couldn't believe more: that the Templar weren't dead already or that he wasn't.

I'm just going to get killed, Warren thought to himself. But he knew if he didn't go Merihim would kill him. He went, almost stumbling over himself.

Only a few feet ahead, he watched as Hargastor slammed one of the Templar against another and turned to the slim, black-clad female in front of him. Another Templar was just getting to her feet. A fourth lay unmoving on the floor. Darkspawn sprawled in death all around them.

Kill him, Merihim ordered. *While his back is to you and he is at his weakest, kill him.*

Warren felt that he was only going to draw the demon's wrath to him once more. But he summoned the energy to him as he took up a position less than twenty feet behind Hargastor.

"Let me take you out of there," Naomi called to him. "You're dying. I can feel it."

Warren felt her pulling at him, but he forced her away.

"Take heart," the voice told Warren. "Your master can't completely forsake you."

Warren didn't know that he believed that. He'd felt certain over the last four years that Merihim would leave him whenever he felt like it.

Or whenever Warren got too close to whatever secret desires the demon followed.

"Merihim has his secrets," the voice said. "All of them do. And when you discover what it is, you make them weak."

It doesn't matter if I don't live long enough to save myself, Warren thought bitterly.

Hargastor's attention was on the black-clad female. The Templar behind him scarcely noticed Warren because she was so intent on the demon's back.

Then one of the fallen Templar pushed himself up and

stood between Hargastor and his chosen prey. Recognition flared through Warren as he surveyed the dark blue and silver figure before him.

It was the Templar that he had met four years ago. The same one that had taken his hand and allowed Merihim to possess him. The armor's coloration—unique as far as Warren knew—wasn't the only thing that gave away the man inside. He also *felt* the man inside.

Warren's focus shifted as his rage and pain outweighed his fear. The Templar had been the one who had left him cursed that night. If he hadn't taken his hand, Merihim would never have given him one of his to wear in his service. He might still have been a free man and able to leave London when so many others had.

Good, Merihim said. *Use the anger you feel. It will make you stronger. Bend it to your need. But destroy Hargastor.*

Warren wanted to wait before striking until Hargastor had killed the Templar. He could see it all in his mind's eye. It would have been revenge of sorts, and almost by his own hand since he hadn't prevented Hargastor from killing him.

Except that if Warren wasn't strong enough to destroy the demon, there would be no one to save him. He'd seen enough of the Templar to know that the ones in the passageway wouldn't have been able to simply leave him there once he attacked.

Do it, Merihim growled.

Power flooded into Warren. Pain fled. In the space of a single breath, he was once more clear-headed. He channeled all the power he had—his and what he took from Merihim—and unleashed it through his demon's hand.

A shimmering shower of falling stars flew from Warren's hand and crashed against Hargastor. The demon staggered as purple pustules suddenly sprouted all over his back. Something writhed inside them, growing larger and more active as Warren watched.

Hargastor howled in pain and fear, something that Warren had never thought he would hear. He turned around and faced Warren.

"What have you done?" Hargastor demanded. "What have you done?"

Not knowing what to expect, Warren stepped back. He'd used every bit of the power Merihim had given him. And he'd used up his reserves as well. There was nothing left. He could barely stand on his feet.

"Who are you?" Hargastor asked.

Warren wasn't going to say anything, but his mouth opened and he said, "I'm your death, dung fly. Your true and final death today. Let your master hear your mortal cries of anguish."

Hargastor screamed in pain and thrust his hands out.

Warren dodged weakly back and covered his head with his arms but nothing happened. His breath caught at the back of his throat when he realized that he could hardly move.

"Warren," Naomi called.

"Wait," the voice said.

Merihim hovered nearby. Warren felt the demon watching through his eyes.

Frustrated and screaming for vengeance, Hargastor started forward. He managed two steps before the pustules began bursting and unleashed small salamander-looking creatures that immediately attacked their host.

The strength went out of the demon and he dropped to his knees. His face screwed up in disbelief and agony. "No! This can't be happening! Fulaghar!" He held his hands up to the ceiling in supplication as more pustules burst and more salamander-things chewed on him. "Fulaghar! Save me!"

No one came, though.

As Warren watched, all semblance of life drained from Hargastor's face. His beseeching arms dropped to his sides and his eyes rolled back up into his head. He fell forward and hit the ground without trying to stop himself.

The salamander-things started feasting in earnest.

You can go, Merihim said. *Find the remaining two. Then we will destroy Fulaghar.*

"*We?*" Warren thought weakly as he started at the demon corpse the salamander-things had been born in and now devoured. Merihim didn't hear his thought, though, or chose not to react to it. Warren felt the demon draw away from him.

"It's over," the voice said. "Go while you're still able."

But Warren couldn't. Too much remained yet to be explored. He stared at the Templar in dark blue and silver standing on the other side of Hargastor's corpse.

"Warren, let me bring you back," Naomi pleaded. "You've got to hurry. I feel you getting weaker."

Listening to his own heart, Warren knew that he was dying—that he would die if he didn't return to his body where Naomi watched over it. But he stared at the blank face of the Templar's helm.

"You owe me," Warren told the Templar. "You took my hand and bound me to a demon." He tried to find additional energy within himself, anything to strike against the Templar. The man inside the armor was barely standing as well. "I will kill you."

Without a word, the Templar lifted his sword in his left hand. Energy crackled across the blank faceplate.

"You're in league with the demons," the Templar accused.

Warren couldn't believe it. "I just killed a demon about to slaughter you."

"That's your interpretation, mate." The other male Templar had his pistol leveled at Warren. "We had him right where we bloody wanted him. And you're not in a good place to be making threats."

The slim black-clad woman pointed her rifle at him.

"Another time, Templar," Warren said. He couldn't help feeling the threat was lame, like it was ripped right out of a comic book that he'd read. But what else could he say that would get the point across?

He felt frustrated that his rage and hate could feel so strong and so sure, and that he couldn't articulate it any better than that. But then he thought that maybe emotions felt so much could only be spoken of in simple terms. There was nothing complex about revenge.

"Another time," the Templar agreed. He saluted Warren with his blade.

At first Warren believed the response was grandiose, driven by ego. But when he searched for the man behind the metal face, he sensed none of that. The gesture was eloquent and meant without hypocrisy or cheap theatrics.

"Warren." Naomi sounded far away.

Silently, Warren let down his defenses and let her call him back across the yawning blackness that separated his sanctuary from the sanitarium. He felt as if he'd taken a step to the side and turned inside out.

THIRTY-TWO

S imon watched the man with the demon hand fade from view. In seconds, there was nothing left of him to show that he'd ever been there.

Except the dead demon stretched out on the floor. The body jiggled and jerked as the salamander-things tore chunks of flesh from it and devoured them in gulps.

Simon crossed the room and recovered his Spike Bolter. Lifting the pistol, he took aim and killed the salamander-things with quick bursts. Danielle and Nathan joined his efforts. No one wanted the things turning on them in case their armor offered no more protection than the demon's hide.

He stepped to the fallen Templar. His name was Mathias Birch. He was a year or two younger than Simon.

"Are you still with me, Mathias?" Simon asked. He dropped a hand on the Templar's armor and got a medical readout. Mathias was in shock and struggling to breathe. A broken rib had punctured his lung. There were other broken bones as well, but the lung was the worst of it.

"I am," the Templar whispered weakly.

"I'm going to put you into stasis to get you out of pain," Simon said.

"I can handle it, Simon." Mathias lifted a quivering hand. "Just give me a hand up and I'll be right as rain. You'll see."

Simon didn't want to argue. If the younger man tried moving around too much, the lung could completely collapse or the rib might move farther and damage his heart. He took Mathias's hand.

"Thanks, Simon. You'll see. I'm not going to fall behind. And you're not going to have to lose another warrior because I've let myself get bollixed up."

"This isn't your fault, Mathias." Simon interfaced his suit's AI with that of the younger man and overrode the other AI's system. He triggered the stasis function and Mathias went limp inside the suit.

Gently, Simon laid the young Templar on the ground. He ran his hands over Mathias's torso and locked sections of the armor into place so they wouldn't move. They would also provide better support during transport.

"Stasis effective," the suit's AI said. "Mathias is resting. Life-support systems control subject's autonomous system."

"Good," Simon said. "Take care of him."

"I will."

"Christopher," Simon said.

The other young Templar standing nearby came forward. "Yes."

"I need you to get Mathias out of here," Simon said. "In case we run into any more trouble."

"All right."

"Nathan. I'll need a hand."

Together, Simon and Nathan lifted the unconscious Templar and strapped him to Christopher's back. Once they had him in place, the Templar walked back down the passageway.

Simon hoped that both of them would arrive safely. Then he freed his Spike Bolter and continued down the corridor to find the *Goetia* manuscript.

* * *

"Did you know him?" Nathan asked as he and Simon checked another pair of cells. "The man with the demon's hand?"

"His name is Warren," Simon answered. If the suit's AI hadn't retained that information from the two encounters he'd had with the man, he knew he wouldn't have remembered. There had been too many things happening since that time in the basement four years ago and on the train Simon had arranged to take so many of London's survivors from the city.

"Warren what?"

"I don't know."

"How do you know him?"

"The last time we saw him, he tried to kill us," Leah said.

Nathan turned to her. "So you know him too?"

"Yes. But that's all we know about him." Though her faceplate remained implacable, her voice took on another timber. "We'll know more about him next time."

"'Next time?'" Nathan snorted. "Maybe you didn't notice, but that guy just bloody leveled a demon that was about to hand us our heads."

"I thought you didn't see it that way," Danielle said.

"I was trying to sound convincing. I did sound convincing, didn't I?"

Simon kept going forward and ducked into the next cell. The manuscript had to be somewhere up ahead. They were running out of places to look.

Rage and helplessness, both old and familiar companions, surged through Warren as he returned to his body. He'd battled both when he'd lived with his mother and stepfather, then again throughout his foster care. He knew what to expect from them.

But the weight across his chest was totally unexpected.

Weak and somewhat disoriented, Warren opened his eyes. Naomi lay stretched across his body. At first he feared that she was dead. Guilt ratcheted into the emotional cocktail exploding through his veins. If he'd stayed too long, if he'd cost her too much, he didn't know how he was going to handle that.

A shallow pulse beat at the hollow of her throat. Her breath coasted across his cheek.

Tenderly, Warren moved her weight off his body so he could breathe easier. She slumped to the floor beside him. The fear didn't go away. Just because she was breathing didn't mean some kind of brain damage hadn't taken place. He'd seen several Cabalists suffer severe mental problems brought on by trying to get closer to the arcane energies the demons wielded.

On more than one occasion the Cabalist seeking to improve his or her understanding of those energies had been completely mind-wiped. When they'd returned from the trances they'd undertaken, they'd been vegetables. Others lost motor control of parts or all of their bodies, reduced to physical cripples that could no longer even care for themselves.

A few others hadn't returned, but *things*—lingering impressions of the dead who had once lived in the house where the arcane procedure took place and demons—had come back in their stead. Usually those instances were just as devastating for the Cabalists around those afflicted by possession of one sort or another.

The "lingering impressions"—called *ghosts* by some, not because they believed in ghosts but because they lacked anything better to call them—were usually malevolent and displaced. Those impressions knew nothing of the world today.

Some of the Cabalists, those who believed in unquiet

spirits, also chose to believe that the spirit world was trying to connect with them to give them more information. Warren didn't think that. The dead were dead and gone. That was the long and the short of it.

He forced himself up and into a kneeling position as he checked Naomi. He checked her airways and found them unobstructed, then watched the slow, rhythmic rise and fall of her breasts as she breathed. When he felt for her pulse, it was slow and steady.

Nothing appeared wrong.

"Naomi," he called.

She didn't reply, but one eyelid flickered a little.

"Naomi."

Still no reply.

Warren slipped a hand beneath her head and shook her shoulder a little. She didn't react. He felt tired and drained, as if he was going to fall over at any moment.

"She's all right," the voice said. "She's just sleeping."

"How do you know?" Warren demanded.

"Because I do."

"You're a book. You don't know everything."

The voice was silent for a moment. "I'm not the book, Warren Schimmer. The book is merely a gateway, a conduit I use."

"You said you've been locked away for years."

"I was. I still am."

Warren looked down at Naomi and tried to will her awake. He didn't want to be alone right now. Not when he felt so horrid and about to throw up because he was sick and scared.

"How can you be locked away?" Warren demanded. "You're here. With me."

"No. That book is the key to allowing me to interface with this world."

"What are you saying? That you're not here?"

The hesitation stretched out again. "I'm here, Warren. In this world. Just locked away from it."

"I don't understand."

"I was . . . bound."

"'Bound?' Bound by whom?"

"The demons."

"Why would they bind you?"

"Because I don't want them to have the power here that they want."

Warren thought about that as he held Naomi. "Could you have kept them from it?"

"It's possible I could have kept them from this world entirely."

"How?"

"Now isn't the time to go into that."

The urge to argue and push for answers gripped Warren. He pushed that feeling aside and tried to concentrate on Naomi instead. "When will be the time?"

"I don't know. There's still so much you have yet to learn."

Warren laughed at that, but tears rolled from his eyes. "I won't have a bloody lot of time to learn whatever it is you're going to show me. I've still got two demons to kill. And Fulaghar."

"I know."

"Unless you know of a way I can destroy Merihim." The thin hope dawned inside him before he knew it.

"You have to be patient. Merihim sows the seeds of his own destruction. That isn't for me to do. Nor you."

"I'm bound to him." Warren was conscious of the tears streaming down his face.

"You don't always have to be."

"How can I separate from him?"

"Now isn't the time for this."

"I don't *have* a lot of time."

"Neither does the world."

Warren wiped his face. "What are you saying?"

"I'm here to save the world, Warren. If events work out well, I'll save you too."

With Danielle at his side, Simon led the way through the passageway. They walked through the area where the demon Hargastor had been holding the humans it had captured.

"Why was the demon holding captives here?" Leah asked.

"Because this is where it was," Simon answered as he looked down at the corpses of Darkspawn and humans. Part of him felt as though he'd failed. There shouldn't have been any innocents on the battlefield, but he knew that wasn't how this war was going to be fought. The innocents were the prizes the demons sought.

"I don't understand," Leah said. "The demon said it was down here looking for a book. I assume that book is the same manuscript that we're looking for."

"This place isn't stocked very well as a library, now is it?" Danielle asked.

"No, but that doesn't explain why the demon would have people caged down here while it searched. There isn't anyone alive in these levels. It had to have brought them here. I don't understand why it felt the need."

"To torture them and kill them," Simon said as he moved on.

"That doesn't make any sense. Having prisoners involved in an operation is a colossal risk."

"The humans were entertainment," Danielle said.

"I have trouble believing that."

"This is what the bloody demons do," Nathan said.

"They torture and they kill anything weaker than they are. When they don't have humans around to subjugate and terrorize, they prey on each other."

Simon listened to the words and remembered how his father had told him similar things all his life. As a child he'd accepted his father's teachings without question. But as a young man he'd challenged everything—including the existence of the demons.

"You've lived through this mess for four years," Nathan went on. "Surely you've learned a few things during that time."

"I'm trying to get a better idea of what they're here to do. Understanding an enemy's wants and needs are tantamount to fighting them."

"Do you believe in good and evil?" Danielle asked.

"They're concepts," Leah said. "Architecture for processing behavior patterns."

"No," Nathan said. "Good and evil exist. At least, evil does. And in its purest form, evil is the demons."

The words sounded eerie and prophetic in the empty passageway. Simon felt chilled inside his armor and thought maybe that was a reaction to the injuries he'd received and the drugs in his system.

"They don't operate on Maslow's Hierarchy of Needs," Nathan went on. "They live to kill everything weaker than them. From what we've learned, they've destroyed hundreds of worlds before they found this one."

"But they're terraforming the city."

"The Burn?"

"Yes. They're remaking it into something they want."

"They're remaking it into a place where anything human can't live," Nathan said. "They're taking away the hiding places and home of their prey. Have you ever seen a forest fire? Not the fire itself, but the aftereffects."

Simon had. He remembered how the grass had been burned to black ash and the trees had been stripped of leaves and small branches by the hungry flames.

"Yes," Leah answered.

"The Burn is like that. It strips and changes everything. The animals that are there, the ones that miraculously lived through the fire, are generally sickened by exposure to the fire. And they have no place left to run."

"We—I—thought that the Burn was meant to acclimate our world into something resembling theirs."

"So they could live here?"

"Yes."

Nathan laughed. "You're naïve."

Leah whirled on the Templar and brought her rifle up. Simon halted and turned back to watch even though he could see everything that was happening on his HUD. Danielle started to step forward.

Simon placed a hand on Danielle's shoulder and opened a private communications channel. "No."

"She's going to attack him," Danielle objected.

"Wait." Simon watched Leah. After having known her for four years, he felt certain that if she'd decided to attack Nathan she would have already done so. However, the possibility of an attack still lingered.

THIRTY-THREE

"I'm not naïve," Leah said in a hard, cold voice. Anger twisted violently inside her. It was everything she could do to keep from hammering the Templar before her with the butt of her rifle.

The sights she'd seen down in the sanitarium were horrible even before they'd encountered the demons. She'd grown up with man's inhumanity to man. Her own family was dysfunctional. She'd become what she'd become in order to get away from them.

"I've spent four years watching men, women, and children die and have been unable to do anything about it," she continued in a thick voice. "I know how evil the demons can be. I just want . . . I just want to understand them more."

"That's where you're making your mistake," Nathan said softly. "You can't understand them."

"We've had our share of monsters too." Leah had personally encountered a few of them. The worst were those that had lived under the same roof with her.

"We're not like them," Nathan insisted. "Not even the worst of us on our worst day. No one we've designated as evil incarnate comes close to being as malevolent as the demons. Not Hitler. Not the Countess of Bathory. Not Vlad Tepes, also called Count Dracula."

Leah recognized the names, but it took a moment to

put them into context. As evil as those beings had been, she had to admit that they paled in comparison to the demons.

"All of those people wanted something," Nathan went on. "Even it if wasn't something we would want for ourselves, we could at least try to understand what motivated them. Control of the world. Eternal youth. To create fear in enemies. Killing, horrible killing and mass killing, was only a means to an end for them. For the demons, there's only the killing."

Leah still struggled with the concept. "What you're describing is a rabid animal."

Nathan's voice remained compassionate and understanding. "No, because rabid animals are diseased. They don't have complete control of their faculties. The demons aren't diseased or suffering dementia. Have you ever read H. P. Lovecraft's stories about Cthulhu?"

"When I was younger. They were too hard to read and I didn't understand them." Leah hadn't cared for them even though many of her fellow students had thought they were brill.

"We believe he was one of the people who came closest to understanding the demons," Nathan said. "The Templar think Lovecraft had an arcane ability—everyone knows he had an interest in such things—to touch the minds of things that lie beyond human understanding. When he wrote his stories, he gave flesh to some of the visions he'd seen in the minds of demons."

"What demons? That was a hundred years ago. The demons weren't here then."

"We believe the demons have been here for hundreds of years. They've been gathering information and preparing for the invasion. The Order found proof of them and tried to bring it to the attention of the world. In return, the Templar were stripped of their lands, wealth, and titles. There's some rumor, though it was never proven, that the demons had a hand in that as well." Nathan fell silent for a moment. "That's why we went underground and hid from the view of the world."

"How can you expect to win against opponents like those you're describing?" Leah asked in hoarse voice. It all sounded impossible to her. Her superiors had already accepted the inevitability of loss. Even the main Templar Order that Simon had separated from seemed to accept that.

Only Simon Cross and his group seemed determined to fly in the face of the odds.

"We don't have a choice," Nathan answered. "If we don't think we can win, if we don't believe we can save the world, why should we do anything?"

"Because we can't let them win," Leah said. Everyone in her group held onto that one absolute. If they couldn't win, then they also couldn't allow anyone else to win. It wasn't a victory, but it wasn't defeat.

"What does it matter if there's nothing left to save?" Nathan asked.

"We can't save this world, but perhaps we can save the next."

"You've already given up on saving this world?"

Leah squirmed under the mild rebuke she heard in his voice. She sensed Simon watching her and she imagined his disappointment. *You've got to accept the truth,* she told herself. *Don't give in to their foolishness. If you reach beyond what you're able to do, you'll fail at everything you attempt.* "Even if we could, everything we've known has been destroyed."

"If enough of us survive, we can rebuild the world," Nathan said.

"It won't be the same."

"Nothing is ever the same. The world changes and evolves and moves on every day even without being destroyed."

"But London—"

"Has been semi-destroyed a number of times," Nathan said. "The Black Plague. The Great Fire. The exhaustion of natural resources. The bombings in World War II. This is a great city. One of the eternal cities of our world. London will come back. We just have to clear out the infestation so that she can once more take root."

Leah stood silently.

"Look," Nathan said, "I don't know what your training is. I don't know what group you're affiliated with. But you—and they—don't know as much about demons as you think you do."

"They think that the Templar are fools."

Nathan chuckled. "Then they don't know much about us either."

"No," Leah agreed. She'd never met any warriors like the Templar. Not even those she'd served with. "I don't think that they do."

"Are we all done here?" Danielle asked. "Or do we want to hang around long enough for some other demon to come around looking for the one we just killed?"

Laughter exploded from Warren when he thought about what the voice had just told him. "You're here to save the world? That's what the bloody Templar claim they're trying to do."

"The Templar are trying to destroy the demons," the voice said softly. "That isn't the same thing."

"If you ask them it is."

"They don't know everything."

"I've heard the Cabalists talk about the Templar. The Templar have been studying the demons even longer than the Cabalists have been examining the powers of the demons. If there's anything they don't know—"

"They don't know what I know."

"I don't believe you."

"What you believe doesn't matter."

Warren hated the fact that the voice didn't have a face to look at. He would have stared it in the eyes and called it a liar.

"What would you do," he asked, "if I chose not to believe in you?"

"I would wait."

The quick answer unnerved Warren. He thought surely the threat would at least cause a momentary consternation.

"Wait for what?" he asked.

"For another who will believe."

"What if I destroyed the book?" Even as he asked that, Warren knew that he couldn't do that. There were too many unanswered questions he had about it.

"You can't."

Warren looked at Naomi lying cold and still on the floor in the center of the protective barrier he'd drawn. He wished she would just wake up. He didn't want to be alone.

"The book can be destroyed, Warren," the voice said. "But the idea behind it can't. When the book that you have is no more, another will appear just like it. The weaving was long and arduous, and it cost me a lot to do it, but it had to be done and I did it properly. I would do it again if I had to."

"How did you manage that if you're bound?"

"I'm bound. Not helpless. If I were helpless, I wouldn't be able to aid you."

"I can't see that you've aided me."

The voice was quiet for a moment. "I can help you now."

Warren waited. He wanted—no, *needed*—the voice to prove itself.

"You want the female to wake. I can help you wake her. And I can take away your pain."

Warren didn't say anything.

"Hold your hand over her forehead."

Gently, Warren placed the demon's hand over Naomi's brow.

"Not that hand," the voice said. "The other hand. The hand that is truly part of you."

Taking the demon hand back, Warren felt helpless. "I can't use the energy with my hand."

"You can."

"I *can't*," Warren replied angrily. "I've tried." That had frustrated him as much as anything. It was like the power that he used all the time tied him directly to Merihim.

"You've allowed yourself to become dependent on Merihim's hand because it was easier."

Warren shook his head. "No. That's not true. I can't get the energy to flow through my own hand."

"You were able to change your sight at the first meeting with the Cabalists four years ago. You've sensed danger all your life. You convinced a demon that it didn't see you when you first encountered one. You bound Kelli to you when you needed someone to guard you while you recovered from the wounds you suffered when Merihim arrived in this world."

All of those things were true. What astounded Warren was that the voice knew about them.

"More than that," the voice went on, "you used your gift to save your life when you were only a child."

Warren closed his eyes as the images filled his mind of his stepfather holding the gun on him after killing his mother. He remembered how fear had scored his stepfather's face when he turned the gun on himself and pulled the trigger.

"How . . . how did you know that?" Warren asked hoarsely.

"I know you," the voice said. "I know your secrets. I know things about you that you hide from yourself." There was a pause. "Now hold your hand over Naomi's brow."

Warren did.

"Feel for her using your powers," the voice instructed. "I'll guide you. After I show you this, you'll always be able to do it."

Warmth spread across Warren's palm. Vibrations shivered through his flesh. The skin across his shoulders tightened and turned cold.

"Her heartbeat is there," the voice said. "All you have to do is find it."

Closing his eyes, Warren felt. When he was about to give up, he felt the *thrum-thrum-thrum* of her heart. It felt muffled and almost hidden away.

"You feel it," the voice said.

"Yes." Amazement filled Warren and drove away most of the uncertainty and anger that coursed through him. "That . . . that's incredible." He stared, conscious of the fact that his hand was inches from Naomi's flesh.

Then he felt a *wrongness* in her heart. It was something that somehow didn't fit.

"What is that?" Warren asked.

"An imperfection."

Warren regarded the feeling. As he did so, an image formed in his mind. He remembered some of his biology classes. The heart was a muscle composed of four different compartments. All of them had valves that opened and shut. One of those in Naomi's heart felt weak and thin. It quivered beneath his touch.

"If that imperfection is left alone, it could kill her," the voice said.

Warren grew afraid. Few doctors were to be found in London these days. And the ones that could be found couldn't do something as demanding as heart surgery.

"Warren," the voice said softly, "you don't have to let it kill her."

"Then what?" His voice broke at the thought of being alone.

"You can fix it. I can help you."

"When?" The idea of letting Naomi live another moment with the weakened heart valve was intolerable.

"Now. Concentrate on that piece of her heart. Visualize it in your mind. I can see by your thoughts that you're familiar with what you're seeing."

"Yes."

"Concentrate on that piece and make it healthier."

Warren tried. He felt the heat and quivering in his palm grow stronger. But he felt the heart valve grow stronger as well. He visualized the valve getting thicker with muscle.

Suddenly the *thrum-thrum-thrum* of Naomi's heart grew more sure and more steady.

"You've done well," the voice said. "Do you feel the wrongness anymore?"

When he passed his hand over Naomi's heart, Warren didn't feel anything out of place. "No."

"Good. Perhaps you've saved her life."

Warren liked the idea that maybe he'd saved Naomi's life, but he knew that the voice could only have fooled him as well. The whole experience could have been only the power of suggestion.

"It was real," the voice insisted.

Warren hoped so.

"Now," the voice instructed, "reach into her thoughts and wake her."

Placing his human hand over Naomi's forehead, Warren felt for Naomi's attention. Images of the past few days, all of them from the young woman's point of view, flooded his mind's eye. Softly, he called her name.

Naomi looked up at him. "Warren?"

"I'm here," he told her.

"I thought I'd lost you."

"No."

"Hargastor is dead?"

Warren nodded. She tried to stand and he helped her to her feet. She stood for a moment and gazed around at the darkened room.

"Why didn't you tell me about your heart?" Warren said.

She looked at him. "What are you talking about?"

"You had something wrong with your heart." Warren couldn't let it go. He had to know if the voice was telling the truth or if it was lying to him.

"A murmur," Naomi said. "That's all the doctors told my parents it was. It was nothing to worry about." She knitted her brows as she regarded him. "I mentioned that while I was out? What an odd thing to do."

Warren shook his head and was shocked to learn he was smiling. "You didn't mention it."

"Then how did you know?"

"I learned something." Warren took her right hand in his. Half-healed cuts twisted around her fingers and across her palm. He hadn't even known they were there before, but he could sense them now. He passed his hand over hers, and when he did only smooth, unscarred flesh remained behind.

Naomi looked at her hand in amazement. "How did you do that?"

"With my power. Not Merihim's."

"Merihim chose you," the voice said, "because you already possessed this kind of power. He bound you to him to make you afraid and dependent on him. And to keep you from becoming all that you could be. Demons never do favors. They always strive for what is best for them."

Even you? Warren asked.

"Yes."

And what do you want?

"I've already told you."

To save the world.

"Yes."

I only want to save myself. As he looked at Naomi, though, Warren thought perhaps he might set his goal a little more generously than that. But only as long as both could be saved. He didn't want to die attempting to save her if that were impossible.

"You're part of the world," the voice said. "I want to save you too."

Warren didn't wholly believe the voice. He'd never wholly believed anyone except people who offered him harm. The voice still hid something from him, though. He didn't fool himself about that.

Naomi looked up from her hand and into his eyes. "Can you teach me this?"

"Perhaps." Warren strode from the protective circle and she followed. His thoughts were on Merihim. There were still two of Fulaghar's lieutenants to track down and kill.

If they didn't track him down and kill him first.

THIRTY-FOUR

"Sensor array available," the suit's AI stated.

"Execute," Simon said. The HUD flickered for just a moment as the system shifted from Danielle's borrowed sensors to the repaired system in his armor. Then he was whole once more.

The repair coming online also made Simon aware of how much time they'd spent in the sanitarium. Despite the fact that the higher demons often worked independently, the one they'd killed—or helped kill—would have been responsible to another demon. Someone would come searching.

He flipped through the button cams he'd left in strategic points throughout the underground levels. He saw the Templar they'd left on guard behind, but nothing else.

Only a few cells yet remained to be searched. The horror story of what had happened to the sanitarium's "patients" continued. Simon felt the heaviness of Leah's doubts and concerns. Despite whatever training she'd received and the four years she'd experienced, she hadn't been prepared for the war against the demons.

He wished he had words to say to her, but Nathan had told her as much as anyone could. From this point on, choosing what to fight for was a personal matter.

The next room Simon investigated had suffered a fire that had killed the person within. The skeleton lay curled up in a fetal ball in one corner of the room.

"When did the room burn?" Nathan asked.

"When this person was alive." Simon knelt beside the skeleton and picked up the tin locket that had corroded from moisture. Black carbon covered the locket's exterior.

"How do you know that?"

"The body's curled into a fetal position," Simon said. "Fire victims are usually found like that."

"Because they're trying to hide from the fire?"

"The fire burns the fluids out of the cartilage and tightens the victims up till it pulls them into that position." Simon gently brushed the corrosion and carbon from the locket. He wondered what would be inside: a picture of a loved one? A child? Parents? A lover or husband? The face of someone who had lost her or someone who had betrayed her? He knew the victim had been female because of the width of her pelvic bones.

When he opened the rusted-out locket, only ash spilled out. Whatever had been inside was gone. Tenderly, Simon placed the locket back on the corpse's chest.

"What started the fire?" Danielle asked.

"I don't know." Simon straightened and studied the scorch marks on the ceiling, floor, and wall.

"It started around the corner." Leah reached up and touched the low ceiling.

"How do you know that?" Nathan challenged.

"Part of the training I had." Leah walked out of the cell and back into the passage way. "You know demons. I know mayhem. My visual enhancements come with a fluoroscopy subset. I can see the burn patterns. The fire started in this cell."

The door was locked at the next cell. A burned skeleton lay at the foot of the bars. The entire interior of the cell was covered in soot.

"It was a chemical fire of some kind," Leah said. "Probably coal oil–based from the signature I'm reading."

"Then it was deliberate," Simon said. The thought chilled him as he looked at the small skeleton curled up at his feet.

"No doubts about that," Leah replied. "Whoever put the coal oil into this cell put plenty of it. Probably splashed some of it onto the bedding in the cell next to this one."

Simon glanced at the bronze plaque above the cell.

313

"Coincidence, mate?" Nathan asked. "Or is this cell directly below the other one?"

"Don't know." Simon called up a schematic on the HUD. The AI immediately calculated the distance they'd traveled since entering the sanitarium. The cross-sectional view of all four underground floors placed the new cell more or less beneath the one that had the walls covered with strange symbols. "Yes."

"Then I'd say that isn't a coincidence."

Simon silently agreed. Then he broke the padlock on the door and entered.

The interior of the cell was filled with black soot and ash. It hung thickly on the ceiling and walls and was thick as a carpet on the stone floor. Simon would have been reluctant about walking into the room without a filtration mask of some kind.

A skeleton lay curled at the back of the cell. This one was male, but almost child-small. There was no doubt about what had killed the victim: half of the head had been caved in. Soot caked the ivory bone.

When Simon knelt, a puff of black soot leaped into the air and temporarily obscured his vision. He wiped the soot from the broken skull.

"Looks like someone clubbed him to death, mate," Nathan said from his position at the doorway. "Maybe set the fire afterward to cover it up."

"Probably." Simon checked the rest of the body looking for clues about the victim's identity. "But why?"

"These people, the jailers and the patients, weren't the best of people, mate. We may never find out."

"And where did the extra ash come from?" Simon drew a forefinger through it and found it almost a half-inch thick.

Danielle knelt down and picked something up that was under the bars and partially in the passageway. She held up her prize. "Looks like part of a sheet. Whoever burned this person might have shoved laundry in here."

Leah joined Simon. "Let me see the skull," she said.

Simon slid back to allow her better access to the skeleton. When Leah tried to turn the skull, the spine snapped and it came off in her hands.

"Sorry," she said. "Didn't mean to do that."

"I don't think he's going to mind," Nathan said.

Leah held the skull in front of her.

"What are you doing?" Simon asked.

"Capturing images of the skull. We have programs capable of rebuilding faces from the bone up. Do the Templar have anything similar?"

"No." Simon knew the Templar would never need anything like that. But it raised several questions about Leah's "we" and what "we" did with information like that.

"How are you going to match that face?" Nathan asked.

"Through a database search." Leah gently returned the skull to the small skeleton.

"You people have everybody in your database?"

"I can check to see if there's a match here." Leah stood and gazed around the room. "There has to be a reason why he was killed. When did you say this part of the sanitarium was shut down?"

"I didn't. It was in the 1920s."

"No one's been here for a hundred years. Seems like someone would have wanted to bury these people."

"These people were put here to be forgotten," Leah said. "The fire just gave them a good excuse."

"The demon and the Cabalist were here tonight," Simon said. "Others could have been here before that."

Leah looked down at the small skeleton. "Whoever this was, he was killed down here and buried when the underground floors were sealed off." She paused. "And he was killed under mysterious circumstances in a location we're interested in."

"Your *we* or *our* we?" Danielle asked with only a hint of sarcasm.

"The database I'll be using is restricted. I'm going to share whatever I find out with you."

"Without trying to sound overtly suspicious, why would you do that?" Nathan asked.

"Because you can do more with the information than we can," Leah said. "For the same reason we turned Macomber over to you."

"Only to lose him to Booth's men," Danielle added.

Leah was silent for a moment. "I—*we*—didn't have anything to do with that."

"You could be playing both sides against each other."

"We're not."

"Did it ever cross your mind that whoever you're with might not be telling you everything?" Nathan asked.

Leah didn't reply.

"Something else I have to ask you," Nathan said. "What makes you think you're going to get the chance to return to whoever it is you work with?"

"We're going to let her go," Simon said. He didn't need to turn around to see them look at him in surprise. He saw their reactions on the HUD. More than that, he felt them looking at him.

No one said anything.

A moment later, Simon spotted a hairline crack revealed through the HUD. "Magnify."

The HUD's perspective changed as he focused on the fissure. It outlined a rough oblong near the bottom of the cell.

Simon leaned forward and formed "claws" at the ends of his gloves. He thinned them so they slid into the fissure easily.

"What is that?" Nathan asked.

Leah knelt down beside Simon.

"A hiding place." Simon popped the cover off. The piece of rock didn't fit exactly. It touched the outer perimeter of the hole hidden behind it in five places.

"The hole was dug out," Leah said. She dragged her gloved fingertips over the nearby stone surfaces. "Then the cover was chipped from another surface to make the cover."

Simon had guessed the same thing.

"Considering that such a feat took a lot of time because whoever did it didn't have proper tools, he must have been extremely determined."

"Or desperate," Simon added. He leaned down and looked into the hole behind the opening. His HUD cycled and increased his night vision.

A metal tube as thick as his wrist and as long as his forearm lay inside. Soot covered the tube and the inside of the secret vault.

"The soot drifted in through the cracks between the

wall and the false front," Leah said. "It wasn't airtight. That means the flames could have gotten in as well."

Simon hoped not. Gingerly, he reached inside and removed the tube.

"It's metal," Nathan said.

"That doesn't mean it was protected," Leah said. "Paper has a low flash point. I don't remember what it is, but I know it's highly combustible once it's exposed to enough heat. Judging from the condition of this cell, I'd say there was enough heat."

The tube was cast iron, not steel. It sagged at one end as though the fire had gotten almost hot enough almost long enough to melt it. A cap screwed on one end.

Excitement flared in Simon as he examined the tube. It looked old, even older than a hundred years. Markings scored one side but Simon couldn't read them. He'd studied a variety of languages, most of them orally but a few of them written. The markings in no way looked familiar.

He offered it to Danielle. "Do you recognize it?" She'd had more linguistics than he had.

Danielle studied it for a moment without taking it. "No."

Carefully, Simon gripped the cap and twisted. The wrenching shriek filled the cell. His audio dampers kicked in automatically to protect his hearing.

"Easy," Leah said.

Four full rotations later, the cap came off. Visions of the illuminated manuscript filled Simon's mind as he peered inside. Then those vanished as disappointment and outrage filled him.

"They're burnt," he whispered.

Thin curls of vellum had turned black. The sheets remained whole, but they weren't legible.

Simon started to toss the tube aside. He'd captured the

image of the tube's inscription. It was possible that they could uncover something about it in the Templar files he had access to.

"Don't." Leah grabbed the tube. "Be careful."

"It's no use," Simon growled. "The manuscript is ruined." He didn't let Leah take the tube, though.

"Maybe not," Leah said. "This isn't regular paper or it would have been gone. Some of the people I work with are artists at recovering lost documents." Her faceplate opened and she looked at Simon. "Please. Let me try to help you with this."

Silence filled the cell.

Simon didn't know what to do. Nothing the Templar had could recover the documents. *But do you want Leah and whoever she's working with to see these documents before you do?*

There was no easy answer.

"Simon," Danielle said.

"What?"

"Either you trust her or you don't." Danielle's voice was soft and easy.

Simon never took his eyes from Leah's face. She was beautiful and brave, and she'd placed her life on the line to save his. *That doesn't mean that everything she's done for you hasn't also served her.*

"Do you trust her?" Simon asked.

"It's not my decision," Danielle said. "You're the one that has the history with her."

"Nathan?" Simon asked.

"Like Danielle said, mate: if you trust her a little, you've got to trust her all the way. If you ask me, I think those papers are burnt beyond recognition. Anybody gets anything out of them, it'll be bloody magic. I don't see you got anything to lose."

Simon pulled the tube back and placed the cap back on it. "Let me think about it."

Leah's face didn't show anything, but her faceplate closed and sealed. "It's your decision, Simon." Her voice held no emotion.

Simon nodded toward the cell door. "Let's get out of here."

Leah accompanied the Templar back up to the surface. She remained aware of being an outsider the whole way. *It's your own fault,* she chided herself. *You need to pick one side or the other. You can exist in two camps, a good double-agent always can, but you can only swear loyalty to one.*

That was one of the first rules she'd learned in the deadly game she'd played since she'd turned twenty-one. Even back at university she'd been apart. Her family had taught her to live that way, alone and apart and whole on her own.

Simon didn't speak to her, and she was decidedly conscious of the fact that she wasn't going to talk to him. She was angry at him for holding back and not talking his feelings out. She didn't blame him for that; she didn't want to talk about her feelings either. In fact, she wasn't sure what she was feeling. Everything was mixed up. And that was stupid because it wasn't like any of them had a future.

A few minutes later, they stood once more outside Akehurst Sanitarium. The wounded Templar still rode the back of another. Simon checked on the wounded man, and Leah liked that he did that. But it reminded her how open the Templar armor was to attack from within. All of their armor was designed to support the unit so that subsystems overlapped. Leah's wasn't like that.

Simon turned to her and his faceplate irised open. She

was immediately struck by how tired he looked. He also looked uncertain.

Leah thought about the hidden fortress he'd established outside London. So many people, civilians and Templar, depended on him to be right. And he was so young, only a year or two older than her.

If the roles were reversed, would you be able to handle everything this life has asked him to deal with?

Leah didn't know the answer to that. She only hoped she'd never be in the situation Simon Cross had found himself in. Given her circumstances, she never expected to be.

"Where can we leave you?" Simon asked as they stood there in the overgrown grounds of the sanitarium.

An uncomfortable feeling of loss squirmed through Leah's stomach. She'd wanted to be released from the Templar, but she didn't know where the separation would leave them. If Simon told her to never come back or be in touch with him, she didn't know what she'd say. She only knew that she didn't want him to do that.

But her alliance to him—to whatever degree—was going to be a problem with the people she'd sworn her allegiance to. She cursed herself for getting into the position she was in. It was her fault.

"I can make my way from here," she told him.

He frowned in annoyance at that.

Leah knew he felt responsible for her. That was his nature, and it was partly why she had gone out of her way to help him when she had. Simon Cross was one of those individuals who could be given to, then counted on to give back at the appropriate time.

That made dealing with him difficult as well.

"I'm not comfortable with that," he said.

"Comfortable or not, that's how it's going to be." Leah

knew she was deliberately being stubborn. She could have allowed him to accompany her close to where she needed to go to rejoin her group. At the very least she could have pretended that.

Except that she had the distinct feeling that he would know if she were lying to him. She sighed in frustration. Dealing with him was hard.

"I want you to be safe," he told her.

"I've been taking care of myself in London by myself a lot more than you have," Leah pointed out. "I don't travel with a group as a general rule." Both of them knew that was true. Every time they had met up she'd been on her own. "What I'm able to do, I'm best able to do on my own."

"All right." Simon reached into his shoulder bag and took out the tube. There was no hesitation in him when he handed it to her. "If you get anything from this, you'll let me know."

"Immediately." Leah knew that she wasn't just accepting a task. She was accepting a responsibility that came along with a lot of strings. And she was accepting his trust in her.

She was also walking on the knife-edge of compromising herself with one side or the other. She put the tube in a rucksack on her back.

"It would be best if we got whatever information you might recover first," Simon said.

"I know," Leah said. But she was aware that both of them knew she hadn't agreed to his terms. She wasn't that free with her commitment.

"Be careful," Simon said. His faceplate irised shut. Then he turned and walked away into the shadows.

For a moment, Leah watched him go. Apprehension vibrated inside her as she wondered if she would see him alive again. She knew she would miss him if something happened to him. The world would be a lot colder place without him in it.

When she could no longer see him, Leah turned to go. She amped up her suit's camouflage capability and faded into the darkness.

THIRTY-FIVE

Warren sat in front of the book and flipped through the pages. Images stirred on them, but none caught his interest. He tried talking to the voice, but it was silent. He didn't know if that was because the voice didn't want to talk to him or because it had been more exhausted than it had let on.

Naomi slept in his bed. She'd been too worn to do much more than walk up the steps and lie down. Warren didn't know if her fatigue was from the energy she'd used from helping him or from his healing her heart valve.

The fact that he'd done so amazed him. He'd read about power like that. Eastern medicine gave the healing power several different names, but they'd all claimed it had existed.

He raised his human hand and flexed it. On impulse, he closed the book and got up. He walked to the bathroom and stood there for a moment.

With his enhanced vision, he saw the curtain draped over the full-length mirror on one side of the room. When he'd first moved in, he'd covered the mirror immediately because he could no longer face the monstrosity he'd become because of the patchwork demon skin stretched across his features. That alien skin had grown back in the areas where the burns had ravaged him worst four years ago.

He steeled himself, then stepped forward and waved—

his human hand—at a row of candles on the edge of the sunken tub. Flames sparked on the candle wicks and grew stronger as they burned. Then he pulled the curtain from the full-length mirror and gazed in numb horror at the ghastly sight of himself.

Even after four years of seeing himself, inadvertently at times, he still wasn't inured to the sight. These days there were other Cabalists who actually looked worse, but they did so by design and reveled in their appearance. Warren never would.

You're a monster, he told himself. *As foul-looking as any demon you've ever seen.*

Fearing the results, Warren raised his human hand to his face. He held his hand within inches of the demon's scales that covered his cheek. Then he willed himself to be healed.

Shimmering force passed from his hand to his face. But nothing happened. He tried again with the same result. Cursing, he gathered his power and blasted the mirror into a million gleaming shards that dropped to the floor and shattered again.

"What are you doing?" the voice asked.

"Nothing," Warren answered. "I was a fool. I did a foolish thing."

"Tell me."

"No." Warren figured that if the voice didn't know what was wrong with him, it wouldn't understand anyway. "It was a private matter. I'll be better served trying to figure out how to find Fulaghar or his remaining lieutenants."

"You're displeased with your appearance," the voice said.

Warren started to deny that, but he knew his feelings were so strong that he wouldn't be able to get away with that lie. "Yes," he whispered. "I'm horrid-looking and I can't bear it."

"Are you?"

A bitter laugh erupted from Warren. "Can you not see me?"

"Of course I can see you. You look a lot like most of the Cabalists. More fearsome than most."

"I'm not a Cabalist."

"You spend most of your time with them."

"Only because no one else would accept me." *And because of Merihim.*

"The Cabalists respect your appearance."

"That's not how I want to look."

"I thought your appearance was very unique."

"I don't want to look unique."

"Then how do you want to look?"

Warren looked down at the myriad images of himself looking back. "I want to look like me. Like the way I used to look."

"Show me."

"I don't have any pictures." Over the last four years, everything Warren had owned that was personal had been lost. After living in foster care, there hadn't been much of it anyway.

"Show me in your mind," the voice coaxed.

Quietly, Warren took a deep breath and pictured himself as he'd been. He saw his face as smooth, unblemished ebony. He'd been handsome, he knew that. Women and girls had told him that. He'd kept his hair cut short, not shaving his head until after he'd lost a third of his scalp in the fire. He'd always wanted to grow a mustache and goatee, but four years ago when he'd been twenty-three, he hadn't been able to.

"You prefer this appearance?" the voice asked.

"Yes."

"It isn't so different from the face you wear now."

"That was *my* face," Warren grated. "Not this patchwork horror."

"You can look like that if you wish."

"I can't. I tried."

"You tried to heal yourself," the voice said. "You're already healed."

"I'm not healed. I suffered third-degree burns. My own flesh died and was replaced by the demon's hide from my hand."

"I can help you look the way you wish."

Warren didn't want to get his hopes up. "The demon hide has claimed my face and my arm. My torso and legs are covered by more scales."

"You tried to eradicate the demon skin."

"Yes."

"You can't do that. It's become too much a part of you. You have to accept it."

"I have," Warren said. "I've accepted the fact that I'm going to look like this the rest of my life."

"Not if you don't want to."

Warren glared at his images. "How can I change this?"

"Let me help you. Reassemble the mirror."

Almost without thinking, Warren gestured toward the mirror fragments. The leaped from the floor and fitted themselves back to the mirror frame. In less than a minute, every piece had slid back into place and left the cracked surface facing Warren.

Then the mirror rippled, lifting and falling back into place. As it fell back into the frame, the mirror was once more unblemished and whole.

The horror that was him looked back at him. He wanted to shatter the mirror all over again.

"Try again," the voice coaxed. "This time don't try to heal yourself. Try to . . . sculpt."

"Sculpt? I'm no sculptor."

"You liked art as a child."

Warren's surprise grew. The voice knew so much about him it was unsettling. When he'd been a child he'd drawn the comic book heroes he'd read about. He'd also experimented with modeling clay. But he'd never been satisfied with the results.

"Try," the voice entreated.

Fear told hold of Warren then. He thought about how he'd been able to heal Naomi's heart valve. What if he really could reshape his face? Could he make it better? Or would he make it worse? Even more frightening, what if he'd do something irreparable to himself? What if he blinded himself?

"You won't do any of those things," the voice said gently. "Trust me."

Warren knew he had a hard time trusting anyone. He'd spent his whole life trying to live small, to be inconsequential and fly beneath everyone else's radar. But his stepfather had hated him enough to kill his mother and try to kill him. His flatmates had hated him in spite of the fact that financially he'd pulled more than his weight. He'd been passed over for promotions and fired from jobs because he'd drawn the ill will of others.

And he'd become enslaved to a demon and haunted by a talking book.

"I am not the book," the voice reminded. "The book is the key."

He'd had more than his share of bad luck.

"Trust me," the voice repeated.

Warren lifted his human hand. "All right."

"Close your eyes and think about how you want to look."

* * *

When Warren first began using the energy, his face turned hot. In places it felt as if it *slipped*. He started to open his eyes.

"Don't," the voice said. "This is very careful work and you're changing areas close to your eye."

Warren made himself wait. The movements of his hand weren't his own. A moment later, fierce bee stings ignited in his face along his chin. The flesh had burned away to the bone there.

Unable to keep his eyes closed, he looked at the mirror. His surprise muted the pain he experienced. Waves of shimmering force radiated from his hand and touched his face. Where the energy touched his face, new skin grew *over* the demon's scales. But the new skin was smooth, unblemished ebony just as he'd imagined.

"You can't reject the demon side of yourself," the voice said. "It will always be part of you now. But you can clothe it in your own flesh."

Warren watched in stunned fascination as the process continued. He controlled the pain and pushed it to the back of his mind.

"I apologize," the voice said. "There's nothing that can be done for the pain."

"It's all right," Warren said. "I've handled pain all my life. Continue."

Long minutes later, Warren looked at the face he'd imagined in the mirror. He couldn't remember if he'd ever looked exactly like that or if the features were idealized from what he could remember. In the end, it didn't matter. He looked human again.

Perspiration coated his face from the strain and the discomfort he'd suffered through. He was afraid that the thin coating of perspiration would wash away what he and the voice had accomplished.

"That won't happen," the voice said. "The changes you have made are permanent. Unless you're damaged or wish to change your features again."

"What about my power?" Warren asked. For the first time he thought about that. "The Cabalists scar and tattoo themselves to use the arcane energies that the demons brought into this world."

"Only because they believe they have to. Or because they wish to. Those who tap the Well of Midnight and choose a path through Darkness are marked in other ways that don't show on their bodies. Your power grows, Warren. Where the others borrow that energy, you've got Darkness inside you."

"What do you mean?"

"The Darkness is part of your being."

The thought twisted and writhed in Warren's head. It caused the pain at his temples to beat even more harshly. "Because of Merihim?"

"Merihim didn't put it there," the voice said. "It's always been there."

"Why?"

"I don't know. But it was probably what saved you from Merihim's attack four years ago."

"He said he spared me."

"He lied."

"Could he have destroyed me?" *Can he now?*

The voice hesitated, then answered. "Yes. You must be careful. The Darkness within you is strong, but it's not as strong as a demon. However, that Darkness within you is still growing."

Warren thought about that and was afraid. If he was tied to the Darkness, did that make him evil? Was that why no one had ever cared for him? Because they somehow sensed the taint?

"The Darkness isn't evil," the voice said. "Light and Darkness are merely two separate paths. Acceptance between those who walk separate paths is hard-earned."

Warren looked at his face and touched it with his human hand. A thin line of beard, just as he'd imagined it, ran from his sideburns to his chin. He'd never been able to grow that before.

He tried to comprehend the explanation he'd been given.

"Do you see Merihim as evil?" the voice asked.

Warren thought about all the things he'd done in the demon's name over the last four years. He'd snuffed out lives and taken things—like the book—that Merihim had wanted. And he'd given no regard to those lives because it came down to a decision between their lives or his.

"Yes," Warren answered.

"Merihim—and all of demonkind—is evil because he wishes to be. Even if he was allied with the Light, which would never happen because the demons were shut away from that path a long time ago, he would be evil. Light and Darkness are beginnings after a fashion. And an end. What a being does with the powers in between is up to that individual being. Do you understand?"

"I think so. But how does that apply to me?"

"Do you see yourself as evil?"

All the deaths at Warren's hands—*hand,* he corrected himself—swirled through his mind. People had died screaming from wounds he'd caused. They'd gone down beneath zombies he'd raised.

"No," he whispered. It had been their lives against his. No one could fault him for saving his own life. People in natural disasters did that all the time. No one would argue that the Hellgate was the worst disaster to ever occur. "I'm not evil." But he knew that others would think he was.

"Then you're not."

Warren tried to take solace in the explanation he'd been given, but he didn't know if everything could be weighed so simply. He peered at his image in the mirror. He certainly looked less evil than he had. But the demon hide still gleamed dark and liquid at his throat.

"Can we continue?" he asked.

"Yes."

THIRTY-SIX

"**Y**ou should get some rest, Simon. Standing there isn't going to heal young Mathias any faster."

Simon had to admit he was nearly out on his feet as he stood staring through the glass of the infirmary they'd built in the fortress. On the other side, Mathias was wired into a dozen different machines they'd salvaged from hospitals throughout London that no longer had the power or personnel to man them. They'd even gotten a few of them from Templar Underground areas that had been evacuated after the All Hallows' Eve battle at St. Paul's.

"I will," Simon replied. "I'd just like to spend a few more minutes here and make sure he's going to be all right."

Wertham joined him at the window. The other Templar was in his sixties, worn and haggard-looking from a lifetime of fishing on the Thames and in the North Sea. He'd been one of the Templar who'd lived full lives outside the Underground. His hair was a peppered mix of sandy blonde and gray. He wore a squared-off short beard that framed a generous mouth. Like the other Templar, he wore his armor everywhere throughout the redoubt except in his sleeping quarters.

"You've been standing watch for over two hours from what I'm told," Wertham said.

Simon didn't know that. They'd managed the journey back from Akehurst Sanitarium and hooked up with an

ATV without incident. There had been a brief encounter with a party of Gremlins, but they'd quickly evaded them and sped out into the countryside.

The surgeons, some of them Templar-trained and others recruited from London, had moved Mathias's broken ribs back where they belonged and used nanobond molecular adhesive to hold them there, reinflated his collapsed lung, and repaired other damage. The jury was still out on whether he would live.

"I felt that as long as I was watching him nothing would happen," Simon said.

Wertham nodded. "I understand the thinking, lad, but we've both been through enough battles that we know that isn't true."

"I know." All the same, Simon couldn't help doing it.

"You brought Mathias home. That's the most he could ask for under the circumstances. You and I have both come home without mates and fellow warriors we stood side by side with over these past four years."

Too many, Simon thought. He didn't say anything.

"I don't suppose you'd mind if I kept you company for a while," Wertham said.

"No."

For a time they stood in silence.

"You've talked to Nathan and Danielle?" Simon asked.

"I have."

"They told you I let Leah go?"

"They did."

Simon's eyes burned from lack of sleep and his body ached from the accumulated bruises. "Do you think I did the right thing?"

The old Templar looked at Simon. "I think you shouldn't be asking such things."

"Maybe I'm trusting her too much."

"Simon, if I can speak freely."

Simon nodded. "There's never been a time when you couldn't."

Wertham had been instrumental in helping assemble the train that had gotten so many out of London four years ago. He'd been at Simon's side ever since as they'd assembled the Templar and started waging their quiet war against the demons to free others that had been left trapped in the city.

More than that, Wertham had been largely responsible for getting Simon out of the Templar Underground after he'd fought with Terrence Booth, whose parents had died at All Hallows' Eve. None above Booth or of equal ranking stood beside Simon at that time.

"That's another thing I wanted to talk to you about," Wertham said. "I think you're far too lenient letting others talk to you and tell you their opinions."

"How else am I going to get their counsel?"

"There should be an order to it. A time and a place. If everybody keeps talking to you willy-nilly, nothing's going to get done."

Simon smiled. "And yet look at all we've accomplished."

Wertham frowned. "There needs to be more respect for your position, that's all I'm saying."

That jarred Simon and he didn't much care for the implication. "I don't have a position." He'd never assumed any position of authority. He felt he'd only guided.

"You're the leader here. You're our Grand Master."

"No," Simon said immediately. "The Grand Master is in the Templar Underground." The position was hereditary and always came through House Sumerisle. The Templar had always served the Sumerisle family, and they always would.

"We're split off from them," Wertham argued, "and have been for four years with no end of it in sight."

"That's a mistake. It will rectify itself." Even as he said that, though, Simon didn't know if it was true. Those who remained in the Templar Underground believed they should hide out from the demons until they were once more strong enough to take them on. After all the deaths at St. Paul's, though, that could take generations.

During that time the Burn would continue changing the world and the demons would continue to fill it. Simon hadn't been prepared to live with that. As it had turned out, other Templar—like Wertham—were of the same mind-set.

"We're waging our own campaign," Wertham said.

"We're saving people," Simon said. "And we're gathering information about our enemy."

"I understand that," Wertham said gently. "But I also know that the Templar were born and bred to order. To rank and file. For four years, we've more or less winged that down here."

"It's worked."

"Maybe so, but it's not going to work any more. Four years ago, when we started this thing and knew we might be dead tomorrow, we didn't have to worry about how we were doing things. Survival was the best we could hope for."

"It still is," Simon said.

"We've gotten larger than those few that came out of London on that train that night," Wertham said. "More Templar have come to serve with us."

Serve. The term bounced crazily inside Simon's head. Dying while losing to the demons wasn't a higher calling. Dying while triumphing over them was. It was all a matter of which way the body count went. At the moment, there were far too many demons.

"We're no longer so few and we're no longer so desperate," Wertham said.

"That could change in one day," Simon whispered hoarsely. It was a fear he lived with every day. "If the demons find us, we could be right back where we were. Where all of London is."

"But we're not, lad. And that's the thing."

Simon met Wertham's honest gaze but he couldn't bring himself to say anything.

"We need to form our own groups," Wertham continued.

"No," Simon said.

Wertham pursed his lips unhappily. "I'm not the only one who feels this way."

"Then there are a lot of you who aren't thinking clearly."

"They want to start a new House, and they want to call it House Cross."

Simon turned toward the older man and tried to keep a rein on the anger that filled him. He hadn't asked for this. He hadn't asked for any of this. "We are of the House Rorke."

"You and I may be," Wertham agreed. "And a few others. But there are more besides that are from all the Houses. Even some of them from the House Sumerisle are with us and want to be united."

"Splitting the Templar isn't the way to do it."

"Then you need to tell them that." Wertham crossed his hands over his broad chest. "Because that's what they want to do."

"I'm not going to allow them to start up a House in my name."

Wertham nodded. "It's not in your name. It's in your father's. Whether you know it or not, many of the Templar with us now were trained by Thomas Cross. They wanted something of him to live on."

Unable to speak, Simon turned away.

Leah made her way through the Ellis Building in the Limehouse District. Her destination wasn't far from Akehurst, but she'd taken her time getting there. What she was about to do and the probable reception she had waiting for her weighed heavily on her mind.

Not only that, but the way had been more difficult than usual. Demon patrols had taken to the streets with a vengeance. She didn't know if it had anything to do with what had taken place at Akehurst Sanitarium or not. She suspected that it might.

The Limehouse District lay on the north side of the river between Shadwell and the Isle of Dogs. In the past, it had been a major port for the English Navy. The locals had been called limeys due to the numerous limekilns in use at the various potteries that existed in the area. Gradually the name had spread to the English sailors, who'd been forced to drink rations of lime juice to prevent scurvy.

The Ellis Building had been erected in 2014 and named after a popular English writer. It had also been put to use by those that Leah served.

Staying to the shadows, mindful of the Soul Reaper clinging to the top of the eight-story building, Leah went up the steps. The Soul Reaper didn't overly worry her. The demon only preyed on the bodies of those recently slain. Living beings didn't interest it.

They tended to be crudely formed of writhing flesh and pulsed with what the Cabalists called "spectral" energy. This one looked like a cowled man from the waist up but had a serpent's tail that flicked restlessly. Four tendrils of purple-white energy opened and closed around it.

Leah went through the shattered doors and stepped into the lobby. Framed pictures of the author's creations hung on the wall and looked out of place in the devastation. Debris and corpses lay scattered on the floor.

Before the Hellgate had opened, the Ellis Building had housed independent businesses that included a travel guide, a temporary personnel placement office, an independent film studio, clothing shops, and other businesses. The upper four floors had held apartments.

Now they held nothing but the secrets concealed in the lower levels.

Leah entered a style shop containing swivel seats, sinks, and shelves that had been filled with product. All the product had been stolen in the early days after the invasion.

That anyone would steal hair care product at a time when London was being razed by demons had amazed Leah. Food and water were common sense, but gels and sprays were pure larceny. Of course, with her training those things could be used as weapons.

At the back of the style shop, Leah stepped into a closet and pressed a hidden switch over the door. The setup at the time had been a joke, an acknowledgement of a famous television show that had been on sixty years ago.

A hidden door opened in the back of the closet. Leah hesitated a moment before she entered. *This could be the last free breath you take,* she told herself. Then she stepped inside.

"Warren?"

When he heard Naomi's voice, Warren turned from the window where he'd been standing and letting the sun fall across his face. For four long years most of his face had been dead to the touch, all the nerves killed by the fire. Now he felt the warmth again.

"Yes," he said.

Shock filled her features. "Your face."

Warren smiled. "It is," he agreed.

"How did you do that?"

"I've learned more since you slept."

Naomi walked over to join him. She studied him with open fascination. "Is this really you?"

"It is." Warren captured her hand in his human one and brought her fingers to his face. He felt her touch against his skin. She was warm and smooth.

Her fingers started to peel back the turtleneck he'd put on to cover his throat.

"No," he said. "It is finished."

Naomi took her hand back. "This is what you looked like before Merihim claimed you?"

"Mostly. I don't have any pictures to go by. All I have is what I remember." Warren took one of her hands and turned the palm up. The scar that he remembered was there. He couldn't remember how she'd gotten it exactly. There was a half-remembered tale of a chase through an alley.

He concentrated for just a moment, imagining the skin whole and unblemished. Shimmering force radiated from his palm. The scar vanished.

Naomi took her hand back. "That's amazing. The Reiki teachings say that people can learn to do things like this for themselves, but not for others."

"They're wrong," Warren said. He studied her horns and the tattoos she wore.

The horns had been grafted to her head by small demon symbiotes the Cabalists had learned to control. Most of the grafting had been done through arcane energy or fire, sutures or symbiotes. In some cases, the most desperate among the Cabalists used a blend of technology and arcane forces.

"I could remove those horns and erase those tattoos," he told her. "Like they'd never been."

Naomi quickly stepped back and raised a hand to protect herself. "No."

"You don't need them."

"They help me use the power," Naomi said. "I won't give up what I've learned."

"The power doesn't come from those things," Warren said. "It comes from inside you."

"A little of it comes from inside me. I've never been as powerful as you have. I *borrow* the power. I don't create it and command it the way you do."

"Do you like looking like that?"

Hurt gleamed in Naomi's eyes. "You've never said there was anything wrong with the way I looked."

"I'm not saying there is now." But Warren knew that he wanted to see what she had looked like before she'd grafted the horns on and inked the tattoos. In his mind's eye she would be beautiful. "But you could go back to the way you were. I could give you that."

Naomi crossed her arms. "You could also take away my power and leave me defenseless. Is that what you want to do?"

Warren let his hand fall to his side. "No."

"I'm not Kelli," she said. "I can stand up for myself. I can take care of myself." She paused. "I won't give that up. Not for anyone."

"I could take care of you."

"I don't want to be taken care of. I don't want to have to trust anyone to take care of me."

"I trusted you to take care of me last night."

Naomi eyed him harshly. "That was one night, Warren. And you didn't have a choice. Merihim pushed you into that confrontation. If I hadn't been here, you still would have had to have gone. That's not trust."

Knowing that what she said was true pained Warren. He'd made deals with other kids in foster care. While they'd been together in one house or another, they'd watched each other's backs. Trust still hadn't been easy.

"If you don't trust me, why do you come here?" Warren asked.

"Because I can learn from you. The way you used to learn from me."

"What if you couldn't learn from me?" Warren stared into her eyes.

"Are you telling me you're not going to teach me?"

"What if I did?"

Naomi's eyes turned flat and cold. "Then I would find someone else who could teach me."

Warren turned from her and walked back to the window to stand in the light. He'd liked her more when she was asleep.

"I don't have a choice either, Warren," she told him. "You're serving a demon. And I've got to survive in a city that's overrun with demons. I have to learn everything I can every day. Just to stay alive. I can't control zombies the way you can or stand toe-to-toe with demons like Hargastor."

For a moment Warren thought he heard jealousy in her words and it surprised him. He couldn't imagine that he had anything anyone else would want.

"I like you," Naomi said in a softer voice.

"Because I can teach you," Warren said with soft sarcasm.

"That's part of it. I have to admit that or I'd be lying to you. But that's not all of it."

Warren heard her approach him and he thought about telling her to stay away. He would have if he didn't dislike being alone so much.

"I'm sorry if I hurt you," she said.

"You didn't hurt me," Warren said in that old litany he'd learned in his childhood. "I was just foolish enough to hurt myself."

"I'll go if you want me to."

Part of him wanted to tell her to go, but he wasn't strong enough for that. He'd let her into his world, and now he was going to have to suffer the consequences.

"No," he said. "I don't want you to go."

Naomi took his hand and held it tightly. It took him a moment to realize that she'd taken the hand that Merihim had given him instead of his human hand.

THIRTY-SEVEN

S tanding in the elevator and waiting for the cage to descend, not knowing if it would or if she'd be sprayed with a nerve toxin that would kill her in seconds or vaporized with energy beams, Leah knew she was being surveyed by sophisticated equipment that peeled her clothing and her flesh away, and even scanned her skeleton.

"Leah Creasey," a mechanical voice said above her.

"I am Leah Creasey," she said automatically. "I'm a citizen of Great Britain and will lay down my life for my king and my country."

The response was necessary and allowed the security systems to compare her voiceprints with records on file. She had to update the file on a weekly basis to keep it current.

"Open your suit."

Leah did, but she took a deep breath and held it in case the elevator cage suddenly filled with gas. It was a ridiculous response to the possibility. If the cage were flooded with gas, she wouldn't have to breathe it to be dead.

And it would be colorless anyway.

"You can breathe, Leah," a male voice said.

"Thank you," Leah said, feeling foolish. Still, she was tense as she breathed in, and maybe a little surprised when she remained conscious.

The elevator cage dropped. For a moment Leah felt weightless. Then gravity returned and tried to claw her to the floor. She knew she'd dropped over three hundred feet.

The Templar weren't the only ones with secrets.

"I'm powering your suit down," the male voice said.

Leah felt the extra weight of the suit suddenly pull at her. She knew the exoskeleton built into the suit had a lot of the same designs the Templar armor had. After all, the designs had been *lifted* from the work the Templar had pioneered, then reverse-engineered and rendered into something that fit more in with how she was expected to use it.

Despite the outside control, Leah's suit had been built to deny the power-down command. That was solely within her discretion. But if she hadn't powered down, she'd never have made it out of the elevator alive.

"There is an escort waiting for you," the male voice said.

"I understand," Leah said. "But I need to speak to someone in Ops."

"Go through channels. Speak to your handler."

"Affirmative." Leah stood straight and tall.

When the elevator doors separated and opened, six armored men and women stood waiting to receive her. All of them carried small arms naked in their fists. With their helmets in place and their armor unmarked, Leah didn't know if she knew them or not.

"Let's go," one of them said as he motioned her out of the cage. They took the metal tube containing the burned manuscript.

"Be careful with that," Leah said. "It's important."

"We just want to make sure it isn't a bomb," the man said.

"If someone thought it might be a bomb, I'd never have been allowed down here." Leah knew her voice was tight with anger despite her best intentions not to feel that way.

Leah knew the underground complex wasn't large. Their operations weren't meant to be. They were self-contained units with limited manpower and limited risk of exposure.

The six guards took her by the shortest route to her room. One of the guards even told her that they had *her room* ready for her.

It was a joke. No one lived in the underground complex. Her quarters was a small room set up with two bunk beds for wounded or unassigned to float until arrangements could be made.

"I need to speak to my handler," she told the leader of the six-man team.

He was a young man about her age with a military haircut even four years into the demon invasion. Scars that looked like barely healed weals from a demon's claws marred the right side of his face. He looked like he'd been lucky to keep his head.

"Sit tight," the man said. "Someone will be with you."

"What I've brought is hot. I don't want to let it cool."

The man gave her a stone face. "Someone will be with you," he repeated. Then he closed the door on her "quarters" and locked her in.

A selection of paperback books and vids occupied a small shelf on one of the walls. As usual, the selection was eclectic and consisted primarily of whatever people brought in.

Tension tightened Leah's nerves, but she didn't want to let it show. She knew she was being observed through concealed video and audio systems. It was standard procedure for an agent who'd been out in the field.

Especially one that's been off the grid, Leah thought sourly.

She stripped out of her armor and hung it in one of the metal lockers. A quick check, standard operating procedure on her part, revealed that no one else was currently checked into the room.

She took a quick shower because she hadn't been out of the suit in hours, then tended to it, cleaning it inside and out. Antibacterial nanobot foam zipped through the armor in seconds and left it operating room clean.

Dressed in khaki shorts and a sleeveless olive T-shirt, Leah pushed her frustration aside and concentrated on filling her time. That was what she was supposed to do when she was confronted by a situation like this.

A quick check through the library netted a techno-thriller that had all the equipment and SOP errors marked in the margins, as well as a few choice comments about the author's lack of military experience. She chose a fantasy novel that she'd read bits and pieces of before the Hellgate had opened and settled back onto one of the beds.

With her memory enhanced with X-Brain neural implants created by SofWire, she picked up on the exact page she'd last been reading. After a while, even though the writing was sharp and clever and the hero's perils were many and large, she pulled the book down onto her chest and slept.

"The Templar is in disarray, Simon." Wertham sat across from Simon in the small room they'd claimed after Mathias's condition had improved.

Simon ate the pork chops, potato soup, and fresh-baked bread listlessly. He was tired and wanted to sleep, but he knew if he didn't sleep deeply enough all he'd have were nightmares and he wouldn't rest. Food would put him to sleep better, and he needed to build his strength. He'd lost weight lately.

"Grand Master Sumerisle died in the Battle of All Hallows' Eve," Wertham went on.

"I know," Simon said. "The Grand Master led the charge." He'd met Patrick Sumerisle on a few occasions and had always been impressed by the man. Thomas Cross had respected him like no other.

The Grand Master had lived out in the public eye. He'd been involved in the British military and had been a member of the Home Office Ministry.

"A finer man never walked this earth," Wertham said. "But his brother Maxim is another matter entirely."

Simon knew that no one had cared much for the Grand Master's younger brother.

Wertham broke a loaf of bread and pushed a chunk into his soup bowl. "You've heard that Maxim tried to take over as Grand Master?"

"Yes." Simon didn't elaborate or venture an opinion either way. What the Templar Underground did wasn't his concern. He concentrated on saving lives.

"Nearly every other House voted against that," Wertham said. "As well they should have. Maxim is a madman."

Simon concentrated on his dinner. As soon as it was finished, so was the conversation. He fully intended to go to bed.

"But it didn't stop him from becoming Seneschal and High Lord of House Sumerisle."

"It was his right," Simon pointed out.

"Oh, and I agree." Wertham's face softened and some of the craggy wrinkles smoothed out. "Don't get me wrong,

I'm not here to simply cast stones. I want you to take note of what the Templar Underground is dealing with."

"There is Jessica Sumerisle," Simon said. His father had known all the members of House Sumerisle. As a result, so had Simon. "I've heard she's intelligent and shows a lot of promise."

Wertham snorted. "She's just a girl. Barely twelve years old, if that."

"The demons went after the Sumerisle family the night the Hellgate opened. Jessica Sumerisle was one of the targets. From what I hear, she barely got away that night. A lot of people didn't."

"She's years from being able to lead her House, much less the Order."

"There's another Sumerisle." Simon barely remembered the girl.

"Avalon." Wertham nodded. "She's seventeen now." He sighed. "Most of those with experience to lead the Templar during these times were wiped out in the battle four years ago." He looked at Simon. "This is why we need someone to stand up for us. For all of us. Maybe then the Order can be reunited and grow strong again."

Simon shook his head. "That's not me."

"It could be."

"It can't be." Simon drew a deep breath and pushed his food away. He'd had all he could stomach. "I turned my back on the Templar two years before any of this happened. I abandoned them. I didn't believe in my father or the way I'd been taught all my life."

Wertham was quiet for a moment. "We've all had our moments of disbelief, lad. All our lives we'd prepared for a war with the demons, and—before All Hallows' Eve— none of us had ever seen one in the flesh. Your mistake has been forgiven. They've seen what you've done."

"Since I turned my back on them again? Since I let them know that I didn't believe in the Templar way a second time?"

Wertham frowned. "It's not like that. Four years, filled with death and sorrow and misery and fear, is a lifetime. People forgive and forget."

"Not everyone has forgiven me," Simon said as he stood. He reached down for his helm. "*I* haven't forgiven me. Four years isn't even long enough." He turned and walked to the door. Then he paused. "Tell the others to give up trying to make me out to be anything more than I am. Let me serve as I can to save those we can and fight the demons when we're able. That's all I ask."

Simon left the room and headed for the barracks. He had to get some sleep before he fell over.

Wake up!

Merihim's command exploded inside Warren's head and yanked him up from blissful slumber. He'd slept on his back, with Naomi's cheek against his and one of her horns pressed to his forehead. The pain of the demon's voice drove him from the bed to his knees.

What do you think you're doing? Merihim demanded. *You're supposed to find Fulaghar's lieutenants.*

"I will," Warren said.

Across the room, a pair of eyes opened on the book. They regarded Warren in silence. But as soon as those eyes made contact with his, some of the pain in his head dissipated. He got control of the nausea cycling through his stomach.

You're wasting time.

"I don't know how to find them."

Then come. I'll show you.

The pain dragged Warren to his feet and out onto the

balcony. He hated being there. Toxic rain fell from the leaden sky masking the moon and spattered across his naked shoulders. The drops left chemical burns behind.

Below in the city, the demons prowled and some of the braver humans hunted for enough food to get them through another day or two. Warren feared that he would attract a demon's attention, and he kept imagining that he heard claws clicking against the rooftop overhead.

A Blood Angel swooped through the street in front of Warren. She never turned in his direction.

Her, Merihim said. *Use her. She can find Knaarl.*

Warren recognized the name as that of one of Fulaghar's lieutenants. "How am I supposed to use her?"

See through her eyes. Just as you use the other Blood Angel eyes you have.

Warren wanted to point out that he'd bound those eyes to him, and that he'd spent days doing it. But he knew it would be no use. It was better to try and fail.

Unless Merihim killed him out of frustration.

"He won't kill you," the voice said. "Not yet. He needs you too much."

The pain inside Warren's head exploded again. He almost dropped to his knees and reached out to the balcony railing for support. His vision turned red—

Then it cleared, and he realized he wasn't seeing through his eyes any more. As he stared, his head pounding somewhere far away, he watched the London cityscape spin by below him. His vision was incredibly sharp, even clearer than it was when he enhanced it. For a moment he saw himself standing in the rain on the balcony. The rain drummed down on him and he felt burning sensations, but they were so far away they seemed more irritating than harmful.

The Blood Angel saw everything with more color and

vibrancy than anything Warren had ever experienced. There were colors that he had no names for. And seeing prey was simple.

Warren watched in amazement as the Blood Angel spotted a man edging through the darkness near a tube station. Heeling over, the demon went in pursuit, dumping altitude like a fighter jet as it whipped through the city.

The man never knew what hit him. He was alive one moment and dead the next. Hooking her rear claws into the dead man, the Blood Angel flew her prize to the nearest building and tore the corpse to pieces to feed to a nearby group of Stalkers.

The Stalkers growled and fought among themselves for the remains.

Overcome by revulsion, Warren vomited. He was weirdly aware of being in two places at the same time: on the balcony and inside the Blood Angel's head.

Knaarl, Merihim said.

Warren knew the Blood Angel heard the name as well. Her perspective changed as she peered around. Then she took wing once more and Warren's sight rode along with her.

THIRTY-EIGHT

While he stared at the city below him, Warren wondered why Merihim didn't simply use demons as his servants instead of him. They would have gotten around much more easily and been less noticed.

"Because they don't have the untapped power that you do," the voice said. "And because other demons would eventually resist Merihim's control because he has no right in this place to command them. The Blood Angel is a deadly foe, but she'd be no match for Knaarl. She wouldn't have lasted against Hargastor either."

"But if Merihim could bind more than one demon to his will—"

"He can't. Not without losing a measure of control. As you can see now, even you have your secrets from him. It helps that you have my protection, but Merihim isn't as invincible as he'd like you to believe. Not in this place."

Warren couldn't get the night of destruction that Merihim had arrived in London out of his mind. Cabalists had died by the dozens. Invincible or not, the demon was deadly.

"If he isn't so invincible," Warren said, "then why don't you confront him?"

"Because I'm not strong enough to defeat Merihim. As I've told you, I'm bound. All that I have open to me is subterfuge. My powers will grow just as surely as yours are. It will just take time."

Time was one thing Warren wasn't sure he had, though. He was surprised that Merihim didn't say anything about the way he looked. To him, his appearance had drastically changed.

"He doesn't see you," the voice stated. "He only sees the power you can wield for him."

Minutes later, the Blood Angel glided to another building, this one overlooking the British Museum. The demon held her position there and studied the structure.

Knaarl is here, Merihim said. *Doing his master's bidding.*

"Why is he here?" Warren asked. He drew back from Merihim's instant anger and almost lost touch with the Blood Angel Merihim had enthralled. "I need to know if I'm going to hunt him. Will Knaarl be here long? If not, will he be here again?" He waited silently for the blow he felt must surely be coming. Even out of his body, he knew he would feel agony if the demon wanted him to.

Merihim stayed his hand, though. *As Hargastor did, Knaarl hunts for an artifact that Fulaghar wants.*

"What artifact?"

Teeth.

"What kind of teeth?" Warren asked.

In Greek myth, Cadmus sowed dragon's teeth and mighty warriors sprang up from them.

The answer astounded Warren. His mind reeled for just a moment. "Dragons never existed."

"Yes they did," the voice said. "Humans have just never recognized them for what they were."

It doesn't matter, Merihim replied. *All that you need to know is that Knaarl will be here looking for the dragon's teeth. You have to come here and kill him.*

In the next instant Warren stood once more on the balcony of his sanctuary. Pain from the acid rain ate into his shoulders. He grew conscious of Naomi pulling at him.

"Get in out of the rain," she pleaded.

Warren turned and walked back into the room.

"What were you doing out there?" Naomi retreated to the bathroom and returned with towels. She mopped at the rain that still covered him and sizzled against his flesh.

"Merihim summoned me. I had no choice." Warren seized her hands in his and stopped her toweling efforts. She was only spreading the caustic liquid. Blisters rose on his skin.

"You need to take a shower before you're poisoned." Worry pinched Naomi's features.

Instead, Warren concentrated and tapped into the energy that filled him. He found each of the burns and healed them swiftly till he was once more whole and pain-free.

Naomi gazed at him in a mixture of envy and admiration. She ran her hands along his unblemished skin. "I can't believe you do that so effortlessly."

The healing wasn't effortless, though. Warren felt the drain and knew that he would have to rest to replenish what he'd lost.

"What did Merihim want?" Naomi asked.

"He's found one of the other demons. I have to destroy it."

"When?"

"Soon." Warren thought about the British Museum and how hard it would be to sneak up on the place. There was only one approach to the building, and the road to it was narrow and winding. The slim entrance to the courtyard was a perfect place to be ambushed.

"I can help you find a way," the voice said. "There are secrets that even Merihim doesn't know."

Warren didn't doubt that. The voice had its own secrets. He just wondered what the voice would do when their desires and needs no longer paralleled. He was just as much at the mercy of one as he was of the other, and he didn't know which offered the greater threat.

Simon worked out on the gymnasium floor. He flowed through the unarmed katas his father had started training him in since he could walk. It was there, on whatever space he had available to him, that he felt closest to his father.

He wore only sweat pants, went bare-chested and barefooted. Perspiration dappled his body and heat filled his muscles. His head was clear and he was more focused than he had been in days.

All he had to do was close his eyes to see his father standing at the sidelines or beside him. They'd often worked out together, going through the forms, then battling each other with empty hands or practice swords till one or both was rubber-legged and could no longer stand.

It was also during these times that Simon missed his father most. No matter how hard they pushed themselves, or how long they had been at a session, Thomas Cross had always seemed to have enough breath to speak.

Sometimes his father had offered only further instruction, or bits of history about the Templar Order and the various Houses. Hundreds of years of history—filled with wars and subterfuge and feats of derring-do—waited to be brought to life with Thomas Cross's natural storytelling ability.

Simon had been held enraptured as a boy and a teen, and sometimes even as a young man, by those stories. No one, it seemed, knew as many stories as his father. Even the ones he told over and over again, to illustrate a virtue or put a fine point on a lesson, held Simon's attention.

But it was the ones about Simon's mother that Simon treasured most. He had never known Lydia Cross. Despite Templar technology, she'd died in childbirth and had held her son for only minutes before death stole her away. Simon's father had told him that he favored her, and sometimes Simon would catch his father gazing at him and see the pain and loss in his father's eyes.

Finished with the latest form, Simon stood and drew in a breath. He was aware of some of the other, younger, Templar watching him. A few of them were barely in their teens, and their youth had troubled him.

When the first of them had shown up in the care of other Templar, Simon had wanted to send them back. They'd slipped away from the Templar Underground, and Terrence Booth and the other Lords and Ladies of the Order had been understandably upset.

Taking the fugitives back had proven problematic. The first few that had been returned had quickly run away again. A few of them hadn't made it through the demon patrols the second time.

Simon had also found out that all of the young Templar coming to join him had been orphaned by the Battle of All Hallows' Eve. Booth and the others protested the loss of the young Templar, but they'd been determined to come once they'd found someone that could guide them to the hidden fortress.

None of them had come without sponsorship, and Simon had given up trying to find out who was responsible. Wertham and the others had remained closed-mouthed in the matter. In the end, Simon had stopped sending the young Templar back and had chosen instead to let them live among his group.

His group.

The thought stuck in his head and he recalled Wertham's argument that they should start a new House. He was torn. It would be a fine tribute to his father. Thomas Cross had been one of the most loyal Templar ever to wear the crimson cross of the Order. Everyone knew that. Whatever problems the Templar had with Simon weren't visited on his father.

"Lord Cross," Anthony, one of the teen Templar, called out.

Simon wasn't used to being addressed as such. His father had been Lord Cross of House Rorke, and even Thomas Cross hadn't often gone by his title, choosing instead to be known by his station as a Knight of the Order. The Cross lands and holdings had been meager, grown so by the constant and unswerving service of the family to their House and to the Order.

"Yes, Anthony." Simon also made it a habit to know everyone in the fortress. The boy preened at the mention of his name, then quickly hid his reaction. Simon picked up a towel from his gym bag and wiped his face and upper body. He was surprised at how many of the young Templar—boys as well as girls—stood in attendance. There were at least forty of them, almost enough to fill the gymnasium floor.

"I would ask a favor of you, Lord Cross." Anthony was dark-haired and blue-eyed. He might have been all of eleven years old.

Simon was conscious of the attention of the rest of the group on him. A few adult Templar stood nearby and watched.

"What do you wish?" Simon asked.

"Would you lead us in the Way of the Sword?" Anthony replied.

Simon looked at the youthful faces. "There are others more skilled than I am in the sword."

"I've heard that isn't true, Lord Cross. I've been told that none are as skilled as you."

Embarrassment flushed Simon's features with sudden heat. "Did Nathan put you up to this?"

"No, Lord Cross." Anthony looked pensive. "I'm sorry if I offended you. I offer my apologies."

"You don't need to apologize." Simon felt even more awkward. He'd only come into the room to stretch out a few kinks and limber sore muscles. And to forget that Leah hadn't yet gotten in touch with him. "You haven't offended me."

Anthony bowed and started to leave the mat. The other young Templar stepped back as well.

Danielle stepped from the sidelines. "Don't you dare let them leave this floor feeling ashamed," she whispered. "It took quite a lot for them to get the nerve to ask you."

"'Them?'"

"You don't think Anthony went to the others, do you?" Danielle asked. "They forced Anthony to ask you." Her eyes flashed. "All they want is some of what they perceive to be your strengths and courage to rub off on them."

"That's foolish," Simon said.

"Not to them. To them you're Simon Cross. *Lord* Cross. And you're the bravest Templar they've ever seen. You fight demons on a regular basis, and you win. They want to know that they can be part of that."

"I'm nothing special," Simon protested.

Danielle stared at him fiercely. "To them, you are. It's hero worship."

"It's misplaced."

"Who else should they put their faith in?"

"Themselves."

"They're not ready to do that yet. Don't you remember what it was like to be their age?"

Simon did.

Danielle nodded over Simon's shoulder. "Are you going to let them just walk away?"

Simon wheeled and looked at the young Templar. None of them looked back. All of them were walking away without a word.

"Anthony," Simon called.

As one, the young Templar stopped and turned back. All eyes focused on Simon.

"Yes, Lord Cross," Anthony said.

"I have to apologize for my behavior," Simon said in a formal tone. "I've done you a disservice. All of you."

"You've done us no disservice, Lord Cross. We should not have bothered you."

"I should have listened to you better, little brother," Simon said. "You asked for instruction. I'm bound by my honor to teach you what humble skill I have in the Way of the Sword."

Anthony grinned.

"On the mat," Simon said. "All of you."

Quickly, the young Templar lined up in four rows of eight with two stragglers in the fifth row. They moved with military precision and gave themselves plenty of room. All of them carried palladium swords smithed to a size that properly fit their hands. New swords would be forged as they grew.

"Take up your swords." Simon took up his own and stood in front of them. Instead of holding it in his left hand, he held it in his right. He was naturally left-handed, and his father hadn't tried to correct that as so many Templar fathers did. Instead, Thomas Cross had taught him to fight with either hand. Thomas Cross had also trained himself to be ambidextrous.

"Lord Cross," Anthony said, "you're left-handed."

Simon was surprised they would know that about him. When he did forms, he kept all the exercises balanced. Battlefield conditions changed constantly. Not everyone could make adjustments like that.

"I can wield a sword with either hand," Simon replied.

"So can we." Anthony presented his sword and switched it to his left hand. As one, the other young Templar did the same thing.

Stifling a grin, shocked that he could be amused while still aware that the young boys and girls before him might one day fight and die while using the same skill set they were preparing to exercise, Simon shifted his sword back to his left hand.

"All right," he said. "Let's begin."

Leah woke when the locking mechanism activated. She didn't move from the bed and kept her arms crossed behind her head while she lay on her back.

Instead of the six-man guard unit Leah expected, only one woman stood there. She was of medium height and had fair hair chopped at shoulder length. Green eyes regarded Leah coolly. Thin and athletic, she looked as if she was in her mid-thirties, but only because Leah automatically assumed the woman was older than she was. Her right temple and cheek held a faded webbing of scars. She wore black armor and carried the hood tucked into her belt. She carried no weapons outside of those built into the suit.

"May I come in?" the woman asked.

Leah smiled. "Politeness from the jailer?"

"I'm not your jailer."

"The inquisitor, perhaps."

The woman smiled, and it was an honest and good smile. "Not even that."

"Are you Greek then? I don't see a horse in sight."

A frown creased the woman's face. "Sarcasm wasn't overly noted in your field service report."

"It's a newly acquired skill."

"I doubt that. You're flirting with insubordination."

"It's hard not to be insubordinate to a command structure that throws you in lockup."

"Yes it is. A few years ago, I found I wasn't terribly fond of it either."

Leah studied the woman and wondered if she were being played. Was this Command's version of good cop/bad cop? She wasn't sure. The woman had sounded sincere.

"If this isn't a good time, perhaps I could come back later." The woman reached for the door control.

Leah wanted to force the issue and find out if Command would put her back on ice again. Unfortunately she felt certain the answer was yes.

"Come in," Leah said. She threw her feet over the side of the bed and sat up.

As the woman entered the room, the door slid shut and locked behind her. "I'm Lyra Darius."

The name didn't mean anything to Leah. Of course, it could have been an alias. People in her line of work often had two or a dozen names.

"I'm afraid there aren't any chairs." Leah waved to the bunk opposite the one she sat in.

Lyra sat without hesitation. "So," she said in an amiable manner, "here we are."

Leah waited.

"I asked to debrief you," Lyra said.

"I don't know you."

"Nor should you. We've never met."

"Why are we meeting now?"

"Because, like you, I have an affinity with the Templar. I outed Patrick Sumerisle from the Home Office Ministry before he died at the Battle of All Hallows' Eve."

THIRTY-NINE

"I was the one who confirmed the existence of the Templar," Lyra Darius continued. "Until I discovered that proof, they'd just been a myth, an urban legend that had been handed down from the days of King Arthur."

Leah's attention sharpened. "How did you manage that?"

Lyra smiled. "It was more luck than skill. As you know, the Templar are quite the masterminds when it comes to covert matters."

"Yes they are."

"I was still with MI-6 during those days," Lyra explained.

"MI-6? But that agency is tasked with threats from foreign powers. The Templar aren't foreign."

"We didn't know that at the time. We only knew there were stories that wouldn't go away. Then the demon murders started. Do you remember those?"

Leah nodded. Prior to the actual opening of the Hellgate, ritual murders had taken place on October 13, 2020. The Metropolitan Police had drawn enormous negative publicity for their inability to solve the crimes. Four days later, a police constable was killed by what was then believed to be a wild beast.

"After that the killings escalated," Lyra went on. "With

everything that was going on in the world at the time, the Home Office chose to view the attacks as terrorist-based."

"Because it was easier than believing in demons," Leah said.

"Yes." Lyra kept her face neutral. "MI-6 rolled in under the radar of the local media, but that was easy with all the military units that were mobilized to deal with the threat of the beasts. By that point everyone was convinced there was more than one."

Leah remembered. She'd been assigned to South Africa at the time to work on a real terrorist threat that had melted in light of the Hellgate. When the call had come through for her to pick up Simon Cross's trail in Cape Town, she'd already been in place.

"I'd been assigned to monitor Patrick Sumerisle," Lyra said.

"Why?"

"His . . . *specialized* interests had become known to us. As you know, having to live a dual life is difficult. Sumerisle's life—*lives*—was even more so. He had a long military service and was part of the Home Office Ministry's Internal Affairs unit. Doubtless that was to keep us monitored in the same fashion that we were later trying to spy on him."

"The Templar also helped increase the military's technological advantage," Leah said. She didn't care that she was being openly supportive of the Templar. There was a lot to like about them. Even if they were idealistic dreamers. "The suit you're wearing came from Templar designs."

"I know. I've become quite enamored of what they've done in the last few hundred years. I've also learned a lot more about them. Unlike you, I've never had the opportunity to wander their Underground bunkers."

Leah didn't say anything. Everything she'd had to say about the Templar Underground was in the reports she'd filed.

"But I did get the opportunity to save Jessica Sumerisle before the Battle of All Hallows' Eve."

When Simon finished the primary Way of the Sword drill, he turned to the young Templar and saluted them. They were all seriousness for about five seconds, then they burst out cheering and high-fiving each other.

Simon grinned in spite of himself. At this moment, in this room, death and destruction by demons seemed a million miles away.

"Not exactly proper decorum, now is it?" Danielle asked.

"No," Simon agreed. But he had to admit that he felt better now than he had after his own workout. He also noted that the exercise had drawn a larger crowd than before. Male and female Templar and civilians who had been drafted to the cause filled the area to standing room only. Simon had no clue when they'd started trickling in.

Wertham was there as well, and the old Templar wore a big smile of approval. He shot Simon a glance, tossed in a wink, and left the room.

"Maybe you should think about making this a regular event with the young ones," Danielle said.

Simon shook his head.

Nathan joined them. "She's right, you know. What you just did with these kids was a bloody righteous thing, mate. You gave them hope and spirit."

"I don't want them to think they're invulnerable," Simon said.

"Yeah," Nathan said sarcastically, "I can see your point. It would be much better if they cowered in fear in this place and grew more certain that today was the day the demons were going to find them and kill them."

"That's not what I meant."

Nathan placed his hand on Simon's shoulder and looked him full in the eye. "Hope and spirit are two of the best things you can give these kids. They're going to be asked to die before their time. All of us are. We risk death every time we leave this place, and the only way we can stomach that is to think that we're strong enough and smart enough to do it. If you try to take that away from them, they're not going to listen to the other things that you can teach them that *will* save their lives." He paused. "It's the same thing your father did for you, mate. And for me and a lot of the other Templar you've been leading into London."

Simon took a deep breath and let it out. "It's easier," he said, "when you're on the receiving end of it. Not when you're dishing it out."

Wertham reappeared and his face was tight with tension. Simon went to meet him.

"Terrence Booth has just sent a group of Templar into the area," Wertham said. "They've sent us a tight-beam communiqué."

Tension ratcheted up inside Simon. After what had happened with Macomber, it wasn't surprising to learn that Booth and maybe the whole Templar Underground knew the location of the fortress.

"What do they want?" Simon asked.

Wertham shook his head. "They said they'd only talk to you."

"All right." Simon leaned down and picked up his sword and gym bag. Whatever Booth wanted, it couldn't be good.

* * *

"When the Hellgate opened," Lyra Darius told Leah, "Sumerisle contacted me and asked me to watch over Jessica."

As Leah watched the older woman, she heard the pain of the memories in her voice and saw the strain in her face.

"Jessica was just a girl," Lyra said. "Eight years old. The demons were making a concerted effort to destroy the Templar. They obviously knew who Lord Sumerisle was because they came after him. When the Hellgate opened, I was with Lord Sumerisle trying to get Jessica to safety. At that point I didn't know for sure what he was going to do."

Leah sat silent and still. If Lyra Darius was playing her, it was the best work Leah had ever seen.

"We were trying to get to Temple Church," Lyra said. "We didn't make it. The caravan of ATVs Lord Sumerisle arranged was attacked by demons. The vehicles were demolished. We almost lost our lives. That was the first time I saw what a fully armored Templar could do. And I knew that the armor the military and we were given paled in comparison."

"They couldn't give away everything," Leah said.

"I know. They have to protect their knowledge." Lyra took a deep breath, but Leah knew the woman wasn't in the barracks room anymore; she was back on the road to Temple Church four years ago. "Lord Sumerisle had me take Jessica. There was an underground tunnel to the heart of a Templar fortress under Temple Church. Keira Skyler was with us."

It took Leah a moment to recognize the name. Keira Skyler had been one of the first Cabalists to come forward when the ritual murders started. She'd told everyone that the attacks were demonic in nature.

"But no one believed her." Leah remembered the scuttlebutt that had come down the pipe at the time.

"No one. Except Lord Sumerisle."

"Because he already knew that."

"Yes. Lord Sumerisle and Keira Skyler were together that night when we were attacked. They'd planned on working to unite the Templar and the Cabalists to repel the demons. For the most part, those two groups don't know much about each other."

And those that do don't trust each other, Leah thought. She remembered the black Cabalist with the ragged face who had been inside Akehurst Sanitarium. Simon had already battled him at some point.

"The Cabalists want to learn to control the demons," Lyra said.

"The Templar want to destroy them," Leah said.

Lyra smiled sadly. "So you can see how Lord Sumerisle and Kiera Skyler had a lot to work out."

"It wouldn't have happened even if they'd lived. The Cabalists and the Templar are too far apart."

"And we're not?"

Leah didn't reply. Everyone had a side in the war being fought throughout London now.

"That night, Kiera and I tried to get Jessica to safety," Lyra continued. "A second wave of demons followed the first. They attacked us at the church as we made our way through the graveyard. I got Jessica inside, but it was a close thing." She quieted for a moment, took a breath, and went on. "Then everything went to hell in a handcart."

"Simon Cross?"

Seated in front of the comm array in his armor, Simon turned his faceplate translucent and allowed the Templar at the other end of the connection to see his face.

"Yes."

The Templar was young, but his face held scars and a

wariness that only close combat gave. "High Seat Booth sent me to speak with you."

"He should have come himself," Simon said. "I'd have been more interested in talking."

"He wants you to come to the Templar Underground."

That puzzled Simon. He sat back in his seat. "Four years ago, the last time I saw High Seat Booth, he told me in no uncertain terms that I was unwelcome there."

Displeasure showed on the Templar's face. "Things have changed."

"What things?"

"I'm not at liberty to go into that."

Simon gave the man a cold smile. "Then we're going to have a short conversation. Tell Booth when he's ready to speak to me, I'll be here." He reached forward to break the connection.

"Wait."

Simon held his hand on the disconnect key. "Give me a reason."

The Templar thought quickly. "High Seat Booth wants to talk to you about *Goetia*. He knows about the manuscript from Akehurst Sanitarium. He says he can help."

Simon also knew that Booth wouldn't help anyone but himself if he could help it. But the fact that Booth had sent men out into the wilderness and across London told Simon that the High Seat didn't know the manuscript had been burned to a crisp.

But Booth did know something.

"Where can I meet you?" Simon asked.

"A Reaper demon broke into the church where I'd taken Jessica," Lyra said. "It had Keira in one hand. Before we could do anything, it killed her. Right there in front of us." Unshed tears showed in her eyes. "There was nothing I could do."

"That must have been horrible," Leah said.

"We weren't friends," Lyra said. "I'd only met her the one time. But I could tell she was a good person. In spite of the horns and tattoos. In the end, she gave her life to protect Lord Sumerisle's granddaughter as she'd promised she would."

"But you got away," Leah pointed out.

"Almost," Lyra said quietly. "I fought with the demon, but it was too strong. I got Jessica to safety, though. I'd almost joined her when the Reaper demon caught hold of me and pulled me from the tunnel entrance." She paused. "I knew I was all but dead then. So I did the only thing I could do. I had a sonic grenade and I used it, fully expecting not to survive."

Leah watched as Lyra ran her left forefinger along the sleeve of her right arm. The armor obediently opened up and revealed a gleaming prosthetic arm.

"I'm not exactly sure how I survived that encounter. The next thing I remember was waking up in a medical facility that hadn't been overrun with wounded and dying from the demon attacks. At that point, the British military was dead in the streets. Tanks and fighters jets littered Greater London. And the Templar were shedding their life's blood at St. Paul's."

Leah stared at the prosthetic arm. She'd read about them and knew they were part of emerging technology, but she hadn't known they were being used in the field.

"The injury should have mustered me out of MI-6." Lyra smiled. "If the demon invasion hadn't taken place, if London hadn't become occupied territory, it would have. Instead, since I had been close to Lord Sumerisle and the Templar, I was repaired and put back into the field."

Repaired. The term jarred Leah's thoughts when she contemplated how the woman had been *repaired* like a piece of equipment and returned to service. But in the end, that's all any of them were: parts of a well-oiled machine.

They were supposed to perform like a well-oiled machine, too. She hadn't the past couple of days. By now Command probably knew it had been longer than that. Which was why she was where she was.

"Not many of our people believe in the Templar," Lyra said.

"Command isn't comfortable knowing anyone has had more information than they have," Leah replied. "Especially not by a few hundred years' worth."

"The Templar haven't been the only ones who knew things. We've had data. We just didn't know how to interpret it. Like the tube you brought in with you. We've known about *Goetia*. We just didn't know it applied to this mess we're in now."

Leah looked at the other woman and took a deep breath. *All right, then. This is where we get down to it.*

FORTY

Warren trudged through the dank expanse of the tube station in Bloomsbury. Night had fallen over the city again, and the demons hunted fearlessly. So far he had missed all of them.

Fear remained his constant companion. And the voice that haunted the back of his mind.

"I'm here," the voice said. "Don't be so tense. We've made a good plan, you and I. This time we have more control of the playing field."

Warren wished he felt as confident as the voice sounded. Merihim had visited him earlier to make sure he was taking up the hunt for Knaarl. When he'd been satisfied Warren was properly fearful, he'd vanished. But Warren had gotten the feeling that whatever the demon was working on was building to a crescendo.

Merihim's obvious lack of interest in what Warren was doing bothered him. For four years he'd served the demon, not faithfully but out of self-preservation. He'd wanted to believe what he was doing mattered more than was apparent now.

"What you're doing matters to Merihim," the voice said. "More than you can know at this juncture."

"Why is it more than I can know?"

"Because certain events have yet to be played in this. If

you know everything you shouldn't, you may change the things you are going to do."

Warren came to a full stop in the deserted tube station. Buckled cars filled with the skeletons of unfortunates who'd died during the wrecks when the systems went offline occupied the dead tracks. More corpses that had been prey to demons occupied the empty spaces. Warren had learned to simply walk over them. Bones crunched under his combat boots.

"You can see into the future?" Warren asked.

The voice was silent for a time. "I can't *see*, but I can make predictions based on factors that I'm aware of."

"Can you make a prediction about tonight? About what I'm getting ready to do?"

"Yes. I predict that you'll have success if everything goes as we've planned."

"You'll forgive me if I feel somewhat underwhelmed by that announcement."

"There are always mysteries that we cannot understand," the voice said.

"That's right. You didn't exactly set out to get yourself bound, did you?" Warren wished he could have kept his mouth shut. But the words had tripped over his lips before he could stop them.

"No, I didn't. That was an x factor at work. But so was the fact that I could communicate with anyone. My captors couldn't have counted on that."

In the cold dark of that tunnel, Warren suddenly realized something else that he knew he should have seen. "I was an x factor too. If you could have talked to anyone else, you would have."

The voice didn't say anything.

"Admit it," Warren said angrily. "You couldn't have just talked to anyone else."

"You're right." Instead of sounding chastised, the voice held a dangerous tone for the first time. "But we need each other to be free. Neither of us can do it alone. And I've already been waiting for hundreds of years. Could you wait so long?"

Some of Warren's newfound confidence and feelings of success evaporated. Mortality was an issue. He'd already spent four years in service to Merihim. How many more could he spend with the demon constantly putting him on the firing line before his luck ran out?

"We need each other," Warren said.

"Yes."

But it remained to be seen who didn't need who first. The thought chilled Warren as he started walking along the tube from the Holborn station toward the British Museum again.

Little more than an hour later, Warren reached the tunnel that the voice had told him would be there. The tunnel wasn't open, however. It lay on the other side of the concrete wall that separated it from the tube line.

When the British Museum was established in 1753, complete with the massive underground storage facilities for exhibits and items that had yet to be sorted out, the founders had also built service tunnels to them. During the intervening years, all of them had been closed, walled off in one way or another. But they hadn't been filled.

Warren used his human hand to feel for the void beyond the wall. When he found it, he concentrated again and felt for the spaces between the atoms of the chemicals that made up the concrete and wood that sealed the tunnel off.

Once he had mapped the atoms in his mind, he stepped

up against the wall and pushed. Slowly, as if moving through mud, he slipped through the solid wall.

On the other side, Warren stood for a moment and re-grouped himself. The spell he'd used to slip through the solid surface was demanding, and it didn't always leave him feeling well. A headache pounded between his temples, and his stomach lurched sickeningly.

When he felt better, he continued.

The tunnel ran for a quarter mile. Scars from pickaxes, shovels, and blasting powder peppered the wall. Ruts from ironbound wheels scored the rock floor and made treacherous footing on either side of the narrow gauge rail track that ran through the middle of the tunnel.

Almost before he was ready, Warren reached the other end of the tunnel. Engineers had constructed a concrete plug to fill in the entrance to the British Museum's lower levels. The oblong plug was twelve feet across and three feet thick. Evidently whoever had given the order to close the tunnel had planned to never use it again.

Warren placed the hand Merihim had given him against the rock. He gathered his energy, then *pushed* and *twisted*.

Slowly, then with greater speed, the concrete plug gave way and rotated free of the tunnel mouth. Thankfully the grating wasn't overly loud, but Warren had worked to dampen that as well.

A moment more and the plug was free. He pushed it forward just enough to clear his body. From the drawings the voice had shown him of Knaarl in the book, Warren knew the demon was larger than he was.

The darkness in the lower room was complete, but Warren's enhanced vision allowed him to see perfectly. At some point the museum had been invaded by scaven-

gers that had thrown priceless artifacts around. They'd
somehow gotten access to the hermetically sealed vaults
that held the various exhibitions not currently on display.
Paintings littered the floor, accompanied by shattered
vases, plates, and other pottery from around the world.

A little farther ahead, an Egyptology exhibit Warren
had read about in the research he'd done on the British
Museum lay in disarray as well. Twenty-three Egyptian
mummies occupied sarcophaguses that had been stripped
of gold and gems. At one point after Howard Carter's
discovery of the Valley of Kings, mummies had been big
business. England had especially taken an interest in the
stories.

Another room was filled with Greek and Roman artifacts that had brought in from the Greek islands, Rome,
and the Aegean Sea. Statues, broken and missing pieces,
lay like broken toys.

"Knaarl isn't here," the voice said.

Warren walked through another room filled with Afri-
can tribal instruments and weapons that was more debris
than display now. The founders of the British Museum
had sent archeologists in all directions to gather exhibits.

On the other side of the room, Warren walked down
the stairwell to reach the second underground room. Candles burned there. The rancid tallow and the acrid smoke
tickled his nose and almost made him sneeze.

The second floor held glassed panels of dried flowers,
seeds, and roots that lay in ruins. Most of the items had
been mounted for display, but now they were little more
than garbage.

Knaarl and a group of Darkspawn sorted through the
materials kept in the room. They'd been orderly about it,
carefully going through the contents and separating everything out.

The demon stood eleven feet tall. *Stood* wasn't exactly the correct word, though. It was more like he *coiled*. From the waist up, Knaarl was humanoid in appearance, but from the waist down his body was that of a snake.

Broad-shouldered and narrow-hipped, the demon was covered in purplish-red scales the size of one-euro coins. A single row of black and green horns stood out above his three black eyes set into a pyramid shape above his thin-lipped mouth. He had no nose. His ears were straight and flat, and they pulsed like a fish's fins. His lower body turned more purple and the scales were larger.

It wore a protective vest made of some bilious green hide with strange sigils carved into it. A long, curved sword hung down its back in a scabbard carved of red and black bone.

When he spoke, his voice came out in a trill. The Darkspawn worked harder, but it didn't keep Knaarl from lashing out with the whip he carried. The braided length opened flesh wherever it touched. Two Darkspawn lay nearby on the ground. Neither of them moved and Warren didn't doubt that they were dead.

You've found him. Good. Merihim's voice echoed in Warren's mind. *Now deal with him.*

Without warning, Merihim suddenly stepped through a tear in the darkness and entered the underground room. He stood savage and terrible in the darkness.

"Knaarl," Merihim called.

The demon wheeled around at once. His three eyes locked on Merihim. Then the lipless mouth curved into a smile that revealed a double row of fangs.

"Merihim," Knaarl said in a thunderous shrill that pealed across the open space of the cavernous room. It almost sounded like the high-pitched squeals of a dolphin. "Fulaghar said he'd chanced upon you in this world."

As he listened to the awful sounds, Warren was certain no human ear could have understood what the demon was saying. He wasn't sure how he was able to.

"It is Merihim's doing," the voice said. "Your ties to him have enabled you to understand the demon tongue."

"Why is he taking part in this?" Warren asked. "He wasn't there when I confronted Hargastor."

"Merihim and Knaarl have a long and sordid history together."

Warren couldn't help wondering how the voice knew that, and why it didn't elaborate on that history.

"Did Fulaghar speak of me in fear?" Merihim responded.

Knaarl smiled even more broadly. "No. He spoke of you in annoyance. As he would any pest. Or lord of such."

"Stay back out of this for the time being," the voice warned Warren. "This isn't your fight. Yet."

Warren was more than happy to stay out of the way.

Knaarl cracked his whip. The Darkspawn turned around, instantly attentive.

"You weren't invited to this place," Knaarl said.

"I was," Merihim countered.

"Not by any of the Dark Wills who claimed this place as prey."

A Dark Will was a demon that had consumed countless billions. Warren knew that from his reading. But now he knew that more had to have been involved in rising through the demon hierarchy.

"I didn't need their invitation," Merihim growled.

"You're not a Dark Will, Merihim," Knaarl declared. "You only wish to be one."

"I *will* be one," Merihim roared. "After all my years, I deserve to be one."

Warren heard the anger in the demon's words.

"The Dark Wills won't accept you because they don't trust you," Knaarl said. "They will never give you that kind of power."

"I don't have to have it given," Merihim snapped. "I'm strong enough to take it."

"Fulaghar sees only that you are greedy enough to get yourself killed in this world. You would have better served yourself if you had maintained your alliance with him."

"That was no alliance. He granted me a life of subservience. The same life that he gave you, Hargastor, and Toklorq. Are you happy being a slave?"

Knaarl waved at the Darkspawn clustered around him. "We're all slaves to Greater Evil, Merihim. Only you—and perhaps a few others—aren't happy with that. And most of those have died the Final Death."

"I don't choose to be a slave. At least the Darkspawn, Gremlins, and Imps aren't intelligent enough to see how badly they're used."

"So it would be better to be reduced to something barely above animal awareness?" Knaarl licked his lipless mouth.

Merihim didn't say anything.

"You managed your appearance here with another of your little baubles, didn't you?" Knaarl asked. "One of your little treasures you sow among the humans to get them to call upon you."

"We're all allowed access to unclaimed worlds," Merihim said.

"That changes after a world has been targeted for a Hellgate and a Burn." Knaarl slithered closer and shook out his whip. "Only then, under the auspices of the Eldest, may we take part in a Burn that purges a world of Light. You were not named to take place in this. Fulaghar was."

Merihim scowled. "Fulaghar doesn't deserve a world this full of prey."

"Have a care with your viperous tongue," Knaarl warned. "You speak of my master."

"All those years ago you chose masters wrongly."

Knaarl's grin was obscene. "Because I didn't choose you, my lord?" The sarcasm carried through the shrill tone.

"Yes."

Knaarl cocked his head to one side. "Your vassals seem to come to quick, untimely ends." The three black eyes regarded Warren. "And you oftentimes choose them unwisely."

Warren got them impression that he'd been judged, threatened, and dismissed all at the same time. If he hadn't been so frightened, he might have felt demeaned and outraged. But part of him knew he might die in the next few minutes.

"None of those that chose you back in those days are still alive," Knaarl said.

"Through no fault of my own."

"Forgive my impudence, Begetter of Pestilence, but you either chose unwisely or you broke your toys by risking too much."

Merihim grinned crookedly, and the demon's delight was a horrible thing to behold. "Have you talked to Hargastor lately?"

Knaarl cocked his head. His arm twitched and his lash slithered along the stone floor like a live thing. Several of the Darkspawn backed away from it fearfully.

"Hargastor was slain in a battle against Templar," Knaarl said.

"No, he was slain by another."

"The Darkspawn who were with Hargastor and escaped

with their lives said they'd fought Templar. They were put to death for abandoning Hargastor, of course." Knaarl licked his lips. "Thus far, you're the only act of insubordination to Fulaghar that has lived. If you choose to stay in this place for long—"

"I am staying here," Merihim said.

"—then that oversight will soon be rectified." Knaarl cracked his whip. "I look forward to telling my master of your demise. Especially if you had a hand in Hargastor's death."

Merihim stood his ground fearlessly. "Out of respect to our past friendship, I offer you this chance to live."

Knaarl laughed and the explosive squeaks nearly deafened Warren.

"You can't touch me here, Merihim," the demon replied. "If you act directly against me or Fulaghar, you will draw the dire wrath of the First."

"The Great Eye allows power struggles among the Dark Wills and the Eldest," Merihim replied. "Only the strongest are fit to stand at his feet."

Warren had read about the First, also called the Great Eye. The demon had been created out of the Shadow in direct opposition to the Light. The First was eternal and unforgiving. It was he who kept the Eldest and the Dark Wills in line.

"Not in this place and time," Knaarl said. "The Burn must run its course on this world first. If you wish to challenge my master after that, then you may ask for your doom." He smiled. "If Fulaghar is generous, maybe he won't torture you before destroying you forever."

"Perhaps I can't raise my hand against him," Merihim said, "but others may in my stead."

Knaarl gazed at Merihim. "You have a Chosen?"

"I do." Merihim swept a hand toward Warren. "And he

has come here to kill you and deprive Fulaghar of another of his vassals."

With a quick, serpentine twist, Knaarl looked past Merihim at Warren.

"A human?" Knaarl crowed in delight. "From all that you had to choose from, and you chose one of the pathetic creatures we kill effortlessly every day." He cracked his whip. "You would have been better off to strike a bargain with the Templar."

"The Templar will never deal with a demon. And I've chosen more wisely than you think."

"We'll see." Knaarl flicked his whip without warning. The braided length sped toward Warren's face like a lightning strike.

FORTY-ONE

Time slowed as Warren's senses churned into over-drive. As the whip came closer, he saw that it had been braided of long, thin snakelike demons. All of them had their mouths open, fangs glistening.

Merihim made no move.

Knowing he could never hope to avoid the whip, Warren reached up with his demon hand and stepped forward to intercept the blow. He caught the whip a few inches back from the barbed end. Several of the braided demons sank their fangs into Warren's hand. Poison burned through his veins.

Knaarl cursed and yanked the whip back. The braided demons in Warren's hand turned loose and curled around to attack in earnest. They slithered up his arm and came immediately at his face.

Warren's first instinct was to run.

"Don't," the voice said. "If the demons don't get you, your exertion will only pump the poison through your heart faster. If that doesn't kill you, Knaarl or Merihim will. Fight them. You have the power."

Steeling himself, Warren took hold of the arcane forces seething through him. He pushed heat out of his body and felt his bones grow cold. But when the heat touched the air outside his skin, it turned to white-hot flame that crisped the slithering snake-demons to gray ash. He shook himself and the ash fell away from him like powdered snow.

"Good," the voice said. "Very good."

Warren eyed the approaching demon and concentrated again. When Knaarl flicked the whip once more, Warren stepped to the side and it missed by inches. He thrust out his hand and picked up an empty crate that the Darkspawn had rifled through.

Knaarl drew back his whip and shook out its length again. "Going to throw that at me, human?"

With a quick gesture, Warren did. Knaarl lifted an arm lazily, as if he were just going to brush the crate aside. Instead, only a few feet from his opponent, Warren shattered the crate into jagged shards.

The wooden shrapnel pierced Knaarl's thick hide in several places. Most of the shards glanced off because they weren't heavy enough to smash through the demon's skin or because they hit at an oblique angle and slid away. But dozens of others embedded in Knaarl's face and upper body. One of the three black eyes took a direct hit and wept blood down his face.

Knaarl roared in pain and rage as he wiped at the offending splinters. He cracked the whip at Warren so hard that part of the snake-demons shot off the end. Several of the Darkspawn picked up their swords and axes and ran at Warren.

Working quickly, Warren levitated other crates—some empty and some full—at the Darkspawn. Seeds and books flew in all directions when the crates impacted against the Darkspawn. Their energy weapons blasted the walls and produced pools of acidic poison or started fires. Several of them when down.

Warren turned and fled back up the stairway to the chamber above. When he reached the landing, he angled for the corner that held the Egyptian artifacts. He poured arcane energy out of himself as footsteps and the sound of coiling scales pursued him.

By the time the Darkspawn reached the chamber, the Egyptian mummies were climbing from their sarcophaguses. Animated by the dark forces that Warren supplied, the mummies tore into the Darkspawn with grim and savage abandon.

Desiccated flesh, bones, and natron salt–soaked linen quickly covered the floor as the mummies came apart. But the Darkspawn fell too, dragged down by the mummies.

His two remaining eyes blazing, Knaarl slithered into the room and searched for Warren. As Knaarl drew the whip back, Warren unleashed a wave of flames that washed over the demon and the nearby Darkspawn. The mummies went up in flames at once and wreathed the demons in them.

Knaarl drew back as the flames ate through his hide and burned him. His whip abandoned him as the snake-demons unbraided themselves and fell to the floor. They burned there and never made it out of the flames.

Behind Knaarl, Merihim stood looking on. Warren couldn't tell what emotion was showing on the demon's face. Merihim's attention was divided between Warren and Knaarl.

"Merihim knows you've gotten stronger," the voice said. "That unsettles him."

"I don't think he wanted me to die," Warren said.

"No, but he wouldn't have been surprised."

"Then who would he have gotten to do his dirty work?"

"Merihim never counts on any one strategy," the voice said.

While Warren was trying to figure out what that meant,

Knaarl broke free of the flames and came at him. The demon drew the curved sword from over its shoulder. Silver fire glinted along the razor-sharp edge. Knaarl seemed almost to spring forward.

"Now," the voice urged. "Strike now while he's concerned about the flames and his wounds from the wooden splinters are still open."

Warren reached into the pocket of his duster and pulled out a glass globe he'd prepared under instruction from the voice. The globe was filled with orange and white froth, but three dark blue arrowhead shapes swam within the liquid. They each had one eye and a thin, barbed tail twice their length.

The voice had called them heart-renders and stated that Knaarl would be vulnerable to them. Warren hoped that was true. He held the globe on his palm and *pushed* it forward.

The globe spun through the air. Knaarl saw the projectile too late to avoid it. When the globe struck the demon just below the collarbone, the force was great enough to knock him backwards. His upper body swayed on the coils of his lower half so far that for a moment it looked like he might tip over. He put a hand back to steady himself.

The globe shattered and released its contents. Glass embedded in the demon's flesh. Orange and white froth ran down his chest. The heart-renders surfed in the froth and each found entry into the demon's body through open wounds left from the wooden shrapnel. The heart-renders' arrowhead-shaped bodies disappeared almost immediately.

"No!" Knaarl roared. Panic tightened his features. He dropped the sword and stabbed his talons into his wounds in an effort to get to the heart-renders as they burrowed deeply.

Merihim stared at Warren.

Knaarl managed to get one of the heart-render demons out of his body. It flopped between his bloody fingers before he gutted it with a talon.

The other two escaped him. From what Warren had understood of the demons as he'd summoned them to him and trapped them in the globe, the heart-renders burrowed into a demon's veins and let the pulse carry it to the demon's heart. Once inside the heart, they flicked their barbed tails and sliced the heart to pieces.

Knaarl took a long time in dying. The demon collapsed in pain and lay on his side while blood pumped from his nose and mouth. Soon his lungs filled with it and he shuddered for a time before lying still and lax.

Afterwards, Warren walked numbly through the burned and broken bodies of the Darkspawn. Three mummies still stood at attention. Another, missing both legs, poised on its arms.

Warren waved at them and released them. They fell in heaps to the ground like unstrung marionettes.

Two of Knaarl's dead eyes stared sightlessly. The wooden splinter still pierced the third.

Wary of the heart-render demons, Warren stayed well back of the demon's corpse.

"You have learned much," Merihim said.

Not knowing how he was supposed to respond, Warren turned to the demon and said, "With the tasks you've given me, I've had no choice."

"Where did you learn about those demons?"

"I learned about them from the Cabalists." For a moment Warren thought Merihim was going to challenge the lie.

"He won't," the voice said. "He still needs you."

Warren hoped so. Otherwise he was going to die in the next moment.

"Even now," the voice told him, "Merihim may not be able to kill you."

May not, Warren repeated to himself. *There were no assurances.*

"At least it's not a certainty."

Warren quietly conceded that, but his knees shook all the same.

"One of Fulaghar's lieutenants yet remains," Merihim said.

"Toklorq," Warren said. A vague stirring rose within him when he mentioned the demon's name. When he concentrated, he felt a directional pull.

"Yes," Merihim said. "With two of Fulaghar's minions dead, the third should be easier to locate."

"I think I can find him."

"You'll be able to," the voice said. "I'll help you."

Merihim kicked the dead demon in the side. A heart-render leaped through Knaarl's unmoving flesh and sailed toward Merihim's foot. Almost lazily, Merihim lifted his trident and brought the haft down on the small demon. He pinned it against the floor and crushed the life from it.

"Toklorq will be harder to kill in some ways," Merihim stated. "He is an automaton, a weapon created on forges, birthed of steel rather than flesh and blood."

"I'll find a way," Warren promised.

Merihim regarded him. "You've proven exceptionally surprising."

Warren nodded. He knew he would have felt pleased if he hadn't been so afraid. Praise had been a seldom thing in his life.

"That isn't necessarily a good thing," the demon said.

Reluctantly, Warren bowed his head. "I'm only trying to serve. I want to live."

"I don't doubt that, but you humans are a treacherous lot."

A pale blue circle opened in mid-air above Knaarl's dead eyes and Fulaghar's features formed within it.

"Another of your thralls grows cold in death," Merihim taunted. "Do you want to mourn him now? Or would you rather spend your time fearing your own coming death?"

"You're a blight, Merihim. Even now, when we should be working together because this world is still so young in the Burn and there remains so much at risk, you think only of your own wants and desires."

"If I had what I deserved, I could think of other things. But the injustice that has been done to me—because of your interference—consumes me."

"You deserve only a lingering and excruciating death. I only wished that I could give it to you now instead of when you finally grow too bold."

"The Dark Wills and Elders won't act against me unless I act against a demon of my own ranking. That's why you have your pawns and I have mine."

"You can attack me," Fulaghar said. "I am above you and fair game for your attempt to become a Dark Will."

"It's the way of the demon hierarchy," the voice whispered in the back of Warren's mind. "Demons may not attack demons of the same station or those below—unless they are the mindless beasts like the stalkers or those of limited intelligence like the Darkspawn and Gremlins. But they make attack those above to try and take their place. The First had decreed this so that only those demons strong enough to rule will. Of course, once a lower caste demon has made an attack and hasn't been successful, that demon's protection from the higher ranks is null and void. They're also allowed their pawns to carry on their rivalry without them because not so much is at risk."

Survival of the fittest, Warren thought. *It's the most basic rule of the predator.* And it kept the demons from utterly annihilating themselves.

"In time, I will attack you and I will kill you," Merihim promised. "But not until you're bereft of your protectors. If I'd attacked you while they were still alive, you would have called them to your aid."

"If you ever get up the nerve to attack me," Fulaghar said, "I won't need to. I'll take your head myself."

"Tell Toklorq to watch out for himself. I'll be there for you soon." Merihim gestured and Knaarl's body burst into charred embers. Warren never even saw the fire that burned it. The pale blue circle containing Fulaghar's likeness disappeared.

Warren's fear increased. Before he wasn't sure if Fulaghar had known who had killed one of his minions, or that Merihim was responsible. Now there was no doubt.

Merihim faced him. "You'll have to be careful now. I don't want you to die before you've finished the task I've given you."

What about after? Warren wondered.

"Don't worry about that now," the voice told him. "By that time you'll be able to handle yourself."

Warren didn't believe that. He only hoped he found a way out of his present situation by that time. But now he was marked by Fulaghar.

Merihim lifted a hand and sliced into the air to open a doorway to somewhere else. "Find Toklorq."

Warren nodded.

"Then kill him when you do. After that, I'll tend to Fulaghar." Merihim stepped into the hole he'd cut into the air and disappeared.

"There's someone else at the other end of that rift," the voice said.

Warren sensed that as well. He tried to peer into the rift but couldn't see anything. However, he gathered impressions of the person at the other end of the rift with the psychic abilities he was still developing.

The person at the other end of the rift was young and female. Her power was strong, but she was awkward.

She also seemed familiar.

Then the rift was gone.

"You sensed her?" the voice asked.

"Yes."

"I saw that you're familiar with her."

"Perhaps." Warren wasn't convinced of that. He was surprised at how much it bothered him to think that Merihim was depending on someone else. The sane thing would have been to be happy. If there was someone else, maybe he could escape the demon's wrath.

Or maybe he already has your replacement.

Warren started to turn and go.

"Wait," the voice entreated. "There's something that Merihim didn't notice."

"What?"

"Look to Knaarl's sword. There in the hilt."

Warren walked to the sword and picked it up. The weapon was far too large to be used by him—or anyone human. He examined the hilt, which was encrusted with gems that would have probably been a king's ransom if the world had still been as it was before the Hellgate opened. Now cans of food and bottles of water were far more precious than diamonds or rubies.

Gold wire wrapped the hilt and almost disguised the secret hiding place built into the sword. Warren's clever fingers found it after a brief search. While in foster care he'd learned to search out all kinds of secrets and hiding places for money and other things he'd needed.

The compartment was locked by a three-ring mechanism that had to be lined up. Warren twisted the rings and heard the *snik* of the lock opening. When he slid the compartment back, he saw the three teeth inside. They were large and triangular, looking sharp, flat, and dull green. With effort, he got the sword over his shoulder and poured the teeth out into his palm.

"Knaarl found them," the voice whispered in disbelief.

"These are the dragon's teeth?"

"Yes."

"How do you know?"

"Because I've heard them described. And because, through *you*, I can feel the arcane energy within them."

Warren knew that the seeds possessed power. He felt it in them. "Where did the dragons come from?"

"They belonged to another demon that has lived here for thousands of years. She's called Lilith."

"Adam's first wife," Warren whispered, remembering the old stories he'd read in the occult books his mother had studied. "She was supposed to be the mother of vampires, demons, and wicked things."

"She's all that," the voice said. "And more."

FORTY-TWO

"Where did you find the manuscript?" Lyra Darius asked.

"At Akehurst Sanitarium." Leah didn't bother to withhold the information. There was nothing to be gained. Command now had the manuscript, and it couldn't be used without their assistance. There was also the possibility that the manuscript was burned beyond recognition and couldn't be recovered at all.

"How did you know it was there?"

"Macomber told Simon Cross."

"Yet Macomber never mentioned that to us."

"He felt the information was better off in Templar hands."

"What do you think?"

"It doesn't matter, does it?" Leah asked. "Command has the manuscript now, and it's burned almost to ash."

"Tech Ops believes they can recover the pages."

Elation soared within Leah but she kept her face a blank. She also monitored her heartbeat and respiration because she figured the room was totally wired for bio readings.

"Do you know what the manuscript's about?" Lyra asked.

"It was supposed to be written by King Solomon and detail the seventy-two demons he called forth and locked in a jar. The title's misleading, though, because it could be read as the invocation of angels or the evocation of demons."

"According to the legend, Solomon bound the demons but never got around to calling on the angels. The Cabalists would have a field day with this because they believe the demons can be mastered and used to benefit mankind."

"Not any of them I've seen," Leah said.

"I would agree," Lyra said. "Except that I saw firsthand what Keira Skyler was able to do with the powers she learned from her studies of the demons." She shook her head. "I can't even begin to imagine what that woman would have known by this time if she had lived."

"The Cabalists are opening doors they can't close. During my trips through London, I've seen several of them driven mad by forces they tried to use. Or physically crippled."

"But there are some who have become quite powerful."

"For now," Leah agreed. Despite the successes she'd seen, she didn't trust the power of the demons. The black man wearing the demon's hand was the perfect case in point.

"Why did you bring the manuscript here?" Lyra asked.

"Because I thought Tech Ops might be able to ferret out the information contained on those pages. I've seen them work their own particular brand of magic."

Lyra smiled a little at the pun. "You knew you were listed as a potential threat."

"Of course."

"Why didn't you check in when you were supposed to?"

"The Templar held me captive."

"How did you fall into Templar hands?"

"Simon Cross saved my life a few days ago."

"According to the reports I read, you were only in danger because you went to warn him about a demon trap involving Templar used as bait."

"That's true." Leah was determined not to lie if she could help it.

"You've fraternized with the Templar even though you were given strict orders not to."

"Yes."

Lyra shrugged. "Would you care to elaborate?"

"For the record?" Leah smiled, but there was no mirth in her expression.

"Definitely for the record."

Leah took a breath and knew that she was about to make or break her career. "Because I believe the Templar are an important factor in how we handle the rest of this engagement."

"'Engagement?'"

"You have another word?"

"Our very survival is on the line. I think 'engagement' is bloody well taking things too lightly." There was no animosity in Lyra's words.

"I'm not taking things lightly," Leah agreed. "That's why I've gone beyond the scope of mission parameters the way I have with the Templar."

Lyra arched a brow. "But it isn't just the Templar, is it? You've been concentrating on Simon Cross."

"Yes."

"Why?"

"Because he and his people seem to honestly care if this world continues." Leah paused. "He still believes he can beat the demons. That's more than Command thinks these days."

Lyra pursed her lips in annoyance at that. Leah could immediately tell she'd transgressed some kind of boundary.

You should have stayed with commentary on the Templar, she chided herself. *That was evidently the safe area.*

But she'd wanted Command to know what she thought of them and the current vision for mission ops.

"We've been dealt extraordinary circumstances," Lyra said. "We're all still trying to make the best of it."

"While we hunkered down," Leah said in a measured tone, "Simon Cross got busy getting people out of London. Four years later, even with the ship runs more or less a thing of the past, he's still trying to do the same thing."

"Are you involved with him?"

The question caught Leah completely off-guard. She hesitated, opened her mouth to speak, tried to figure out what she was going to say, then closed her mouth. She tried again. "No."

"I've seen his pictures. He's a handsome man. It would be easy to understand."

Despite her training and her intention of not showing emotion, Leah felt her face burn slowly. At any other time, about any one else, she was certain she'd have revealed nothing.

"If I were younger," Lyra said without breaking stride, "I'd probably be interested myself. Of course, maybe he favors older women."

"No," Leah said, too quickly. "He doesn't."

Lyra looked at her and cocked a brow.

"No offense intended," Leah said.

"None taken. You have Simon Cross's preferences on good authority?"

"No."

"But you seem so certain."

"In all the years that I've known him, Simon hasn't seemed interested in anyone."

"There are plenty of Templar women. Perhaps one of them then."

"I wouldn't know." Even as she said that, though, Leah felt certain that she would. "Simon is fixed on the war effort against the demons at the present."

Lyra regarded her silently for a moment, then nodded. "I've known people like that. Several of them are in this unit."

Leah nodded.

"The problem is that Simon Cross seems to have something of a checkered past."

"And I submit that no one's perfect. I'm judging him on the man I've seen in action. Not the one that became an expatriate of London all those years ago."

"You certainly seem adamant."

"I am."

"Good. Then maybe we can get something done." Lyra stood.

Leah fully expected to be abandoned at that moment and wasn't looking forward to it. She could deal with being alone. Isolation was often a part of her job. She just didn't like knowing that nothing was getting done.

"Control," Lyra said, confirming Leah's suspicions that others were listening in to the exchange. "Break silence."

"Control here," a male voice responded.

"Bring Leah Creasey's armor to this room and countermand the orders to hold on sight."

"That's not how we were told to handle the interview."

Lyra's tone changed to one of steel and fire. "You'll do it now, on my authority, or you'll answer to charges."

"Yes, ma'am."

"And open this bloody door before I do it myself."

The door unlocked immediately.

Leah followed Lyra Darius through the narrow, twisting hallways of the underground complex. The unit's headquarters were kept deliberately small. It didn't take much to take care of the operation she was part of.

"Tech Ops tells me it's only going to be a few hours before they have the burned pages of the manuscript you found—"

"Simon Cross found," Leah interjected. She accepted her armor from a man who came to her at a dead run.

"—and that they're expecting a full recovery of the data on the pages." Lyra stood in the hallway while Leah pulled her armor on. The older woman even turned her back and provided a modicum of privacy by staring back any passersby of the moment.

When she had herself presentable, once more comfortable in the armor she'd worn nearly every day for the last four years, Leah said, "Thank you."

Lyra set off at once. "The thing that stood in your stead is your years of service prior to the demon invasion. And the fact that I'm predisposed to the notion of the importance of the Templar myself."

"Yes, ma'am."

"I also liked that you brought the *Goetia* manuscript here."

"When Simon found out it was burned, he thought he had no choice. I thought recovery was possible."

"I think it would read better in your report that you simply seized the first opportunity to bring the manuscript to our attention. Your motives aren't quite so questionable that way."

"Yes, ma'am."

"You can oftentimes disguise your motivations by simply stating your actions."

"Duly noted."

The Tech Ops room was compact. It was wall-to-wall with computer hardware and special peripherals. Three people, two men and one woman, sat at the screens and spoke commands to the AIs.

"Jenkins," Lyra said.

"Here." One of the young men swiveled around and looked at her. He looked as if he was fresh from Academy somewhere, but since there'd been no new recruits in four years, Leah knew that was impossible.

"You're working on the manuscript," Lyra said.

"I am," he agreed.

"What do you have?"

Jenkins swiveled back around in his chair and spoke commands quickly. "The original document you brought me was badly burned. Fortunately, there hadn't been any additional damage to the baseline structure of the pages. Separating the pages was logistical nightmare. I won't bore you with the details of using the electromagnetic stasis nanostabilizers to fix the print—"

Lyra held up a hand.

"You have a question, ma'am?" Jenkins asked.

"No. I'm voting for not being bored."

"Oh." Jenkins looked properly flummoxed. "Of course, ma'am." He turned his attention back to the monitor. "In the end I overlaid the stabilized pages with a molecular Gutenberg imprint scanner tuned to the chemical compositions of the inks—there were six identifiable kinds—and *lifted* the text and images. Once I had them, I uploaded them to the computer and started using de-encryption programs."

"There were images?" Lyra asked.

"Yes, ma'am. I've managed to render them, but I'm not certain how much of that is pertinent."

"Why?"

Jenkins hesitated. "Because they're . . . strange." He voiced a few commands and images came up on the monitor.

Leah leaned in for a closer look. The images were drawings done in exquisite detail. But they were of horrendous beings.

"Demons," Leah said.

Jenkins nodded. "There are names given here. And they coincide with the *Goetia* book as we know it."

That announcement threw Leah for a moment. "What *Goetia* book as we know it?"

Jenkins glanced at Lyra, who nodded.

"*Goetia* has been a popular entry in supernatural works. Or New Age as many of them came to be called." Jenkins spoke quietly and book covers took shape on the monitor next to the one showing the demons. "All of them are supposed to have been penned by King Solomon. One of the most famous was a rendition by Aleister Crowley in 1904. It was called *Ars Goetia*, and Crowley maintains that the book was written as a means of psychological exploration."

"But that's not the book we're looking at here," Lyra asked.

"No, ma'am. Not only that, but this book has another book hidden within it."

"What do you mean?"

"There's a secret text hidden in what you see here." Jenkins brought up more pages. These were filled with text in a language Leah couldn't identify.

"Language has never been my strong suit," Lyra admitted.

Leah's background had included encryption, but not linguistics. If someone tried to hide information in English, French, or Japanese, she could ferret through most of those and find suspect passages.

"What you're looking at here is Coptic Egyptian," Jenkins said. "Presumably the language King Solomon might have used for scholarly works."

"Where's the secret text?" Lyra peered more closely.

"Here." Jenkins spoke commands and certain words and phrases were highlighted on the monitor.

"This looks like a different language," Leah said.

"I wouldn't have known that," Lyra said.

"I've a bit of a background in linguistics," Leah admitted. "Nothing sharp enough to handle something like this."

"You've more than I do," Lyra said. "I can speak passable French and Italian, but I have extremely limited use of those written languages."

"That is a different language," Jenkins said.

"What language?" Lyra asked.

"We don't know." Jenkins sighed in an enervating manner as only the young can do. "I've sent it round to the experts in documents, but they've yet to identify it either. And I must admit I'm pretty keen on languages myself."

"How did you find it?" Leah asked. "It looks seamless."

"It is seamless. The conjugation of the verbs and the syntax is faultless. However, the molecular scan revealed the hidden words because they were always shown with two layers of ink. One was written right over the top of the other."

Jenkins spoke commands and one of the words overlaid another. The letters were formed differently.

"Those aren't a match," Leah said.

"No."

Leah stared at the jumble of letters. "Something as atrocious as that should have been immediately apparent."

"If both inks were written so the human eye could see them, it would have been."

"Explain," Lyra said.

Jenkins faced her. "The second layer of ink was invisible to the naked eye. Judging from the chemical composition we were able to extract from the burned vellum sheets—and heat does change a chemical signature, mind you—we've made a tentative match to one of those chemicals used by the Cabalists."

"A Cabalist wrote this?" Lyra asked.

Leah felt her stomach knot up. If that was true, it might screw up her hopes of getting the translation back to Simon and the other Templar.

"We don't know that a Cabalist wrote this," Jenkins said. "Given the time that we think this manuscript was written, based on the chemical composition of the paper and the inks, it's possible someone else was using the ink as well."

"But you don't know what it says?" Lyra asked.

Jenkins shook his head. "We have no clue at all."

FORTY-THREE

Eleven-point-seven miles east of the Templar fortress, Simon stood on the lee side of the ATV he'd used to arrive at the rendezvous. He scanned the surrounding darkness through the HUD.

Nathan and Danielle stood at attention nearby. Other Templar secured the perimeter.

In the distance, Simon could see the London landscape. Black smoke from the Burn occluded the sky. Even after four years of seeing it, the fact that the city was unlit at night was strange and foreboding.

"Simon," the ATV comm ops radioed. "I've got two unfriendlies onscreen."

"Put them through," Simon said. In the next moment the two unknown vehicles ghosted onto his HUD.

"They're on a direct approach vector," the comm ops man stated coolly. "At thirty-seven miles per hour."

"Can you give me an ETA?" Simon asked.

"Given the terrain and based on the fact that they're pretty much maxing out the ATV, I'd estimate between twenty-two and twenty-six minutes."

Twenty-four minutes later, the two ATVs rolled up onto the tree-covered hill where Simon and his crew waited.

"Simon Cross," someone radioed from one of the ATVs.

Patched into the comm channel from his ATV, Simon saw the Templar's face appear on the HUD. He opened the channel at his end so his face could be seen as well.

"I'm here," Simon answered. He recognized the Templar's features although it had been years since he'd seen the man.

Donald Pettibone was in his forties by now. His face was lean and haggard. A thin salt and pepper mustache framed his upper lip. He was a sergeant of the House Rorke and had trained many of the Templar in small-unit maneuvers. The Fists, as they were called, of the House Rorke were some of the most disciplined of all Templar.

"It's good to see you again, Simon," Pettibone said. He smiled a little, but there was no warmth to his dark eyes.

"I'm glad you're well, Sergeant Pettibone. Still training?"

"Always."

"I'm surprised you're away from it now."

Pettibone hesitated. "The High Seat felt it would be better if you saw a friendly face."

Friendly face or not, Simon still didn't trust the situation. "What does he want?" He didn't feel generous enough to refer to Booth by either his name or his rank.

"To talk with you."

"He could have come himself."

Pettibone pursed his lips in distaste. Simon wasn't sure if it was because he'd suggested Booth come or because he'd forced Pettibone into admitting the High Seat didn't want to do that.

"He feels it would be safer if you visited the Underground," Pettibone said.

"Then we're at an impasse," Simon said. "Booth has wasted both our times." He started to turn away.

"Lord Cross."

Pettibone's use of the hereditary title froze Simon in place.

"That was my father's title," Simon said, "and he chose not to use it except at House functions. He saw himself as a knight first, a Seraphim and defender of the House Rorke and the Order."

"I know that, Simon," Pettibone said. "I'm only reminding you that the title is yours now."

"Why?"

"Because there are some who feel you should be treated accordingly."

Simon studied the man's face. There had never been any deviousness in Sergeant Donald Pettibone. He was as truthful a man as ever served a House.

"When I left the Templar Underground four years ago," Simon said, "there was no mention of the title or my station."

"The situation was still very raw then." Pettibone blinked and pain showed in his unwavering gaze. "We had lost so much and things were confusing."

"And that's changed?"

"It's more settled these days."

"Yet I don't see Templar in the streets fighting the demons."

"Not to be disrespectful, but you're not massing an army against them either," Pettibone said. Hurt pride tightened his jaws.

Touché, Simon thought.

"You know as well as I do, because your father—God rest him—and I taught you tactics. Grand Master Sumerisle tried routing the demons through sheer numbers. That didn't work then, and that was when there were more Templar to go to war against the demons. Now it's the demons numbers that have increased, and they're increasing every day. We have to pick and choose our battles."

"I pick and choose mine," Simon growled. "And I see my warriors fall defending innocents or striking against the demons where we can. When was the last time High Seat Booth took up a sword or pistol against a demon?" From what he had heard, Booth hadn't left the Underground except to come strip Macomber away.

"That's disrespectful," Pettibone protested. "Your father would never have acted in such a manner."

"You've known since the day you started training me that I was my father's son but not my father." Even during those early years Simon hadn't meekly accepted anyone's teaching. He had challenged Pettibone on several issues and had tried the man's patience severely. "Tell Booth that I decline his invitation. You may even tell him I did so *respectfully* if you wish."

"Lord Cross . . ."

Simon turned on his heel and walked back to his ATV. "We're leaving, Sergeant Pettibone. I wish you a safe return."

"High Seat Booth offers you the Flag of Honor," Pettibone said quickly.

Without turning, Simon stared into the sergeant's face on the HUD.

"That's right," Pettibone continued when Simon didn't respond. "House Rorke extends the Flag of Honor."

The Flag of Honor hadn't been used in over a hundred years. It had first been established to settle the grievances between rival Lords of a House shortly after the Order had gone into hiding after Phillip the Fair denounced them as heretics. Despite how close-knit the Order was, there were sometimes personality clashes or debts of honor over the hand of another Templar woman that had to be settled.

The Order had wanted those clashes set aside so the Houses wouldn't be divided or conflicted within. It had been a similar clash that had caused House Pherral to fall ·during the Great War over a hundred years ago. As a result of Lord Pherral's actions—and Simon didn't know what they were because those records were sealed—House Pherral was stripped of its powers and privileges within the Order.

While growing up, Simon had known Rorke Pherral, one of the Fallen House's descendants. Pherral had been in line under his father to become the next High Seat if the House had stood. But that line had died when the father and son had died at the Battle of All Hallows' Eve.

"A Flag of Honor guarantees you safe passage," Pettibone said. "And it will give you a chance to be heard before all the Houses of the Order."

"This is about the *Goetia* manuscript, isn't it?" Simon asked.

Pettibone hesitated. "The High Seat wants to see that manuscript."

"How did he learn about it?"

"High Seat Booth convinced Professor Macomber to tell him about it."

"How?"

"Macomber saw the Templar Underground. He knew the secret would be safe with High Seat Booth. The High Seat sent a team to Akehurst Sanitarium, but it was plain that someone had already been there. Given the damage done to the dead demons that we found, we knew it was Templar that had killed them."

"That still doesn't explain why Booth has offered the Flag of Honor," Simon pointed out. "Booth could have petitioned the Order for an army to attack the stronghold we have."

"They'd have had a bloody fight on their hands if they'd tried," Nathan quietly promised.

"The High Seat didn't want to do that. You've become something of a popular figure among the Underground. He felt that many wouldn't agree with that choice of action. Even with the *Goetia* manuscript and the secrets it holds at stake."

Simon couldn't believe that.

"There are a lot of people who are pulling for you, Lord Cross," Pettibone said. "They don't necessarily agree with what you're doing, especially with the young Templar that have slipped away from the Underground to join you like some Children's Crusade, but they know you're out here making a difference."

Simon thought about that and was sorely tempted to agree to the offer. Even though he believed in what he was doing, he also knew he was dragging his father's good name down with him while he did it.

The Flag of Honor would give him a chance to set that right.

Nathan dropped a hand on Simon's shoulder and switched to private communication. "Don't do it, mate."

"It's the Flag of Honor," Simon said.

"But it's Booth that's extending it. I'd feel better if it was some other House making this offer."

"I'm sworn to House Rorke."

"And you've gone rogue of late, mate. We all have. We don't belong to a House anymore. Besides that, there's bad blood between you and Booth, and Booth's not one to let go of something once he's got his teeth in it."

"Booth can't do anything to me under the Flag of Honor. The Order won't let him."

"You'll be stepping right into the spider's web, mate.

That's never a good thing. We won't be able to protect you there."

"Nathan, I appreciate what you're saying, but I've got to do this. The people that have come to us, the civilians and the Templar—including those kids—could use the resources of the Templar Underground."

"They need *you*, mate." Nathan's face was somber on the HUD screen. "If they lose you, then they've lost more than they could ever replace."

"They could lose me tomorrow," Simon said softly. "I'm one man, Nathan. One Templar. The next battle against a demon could be my last."

"Simon, you're my friend and I love you for the courage and good heart that you have. I swear to you that on any battlefield you choose, or that chooses you, you'll never be one man or one Templar Knight standing alone." Nathan stared into Simon's eyes. "But do *not* do this thing. You can't trust Booth."

"I have to," Simon said.

"Let me go. Appoint me as your representative. I'll make the meeting with Booth."

"I can't."

Exasperated, Nathan exploded, "But it makes bloody sense! You'll be safe and we'll find out what Booth really wants."

Simon met his friend's gaze. "You can't go. Even as my representative, you wouldn't be able to speak for me. There are some things I've got to set right for my father's memory. I've got to stand accountable for my actions."

"Then let me come with you."

"You need to stay here. Keep everyone safe till I get back."

Apprehension darkened Nathan's features. "And if you don't come back?"

"Keep everyone safe."

Nathan leaned in and hugged him fiercely. His voice was hoarse when he spoke. "You just bloody well make sure you come back, mate. We need you here."

Tall and straight, Simon turned to Pettibone. "All right, Sergeant. You can let the High Seat know I've accepted his Flag of Honor."

The ATV hatch opened.

"Come aboard, Lord Cross."

Simon entered the ATV and took a sling-seat in the back. No one spoke to him as the hatch closed.

"Just sit back and enjoy the ride, Lord Cross," Pettibone advised. "It won't be long."

The ATV jerked into motion.

For a time Simon kept contact with the other ATV. He saw Nathan and the others load back up and turn the attack vehicle around to head back to the stronghold. Then the connection, kept encrypted and separate from the channel cycling through Pettibone's ATV, was lost.

Simon sat back and was alone in the midst of potential enemies, protected only by a thin veil of honor from an ideal that was nearly a thousand years old and birthed in another world than the brutal landscape that lay around him.

Three hours later, Simon slipped through the shadows surrounding the Elephant and Castle tube station with Pettibone and the other Templar. The House Rorke entrance lay behind a secret door within the abandoned tube.

When Simon had first returned to London four years ago, he'd come through the tube station. He hadn't been back since.

The area was worse than it had been. The Burn continued to scour the city. Huge holes and cracks tore up the streets where demons had battled or Carnagors had tunneled up through.

Pettibone waved them to one side of an alley. The Templar hunkered down with their blades drawn and their pistols in hand.

Simon waited for them, but the sense of foreboding continued to build within him. It didn't make sense that they were holding their present position. There was nothing keeping them from entering the tube station.

"What are we waiting for?" Simon asked.

"Patience, Lord Cross," Pettibone said. "The city continues to grow more dangerous every day. Things could have changed even in the few hours we've been gone."

Simon checked the HUD and noticed—not for the first time—that the other Templar had kept him in the midst of them. He felt like a prisoner, but he knew that what they were doing made perfect sense. Under similar circumstances, he would have done the same thing.

Across the street, a line of Templar came from the tube station and approached. When Simon recognized Booth's distinctive black over red armor design, a sour bubble of distaste burst at the back of his throat.

Simon stood as Booth came toward him. The Templar spread out around them, but two of Booth's personal guard remained close enough to defend him if the need arose.

"Simon," Booth said. His faceplate turned translucent to reveal his face. Despite the ongoing invasion, Booth had gained weight during the last four years. It showed in his features. Simon hadn't been certain of that during their exchange aboard the ATVs when Booth had come for Macomber.

Hiding out seems to have agreed with him, Simon

thought, and he stopped himself just short of making that observation. Instead, he managed a more diplomatic, "High Seat Booth."

"Even with the offer of the Flag of Honor," Booth said, "I really didn't expect you to trust me."

Simon wanted to assure Booth that the matter had been daunting. "We have a common goal," he said.

"The book of *Goetia*." Booth nodded. "Did you bring it with you?"

"No." Simon didn't care to elaborate that it was burned or that it was no longer in his hands. "I have the book. I came to see what you had to offer."

"Ah well, I suppose you possessing the book was too much to hope for. It doesn't really matter. Arrangements can be made. Ransom has always been a part of war."

A high-pitched whine sounded behind Simon before he could move.

"Warning," the suit's AI said. "An electromagnetic neural pacifier has—"

Pettibone threw himself forward with the device clutched in one hand. The pacifier had been designed to take out the armor when a Templar wounded on the battlefield wasn't in command of his senses. It had also been developed in case of possession by a demon or a tainted artifact. The Templar armor was as dangerous as a miniature tank and definitely more mobile. The pacifier also had to be coded to the armor's defense overrides to get through. Each House had their own sets.

Simon tried to block the pacifier, but Pettibone was too quick and too practiced to completely avoid. In addition to that, two of Pettibone's Templar tackled Simon and knocked him to the ground while he was off-balance.

He struck one of them in the faceplate hard enough to rock his head back and succeeded in levering a forearm under the chin of another. He planted a foot and rolled in an attempt to break free of their holds. Before he could get to his feet, Pettibone slammed him with the pacifier.

"Block electromagnetic buildup," Simon ordered.

"Complying," the suit AI responded. "Operations error. Electromagnetic burst is noncombative. No threat perceived."

"Negative," Simon said desperately. "Shut down House Rorke protocol." He'd been a fool to trust Booth, and he'd been an idiot for not thinking the overrides could be used against him. But they'd been necessary among his own teams.

"Hold him!" Booth ordered. "Sergeant! Put him down!"

"Enter password for House Rorke protocol shutdown override," the suit AI said.

Before Simon could respond, Pettibone slammed the pacifier home against the base of the armor's helmet. Then a series of electromagnetic bursts swept through the armor and along Simon's neural pathways. He tried to hang onto his consciousness, but he fell into a deep, black well.

FORTY-FOUR

L eah stood on one side of the conference table in the small room she'd been taken to after Tech Ops had finished the image recovery of all the burned pages.

Jenkins had uploaded the images to a file, then uploaded the images of the secret text as a separate file. He'd given copies of both files to Lyra Darius. Lyra had asked Leah to wait for her in the conference room.

As she waited, impatiently, Leah studied the constant vid feeds pulsing through the monitors on all sides of the room. All of them would go silent at the touch of a button, but anyone in the room also had access to other rooms in the compound as well as to many street level views around the Ellis Building. Some of them also showed nearby neighborhoods.

Night had fallen on the city hours ago. The demons hunted everywhere.

As she watched them, Leah wished Command had given the order to emplace weapons in different parts of the city. At one time that had been part of the plan to deal with the demons. They could have killed them from a distance.

Unfortunately, those weapons would have been found and destroyed almost immediately after use. And Command had worried that the demons might find a way to trace the wireless communication back to the compound. Losing weapons was a problem too, because they hadn't yet found a way to quickly produce them for operatives in the field.

On one of the screens, a group of stalker demons chased a man and a boy. The demons caught up with them in seconds. Leah made herself watch their deaths so that it would be burned into her mind why she would give the demons no mercy when she had them in her sights.

Then the door opened and Lyra entered.

"Have a seat," Lyra invited.

"I don't want to sit," Leah said. "Sitting means staying, and staying means delaying. One way or the other, I need to be somewhere that I can be doing some good."

"All right." Lyra sat on the corner of the table. She looked tired and exhausted. "I ran your suggestion to take a copy of the *Goetia* manuscript to the Templar—"

Leah started to object.

"—to *Simon Cross*," Lyra amended, "by my advisors. To a person, they all vetoed the idea."

Leah's heart sank. *You betrayed Simon's trust.* Despite the setback, she immediately began coming up with plans to strip the files from the computers and get out of the compound with them. None of them seemed particularly easy, but she wasn't going back to Simon without something in hand.

"I pointed out that we would still have a copy of the manuscript to work on ourselves," Lyra went on. "Their response was that the Templar would have a headstart on us because they'd be more familiar with the language."

"Which is exactly why we should give it to Simon," Leah said.

"I made that same argument. I also pointed out that unless we were prepared to keep you on permanent lockdown, we couldn't guarantee the control of the *Goetia* files."

Leah didn't say anything, but a tingle of fear ran through her. She'd been trained to handle incarceration. Out in the field it sometimes happened. But she couldn't imagine being locked away while Simon was still battling the demons and to save those he could in the city.

"I know you could promise me that you wouldn't go near those files," Lyra said.

"I would never do anything to hurt this organization," Leah said immediately, going for the opportunity. "I give you—"

"Stop." Lyra held up a hand. "You lie prettily, but you still lie. You'll do exactly what you think you need to do in this matter. You've got plenty of precedent set up in that regard."

Leah quieted. Her mind busied itself with ways to get out of lockdown. She'd been trained to handle that as well.

"Fortunately for you," Lyra said, "my advisors are that only: advisors. My decisions are mine in this place, and they're not open to review. Therefore, it's my decision that you be allowed to take this information to the Templar—to Simon Cross—with the understanding from you, and I know you can't guarantee an agreement from him, that we share information that becomes pertinent."

Leah couldn't keep the smile from her face.

"Stop grinning like a loon," Lyra ordered in mock-seriousness. "I've just given you orders that put you in harm's way again."

Making her face grim again, Leah nodded. "Yes, ma'am. When can I go?"

"I thought maybe you might want to rest and grab a bite before you—"

"Begging your pardon, ma'am, but I'm rested. And I can eat on the way."

A sad smile twisted Lyra's lips. "Somehow I thought you'd say that. Let me have your hand." She offered her own.

Leah took the other woman's hand.

"Ready for transmission," Lyra said.

"Ready," Leah replied. She closed her helmet and watched as the download application appeared onscreen.

"Transmitting."

The transfer took several minutes because none of the files had been compressed. When the upload bar hit 100 percent, a beep sounded. Leah knew about the AIs that drove the Templar armor, but suits worn by her group and the military didn't feature those.

"Don't make me regret this, Leah," Lyra said. "Don't hold information back on us and bloody well don't get yourself killed."

"No, ma'am."

"You can go. Motor Pool has a motorcycle for you as well as nutri-sub you can eat on the way."

"Thank you, ma'am."

Minutes later, Leah threw a leg over the twenty-year old BMW R 1200 GS Adventure Enduro motorcycle she'd been assigned and keyed the big engine to life. The roar filled the neat garage.

"Command said you were used to this model," the compact mechanic said as he gave the petrol tank a final wipe with a towel.

"I am," Leah agreed.

"I hope it takes care of you."

"I'm sure it will, chief."

"Well, try to bring it back. You've lost two of them and they're getting harder and harder to find."

Leah glanced around the motor pool. There were currently fewer vehicles in the bays than she'd seen at any other time. Tanks, armored cars, jeeps, and motorcycles made up the inventory.

"I'll do my best, chief," she said. Then she twisted the accelerator, let off the clutch, and lifted her foot as she shot forward.

She raced through an underground tunnel wide enough for the military tanks. Two-point-four miles later, she arrived at a security checkpoint manned by a dozen men wearing the same kind of armor she had on.

"Leah Creasey?" one of the men asked.

"Yes." Leah rested on her left foot and leaned the motorcycle.

"Special dispatch."

Leah knew the man was reading the orders on his HUD. "Yes."

"Do you know the area?" the man asked.

Leah pulled down a map overlay of the area. The tunnel let out into an underground parking garage. "Yes."

"Have a safe trip."

"Thank you."

The man signaled the others and they checked the monitors outside the false wall. When they were satisfied there were no spying demon eyes, they opened the wall.

The security chief tossed Leah a quick salute.

Leah twisted the throttle and raced out into the parking garage. Seconds later she was racing through London's broken streets as if the hounds of Hell were after her. And, at times, they were.

Hours later, Leah parked the motorcycle under a tree deep within the woods. She took one of the petrol tanks from the rear of the bike and topped off the tank. Anytime she stopped she made that her first order of business. Running out of fuel while fleeing demons wasn't a pleasant prospect.

Then she changed her communications array to the frequency Simon's Templar stronghold monitored and attempted to contact them. Almost instantly she was put through to Danielle.

"Where are you?" Danielle demanded.

"Only a few miles from the stronghold," Leah answered. "I thought I might call before I just came in." She noticed the tension in Danielle's face and voice even before her suit's analysis programming kicked into play to confirm it.

"That's a good thing. Did you have any luck with the manuscript?"

"Yes. I've got a copy of it with me."

Relief showed on Danielle's face and eased some of the fatigue etched there. "Stay where you are. I have your location. I'll have a team bring you in."

"I could come in by myself."

"In case you're not alone."

Leah peered around the empty woods. "Who else would be here?"

"Hopefully, no one. But just in case."

Irritation chafed at Leah. She suddenly felt more vulnerable in the woods. "What's going on, Danielle?"

"We'll tell you when we have you."

When we have you? Leah didn't care for the sound of that. "You'll tell me now or I'll be gone before anyone can reach me. Where's Simon?"

Danielle took a breath and let it out. "While you were gone, Simon was lured back to the Templar Underground by High Seat Booth. Now Booth has him. We just received a ransom demand. Either we bring Booth the *Goetia* manuscript or he'll stake Simon out for the demons to have."

Leah threw her leg back over the motorcycle. "Clear me through, Danielle. I don't want to wait on your escort." She keyed the engine to life.

Terrence Booth, Leah knew from previous encounters with the man, was a despicable lout. Adding liar and conniver to the list wasn't a hardship. She'd detested him from the moment she'd met him, almost as quickly as she'd come to trust Simon Cross.

It was hard to accept the two men came from the same environs and heritage.

Leah stared at the frozen image of Simon chained to a chair in a small room. His head sagged forward on his chest. He was either unconscious or drugged into a stupor.

For all you know, he's already dead and Booth shot this of his corpse. Leah tried to forget that thought had ever crossed her mind but it was impossible. *Concentrate on the fact that he's alive. If he's not—*

She couldn't finish. If Simon wasn't alive, it was already too late.

Booth's message had been short and to the point. She played the last of it back.

Booth stood in front of the vidcam in full armor. His faceplate was translucent to show his features. Simon sat in the background, stripped of his armor and chains binding his chest, arms, and legs.

"I know you have the *Goetia* manuscript," Booth said. "I've sent men into Akehurst Sanitarium to retrieve it after Professor Macomber told me about it. I found your handiwork. So either you produce the manuscript by sunrise tomorrow or I stake Cross out as demonbait."

The vid blanked.

Leah made herself breathe out. A headache crashed like blazes between her temples. She hated thinking about what might have happened if she'd gotten her freedom any later than she had. "Did anyone talk to Booth?"

"I did." Nathan sat on the other side of the comm control room. He was pensive and had a hard time sitting still. "If I'd been in the same room with him, I'd have kicked his bloody teeth down his bloody throat."

"If that would get Simon back, I'd be all for it," Leah replied. "Until we have that guarantee, we're not going to choose that course of action."

"If he's hurt Simon, I'm going to kill him."

"Calm heads win battles," Wertham stated from the corner. "Not young hearts." The old Templar sat quietly at the back of the room. "If Lord Cross is alive, we'll get him back. If not, then we'll see to his vengeance."

"Can you call Booth back?" Leah asked.

"We don't know," Danielle said. "At the time there didn't seem to be much point in it. We figured the less said, the better. We didn't want to admit that we didn't have the manuscript."

"When did Booth take Simon into custody?"

"Early this morning," Wertham said. "Before first light."

"Why did he go with him?"

"Booth offered a Flag of Honor," Nathan said.

"Tell me again what that is."

Nathan did. "I asked Simon not to go. I offered to go in his stead. But he wouldn't hear of it."

"Why?" To Leah the decision sounded foolish.

"Because Booth played Simon," Danielle said. "He

knew that by offering Simon a Flag of Honor he was essentially presenting Simon a chance to clear his name."

"Clear his name of what?" Leah asked.

"Abandoning the Templar six years ago," Wertham said.

"While he was down in South Africa?"

Wertham nodded.

"But I thought the Templar—at least some of them—were allowed lives outside the Underground."

"Some of them were," the old Templar said. "I was a fisherman for many years. But Simon walked away not only from the Templar, but from his father."

"That's where Booth had Simon," Nathan said. "And Booth knew it. Histories are kept of the Order and the Houses, and the individual nobility that serves them. There's never been a more loyal Knight Templar than Lord Thomas Cross."

"Simon feels he's brought shame to his father's name," Wertham said. "All those years ago, with his father still alive, Simon didn't think about it. He probably couldn't even fathom the idea of his father getting killed. I know he still has a hard time dealing with the guilt involved in that."

"All right," Leah said, "I get that Simon was highly motivated and vulnerable to this deal." With her own upbringing, though, family honor was an alien concept. But she understood the integrity part and knew—at least partially—what kind of man Simon Cross was. "What I want to know is how Booth can feel free to break this offer to Simon? Doesn't that leave a black spot on his honor somewhere?"

"If Simon were in good standing with the Templar," Danielle said, "most definitely. This would be an egregious breach of ethics."

"Templar Houses have fallen over such matters of honor," Wertham said.

"What if we let the rest of the Templar Underground know what Booth has done?" Leah asked.

"For all we know," Nathan said sourly, "one of the other Lords or Ladies came up with the idea."

FORTY-FIVE

"The other Houses in the Templar Underground didn't like it when Simon walked out on them four years ago," Nathan went on, "and they like it even less that other Templar have continued to come to us."

"Did you tell Booth that you would bring him the manuscript?" Leah asked.

Nathan looked guilty. "Yes. I didn't have a choice. I didn't know what might happen if I told him it had been destroyed."

"Good, because now we've got it."

"You're going to give it to him?" Danielle looked like she couldn't believe what she was hearing.

"Of course we are. We can make a copy for everybody. We're just not going to give Booth the file with the secret text." Leah had already briefed them on what she'd found out.

Some of the Templar scholars were already working on the text, but so far they didn't have a clue as to what was hidden in the language.

"Wait," Danielle protested.

Already guessing what was coming, Leah looked at the Templar and waited.

"This is *our* problem," Danielle said angrily. "No one died and made you queen."

Leah let the other woman's emotion roll off her and didn't take it personally. She knew Danielle was dealing with her own guilt and frustration in the matter, and none of that had anything to do with her. "I'm not trying to be queen."

"The way you're trying to take over everything says otherwise."

Nathan and Wertham seemed only too happy to stay out of the discussion.

"You're not a Templar," Danielle said.

"No," Leah said calmly, "I'm not. But I care about Simon. A lot." She felt her face burn a little at the admission and wondered where *that* emotion had come from. "I don't want to see him hurt."

"We can handle this."

"How?" Leah challenged.

Danielle looked at the other two Templar. They both looked elsewhere and didn't meet her gaze.

"We don't have any reason to believe Booth will deal in good faith with us—"

"It's not *us*," Danielle interrupted.

"—in this matter after the way he's treated Simon."

"We don't think that."

"Then what do you plan to do?" Leah asked. "And charging in isn't the answer."

Danielle sighed. "I don't know," she said in a small voice. "But you're right about not expecting the best from Booth. The bad history between him and Simon goes back to the time they were boys."

"Subtlety and subterfuge are my game," Leah said. "If I can put together something we can all agree on, we can get ahead of Booth. But if you try to freeze me out of this, you're going to be losing an asset you need. Trust me on that."

Danielle nodded.

Leah checked the time and found that it was a little after eleven o'clock p.m. "All right, we've got some time to play with. Let's see if we can come up with something that even remotely resembles a plan." She looked at Wertham. "Is there any way I can get a blueprint of the Templar Underground?"

"No. Those aren't drawn out for two reasons." Wertham ticked them off on his fingers. "Number one is so that those plans can never fall into anyone's hands and be used against the Templar."

Leah understood that. Command didn't allow blueprints of their hidden centers for the same reasons.

"The second is because much of the Underground has changed over the years as new construction has taken place."

That, Leah knew, was going to be a problem. "But you can draw a map?"

Wertham nodded. "All of us can."

"Then all of you do it. Without conferring with each other. We'll need to check against error and omission." Leah looked at Wertham. "Can you assemble a team willing to go in after Simon?"

"If the rest of the stronghold knew Booth had him," Nathan said, "we'd have a mass evacuation on our hands. They'd *all* go after him. That's why we've kept this to ourselves."

"All right. Keeping control of the information was good. But you're going to have to put someone in this room who can deal with Booth in case he tries to contact you again."

Wertham nodded. "All of that can be done."

"Then get it done now. We need to be en route as soon as we can be. Without anyone here being the wiser."

The three Templar stood.

"One other thing," Leah said. "Do you have someone who can print the manuscript out and make it look authentic? I don't want to give Booth an electronic copy. Then he'll know we've already gotten copies of it ourselves. And I don't want to make it easy for him to resource. He can do his own bloody scut work."

Pain exploded in Simon's head and drew him back to wakefulness. When he felt the warm spill of blood down his chin he knew he'd been hit again. He ignored the pain and tried to focus on his tormentor. Chains covering his upper body and legs confined him to the straight-backed chair in the small room where he was being held.

"I think he's awake again," the Templar in front of Simon said.

It took a moment of intense study for Simon to realize it was one man and not twins.

"Are you awake, Simon?" Booth asked.

Still weak and partially disoriented, Simon sagged against the chains and turned his head to look at Booth. The High Seat sat across the metal table in the room.

"I'm awake," Simon mumbled through swollen lips.

"I've talked with your friends. They've agreed to exchange the *Goetia* manuscript for you." Booth ate fresh cherries from a bowl.

The Templar Underground gardens were a mixture of hydroponics and mysticism. Almost anything could be grown there because conditions for any type of plant were possible. The systems in the stronghold Simon had established hadn't reached anywhere near the same efficiency or potential variables.

Do to the pain and the drugs coursing through his system, Simon had trouble sifting through Booth's words. "They told you they would trade the manuscript for me?"

"Yes." Booth popped another cherry into his mouth.

Simon hated the High Seat for his excesses, and he was sure Booth knew it. In the stronghold it sometimes became a struggle to feed everyone. Yet the Templar in the Underground produced enough to have surplus and could grow things beyond the staples.

Given the circumstances and the fact that he hadn't been privy to the conversation with anyone Booth had talked to, Simon felt certain Booth wasn't telling the truth. He licked his lips and tasted blood.

"You're lying," Simon croaked. He craved a drink of water. He didn't know how long he'd been unconscious.

Almost casually, Booth tapped a remote control next to the cherry bowl. A tri-dee screen opened on one of the walls and showed Nathan seated at the comm command center in the stronghold.

"—either you produce the manuscript by sunrise tomorrow or I stake Cross out as demonbait," Booth's recorded voice said.

Booth tapped the remote control to freeze the image on Nathan. "That was me, making my demands. This next bit is your friend." He tapped the remote control again.

Nathan stared at the screen for a moment, then said, "We'll bring you the manuscript. But we need more time."

"No more time," Booth's recorded voice replied. "Sunrise tomorrow. After that, Simon Cross is a dead man."

Booth turned off the tri-dee and smiled brightly. "You're going to be a dead man anyway, but he doesn't think so. Yet."

Simon made himself grin. It was hard because his lips

didn't work right in the shape they were in. His nose felt broken and he couldn't breathe through it.

"Nathan knows you're a liar," Simon said. "He already knows honor doesn't mean anything to you."

"What?" Booth feigned surprise. "Because I broke the Flag of Honor agreement with you?"

Simon refused to take the bait.

"You make agreements like that with men *with* honor," Booth said. "Not the likes of you. That agreement is for Templar. You're an outcast. There's no honor in dealing with you."

Something Thomas Cross had told Simon a long time ago came back to him. He hadn't really seen the truth of it until four years ago when he'd come back to find London in the hands of demons.

"Honor isn't something between men," Simon said. "It's something inside a man that can be used to take his measure. And because he has it, he can extend it to others." He pierced Booth with his gaze. "You have no honor."

Booth scowled. "Don't bore me with your platitudes."

"They're not platitudes," Simon said. "They're words my father gave me to live by." He looked at the other Templar in the room. "They're words I'm sure he gave to all of you."

The other Templar dropped their eyes and wouldn't meet Simon's gaze.

Booth nodded at the big man in front of Simon. Knowing what was coming, Simon tried to turn away from the blow. It didn't do any good. The man's hand caught him full in the face. For a moment it seemed like the pain was going to be enough to knock him over into the abyss.

"Don't use your father's good name to hide your shame," Booth said. "There's not a man in this room that doesn't know what Thomas Cross meant to the Order. He never once turned his back on us."

Simon spat blood into the cherry bowl.

Booth cursed him and got up from the table. Unlike the man who'd been hitting Simon with his fists, Booth still wore his armor. If he hit Simon, the blow would undoubtedly kill him.

Simon didn't turn away.

"High Seat Booth," one of the Templar said, "I won't be party to murder."

Booth turned to the man. "Then you should leave, Whitehall."

The Templar drew himself up. "No. I agreed to this because I believe we need to have the *Goetia* manuscript. If what Macomber told us about the protective nodes was correct, we can't continue holding out against the demons without them. If Cross's friends find out he's dead, they won't give us the manuscript."

Rage darkened Booth's face. He curled a hand into a fist and hammered the table, knocking it flat. The *boom* of the impact filled the room.

Simon guessed that the room was soundproofed. Many of the Templar Underground rooms were. But his thoughts centered on what Whitehall had said Macomber had talked about.

"You're being insubordinate," Booth declared.

"No sir. I'm here to get the manuscript," Whitehall said. "All of us are. And we agreed that the Flag of Honor didn't apply to Simon Cross. But we will not permit this. No Templar murders a helpless prisoner."

"Then you're all fools," Simon told them. "Because the manuscript had already been destroyed when we got there. Whatever information it contained was lost a long time ago."

"You're lying," Booth accused.

"On my father's blood," Simon replied.

"Your friend Nathan said he was going to bring the manuscript."

"He didn't have a choice. You told him you were going to kill me." Simon drew a breath. "You're just wasting time and broke what little honor you had for nothing."

Booth stared at him for a moment, and Simon could see the fear in the High Seat's eyes that what he said was true.

"No," Booth said. "That's not completely true, is it? If it were, you wouldn't have agreed to meet me. There's more to this than you're saying."

"I came here to defend my father's honor," Simon said.

"That's true, but that's not all of it. You're hiding something. I want to know what it is."

Simon looked at Booth and firmed his resolve. "The manuscript was burned. It doesn't exist any more."

"We'll see about that." Booth turned to one of the Templar. "Hail Nathan Singh for me."

The Templar stepped to one side and talked quietly for a moment.

Simon tried desperately to force away the pain filling his face and body, but even with all his training it was a hopeless cause.

"I've got the Templar stronghold," the Templar said.

"Put it on the monitor," Booth ordered.

Even though he didn't want to, Simon glanced at the monitor. He recognized Pelter, one of the older Templar at the stronghold at the comm array and couldn't help wondering where Nathan and Danielle were.

"Where is Nathan Singh?" Booth demanded.

"Hold on, High Seat Booth," Pelter said. "I'll have Nathan for you in just a moment." He leaned forward and the monitor changed.

In the next moment, Nathan's image filled the screen. "What do you want?" he demanded, not sounding friendly. The background showed that he was standing in the ATV bay.

The confusing thing was that Simon knew there was no comm array in the caves where the ATVs were stored.

"I've been having an interesting chat with our friend Simon," Booth said.

Nathan jerked a thumb over his shoulder. "If you want us there on time, you'd be better off not wasting my time."

Displeased with the cavalier treatment, Booth scowled. "Simon tells me there is no manuscript. He says that it burned up at the sanitarium."

"So?"

"Did it?"

Nathan cursed. "Simon doesn't trust you, Booth. Obviously he has reason not to. He doesn't want us trusting you either. So he's going to lie to you about the manuscript and tell you it doesn't exist so you'll call the deal off. The way he sees it, he's trading his life for all of ours."

"Then you have the manuscript?"

"Yes." Nathan acted bored with the subject.

"Show me," Booth ordered.

"Show me Simon's still alive."

Cursing, Booth stepped back and waved to Simon. One of the Templar came closer and used a vidcam to capture his image.

"He's alive," Booth said.

"That could be a holo," Nathan argued. "Have him say something."

Booth nodded at the big man, who immediately back-handed Simon in the face before he could get away.

"He bleeds on demand," Booth said smoothly.

Nathan cursed Booth fluently.

"I suggest you stop playing games with me," Booth said. "Show me the manuscript if you have it, or I'm going to have Simon killed right here in front of you."

Nathan reached out of the cam's view and pulled up a sheaf of papers. They looked old and authentic, not like the burned sheets Simon had found in the tube they'd recovered from the sanitarium.

"I need to get moving if I'm going to make your deadline," Nathan said. "Now, if there isn't anything else?"

Booth gave the command to break the comm connection and turned back to Simon.

"It seems you can't speak the truth any more these days," Booth said. He nodded at the big man.

Another cruel blow smashed into Simon's cheek and caught the hinge of his jaw. Pain exploded bright colors across his vision.

Simon tried to speak and deny the existence of the pages. It was some kind of trick. It had to be. But his jaw wouldn't move right and he couldn't form the words. The struggle to speak only increased the pain and he slid over into darkness. His last thought was that Nathan and Danielle were somehow setting themselves up to get themselves killed.

FORTY-SIX

"Comm's cut," Leah said.

Nathan breathed a sigh of relief and leaned back against the tri-dee projector that still broadcast the image of the cave that held the ATVs. Leah had captured the image of the cave before they'd left hours ago.

"Are you sure Booth bought it?" Nathan asked.

"I'm sure," Leah said. "I've spoofed comm a few times during my career."

"What career is that?" Danielle asked.

Leah ignored the suspicion in the Templar's eyes. She knew none of them were completely accepting of her, but at the moment they all had to trust her to do what she'd said she could do.

"Here's a copy of the transmission," Danielle said, changing the topic. She played it back.

Seated in a sling-seat in the ATV they were riding in to get back to London, Leah regarded the finished product. It was good. The computer application she'd uploaded to the stronghold comm array was impeccable.

"What if Booth has the vid checked out?" Nathan asked. "Will he be able to tell it's a fake?"

"Whoever looks at that broadcast would have to be some kind of specialist to tell it's not real," Leah said. "I don't think the Templar have anyone good enough to expose that because you people—quite frankly—haven't been interested in those kinds of applications. You may have the lock on personal defense systems, but there's still a lot you're not familiar with when it comes to other programming and uses for it."

"Not only that, but Booth doesn't want to believe the *Goetia* manuscript is destroyed," Danielle added. "He wants it to be real."

"If the manuscript actually leads to some kind of permanent protection from demons," Nathan growled, "it would make him some kind of bloody hero."

"Let's just see if we can't keep him from becoming Simon's murderer," Leah said. "For the moment, I'll settle for that."

Wake.

Wearily, Warren woke and peered into the darkness of his bedroom. Across the room, the seeds he'd gotten from Knaarl's sword lay beneath the warm earth in a terrarium and considered germinating for the first time in thousands of years.

"What's the matter?" Naomi asked from beside him.

"Merihim," Warren said.

Fearfully, Naomi clutched the bedsheet to her bosom and leaned back against the headboard.

Come. We must go. Fulaghar and Toklorq are closing in on the book Fulaghar has been searching for.

Warren climbed from the bed. Although he didn't want to, his own gaze strayed to the book on his desk. It was still there.

"Where are they?" Warren asked. When he looked at the balcony window, he saw that from the pink sky that sunrise was only minutes away.

At the Tower of London.

Cold dread balled in the pit of Warren's stomach. He'd been there before. Located in the London Borough of Town Hamlets, the Tower of London had always been an auspicious place. Public executions and royal imprisonments had taken place there, and the White Tower—which was actually the whole complex—was the supposed site of a number of supernatural events and powers.

It wasn't a place for demons to congregate.

"Go," the voice said in the back of his mind. "I have seen the future of this. Everything is as it should be."

Warren sincerely hoped so. "I thought you needed me to kill Toklorq before you confronted Fulaghar," he told Merihim.

The demon stood out on the balcony in the waning night. He looked fierce and terrible, his trident clenched in one hand.

It's too late for that. As it turns out, Fulaghar's search for the book Goetia *wasn't foolishness after all. The book exists, and at present it's in the hands of the Templar. Fulaghar has gone there to get it back.* Merihim turned to face Warren. *You and I are going to put an end to him so that I can claim my rightful place as a Dark Will.*

In seconds, Warren joined the demon.

Merihim slid the trident across the air and sliced open a hole. Warren felt the energy pouring forth from it. Then Merihim pushed him into it and followed.

Simon stumbled and nearly fell as one of the Templar dragged him up the steps from the Tower Hill tube station. His jaw pained him terribly, and from the way it wouldn't move properly when he tried to work it, he suspected that it was broken. It was everything he could do to keep it clamped shut so that it didn't produce even more agony.

He was dressed in his armor, but it was powered down by Booth's command. For the first time ever, the armor felt heavy and unwieldy on him. It also felt dead because the suit's AI was off-line. They'd shackled his arms behind him and left his helm open because they'd wanted Nathan to identify him.

Despite everything that had happened, Simon still hoped that Nathan's better sense had returned and he had decided not to pay the ransom anyway. If he had, it was probably going to get them both killed. Simon was certain that Nathan hadn't had the real manuscript to show Booth.

"Lord Cross."

Carefully, still having to match the stride of the Templar who had hold of the chain around his neck, Simon turned around. His head felt so heavy that he almost fell over his own feet.

Professor Archibald Xavier Macomber trudged in Simon's wake. Booth's Templar marched in single file order along Tower Wharf. The Burn had eaten into what had once been beautiful landscaping and trees.

Macomber looked worse for wear. Evidently Booth hadn't been overly gentle with him either. Bruises marked his face.

"I'd heard that you were here," Macomber said tiredly. "I have to admit, I'd hoped that you were still free." He smiled a little. "I'm not a big believer in last-moment rescues like on the vids and holos, but I'd held out for that one."

"Sorry to disappoint you." Simon's words were thick and slow through his mangled, swollen jaw.

"My God," Macomber said. "Your face looks horrible."

"It can't look as bad as it feels," Simon assured him.

The Templar pulling Simon yanked on his chain, nearly driving him to his knees from the pain.

"I was told that Booth is going to be getting the *Goetia* manuscript," Macomber said.

"It was burned," Simon said. "What he's getting is a . . . fake."

Macomber looked troubled. "Then it will probably be bad for both of us."

Simon didn't bother to disabuse the professor of that notion.

"Booth ordered me along to prove the veracity of the manuscript," Macomber said.

Simon nodded, but kept up with the Templar ahead of him. He gazed around at the grounds. The Tower of London held a lot of the city's history.

It had first been erected in 1078 when William the Conqueror had the White Tower constructed. The other buildings had followed, but so had the places of execution and prisons.

During its lifespan, the Tower had provided space for an armory, treasury for the Crown Jewels and more, an observatory, public records offices, and menageries. The most famous animals that called the Tower home were the Ravens of the Tower.

For hundreds of years, there had always been at least six Ravens in the Tower. A saying had sprung to life that if the Ravens ever left the Tower, it would crumble to rubble and disaster would befall England.

After the battle at St. Paul's, Simon had heard that the Ravens had left the Tower. He'd also been told that Blood Angels had stalked them and killed all of them. He didn't know which to believe. The Ravens' wings were kept clipped to keep them from flying away, and they'd been under the care and scrutiny of the Ravenmaster, one of the people selected from the Yeomen Warders.

As they walked along the river, Simon peered into the depths. Only a few inches of foul water remained, and already familiar white shapes could be seen in the mud and the shallows.

"Are . . . are those bones?" Macomber asked.

"Yes," Simon said. There were bones, cars, boats, and ships all mired in the vestiges of the once-mighty Thames. In another few years, possibly only a handful, the Burn would drain it completely and leave it only a cracked and broken ruin.

"I'd heard when the moat that had been around the Tower was drained in 1830 human bones were found."

Simon didn't know if that was true or not. He concentrated on putting one foot in front of the other and not falling down. Ahead of him, safely ensconced between four Templar guards, Booth set the pace in full armor. The High Seat's steps were a lot easier with operational armor.

"I was also told that the mortar used on the stones was mixed with the blood of sacrificial animals. The way the Romans were said to do things."

"I don't know, Professor," Simon said with effort.

"If it's true, that might make these buildings more in the demons' purview than the human races."

Only a few moments later, Simon was gratefully brought to a halt at the outer perimeter entrance across the moat. It had been drained years ago, as Macomber had mentioned, and now remained totally dry. But broken bodies and refuse filled the moat. Evidently the demons had taken to using the area as a dumping ground for carcasses of their victims.

"It appears your friends are running late," Booth said irritably.

Silently, Simon hoped they didn't come. He didn't know if Booth would kill him in frustration or not, but it would be better to die than to be the reason his friends died.

The stench of the Burn was heavy on the air. So was the thick, sweet scent of old death. In the distance, demons heeled over in the sky. So far none of them had taken interest in them.

But it surely wouldn't take much time.

When Warren stepped through the rift Merihim had created, he found himself on a tower. It took him a moment to recognize where he was and realize that he was on the Middle Tower on the Tower of London where it overlooked the outer perimeter entrance.

A group of Templar stood on the wrought-iron railed bridge that crossed the moat. They appeared to be waiting for something.

Merihim stood at Warren's side. The demon tilted his head back and scented the air.

Reaching into his shoulder bag, Warren freed one of the Blood Angel eyes under his control and sent it aloft. When he closed his eyes, he could see through the charmed eyeball.

"Go carefully here," the voice told him. "You're on very dangerous ground this morning."

Warren already knew that. But he also felt the power lurking in the nearby graveyards. All manner of poverty-stricken prisoners had been buried in those graves, but a few of them contained members of royalty as well.

It was an army lying in wait for him and his skills. He concentrated on the arcane forces and got it ready. At a word and no more than a moment or two, he would be able to raise them. Four years ago, perhaps even only four days ago, such a thing would have been even harder.

The power within him was growing. He flexed the demon hand, knowing that much of the dark magic he'd been using was concentrated in it.

"But you're growing from within as well," the voice told him. "You can sense that as well."

Warren was and he could sense that. "Will I ever know who you are?" he asked.

"Soon," the voice promised. "Very soon now."

Warren was surprised that Merihim still wasn't aware of the voice inside his head. There didn't seem like there would be room enough for them both in there.

"I've protected myself from him," the voice said. "Just as I've protected your thoughts from him."

Thinking about that made Warren realize that whoever the voice belonged to was much more powerful than Merihim.

"Once," the voice said, "but not yet again. Soon, hopefully. I need to be free. You would have your vengeance against the Templar that took your hand, and I would have my vengeance against the one that bound me."

Look, Merihim said. He pointed one razor-tipped claw at another group of Templar who were approaching from the other end of the bridge across the moat.

"Where's Fulaghar?" Warren asked.

Merihim scented the air again. *Nearby. We'll see him soon.*

Warren watched the two groups of Templar. One of them—the one with his helmet open—looked familiar. When he nudged the Blood Angel's eye closer and looked down, he saw that it was Simon Cross. Anger boiled up inside him.

I see him too, Merihim said. *And I would have my pound of flesh from him as well after what he did to me four years ago.*

Back then Merihim had learned about the train the Templar had used to get so many of London's survivors out of the city. The demon had intended to sacrifice the lives aboard it for his own reasons. Simon Cross had grievously wounded him. Warren had been surprised that Merihim hadn't tracked the Templar down and killed him for that alone.

But he hadn't.

"The Templar is one to be watched," the voice said. "He's going to be extremely powerful soon."

Simon Cross didn't look so powerful now, Warren thought as he stared at the man with his hands shackled behind his back.

FORTY-SEVEN

L eah watched from hiding down in the moat as Nathan and Danielle crossed the bridge to meet with Booth and his group of Templar. Her suit's camouflage ability blended her in with dried mud, dead vegetation, and refuse that lined the moat.

It also protected her in this instance from Booth's Templar. And that let her know that the programming she'd altered in her suit was working as it was supposed to.

Now if only the rest of it worked.

She brought up the application on her HUD and tried the communications channel. "Nathan. Danielle. I'm in place."

"Affirmative," Nathan replied. Neither he nor Danielle broke stride as they walked over to meet Booth. In addition, the High Seat and the Templar that followed him didn't register the communications either.

"Wertham," Leah called.

"Yes," the old Templar responded.

"You should be shielded too."

"Understood," Wertham said. "We'll begin moving in."

Now for the really scary one, Leah thought. She tuned in the comm channel on Simon's armor and whispered, "Simon. This is Leah. Can you hear me?"

* * *

When Simon heard Leah's voice in his ears, with his helmet open, he couldn't believe it. He glanced at the Templar beside him to see if they'd heard it too. With her voice in the open like that, their suits' audio receptors should have picked it up if their comms didn't.

"Don't act suspicious," Leah said. "Don't look around."

Simon focused his attention on Booth. The High Seat would be the key. Beyond Booth, Danielle and Nathan walked along the moat bridge.

"Booth and his Templar can't hear me," Leah said. "I've jammed their AIs to this frequency. Nod if you understand. If you speak, they'll hear your voice. I can't mask it."

Simon nodded and worked his jaw as if he was trying to find a comfortable position for it. Unfortunately that didn't seem possible.

"Good." Leah sounded almost relieved. "Remember aboard the ATV when I mentioned that the comm relays among your armor might be a vulnerability?"

Simon nodded again.

"Welcome to the proof of that."

A small smile pulled at Simon's lips. If he survived this situation, he definitely had some work to do on the armor of the men at the stronghold. The first priority was going to be to dump all the House protocol. They weren't going to work against the Order, but they weren't going to be confined by it either.

"Nathan told me Booth's first step in holding you prisoner would be to neutralize your armor," Leah said.

Simon nodded.

The Templar to his right looked at him. "Is something wrong with you?"

Simon looked at the man as if he were daft. "My jaw is broken," he said hoarsely.

The Templar watched him a moment more, then turned away to watch Danielle and Nathan's approach.

"I think I can put your armor back under your control," Leah said, "by neutralizing Booth's hold on it. But Nathan said as soon as I do that your armor will recognize that it's in a hostile environment and button you up."

Simon nodded again.

"So I can't do that until we're ready. We're going to need you to hang on just a little longer."

Grimacing, Simon lifted his chin and lowered it slightly. If he didn't black out from the pain of his nose and jaw, he was going to be fine.

"That's far enough," Booth ordered.

Nathan and Danielle stopped less than ten feet away. In the armor, the distance was nothing.

"Let's see the manuscript," Booth said.

Nathan reached over his shoulder and produced a protective metal tube.

Booth reached for the tube, but before he could get it a scaly demon's arm flicked out from a hole in the air, seized it from Nathan's hand, then backhanded the Templar in the face.

Nathan shot backward as if he'd been propelled by a cannon. He tore through the railing and plunged over the side into the moat.

Now! Merihim ordered. *Do you see Fulaghar?*

Warren only saw part of the demon, but he knew where the rest of Fulaghar was.

Anchor him here to this place, Merihim commanded.

Holding on to the arcane energy that filled him, Warren stretched out his hand. A shimmering wave sped across the intervening distance as the Templar on the bridge started pulling weapons.

When the wave hit Fulaghar, it rocked him and drew his attention at once. Warren concentrated on hooking into the demon like a fishing line. He imagined that the demon couldn't go anywhere without breaking an invisible steel cage around him.

Fulaghar squalled in fury. He beat against the invisible barrier. Warren felt the blows of the demon's struggles as if they were blows against his body. He held on despite the pain.

The Templar had unlimbered their weapons. All except Simon Cross, who shuffled back out of the way.

Beside Warren, Merihim leaped out into open space. For a moment he thought the demon had taken leave of his senses. Then Merihim sprouted silver wings from his back and flew toward Fulaghar.

Hold Fulaghar, Merihim said. *Don't let him get away.*

"Look for Toklorq," the voice reminded. "Fulaghar wouldn't have gone far without him."

Warren's brain felt as if it was going to shatter has he held the demon. By that time the Templar were firing away with their pistols. Greek Fire and explosive rounds detonated against Fulaghar's body and inflicted massive wounds. Merihim slid his trident forward and sped straight for Fulaghar.

Then someone—some*thing*—materialized beside Warren.

"Look out!" the voice warned.

Somewhere in the back of his mind, Warren heard Naomi scream.

Leah couldn't believe the demon had shown up when it did. Of course the *Goetia* manuscript was important to them too if it held the power that Macomber hinted that it did.

She lost only a moment as she uploaded the new programming she'd prepared to Simon's suit. The bar raced across her HUD. She hoped he lived through the hellstorm that had opened up on the moat bridge.

"Wertham," Leah called.

"Yes."

"We're under attack. We need you now."

"On my way," the old Templar said.

Stepping away from the underbelly of the bridge, Leah unlimbered her Cluster Rifle and took aim at the demon. Her finger settled on the trigger at the same time she saw the second demon streaking in on a pair of bat wings with a green trident clutched in its hands.

Leah recognized the demon and the weapon from the attack on the train four years ago. *Merihim.* Command had been interested in how he'd arrived in the world since the reports mentioned that he hadn't arrived through the Hellgate. They'd tried to keep tabs on the demon over the years, but it was almost impossible.

She shifted her sights and took aim on Merihim's broad chest, realizing only then that the wings were new.

"AI back online. Going into protective mode."

The feminine voice was music to Simon's ears. Despite the pain he was in, despite the fact that Booth's men surrounded him and a pair of demons had appeared on the bridge, he felt joyous.

The helmet closed over his head as the armor powered up. Strength returned to him. He snapped the shackles that bound his hands behind his back and reached for the chain around his neck.

"Medical assistance required," the suit's AI said. "Suggest emergency repairs under full sedation."

"Negative," Simon countermanded, his broken jaw

screaming with pain over the effort required. "I'm in hostile territory and need to be functional." He gripped the chain, stepped forward to flip the slack around the Templar that had held him prisoner, set himself and called for foot anchors. When the anchors were embedded in the bridge, he twisted his body and yanked.

The Templar spun through the air at the end of the chain. His Spike Bolter dropped as he grabbed for the chain. Then Simon released the chain to fling the Templar toward the River Thames. He caught the Spike Bolter in his left hand and turned back to the demon on the bridge.

"There are other Templar around you," the suit's AI informed him. "They can take responsibility for your safety."

"Negative." Simon squeezed the trigger and palladium spikes shredded demon flesh. "Do whatever medical procedures necessary, but keep me functional."

"Understood. Stand by to set jaw."

Before Simon could say no, the helmet's interior shifted as the nanofluid flowed and pulsed to realign his face. His jaw shifted and the pain dropped him to his knees. Just before he passed out, the suit AI opened up the full range of medical supplements.

Epinephrine pumped through his system. His nose started clearing as the swelling was reduced. He tasted blood at the back of his throat and knew he was swallowing it, but there wasn't anywhere else for it to go. The suit would also make sure he was pumped full of anti-nausea meds as well.

Then, blessedly, the pain started to fade too.

"Stop him!" Booth screamed. "Don't let him get away!"

Simon had no intention of getting away. He stepped

toward the first Templar who came at him and delivered a roundhouse kick that caught the man in the midsection and knocked him from the bridge.

Danielle waded into the thick of things as well, striking out against the Templar as she tried to make her way to Simon. She was a wraith among the Templar, one of the best unarmed fighters Simon had ever seen. Her hands punched like piledrivers and her knees and feet flew in rapid strikes. Booth's men couldn't equal her.

She stripped a sword from one of the Templar before she heaved him over the side of the bridge. Turning, she threw the sword to Simon.

"Catch!" she cried.

Recognizing the blade as his own, Simon swapped hands with the Spike Bolter and caught his sword by the hilt. Firing steadily at the demon standing on the bridge, he advanced on the creature with his sword.

Warren turned, trying desperately to keep Fulaghar locked on the bridge, then saw the demon stepping from the rift beside him.

Nine feet tall and wiry, Toklorq had four arms twice as long as his body and an eye on every side of his head. If there was a mouth, Warren couldn't find it. The demon was covered in bronze and orange scales. The arms were more like tentacles. They whipped out to seize Warren.

Warren tried to slip away, but couldn't. The arms wrapped around him and started squeezing so hard he couldn't breathe. His vision started to turn black, but he tried to hold Fulaghar.

"Let Fulaghar go," the voice advised.

The fear Warren had of Merihim wouldn't allow that, though. He struggled to maintain his hold.

"Warren!" Naomi yelled from back at his sanctuary.

She pulled at him with her power, trying to get him back through a rift.

Warren turned her efforts aside.

"You're going to die!" the voice said.

Warren knew it was true. He could already feel himself slipping over the side, and there was nothing to stop the express elevator down once he went.

Leah squeezed the trigger and felt the Cluster Rifle surge against her shoulder as it fired a missile at the center of Merihim's chest. Some sixth sense warned the demon, though, and he rolled over on his side to let the projectile slide harmlessly by.

He pointed the trident at her. That surprised her because the camouflage ability was still juicing the suit.

Leah saw a mild distortion leave the tines of the trident, then the distortion turned wild and was upon her. The force blew her backwards, and she just knew she'd come apart.

In his HUD, Simon saw the shimmering force leave Merihim's trident and strike ... *something*. He had to guess that it was Leah. He called her name but didn't get a response.

He wanted to go to her, but he didn't even know where the demon's blast had knocked her. She was still invisible to his sensors. He checked for blood, but didn't see any of that either. If she'd been hurt or killed, her suit was still holding together.

Instead, he concentrated on the demon on the bridge. That one at least was within range.

The demon threw a hand out. Flames jetted over Simon and raised the suit's external temperature to smoldering in a heartbeat. By then Simon was on the creature. The palladium spikes from the Spike Bolter weren't doing much damage. The demon was healing too quickly.

Simon drew his sword back, it too wreathed in flames from the demon's attack, and swung. The blade cleaved toward the demon's head, but then Merihim's trident was there.

"No!" the demon roared in his raucous voice. Merihim kicked Simon in the face and sent him skidding back across the bridge.

FORTY-EIGHT

J ust before he lost consciousness, Warren released his hold on Fulaghar and turned his full attention to Toklorq.

"Die, human!" Toklorq hissed. His intelligence didn't seem to be quite on a par with Fulaghar's other two minions. But he was easily as deadly.

Warren pictured a sword in his mind, then built it out of the arcane energy he controlled. With a quick thrust, he shoved it into Toklorq's head. The skull exploded and eyeballs shot in all directions. Some of them plopped against Warren.

Dead, the demon fell backwards as its tentacles lost all control.

Wheezing, barely able to suck air into his lungs, Warren collapsed on top of the Middle Tower. Then he remembered Fulaghar.

When he turned around, Warren saw Fulaghar leap up at Merihim, who was still flying. Both demons hung in the air and became targets for Templar fire.

You witless, gutless fool! Merihim exploded. *We had him beaten!*

Terror flooded Warren's veins when he thought of the demon's wrath. He tried to catch hold of Fulaghar again, but his efforts were too weak and were too easily turned aside

Instead, seeing the Templar in the moat, Warren awakened the dead in the nearby graveyards and called out to them. Then he reached for the dead that he felt in the bed of the moat. Some of them were new, but some of them had been there a long time.

All of them came.

When Leah came back to herself, she was lying flat on her back. Recalling the blast that had hit her, she didn't know how she could still be whole. She relaxed enough to force a breath into her paralyzed lungs.

The readout on her HUD showed that she was intact and able to move.

Then skeleton arms reached up from the dried mud under her and wrapped around her head. She tried to break away, but more joined the first and held her tightly.

In the next moment, a skull popped up and lunged at her throat. Thankfully the armor held for the moment.

"Wertham," she radioed.

"Almost there," the old Templar replied. "Hold on."

Holding on wasn't the problem, though. Getting held was. Leah struggled against her undead captors.

"Oh my God."

Hearing Danielle's exclamation, Simon forced himself to his feet. Despite the meds in his system, he was starting to fade quickly. The artificial vigor could last only so long.

He glanced at the sky where the two demons fought, thinking that was what had caused Danielle's consternation. Then he noticed the hills around them were filled with undead corpses that were converging on the moat. Even more of them were crawling up from the moat bed.

They were surrounded.

Then Simon heard Leah call for Wertham and wondered where the old Templar might be. He'd sounded close enough.

"Nathan," Simon said when he got a lock on the Templar down in the moat. Other Templar, all of them Booth's men, fought against the undead that came up from the moat.

"I'm here, Simon," Nathan replied. "Bloody hell. These things are everywhere."

"You haven't seen anything yet," Danielle said. "I think Anne Boleyn and William Hastings just climbed out of their graves this morning to kick your arse."

"They'll have to stand in line." Nathan swung his sword and shattered two skeletons directly in his face. But there were plenty more where those came from.

"Wertham," Leah called again.

Simon scanned the moat and found a cluster of skeletons that looked like they were fighting themselves. Then every now and again he got a glimpse of Leah's armor. Once he saw her in motion, he saw all of her because the camouflage function couldn't keep up with all her movements.

"We're here," Wertham declared.

Suddenly Simon was aware of jet turbines overhead. When he looked up, he saw a sleek attack helicopter complete with nose turret guns and door gunners. A grin pulled at Simon's face when he realized Wertham must have raided one of the abandoned military air bases to get the helicopter.

The gunners aboard the aircraft opened fire at once. They connected their online systems with the Templar armor and picked discriminate targets in rapid-fire sequence. The HARP and Greek Fire rounds slammed into the undead in the moat and turned them into calcium confetti.

Evidently Wertham had upgraded the weapons systems aboard the helicopter.

Turning his attention back to the demons battling in mid-air, Simon lifted his Spike Bolter and fired continuously into both of them. In seconds both demons were bleeding profusely.

"Wertham," Simon called, as he continued firing.

"Simon," Wertham replied jubilantly. "Good to know you're still among the living."

"Celebrate later," Simon said. "Kill demons now. See the two in the air?"

"Yes."

"Take them out." Simon looked around and spotted Professor Macomber cowering on the ground several feet back. Evidently he'd made quite a bit of distance crawling when no one was watching.

"Did you see all the undead making their way toward you?" Wertham asked.

"Yes."

"You need to evacuate."

"I know. See if you can take out those demons." Simon ran back to Macomber. The drain on Simon's system was getting worse. Despite the exoskeleton, he felt himself getting rubber-legged.

He caught up to the professor and guarded him with his body.

"Stay with me, Professor," Simon said. "We'll have you out of here in just a moment."

"What about Booth and his men?" Danielle asked.

"I'd leave them to rot, mate," Nathan replied.

"I can't," Simon said. "Wertham, is there room?"

"We have room."

The helicopter came around and the nose turret belched a massive Greek Fire shell at the demons. It missed Merihim, though, and got the other one full-on.

The stricken demon dropped to the ground down in the moat and didn't move again.

"Nooooooo!" Merihim screamed in fury. He flapped his wings and sped away. Two more rounds exploded in the air in his wake and rained down fire.

The helicopter juked around and tried to bring the fleeing demon into target acquisition again. Before it had a chance, four flying demons swung to the attack.

"Incoming!" Nathan yelled. "You've got four bogeys on your tail!"

"We've got them," Wertham replied.

The specially made helicopter spun around and brought all guns to bear. Two of the demons blew apart, but the other two slammed against the reinforced nose and hung there by their feet. They hammered their fists against the nose until the surface cracked under their assault.

One of the Templar eased out on the skids with a Blaze Pistol. Once he could reach around the nose, he squeezed the trigger and set both demons afire. They jumped ship and flew away, but there were already more circling the sky.

"If we're going to get out of here, now would be the time," Wertham said. "We're going to be drawing demons from all across London. This thing should be able to outfly most of them, but if it breaks and we have to walk back, none of us are going to care for that."

"Bring it down," Simon ordered. "I've got Professor Macomber with me. I want him protected."

"Affirmative."

Helplessly, full of dread, Warren watched as Merihim wheeled back toward him.

"You've got to get out of here," the voice in the back of his head said.

Warren tried, but he couldn't get his feet under him. "Naomi."

"I'm trying, Warren," she said. "I need you to help me."

Struggling, Warren concentrated but couldn't make the connection. Then Merihim landed in front of him hard enough to jar the rooftop.

You failed me, the demon seethed. *I didn't kill Fulaghar. The Templar did. His death doesn't mean anything.*

"His position still opens up, doesn't it?" Warren asked, trying to back away from the demon. "That's all you were after."

No. It doesn't. But yours is going to. Merihim gestured and another rift opened in the air.

A female Cabalist decked out in horns and a tail and covered in tattoos stepped onto the rooftop. She looked at Warren in disgust.

"He didn't even try to make himself over in your image," the woman said.

You can be everything for me that I wanted and needed, Merihim said. *His gift is yours for the asking.*

"I'll take it." The woman held up her right hand.

In a rush, Warren understood what they were talking about. He tried to push away, tried to reach out to Naomi. But he was too afraid. "Help me," he called out to the voice. "Please."

"He cowers," the woman said.

Merihim whipped his arm and his claws slashed through the woman's forearm. Her hand fell away from her arm. Miraculously not a drop of blood spilled.

The demon reached for Warren's hand—the one Merihim had given him—and grasped it around the wrist.

With a pulling twist, the demon ripped the hand away from Warren and shoved it onto the woman's stump. Merihim waved his hand over the transplant and it was healed almost immediately.

Warren felt jealous when he remembered how long it had taken him to heal after Naomi's Sept had decided to experiment on him. Then agonizing pain shot up his stump, through his shoulder, and exploded into his head. The demon reached for his head, claws extended.

In that moment, mercifully, Warren felt Naomi take hold of him and pull him back. And he blacked out.

"Booth," Simon roared across the intervening distance as Wertham brought the helicopter down toward them.

Booth turned around to face Simon and lifted his pistol. "I should kill you right now, Cross. You're a jinx, and you're constantly pulling us into this war with the demons."

Simon resisted the impulse to lift his pistol. He doubted Booth's pistol could penetrate his armor even at the short range.

"The war is already here," Simon said. "It's not going to go away just because you hide from it."

"Don't you get it?" Booth asked. "Why haven't you gotten it through that thick skull of yours? The war is already over."

Despite the undead closing in around him, Simon was confused. "What are you talking about?"

"The war with the demons," Booth said. "It's over. We lost."

"No. We're just getting started. That's why Lord Sumerisle sacrificed all the Templar at the Battle of All Hallows' Eve. To buy us time."

"Time? Time for what? So we can die more slowly?"

Simon didn't say anything.

"You're an idiot," Booth exploded. "Lord Sumerisle led those Templar into battle thinking that was going to be the *end* of it. They expected to rout the demons and throw them out of this world. They didn't believe for a second that they were going to have their heads handed to them."

"That's not true," Simon said. The story that had been told for four years was an important one. The sacrifice of the Templar was a tale of respect and honor.

"They'd never fought a Hellgate before," Booth said. "Don't you see? They'd trained and practiced for *years*. For *generations*. All to beat the demons in one battle. That didn't happen. They lost." He waved his arms helplessly to point out the undead all around them. They filled the moat now and were starting to climb up onto the bridge. "*We* lost, Simon. The Templar are pathetic. Despite all our weapons and our training, the demons spanked us and sent us home. The one who didn't die immediately in that battle? We're the unlucky ones."

"No," Simon argued. "My father was not a foolish man. What you're describing describes foolish men. That was not Thomas Cross. Not for his life. Not for a night. Not for a moment."

"But it is the truth," Booth said. "And you just keep stirring up the Templar. You keep giving them some kind of hope and spreading the idiocy. If you'd just leave it alone, just die or go away so that we never have to hear of you again, the survivors could just sit back and live out our lives in secrecy."

"That's not how we're supposed to live."

"Then we've been living," Booth argued. "All these years hidden away from the rest of the world? We've already been living like that. But you insist on luring them out of their shells. They're going to get caught, and they're going to give up the Templar Underground so that we're all killed. And it will be all your fault."

Simon thought of the young male and female Templar back at his stronghold and how few—if any—of them would live long lives.

It's not about how long your life is, boy, Simon heard his father say again. *It's about how long it's worth living.*

"Simon," Wertham said. "We're losing our chance to get out of here."

Simon nodded to the helicopter. "We can get you out of here," he told Booth.

Booth shook his head. "I'll take my chances with the undead. They may not get me killed. That's not true of you, Simon. You're going to get a lot of people killed." Without another word, he turned and ran. He blasted undead and used the suit's prowess to leap over them.

None of the other Templar followed him. Two of them had fallen to the undead.

"We'll take you up on your offer, Lord Cross," one of them said.

"You know you don't have to give them a ride," Nathan said. "Kidnappers and torturers, the lot of them."

"No," Simon said, "they're Templar. Our brothers and sisters. We won't leave them behind."

They all loaded onto the helicopter. The pilot lifted them out of the clutches of the undead and unlimbered the jet thruster.

In seconds, the Tower of London was in the distance and Simon was headed for home. He tried to keep his eyes open and couldn't. He sunk down to his haunches and rested his head on his knees. The vibration of the fleeing helicopter lulled him to sleep.

EPILOGUE

S imon woke two days later, but he didn't know it until he climbed into his armor—against doctor's orders—and checked the time. Then he was irritable because he felt like he'd lost too much time.

Also, despite the nanomolecular bonding that had been done on his jaw, it fit differently and gave him a headache. But he could eat solid food and he found he was ravenous. However, he ate on the go.

Word had gotten out about his injuries and—according to Nathan—there was some speculation about whether Simon was going to be able to walk again. So he showed them.

The first thing he discovered was that the stronghold's population had grown again. More Templar had abandoned the Underground and joined his group.

"It's a blessing and a problem," Wertham said. "It's good to have the extra manpower, but feeding and billeting them is becoming a real chore."

Simon sighed, feeling challenged and proud all at the same time. "We're going to have to expand."

"Again, you mean," Wertham said. "And the larger we get, the easier it'll be for the demons to find us."

That was a real concern.

* * *

Fortunately, Professor Macomber thought he had an answer to that. He'd been working with some of the Templar linguists.

As it turned out, the hidden text in the *Goetia* manuscript was actually an artificial language that they were still in the process of deciphering.

"What we've discovered about it is nothing short of amazing," Macomber said when he met with Simon. The professor had been working nonstop since he'd arrived at the stronghold. "If what we think we've found is true, we may have a way of erecting barriers that the demons can't penetrate."

"That would be good," Simon said. "There are a lot of women and children here that could use a safer place."

"But there's more," Macomber went on. "What we've been working on suggests that there lies within this world a way to defeat the demons and reclaim what was lost."

"What do you mean?"

"The Demons are part of the eternal battle between Light and Darkness. The Hellgate, according to the *Goetia* manuscript, will never open on a world that lacks the ability to save itself."

"So somewhere in this world—"

"Somewhere in London, actually," Macomber corrected.

"—there's a way to defeat the demons."

Macomber nodded. "I believe it's true. Everything I've read about the Light and Darkness tells us that a balance must be struck. In order for something to risk being lost, there must also be a way to win it."

"We just have to find it," Simon said.

"And learn to use it," Macomber said.

"While trying very hard not to get killed doing either of those things," Nathan pointed out.

"Well then," Simon said, smiling. "It sounds like we've got it all figured out. That's something."

A few hours later, Simon found Leah outside the stronghold. She was checking over the motorcycle she'd rode in on when she'd brought the *Goetia* manuscript back.

"Leaving?" Simon asked.

She glanced at him over her shoulder. "I didn't want to wear out my welcome."

Simon stood over her and watched her work for a time. "You could have left earlier."

She stood and faced him. "Nope. Not till I knew you were back on your feet."

"Now that I'm back on my feet, you could stay another day or two."

"Could I now?"

Behind his faceplate, Simon smiled. "I woke up feeling hopeful. That's the first time in a long time that I've felt that way. I kind of liked the idea of sharing that with someone."

"There are even more people here to share it with than before," Leah pointed out.

Knowing she wasn't going to let him get by without saying it, Simon told her, "I'd really like it if you could stay a couple of days. I'd like the chance to get to know you better."

She regarded him from behind the black mask, her features expressionless. "We don't even know if we have a chance for a tomorrow. Why should you ever get to know more than you already know right now?"

"Because I'd love the chance to."

"Feeling grateful because I saved your arse?"

Simon grinned. "No. You're a hard woman to get to know, Leah."

"I've lived that kind of life," Leah said. "Didn't have much use for friends or trust when I was growing up."

"I don't have anything else to offer you."

Leah reached behind her head and opened her mask. She shook her hair out and looked up at him. "Who knows? Maybe one day I'll find that tempting." She ran her fingers up under his faceplate and his helmet popped open.

That surprised Simon and it must have shown on his face.

"I've really got to get those security problems fixed," he said.

She stood on tiptoe and kissed him. "But maybe not this one?"

"Maybe not," he agreed.

Warren woke in darkness and pain. He felt feverish and weak. Glancing down at his right arm, he found it ended in a stump that was wrapped in white gauze.

When he'd first regained consciousness, he'd tried to heal himself. The bleeding had stopped and new skin had formed, but he hadn't been able to regrow his hand.

He was a cripple again.

Not only that, but a lot of his strength and power seemed to be gone as well. He was forced to admit that not all of what he'd had was his. It had been borrowed from Merihim.

Now it was gone.

Naomi was gone. As soon as she'd made certain he was going to live—and that his powers had been curtailed— she'd gone.

In a way, Warren didn't blame her. She needed to learn in order to stay alive in the world. He had nothing left to teach her.

Not even the voice had remained.

"I'm here, Warren," the voice said.

Surprised, Warren stared into the darkness because it sounded as if the voice were in the room with him. "Where have you been?"

"Getting things ready."

"Ready for what?"

"You. For your next step in your evolution."

"Merihim took my hand."

"I know. I was there."

"You knew he was going to do that, didn't you?" Warren accused. "You saw that."

"Yes."

"You could have stopped it."

"I didn't wish to. You'd become dependent on Merihim. I wouldn't have been able to break you away. You needed someone stronger, but you didn't know it."

"You?"

"Yes, me."

Warren laughed bitterly. "You're bound. What can you do to help me?"

"I already have. All you have to do is pull me back into your world."

"How?"

"Go to the book."

Warren did, and when she bade him to place his hand upon it, he did. He was surprised to feel a small, strong hand take hold of his. Gently, he pulled the hand free of the book.

A young woman with black hair and dark eyes with a complexion the color of fresh milk stepped out of the book. She leaned forward and kissed him, and it was the sweetest thing he'd ever tasted.

"Thank you," she said. She held up a metallic hand that

was cunningly artificed. "This has a tremendous amount of power. Merihim will regret hurting you. All of them will. And I am going to give it to you."

She held the hand to his stump. A series of metallic pins unfolded from the center and stabbed into his arm. There was only a moment of pain, then Warren felt better than he had in days.

"Who are you?" he whispered.

She smiled at him and kissed him again. "I'm every dark desire you've ever had. Call me Lilith."

THE *HELLGATE*: LONDON SAGA
CONTINUES IN BOOK THREE:
COVENANT

ABOUT THE AUTHOR

Mel Odom lives in Moore, Oklahoma, with his wife and children. He's written dozens of books, original as well as tie-ins to games, shows, and movies such as *Buffy the Vampire Slayer* and *Blade,* and received the Alex Award for his novel *The Rover.* His novel *Apocalypse Dawn* was runner-up for the Christie Award.

He also coaches Little League baseball and basketball, teaches writing classes, and writes reviews of movies, DVDs, books, and video games.

His Web page is www.melodom.com, but he blogs at www.melodom.blogspot.com. He can be reached at mel@melodom.net.